BENDING THE LANDSCAPE

FANTASY

EDITED BY NICOLA GRIFFITH AND STEPHEN PAGEL

Borealis is an imprint of White Wolf Publishing.

White Wolf Publishing
780 Park North Boulevard, Suite 100
Clarkston, GA 30021

World Wide Web Page: www.white-wolf.com

Cover Design by Michelle Prahler
Cover Art by Kevin Murphy

Printed and Bound in the United States of America.
First White Wolf Omnibus Edition: March 1997

10 9 8 7 6 5 4 3 2 1

Table of Contents

INTRODUCTION
BY NICOLA GRIFFITH AND STEPHEN PAGEL — 9

FROST PAINTING
BY CAROLYN IVES GILMAN — 13

GARY, IN THE SHADOWS
BY MARK SHEPHERD — 35

PRINCE OF THE DARK GREEN SEA
BY MARK MCLAUGHLIN — 55

WATER SNAKES
BY HOLLY WADE MATTER — 61

GESTURES TOO LATE ON A GRAVEL ROAD
BY MARK W. TIEDEMANN — 79

THE FALL OF THE KINGS
BY ELLEN KUSHNER AND DELIA SHERMAN — 89

CLOUDMAKER
BY CHARLEE JACOB — 123

MAGICKED TRICKS
BY K. L. BERAC — 135

THE SOUND OF ANGELS
BY LISA S. SILVERTHORNE — 159

THE KING'S FOLLY
BY JAMES A. MOORE — 167

BESIDE THE WELL
BY LESLIE WHAT — 185

THE HOME TOWN BOY
BY B. J. THROWER — 195

EXPRESSION OF DESIRE
BY DOMINICK CANCILLA — 211

THERE ARE THINGS WHICH ARE HIDDEN FROM THE EYES OF
THE EVERYDAY
BY SIMON SHEPPARD — 221

FULL MOON AND EMPTY ARMS
BY M. W. KEIPER — 233

MAHU
BY JEFF VERONA — 249

THE STARS ARE TEARS
BY ROBIN WAYNE BAILEY — 271

DESIRE
BY KIM ANTIEAU — 289

YOUNG LADY WHO LOVED CATERPILLARS
BY JESSICA AMANDA SALMONSON — 305

IN MEMORY OF
BY DON BASSINGTHWAITE — 311

IN MYSTERIOUS WAYS
BY TANYA HUFF — 331

IN THE HOUSE OF THE MAN IN THE MOON
BY RICHARD BOWES — 353

CONTRIBUTORS' BIOS — 372

Nicola Griffith's Dedication:

For those who are brave.

INTRODUCTION

*T*his series of anthologies—the first of which you hold in your hands—is called *Bending the Landscape* because, hopefully, this is what it will do. The stories here will take you to physical, emotional and sometimes moral landscapes that are vastly different from the familiar. Sometimes you will meet a person you know in a place that is unrecognizable; other times both the person and place will feel as comfortable as your slippers...only for you to find their actions utterly unexpected.

Some of these landscapes are as new to the writers as they are to you. It was our aim with this series to have some queer writers write fantasy for the first time, and for some genre writers to explore queer characters. We have lesbians writing about gay men, gay men writing about lesbians, and straight folk putting themselves in the shoes of both. Many are writing about people that the majority of our society would consider outside the norm—extranormal, if you like. Each writer has been asked to peer through a lens that bends their particular daily landscape away from its usual form, and to then describe and perhaps reach some understanding of what and who they see.

According to Samuel R. Delany, the difference between naturalistic and fantasy fiction is one of subjunctivity. While the former portrays events that could have happened, fantasy, on the other hand, describes events that contravene reality. Fantasy is extrareality. It acknowledges the way the world is (or has been, or might be) and deliberately bends it out of true.

Fantasy can take many shapes: myth, allegory, or satire; fairy tale, fable, or urban horror. And its uses are as varied as its forms. Fantasy may serve to take our minds off our own lives; to experiment; to aid our understanding of others; to have fun; to sound dire warnings; or to explain the world. It does all this while saying, quite clearly, *None of this could really happen.* As Joanna Russ has pointed out, this negative subjunctivity is the source of pleasure to be found in reading fantasy. We know it's impossible. That's the point.

Some of these stories might have been called science fiction by other editors—the strange presence in the arid landscape of Gilman's story might just as easily have been aliens as spirits; the biolinks of Lisa S. Silverthorne's piece are SF gizmos—but in each case we decided that the crux of the fiction was some element of negative subjunctivity— something in the story *could not really have happened*—as opposed to the subjunctivity of SF which runs: *this has not happened* (to which some might add *yet*).

This first volume of *Bending the Landscape* is a collection of all-original fantasy stories—but don't expect the usual anonymous fantasy backdrops. Why bother with vaguely medieval European settings when we have much more interesting fare in store? This fiction will take you from North Africa to China, from Florida to Hawaii, from Korea to Montana, from the tract houses of Long Island to a lonely lighthouse in Oregon. The unreal in these real places can be as unexpected as a paper cut—as can be the presence of lesbian and gay characters where one has previously found mostly (presumed) heterosexuals. Some readers might find our presence in "their" fiction to be as unwelcome as that paper cut; others—us included—will be delighted. We all need to see representations of ourselves in the world, whether that world is real or not.

There is another reason why we put together queer characters and the fantasy genre. If part of the excitement of fantasy lies in violating reality, or the norm, then doing so twice—extranormal characters in extrareality—is doubly exciting.

Reading these stories will give you a frisson, a thrill. They are transgressive. They will fizz as they leave the page; they will feel more real than many of the things you know to be true.

Take, for example, Mark Shepherd's "Gary, In the Shadows." Set in both the urban cruising grounds of fifteen years ago and the offices of a 911 operator, it shows us how people can be more real, more present in our lives, as ghosts than as mortals. Holly Wade Matter's "Water Snakes" follows a young girl in an Arkansas town as she learns about injustice, appearances, and growing up—but it is the walking statue that edges her experience with brilliance and burns it into our imagination. Simon Sheppard introduces us to the Magicians of Fez, only to show us that we knew them all along. Don Bassingthwaite takes us from the Sun King's Versailles into the present, and it is the present that is strange and unfamiliar.

This time shift technique is also used to good effect by Jeff Verona, in "Mahu," when an old man returns to Pearl Harbor, the scene of the incident which changed his life—and where his life is about to change again. The past, too, has much to teach the woman in Kim Antieau's "Desire."

In the pages of this book you will meet people who spend time on and in mountains and art galleries, headlands and seas, streets and gardens. Some of these people fall in love. Some part. Some die. Whether successfully or not, they all fight to live their lives the best they can—as we all do, day after day. Some of the women are lesbians, some of the men are gay; some of them are simply observers, straight people whose lives have been changed irrevocably by the struggles of their queer friends, lovers, or neighbors. They are extranormal characters living in extrareality. Take a look. See if anything about their lives bears any resemblance to your own. We think you might be surprised.

— *Nicola Griffith & Stephen Pagel*

FROST PAINTING

BY

CAROLYN IVES GILMAN

*C*arolyn Gilman tells us that the setting for "Frost Painting"grew out of solitary driving trips across North Dakota and eastern Montana. Highway 2, she says, gives you great opportunities for deep thought and contemplation: "You reach a Zen state of mind in which every 'Reduced Speed Ahead' sign is like a koan."

Gilman is perhaps best known for her inviting, lyrical novella, "The Honeycrafters." This story is a different animal entirely. We travel to the mountains of Montana with a knowing and brittle art critic who is faced with a frustrating and ultimately bitter choice.

—N.G.

※

Soon after Galena Pittman's plane landed in Williston, North Dakota, she began to pick up nuggets of valuable information. To wit:

1. They really listen to Country Western music in the country west. Monotonous, whining hours of it, in fact.

2. Edible vegetables are as rare there as art critics.

3. Don't depend on public transportation if you want to get somewhere before dehydration sets in.

"I'll just catch a cab," she said to the woman at the ticket counter in the one-room Williston airport. The woman was dressed in the polyester pant suit all small-town females seemed required to wear, and she had that rural look of certainty that she knew how the land lay. Right now she was regarding Galena as if she were a six-year-old who needed life explained to her.

"The cab drivers will both be at home," she said.

"*Both?*" Galena said.

"It's suppertime," the ticket woman said, efficiently piling up papers.

She cast an eye over Galena, taking in the stylish bolo tie with the ceramic cactus pin, the wide-brimmed hat with the quail feather, the hand-painted cowboy boots. Her eyebrow rose.

"How am I supposed to get to the motel, then?" Galena said. Outside, there was nothing in sight but range land. It was going to be a long walk.

At last the woman sighed. "I'll give you a lift."

Climbing into the woman's pickup, it occurred to Galena that the context had changed the message of her clothing since she had left Chicago that morning. Normally, she took pride in dressing with the kind of riskiness that said to onlookers, "This is a trained professional. Do not try this at home." But here the cultural referents were different.

"I suppose you think I'm intending to be satirical," she said as the truck thudded across cattle grates onto the highway, bouncing her off the seat. "Actually, I'm making a kind of reflexive commentary on the banalization of the Western motif in the mass market."

No reaction.

"It's a statement on Eastern use of Western symbols. I'm satirizing us, not you."

"You heading for the Windrow Mountains?" the woman said.

"Yes." Galena was surprised to be found out so quickly.

"I figured. You're the type."

The type? Galena would admit to being many things, but not a *type*.

"We've been getting a lot of you through here," the woman went on. "Arty types."

Kooks. Weirdos. Galena could almost hear the woman thinking the words. "I'm not going there to stay," she said. "Joining a hive-mind's not my thing. I'm not a Californian."

"Uh-huh," the woman said.

There was something like a siren that went off in Galena's mind at times like this. It was whooping, *wrong, wrong*. She had made a fool of herself again. It was like a career.

The next morning when Galena picked up the white rental Hyundai at the Chevrolet dealership, the boots and bolo were gone. Even so, the car dealer spotted her right away. Guessing where she was bound, he turned suddenly reluctant to rent her the car.

"Look, I'm just going there to see a friend," Galena said reasonably. "I'll be back Sunday."

"So you say."

"You want to see my plane ticket?"

"You all have plane tickets."

Exasperated, Galena said, "Have they ever heard of tolerance in this town?"

"It's easy for you East-Coasters to be tolerant," the man said. "You don't have to live near them. I'll tell you this: If those weirdos ever decide to come out of the mountains, we're going to be ready for them. That is, if you liberals haven't taken away our guns by then, too."

Galena would have gladly gotten into a scrap with the man, but there was no time. She ended up leaving a signed credit-card slip with him to cover the cost of retrieving the car, if necessary.

Unfolding the map on her dashboard, she saw that south and west of Williston was nothing but blank space with anemic gray lines wandering through it. "Road condition unknown," the map said helpfully. "Hi ho Silver," Galena said to the Hyundai. Then she put on her sunglasses and prepared to cross the Great Plains in a Japanese rattletrap.

"I hope you appreciate this, Thea," she said.

"Galena Pittman," a rival columnist had once written, "is aptly named for a poisonous mineral." The phrase had amused Galena's colleagues so annoyingly that she had adopted it, mentioning it so often and laughing so hard that everyone began to realize it stung her.

In fact, Galena had been stinging since she was born. Long ago she had realized she was the world's pincushion, a target for every petty mortification, every nettling slight the world could invent. She could chew her cuticles raw thinking of the condescensions she had to endure in a given day, the premeditated cruelties of cabmen and bureaucrats. The only defense was to attack earlier and more wittily, to wear a coat of banter thick enough to keep the pins away. It rarely worked.

Her mother had a favorite saying: "If you make a bed of nails for yourself, you'd better lie on it, and like it." Galena had spent a lifetime casting barbs at that slogan, trying to find ways to disprove it.

In college, she had wanted to be an artist; but she had soon learned that she couldn't bear to see others looking at her work, thinking thoughts she couldn't control. She had tried to explain herself so intrusively, and annoyed so many people, that it finally dawned on her that the explaining was all she was really good at. So, unable to be criticized, she became a critic.

Galena had actually fallen in love with Thea Nodine's art several minutes before she fell in love with the artist herself. It had happened on a day when her landlord had decided to repair the plaster without any notice, and she had spent most of an hour calling everyone she knew to come help her move furniture, receiving only one recorded message after another. At last, where friendship failed money had to take over. The people at Hank's Hauling had been only too happy to help, once they had taken her Visa number hostage. By evening her apartment was in chaos and Galena was in a state of advanced disappointment with the world. She wouldn't have gone to the opening if she hadn't been paid to cover it for the *North Side Review*.

Standing there in a haze induced by exhaustion, cheap chablis, and whatever nutrition came from brie on rice cakes, Galena saw her first frost painting. It was a feathery, crystalline abstraction on glass—almost an image, like an elusive memory. It had been taken from its refrigeration box and set in a wooden stand for display, and the overheated gallery air was beginning to melt it. She stood and watched as the painting slowly turned to water from the outside in. She couldn't figure out why she found it so moving till someone behind her said, "That's how I feel." Galena realized it was how *she* felt, too—like a fragile thing aging and perishing as everyone stood and watched. She stared until the painting was no more than a sheet of glass covered with tears, and all that was left was a memory of beauty that had changed and passed on, like time and lost youth.

She asked the gallery owner about the artist, and he said, "Oh, you've *got* to meet Thea. She's simply an angel. All her work is perishable, you know. She works with the craziest things—sand, smoke, ice, sparks."

Thea was dressed in an oversized lumberjack shirt and jeans, her tangled brown hair falling around her shoulders. At first Galena wondered what kind of schtick this was—but a look at Thea's young face immediately told her that it was no schtick—the girl was simply unaware of the impression she made. Galena was suddenly seized with an urge to cherish this wisp of smoke, to protect it from all the winds that might dissipate it, to keep it young forever.

She gave Thea a ride home that night. The artist was living in a squalid, firetrap loft with five others, sleeping on old mattresses and cooking on a portable grill. The next morning, Galena bustled to the rescue, transplanting Thea into her apartment. The girl came willingly enough, but without the gratitude Galena expected. She had yet to learn that Thea was oblivious to her environment, existing like an air plant with no soil, just on sunlight and inspiration.

Galena made the nest, brought in the money, and kept out the world. Thea brought into her life almost-forgotten pleasures like scented soaps and silk pajamas, pearly Christmas ornaments and pomegranate seeds. Their relationship had all the hallmarks of permanence: an adopted cat, Chinese takeout in front of the television, Saturday morning errands, repainting the bedroom. Life was so normal, so trustworthy, it lulled Galena into forgetfulness. She almost became amiable.

She missed the signs of Thea's restlessness at first. In hindsight, the whole shift to wind sculpture had been part of it—a yearning attempt to grasp impermanence again. In that sunny spring Galena would come home to find her staring at the vortexes formed in Plexiglas tubes by the wind machines. They were like miniature, multicolored tornadoes, made visible by smoke or sand or bubbles. They had never looked strong enough to sweep any Dorothys off to Oz. Or Montana.

GAS—CASINO—ALIEN CURIOS, said the hand-painted roadside sign. Galena lifted the sunglasses onto her forehead; in the rearview mirror she saw they had left white circles in the dust on her face. Without the green tint of the lenses, the landscape looked bleached into shades of gray. Eroded hills, tufted with buckbrush and jackpine, cooked under the glaring sky. Ahead, hovering above the distant horizon, was a brushstroke of white—not clouds, but the snow capping unseen mountains.

She turned the Hyundai into the gravel parking lot in front of the gas station. The air conditioner sighed wearily as she killed the engine. As she twisted to get out, a sharp pain caught her unawares. She waited, sweaty, till it was gone, thinking: *Serves you right for growing up.*

Outside, the heat radiated off the yellow ground. In a dust-caked pickup by the gas pumps, a young woman waited with a child, her wispy blond hair blowing in the dry wind. The bumper sticker on the truck said, IF YOU DON'T WANT HEMORRHOIDS, GET OFF YOUR ASS. A Western sentiment, Galena presumed.

A wiry, bowlegged man was buying cigarettes at the counter inside. Galena wandered down the aisle of dusty tourist trinkets: rubber tomahawks, dribble glasses, ashtrays with toilet humor on them.

The door closed and Galena became aware of someone watching her. The woman stood motionless at the head of the aisle, not unlike one of the rock formations outside: a wind-scoured, lumpy shape with a cracked complexion that looked hard to the touch.

"Where are the alien curios?" Galena asked, thinking that the woman herself looked a little like one.

The woman pointed to a tabletop display case at the end of the aisle. Galena had to wipe the dust off the glass to see inside. She had expected plastic E.T.'s, but instead saw an assortment of lumpy concretions like fossilized organs. The shop's proprietor eased in behind the case, moving her bulk with uncanny silence. Without asking, she opened the case, took out one of the rocks, and handed it over. It was translucent, like

18

onyx, and threaded through with red-brown veins. Galena suddenly had the feeling she was holding a giant eyeball, and put it down on the counter, a little revolted.

"How do you know it's alien?" she said to play along.

"It sure's hell ain't natural," the woman said. She had a breathy cigarette-voice.

"So what is it? A transdimensional doo-dad?"

"One of the things the Dirigo leave behind."

Galena said, "I thought the Dirigo looked like strings of Christmas lights." That was how *Unsolved Mysteries* had it, at any rate. "No one ever said they left turds."

The woman drew another object from the case and cradled it in her palm. It was the color of a kidney, and shaped a little like one. Its surface was slick, as if wet. "The aliens didn't leave these. The people that let them take over did."

So this was the much-publicized art created by the Windrow Mountain colony. It was not up to Thea's standards. Galena felt partly relief, partly anger that Thea could have been hoodwinked into participating in this travesty.

The woman's mineralized skin did not show a flicker of emotion. "You going up there?" she said.

"Yes. I've got a friend there."

"You think. There's nothing human living up there."

There's nothing much human down here either, Galena wanted to say; but she curbed her tongue.

When she emerged from the shop, a wind brushed by, scented with sage. She turned to look south, where the Windrow Mountains still hovered like an unkept promise on the horizon. "Don't leave, kid," she whispered. "I'm coming."

The reports from Montana had fascinated Thea from the start. There were many versions at first: Remote Montana community taken over by aliens. Demonic possession in Montana wasteland. Mystery Montana disease baffles scientists. Galena scoffed at it all.

After anthropologists at the University of Montana began to

investigate, the explanations still metamorphosed to suit every paranoia. It was a type of mass hysteria. It was a scandalous case of environmental contamination. It was genetic inbreeding. It was a secret government experiment. One debunking journalist concluded that the "victims" were in fact members of a harmless New Age religious community who were being stigmatized by society as "ill" for their nonconformity.

The explanation of the victims themselves never changed. The Dirigo, they said, were enabling them to create art of a type never before imagined.

It was the art that riveted Thea's attention. As pictures finally filtered out, Thea bought all the magazines and pored over them. "Just think," she said, "I could work in real wind, real lightning, if I had their inspiration."

"If you had their inspiration, you'd be in a looney bin," Galena said.

But it did seem as if Thea's creativity was lagging that spring. Her studio was cluttered with unfinished work; it was over a year since she had held one of her famous shows that drew such crowds to see the self-destroying art. As her comfort increased it seemed her drive faded. Galena worried that her own happiness was poisoning the well from which it sprang.

One morning when Galena, ready to leave for work, leaned over the bed to kiss her partner goodbye, Thea looked up out of the rumpled bedclothes and said, "I'm going to Montana." Galena laughed, brushed the scattered hair out of Thea's face, and said, "Ride 'em, cowboy."

When she got home that evening, Thea's suitcase and backpack were waiting by the door. The truth smashed all the elaborate structure of Galena's security. Contentment had come to her so late, so unexpectedly, that she had never thought it, too, could be perishable. She followed Thea around the house, asking questions in a voice like a lost child.

"How can I get in touch with you?"

"What are you going to do there?"

"How long will you be gone?"

"Why are you doing this?"

"When will you know?"

"What about me?"

"What about me?"

To which Thea could only answer again and again, "I don't know."

And that was all Galena had ever gotten out of her. She consented to drop Thea off at the airport, but wouldn't go in with her, and they didn't part with a kiss, or even a handshake.

The road deteriorated as it began to climb. The shoulders were first to go, then the paint, till all that was left was a line of asphalt about as flat as a strip of cooked bacon. Galena's stomach was running on empty, but a touch of nervous nausea kept her from stopping to eat the granola bars she had brought. She didn't know how she was going to find Thea, and she didn't want to be wandering the Windrow Mountains all night.

The mountains wore a skirt of pine forest. The road veered to and fro through the still trunks till Galena began to suspect it didn't know where it was going. Down under the canopy of needles the air was dark as twilight, though the sun had to be in the sky, somewhere.

She rounded a corner and laid on the brakes. Ahead, the road was blocked by a fallen tree. A large yellow sign said, PRIVATE PROPERTY. TRESPASSERS WILL BE PROSECUTED. The sign was pockmarked with bullet holes.

She got out to survey the problem. The air was surprisingly cool; she must have climbed in altitude. The tree turned out to be just a poplar sapling, more leaves than trunk, felled by a chain saw. She seized a branch and dragged it across the asphalt, out of the way.

"If you want to keep me out, you'll have to try harder than this," Galena said to the unknown woodsman.

The effort had winded her, and she sat sideways in the driver's seat a while, her door open on the chill, quiet air. At first she thought that her tired eyes were playing tricks; but no, the shifting points of light were real. Off in the forest, down the winding corridors of pines, some people were carrying candles, or flashlights.

"Excuse me," Galena called out, getting up. "Can you give me some directions?"

The lights winked out. Piney silence surrounded her. Only then did Galena remember the reports—floating strings of lights sighted; gauzy veils, unexplained. She realized she was standing with one arm outstretched, as if hailing a cab. With a nervous laugh at her own absurdity, she headed back to the car and the security of self-examination. One's first brush with the paranormal ought to have more dignity than this, she decided. In her mind she composed the headlines. CHICAGOAN TRIES TO CATCH RIDE ON UFO: "I THOUGHT IT WAS A CAB," CITY SLICKER SAYS.

The road plunged down a ravine, then abruptly emerged from the trees into a barren valley. The setting sun touched the sandstone cliffs, a vivid orange. Lines of erosion made the rock face look like an ancient bas-relief, so worn away that the original sculpture was barely visible. Galena stopped the car to study it. She could almost see figures in motion—no, an inscription in flowing characters. It reminded her vividly of something. It was on the tip of her tongue: she would remember in a second.

It was just a cliff. Frowning at the illusion that had drawn her briefly out of herself, she put the car in Drive again and followed the winding road down into the heart of the valley. Rock formations rose on either side: twisted sandstone pillars that looked like figures hidden in stone cocoons, their protolimbs still obscure beneath the surface. They drew her eyes, as if subconsciously she knew what shapes lay beneath. The valley floor held an army of them in a thousand poses, straining to free themselves. Galena sped through them; they towered over the little car, their shadows lying like barriers across the road.

At last the forest enclosed her again. It was dark now; she turned on the headlights. There was still no sign of any colony—no sign of humans at all. She had passed the last motel just after noon.

At last, a light shone through the trees. She slowed, then spotted the driveway—just a dirt track, really. As she drove up it, the tall grass swished against the car's undercarriage.

It was a log house, probably built as a hunter's lodge. Leaving the headlights on, Galena skirted the stack of firewood and climbed three board steps onto the porch. The screen door creaked when she opened it to knock. It was several seconds before there was any response. Then, hesitantly, the door opened a crack and someone peered out.

It was Thea. "Hi there, kid," Galena said, as if she'd known it was going to be her.

Thea stood staring. "Galena," she said.

Her long brown hair fell in curly tendrils, uncombed but fetching. She looked more thin and waiflike than ever in a flannel shirt and jeans. Her feet were bare. Galena wanted to hug her to make sure that everything was all right, but there was something in her manner—a slight shrinking back, a wariness.

Thea held the door open. "Come in."

The kitchen table was soon strewn with the snapshots Galena had brought—mostly their cat, Pesto, doing assorted catlike things. Thea stared for a long time at one where the flashbulb made the cat's eyes light up like headlights.

"He's gotten to be a real sentimental slob," Galena said. "After you left, he wandered around the house and cried for a few days." *So did I,* she didn't say.

She continued the patter she'd tried to keep up ever since entering, afraid of what silence might mean. "Mr. Garavelli at the dry cleaners told me to say hi to you. They've been repaving the street out front and it's been unbearable all summer: nothing but dust and noise. Workers leaving their shirts on the bushes. Manly sweat everywhere." She took a sip of the tea that was virtually all Thea could offer her; the refrigerator was almost empty. "I had to go in to Dr. Hamer for a biopsy last week. I find out the results Tuesday."

At last Thea's eyes focused on her. "What's wrong?" she asked.

"Getting old, that's what's wrong." *Getting old alone,* she thought. *No one to tell how it feels, no one to give a damn.* "Never mind," she said.

At last silence fell. Inside the wood stove, a log settled with a brittle sound.

"Galena, I can't come back," Thea said. Her voice sounded like a guilty child confessing. "I've made the commitment here."

"Sure. I understand," Galena said, barely hearing the words. "What's important is your work. How's it going?" She glanced around the cabin. There was not a sign of artistry anywhere, just worn Salvation Army furniture.

"I'm working outside now," Thea said. "I'll show you tomorrow, if you want."

"Yes. I want."

Silence again.

"I'd better get my suitcase out of the car," Galena said. There was a twinge of pain as she rose, mocking her. *Think you're brave, do you?* it said. She took care not to react. She couldn't bear to seem vulnerable.

"Sure. You can sleep on the couch," Thea said.

Galena looked at her silently. Thea wouldn't meet her eyes. "What is this, Montana morality?" Galena asked.

"No." Thea's voice was pleading. "I just can't, Galena. I don't want you to lure me back. It will be too hard."

Too hard on whom? Galena wondered. "Okay," she said slowly. "You make the rules."

Suddenly, Thea gave her an impulsive hug. "Thank you," she whispered. As she disappeared behind the bedroom door she glanced back. The light caught her eyes with an odd glint, as if the retinas were brushed metal. For a moment she looked utterly alien.

That night Galena lay alone on the lumpy couch, kept awake by wind in the branches outside, the skittering of small feet across the roof, insect wings on the window screen. None of the soporific sounds she was used to—the roar of garbage trucks, the wail of sirens. No comforting weight of possessive cat on her feet. She wondered if Thea were awake.

This desire to be held and comforted was childish, she told herself. *You're an adult now. You know how to survive.*

Lying in the dark, she imagined a tumor growing inside her, a living thing that wasn't her, like the child she never had nor wanted. Nature had a way of getting back at people who didn't follow its rules. And reproduction was the first rule, the evolutionary imperative.

She had never made a decision to swear off men—just drifted into it, the path of least resistance. Her last attempt at a straight relationship had been a madcap fling with a sculptor. The only time they had had sex together, while she was still basking in the afterglow, he had smiled at her and said, "You look like a woman who's just been fucked."

The statement had jarred her. Why was it *she* that had just been fucked, and not *him?* He had slipped, and revealed the real reason he had done it—not for the enjoyment, no strings attached, but in order to transform her into something she hadn't been before, as if she had been raw material he had made into something. As if he had put his mark on her, like a dog pissing on a lamppost.

From that moment she knew that for men, sex was inextricably connected to power, and always would be. No matter what they said, or how enlightened they acted, sex was dominance to them, on such an instinctual, hardwired brainstem level they could never overcome it. And she had far too vivid a sense of her own individuality to ever imagine herself as a thing marked as a man's territory.

Thea's love had always been free of other agendas. It had never been mixed up with power, or pride, or self. It had been a spontaneous gift, unpremeditated, as if it sprang from the air between them. Galena had never had to give up being who she was in order to be who Thea loved.

She hugged the pillow to the hollow feeling in her body, wondering if loneliness caused cancer.

In the morning, Galena ate a breakfast of granola bars and tea; Thea was not hungry. By daylight, the cabin looked more dilapidated than ever. One of the kitchen windows was broken, and there was an old mouse nest in a corner. "How did you find this place?" Galena asked.

"Everyone stays here when they first come," Thea answered. "It's where you wait."

"Wait for what?"

"For the Dirigo. I'll be moving on soon."

"On to where?"

"The colony. I'm almost ready."

"Will you show me the colony?"

"If you want."

Thea set out as if to walk, but Galena asked how far it was, then persuaded her to take the car. Thea looked at the Hyundai as if she'd forgotten how they worked, then opened the door awkwardly. Galena watched her carefully, suspicious.

"What do you want to see first?" Thea asked.

"What's the choice?"

"There are work sites all around us. The Wind Clock, the Haunt, Nostra Knob."

"What have you been working on?"

"The Flens."

"Let's see it, then."

A few miles down the road, Thea suddenly exclaimed, "Stop! Stop here!"

Galena pulled over. They were high on the mountainside; on their right hand was a steep dropoff, giving them a wide view of a wooded valley that wound into blue distance, interrupted by the outthrusting roots of mountains on either side.

"Look out there," Thea said. "Do you see the painting?"

The vegetation on north slopes, south slopes, and valley floor was a pattern of green, teal, and umber. It was as if someone had taken a giant brush and painted the land to form an abstract of overlapping tints. "Isn't that natural?" Galena said.

"Of course not. This was one of the first landscape paintings the colony did. Here, let me drive so you can watch."

A little reluctantly, Galena got out and went to the passenger side. Thea said, "Unfocus your eyes just a little the first time," then started the car slowly forward.

At first Galena saw a complex patchwork of sunny streaks. Then, as her perspective changed, a dark, spear-shaped wedge began to push its way into the foliage colors. As it touched each band of color, that area went suddenly dark, drab, and uniform. It had almost reached the opposite side when a cascade of rusts, siennas, and lemons erupted from the speartip and turned the landscape bright again.

The car stopped. Galena blinked out at the view, which had been transformed by traveling 300 feet along the road. "How did they do that?" she asked. "By painting the back side of every leaf?"

"I don't know," Thea said. "It looks different at every time of day, and every type of weather."

Galena shook her head. "Landscape painting. I see what you mean.

Not painting the landscape, but *painting the landscape*. How many people did it take?"

"I don't know," Thea said again.

As they continued on, Galena looked on every prospect around her with new attention, to find more *trompes l'oeil* hidden in the leaves.

They arrived at the Flens down a rocky path. At first, it looked like a range of rampart cliffs, formed into organ-pipe pillars of a thousand dimensions. A swarm of people was at work on the cliff face, some on scaffolding anchored into the rock, some swinging on ropes. Though she tried from several angles, Galena could not tell what the sculpture was going to be.

When she asked, Thea laughed. "The sculpture is not in the rock," she said. "The medium we are working in is wind. At sunset, the mountain above us cools faster than the valley, and a wind rushes down the slope. The Flens will catch it in a thousand fissures, and part it, till it forms a shape. We will know we have gotten it right when the rock pipes sing. It's almost done; we are tuning it now."

"You are making an organ from the mountain," Galena said, struck by the strangeness of the concept.

"An organ only the wind can play," Thea answered.

As Galena watched, the workers vacated one area. There was a puff of smoke, then an echoing explosion.

"They use dynamite?" Galena asked.

"We use anything that will do the job," Thea answered.

The workers moved back into the dynamited area, their movements efficient and coordinated. Galena could see no one in charge, hear no shouted orders.

"Who designs the artworks?" she asked. "Who is in charge?"

Thea looked at the ground and shrugged.

"Thea?" Galena said.

"You will just misinterpret it," Thea said.

"Try me. Come on."

"The colonists just *know* what to do. They feel what's right. Imagine having the skill to produce each effect deliberately. Imagine thinking, 'I need pathos here, or an ominous effect,' and knowing exactly what you have to do to create it, as if it were being whispered in your ear. And everyone else knows the same."

"Kind of like having a muse?"

"That's right. The Dirigo are our muses."

Gently, Galena said, "You never needed to use anyone else's inspiration before. You never worked by anyone else's plan. That's what made you so good."

Nervously, Thea brushed a strand of hair behind her ear. "I was never as good as you thought I was."

Galena was about to protest strenuously, but Thea said, "You blew me up so big, nothing I could do would ever justify it. Everyone's expectations were so high."

"Thea, kid, you deserved it!" Galena said.

"You see what I mean," Thea said, then turned back toward the car.

"So is that my sin?" Galena shouted after her. "Having faith in you?"

Thea didn't stop or answer. When they both got back to the car they sat a while in silence. Galena considered, and rejected, half a dozen strategies: conciliatory, wounded, encouraging, authoritative. None of them were sufficient to the way she felt.

When Thea finally spoke, it wasn't about Galena at all. "Here, no one makes the art for any reason but because we want to."

They drove on to other sites. The art was everywhere. It was fashioned from streams and sand, shadows, lichen, and rain. In one place a flight of swallows was an intermittent part of the sculpture. After a while it was impossible to see the landscape as a backdrop, an accidental thing.

"Supposing these Dirigo were real—" Galena started.

"They *are* real," Thea said.

"Okay, okay. Are they trying to tell us something?"

"I don't know. You're the one who gets messages from art."

"Do they talk to you?"

"No. Not the way you mean. We don't know what they want. We're not even sure they know we're any different from the trees and rocks. Except—"

"Yes?"

"Some people feel they're trying to remember something. Something they once knew long, long ago, but now they've forgotten."

"Like us all," Galena said.

The last site they visited was what Thea called the Pivotary. They drove up a long gravel road that climbed past the trees into a cold, bleached world where the very air seemed purified and rare. Through the afternoon an ache had been growing somewhere between Galena's back and gut; when they reached the end of the road she parked and sat a while, waiting for it to subside. The sun was low, but above them the sky was still bright.

They walked side by side up a gravelly path that curved between two spurs standing out from the mountain like rock gates. Beyond them, in a sheer-sided bowl, lay a mountain lake, its surface so perfectly still it mirrored every rock around it. When they came to a halt beside it, and their footsteps ceased, silence settled in. The air seemed so crystalline it might break at a touch.

In a hushed voice, Thea said, "This is where the Dirigo live. They've been here for eons, maybe since the beginning. It's possible that the Blackfeet Indians knew about them. We think other humans may have known, once, in other times and places. We come here to invite them in. Don't worry, they can't inhabit anyone who is unwilling. You would have to go into the lake to make them part of your life."

"Like a baptism?" Galena said.

"That's right."

There was a silence. At last Thea said hesitantly, "You could do it, too. You could join us."

"Oh, Thea. When will you learn? I don't have the talent for art."

"You could. There are people in the colony who never made a thing before coming here."

"So that's what the Dirigo offer? Instant talent?"

"Vision. Creativity. A feel for the elements. If that's talent."

"What a deal," Galena said, stirring a pebble at her feet. "You'd have to be crazy to turn it down." She glanced sidelong at Thea. "But what's the catch?"

"There are only catches in a human context. Catches belong to the outside world."

"The human world, you mean. Catches are part of being human."

"All right," Thea said. "The catch is, I have to hurt you, by leaving you behind."

They stood looking at each other then—communicating, Galena thought, for the first time, though not a word was said. *I need to say it aloud*, Galena thought. *I have to admit how badly I need her.*

As the light shifted with the setting sun, it caught Thea's eyes, and the retinas reflected through, opaque as mirrors, beautiful as gemstones. A chill went down Galena's spine. She grasped Thea's hand. It felt cold.

"Have you already gone into the lake?" she asked.

Thea nodded. "Three weeks ago."

"Can you still back out?"

"I don't want to."

She was the same, but unknowable. Unchanged, yet wholly different. "What did I do to make you want this?" Galena said.

"It has nothing to do with you."

It couldn't be true, Galena thought. Somehow, this was her fault.

"Look!" Thea said, pointing out over the lake. "They've come."

The sun had set, and darkness leaped up from the ground. But the sky was still light, and the lake, reflecting it, glowed azure in the twilight. Above it, a constellation of sparks danced, firefly lights cavorting. Around them the air shimmered as with heat waves. Galena glimpsed something like a shred of iridescent gauze, gone as soon as she focused on it.

"What are they doing here?" Galena whispered. "What do they want?"

"The art," Thea said. "It's all they want. To make beautiful things. They can't do it themselves; they need our hands, our ingenuity."

She was gazing at them entranced. *I am losing her*, Galena thought.

The valley was growing dark; now faint streaks of colored light flashed and disappeared above the lake, like an aurora, or a reflection from a light that wasn't there.

Galena took Thea's hand firmly in hers. "Come on," she said, "I'll drive you home."

30

Following the headlights down the steep road, Galena remembered how, in the days when Thea had still gone down to her old studio to work, Galena had picked her up after work, to drive her home. Sometimes she would climb the steps and hear the artists who shared the space laughing together uproariously, like teenagers. When she entered the room, the laughter would cut off self-consciously. Even if she told them to go on talking, the atmosphere would turn stiff and formal, as if Teacher were watching. It had made Galena hate to go there after a while, and feel out of place, unwanted.

There was an ache in her gut that said, *No more future, no more chances.* Always the future had been there, a sketchbook where she could try out new scenarios. Now experimentation was done; only action was left.

She came to the main road, then retraced the way back past the turnoff to the Flens, past the landscape painting, speeding faster with every mile. As pine trunks flashed by in the darkness, Thea said, "That was the turnoff to the house. You missed it."

"I know," Galena said.

The road curved and plunged downward, into the valley of the stone shapes. Thea said tensely, "Stop, Galena. I can't leave."

"Yes, you can," Galena said. "And I think you'd better, before they brainwash you completely."

She pressed down on the gas, wanting to get past the rock formations that loomed in frozen motion over the road. The passenger side door opened, and Galena heard the pavement rushing past. She reached over to grab Thea's arm, only to feel it pull away. The loony girl was actually going to jump. Galena braked hard, and the car slewed around on loose gravel. For a moment she had a terrifying out-of-control feeling. Then the car came to rest in the roadway, facing back the way it had come. The headlight beams pointed crookedly into the dust and exhaust. The passenger seat was empty.

Galena left the car door open and walked down the harsh beams of light, searching the shoulders for a sign, her stomach muscles clenched. Then, ahead on the roadway, she saw Thea's silhouette, walking steadily away from her. She sprinted to catch up.

"Thea!" She grasped the girl's arm and forced her to turn around. "Are you—" The headlights caught Thea's eyes and they shone back, bright and preternatural.

Instinctively, Galena stepped back. Then a desperate sense that she was losing overcame her, and she grasped Thea by the shoulders. "Fight them, Thea! Be yourself. Don't surrender, don't let them control you."

A wan smile crossed Thea's face, too wise and knowing for her young features. "Myself?"

"Yes." Galena clutched her tight. "The Thea I knew."

Thea's voice was maddeningly adult. "The Thea you invented, you mean. I know all about being dominated, Galena."

Galena loosed her grip, deeply stung. "That's not true! All I ever wanted was for you to be yourself."

"Then let me go," Thea said.

"Not to give up your freedom," Galena said stubbornly. "Not to become something that's not even human."

"The only humanity I lose is the ability to make things ugly."

"Oh, isn't that great," Galena said, bitingly sarcastic. "Why don't we all join the Dirigo, then, and have a world of people who want nothing but beauty. A world of saints and artists."

"Why not?" Thea said.

There was a cloud of sparks around her head, like a halo in a medieval painting, but they cast no light on her features. Half to them and half to her Galena said, "Because it wouldn't be a human world, Thea."

There was a silence. The rock shapes around them seemed to be listening. "Then I don't want to be human," Thea said.

She was leaving her face, retreating back behind those eyes that revealed nothing. When she turned again to walk into the dark, there was no one left to stop.

The shoal of silver slivers that had hung above Thea's head did not leave with her. They still hung in the air, darting about in school formation.

Galena knew that she too could wear a halo of stars if she only consented. There was a heavy lump inside her gut—her own inhabiting being, eating her away from inside.

"Get out of here!" she shouted at the pinprick lights above her. "Let us be! You've got no business trying to make us better than we are."

Her footsteps sounded heavy and corporeal as she walked back to the car. When she had turned it around she paused with her foot on the brake, caught on a snag of grief. For a moment she rested her forehead on the steering wheel, then shifted blindly into Drive.

She had her comebacks ready by the time she got to Williston. When the car dealer's eyebrows cast aspersions her way, she said, "The Dirigo didn't want me. I guess they saw I was already alienated enough."

She would have been ashamed to commit a pun in Chicago, but this was North Dakota.

The sweaty, overly familiar salesman in the seat next to her on the plane found out where she had been and said jocularly, "Did you see any aliens?"

"Not as many as I've seen since coming back," Galena retorted.

As they circled high above the fumes and grime of O'Hare, caught in traffic, she looked down at the barren mess humanity had made of the landscape, and imagined it all melting away like one of Thea's frost paintings.

It would never happen. If humanity were offered salvation on a silver platter, someone would probably just mug the messenger.

She shifted, feeling the bed of nails beneath her.

GARY, IN THE SHADOWS

BY

MARK SHEPHERD

I have known Mark Shepherd for several years; we were both on the same convention schedule for a while. His writing always has a certain indefinable texture. We have all been in situations where we have made a friend, shared a night, or just done something for no particular reason other than that it just felt right. Mark's "Gary, in the Shadows" gives us a glimpse of why we do that, and why against all odds some things just turn out right for us.

— S. P.

※

Midnight, after work, and Sean was driving his battered Volkswagen bug on the deserted downtown streets. Hands shaking, white knuckled on the steering wheel, he tried to put the image out of his head before getting on the expressway.

She died while I listened.

Gotta calm down.

It's what I get paid for.

The bug's front end needed a lot of work, it was all he could do to keep it driving straight. *Cops will think I'm drunk for sure.*

Sean was a 911 operator cursed with an imagination. Tonight a woman had called after someone named Mike had stabbed her. While she was talking, Mike had stabbed her again, and again. The phone was left dangling, and Sean heard everything. His job was to stay on the line as long as possible, while another operator called the location in to the police dispatcher. He listened to the screams with a white face. He saw what was going on, every detail defined to the last blood drop, and he could do nothing about it except listen.

Then silence. A door opened, a door closed. Then nothing at all.

Maybe it was a lover's quarrel.

He knew this was being taped, everything was being taped. So he had to keep talking, which was his job, even though it was futile. His supervisors, police and prosecutors would be listening to this tape an uncountable number of times, and there was always the chance it would be leaked to the press. He kept talking, shouting into the headset, for the tape, for his boss, for the cops, even though he knew she was probably dead. Then the cops arrived, and picked up the phone, not sounding very optimistic when they said, "We're on the scene."

Sean disconnected. "I need a cigarette," he said to Sylvia, his supervisor, who had done all the dispatching for his call.

"Go ahead," she said. "You look like shit."

It was close to quitting time anyway, so she gave him the rest of the night off. He drove around downtown, trying to shake the memory of the voice, and the image of what he so clearly imagined.

He often drove downtown on his break, there being little else to do here this time of night except drive. Nothing happened downtown after the white collar workers went home. Nothing here except the occasional wino asleep in a doorway, or another transient just passing through with a backpack on his shoulders. Plenty of solitude, zero traffic, just the methodical turning of traffic lights for cars that had long since gone home.

He turned right on Main, then again on Tenth. In circles, like he had years before, in a different time for entirely different reasons. In 1980 the traffic had been nearly bumper to bumper, and groups of parked cars would congregate in the parking lots, playing music, their occupants getting stoned while listening to *Donna Summer* or *Gloria Gaynor*. Fifteen years ago, things had been quite different. Downtown was the crusiest and sleaziest place for men to pick up men, and it happened in a parade of cars, driving the loop, checking out the other drivers and the hustlers walking the street, pulling over to talk. Making arrangements. The rustle of money changing hands.

It was a furtive, clandestine festival with very few rules and abundant anonymity. No souls, just bodies, lots of warm bodies, perspiring in the hot summer night. The smell of poppers and cigarettes. Sweat heating up in the frenzy of sex, and cooling as the door closed, the footsteps fading, the car starting and driving away.

As a teenager Sean had discovered it quite by accident. He enrolled in the junior college two blocks down, oblivious to what was going on here until he walked home late one night and saw the strange procession of cars, all kinds, driving a rectangular pattern around the core of downtown. At first he thought it was a funeral, but saw no hearse, and no beginning or end to it. Just a continuous loop, a circle which snaked around the same blocks, sometimes until the sun rose.

Sean was eighteen and had never dated a girl, had never been interested. When he saw the young men getting into the cars with the old men, he knew why. He knew there were bars where this went on, in secret locations throughout the world, but this was right out in the open, and no ID was required. He considered his recent craving for sex, lots of sex, and regarded the street with a hungry eye.

His perspective changed dramatically. He asked his father if he could get an apartment downtown, closer to school, and he had agreed. In the following week he moved into a one room apartment in what had been the Ambassador Hotel, with a manually operated elevator and a clueless old man running the place. Father paid six months in advance, with an allowance, as long as he stayed in school.

He stayed in school, but at night he went out, just outside the hotel and down a few blocks. Another place, another person. He thrived on his double life, dressing down in ragged jeans, tank tops, sneakers, trying to fit into a new mold. The men in the cars mistook him for a hustler, and reluctantly drove away when he turned them down. As for the hustlers, street kids with no family except themselves, they looked upon him as a threat to their livelihood.

All of them, of course, except Gary.

The first night he saw him, Gary was showing off his martial arts in an alley, which would become his usual routine between tricks. Sean noticed right away that he was a small kid, coming maybe up to his shoulder, but he had an upper torso developed like Bruce Lee's, and long blond hair that flew about him like a whirlwind. It was the light, yellow blond of youth, not sun; Sean doubted he saw much sun. He wore jeans, and no shirt…in fact, if he ever owned a shirt, Sean never saw it. He was sparring with a much bigger boy, who acted as if the whole thing was a joke— until Gary took him down expertly with a series of moves which flowed together seamlessly, like pouring water.

After money changed hands among those gathered, Gary walked right up to Sean and poked him in the chest with two fingers.

"What's your name, dude?" he said with a huge smile, which showed two missing teeth. He'd lit a cigarette, though Sean didn't notice when, and was already halfway through it. Even looking down at him, Gary seemed formidable. He had a young, round face, and a tendency to hop around on the balls of his feet. Evidently Gary had been out sparring a bit already; sweat gleamed off his smooth, hairless upper chest. Sean's initial fear turned to lust. The boy was pure porn.

"Sean…" he said. "I go to school. Over there." He pointed at the college.

"No shit," Gary said. For some reason Sean had expected ridicule, but instead sensed admiration. "I saw you moving in. The Ambassador?"

"That was me," Sean said, feeling stupid. *When did I see Gary walking around? Was he invisible?* He knew he would have remembered seeing him.

A big Lincoln Town Car pulled up to the curb and honked.

"Gotta go," Gary said, running to the car.

Sean watched him get into the huge vehicle. It still had the dealer's sticker on the window. The guy even looked rich, if such a thing were possible in semidarkness.

The next day when Sean was getting ready for school, he saw from his seventh story window Gary walking down the street. There were parking meters all down that side, which were nearly as tall as he was. He threw a kick over each one as he passed, his heel just clearing it. Sean had never seen anyone so flexible, not even a gymnast. The possibilities made his palms sweat. Later, he would realize the whole display was for his benefit.

After school Sean looked back to see Gary running to catch up with him. Still, no shirt.

"You wanna get high?" he asked.

"Sure," Sean said. "Let's go up to my place." He'd already smelled dope burning on one of the floors, and knew they could get away with it there.

The place came with a couch and fold down bed, and not much else. Gary sat down on the couch and pulled out a bag of pot as big around as his thigh. Sean put his books down, and when he turned around, Gary already had the first joint rolled.

Sean couldn't help but stare at Gary's chest and flat, ripped stomach, all the more apparent when he laid back and kicked his feet up on the coffee table.

"I'll bet you could light a match off that stomach," Sean said before thinking.

With a white-tipped matchstick, Gary smiled his toothless grin and did just that, with a flick of his wrist. Sean sat down next to him, took the lit joint, and tried to look like he knew what he was doing. He didn't.

"No. Like this," Gary said, and put the lit end in his mouth, pulled Sean's lips roughly toward his, and blew a thick plume of smoke in his face. The gesture was casual and erotic. Sean thought he was going to ooze into the couch, with Gary holding his face like that. He didn't want him to let go.

When they had smoked about half of it, Gary lay the joint on top of an empty pop can. "Come here," he said, and pulled Sean over and gave him a big puppy dog kiss. It was the spark that started the fire.

An hour later they were lying in the fold down bed, naked and sated, finishing the last of the joint. Sean held him as Gary lay his face on his chest. He'd never cradled someone like this, and had always wondered what it would be like.

"Can I stay here with you for a while?" Gary asked, and Sean said not yes, but *hell* yes.

As it turned out Gary was the only truly gay kid working that particular street, only he didn't want the others hustlers to know it. Sean couldn't figure out why, but didn't ask. He gave Gary the spare key to his room, an old rusty skeleton key that actually worked the door, and told him to come and go as he liked.

Gary looked at the key as if it were a bar of gold. "What do you expect, you know, in return?"

At first Sean didn't understand, then he said, "Don't worry about it. I like you. I like being with you."

The boy looked confused and relieved at the same time. "I have to go," he said. "Appointment."

Sean knew he would never be able to change him, and didn't try. If he was going to be a prostitute, there wasn't much he could do about it. What struck him as peculiar about the whole thing was that Gary was adamant about Sean not "hookin' on main," as he referred to it. It wasn't that Sean was considering it, although at the time prostitution had its own lewd appeal. Jealousy had nothing to do with it, either. Gary didn't want him to throw his life away, since, after all, he was going to college. He had a chance to do something besides sell his ass on streetcorners.

Over the next three weeks Gary stayed most of the nights with Sean after an hour or more of passionate lovemaking. If Gary'd already had sex with anyone else that night, it didn't show. Sean was astounded to know the boy didn't have a social security number, and that he wasn't certain how to spell his last name, and had no idea what his middle name was, if he had one at all. He was seventeen, he knew, and Sean believed him. He'd smoked cigarettes since he was ten, and that explained his short build. But he was obsessive about his Tae Kwon Do workouts, going through his katas several times each morning, and again before bed. His parents had beaten him until, age fourteen, he ran away. He showed a scar on his right buttock. "Dad did that with a knife," he said, as if he were pointing out a dent in a car.

One night he came in, limping, beat all to hell. Bloody nose, abrasions all over him, both wrists and an ankle sprained and swollen.

"Queer bashers," he mumbled through his thickening lips. Sean took care of him, even bought him the fifth of bourbon he'd asked for, at the store where anyone could buy booze, to help deaden the pain.

Three days later, he looked ready to leave. "I have to go," he explained, looking sad. "I'm into some shit you don't know about, and I don't want you to get hurt. I'll see ya," he said, before turning around and walking out, without even a hug. Sean knew he would see him again, though that didn't stop the tears. He was horribly in love with him, and was certain Gary felt the same way about him.

For the next month he went about finishing the semester, feeling like his heart had been ripped out of his chest. He let himself cry when he wanted to. He quit going out at night and concentrated on school, deciding he'd had enough of the streets.

One night, though, he took a path home from school that intersected with the old turf. Same parade: fifteen cars following close around the strip. He walked past an alley, where a pickup truck was parked, but running, with its headlights on. From the truck bed he heard grunts, and someone crying out in pain. Someone was getting the shit kicked out of them.

Without thinking he threw his books down and ran up there, finding two reckneckish characters beating up one of the hustlers, a tall thin kid with red hair who had always seemed vulnerable. One was slugging him in the stomach with a baseball bat, while the other held his head back to keep him from doubling over.

"Hey, assholes!" Sean shouted. They both stopped and looked at him. They dropped the hustler, who had passed out, and started walking toward him.

Sean's instinct told him to run like hell, but his feet were frozen in place.

From the shadows came a man-sized cat, with flailing blond hair. His scream alone, which had improved since Sean had seen his last workout, stopped the rednecks dead in their tracks. What followed took about twenty seconds, he would guess later: pivot, kick, and Gary deflected the ball bat, sending it several feet away; kick, kick, and triple punch…one of the rednecks was on the ground, and the other was in trouble. Gary landed his right foot on the guy's shin, just below the knee. Sean heard the *craaack*, saw the impossible angle the man's leg was at now, and the strange color his face had turned. Neither would be any trouble, anymore.

Gary stood back, watching the one on the ground warily, as he was slowly getting up.

"*You shits had enough? You want more?*" Gary shrieked. "*Come on! You want some of this?*" Sean had never seen him this hyped before, and he knew Gary was more than capable of killing these two, if he so desired. His moves so far had served to immobilize. If he went any further, the two wouldn't live another minute.

"Come on…let's get out of here…." one of them said, and helped the one with the broken leg to the truck. A minute later, the truck burned rubber out of there. Sean ignored them and went to the fallen kid, who wasn't moving.

"I'll call an ambulance," Gary said, walking off. "Stay with him."

"Wait, Gary! You're coming back?"

"Cops are looking for me," was all he said, disappearing behind a building.

"Gary?" He was already gone.

Sean slammed the brakes of his bug, nearly running a red light, killing the engine in the process. The lit cigarette fell in his lap. Absently, he knocked it on the floor. His mind had drifted to God only knew where, thinking about Gary, everything that had happened here fifteen years ago. "*Shit*," he muttered, looking to see if there were any cops around. He was halfway into the intersection. Nothing left to do but start the bug and get out of the way. *Go home, Sean*, he told himself, smashing the cigarette with his heel. *Go home.*

Movement, and a broad expanse of bare flesh, caught his eye before he turned right on Tenth. Someone was walking on the right side of Main. Either by instinct, or reflex, he proceeded south on Main to check out the pedestrian. *Just like the old days*, he thought, while at the same time knowing there was no cruising going on here anymore, not really. But still, it was the same pattern, and not out of his way. And half naked, he looked attractive. *What the hell. Looking won't hurt.* Still, he checked both doors to make sure they were locked.

He pulled up beside him, slowing down, knowing this was anything but subtle. The kid had blond hair, like Gary, and wore only jeans, like Gary. In his right hand he held the glowing ember of a cigarette, or maybe a joint. *Bad boys. My type.*

The boy turned to look at him. It *was* Gary.

Can't be, Sean thought, rubbing his eyes. The boy, Gary, whoever, glanced at the bug, rolled his eyes and looked the other way, ignoring him. *Just like Gary to turn his nose up at a piece of shit car like this.* Sean continued to pace him. The cocky walk, the sneer, the missing teeth, the wild, rangy hair. *Jesus Christ, that is Gary. He hasn't aged a day.*

Sean pulled over, put the car in park, a nd got out.

"Gary, is that you?" he called over the roof of the Bug. "It's *Sean.*"

When he said *Sean,* Gary stopped, and looked at the car. He looked sad, perhaps confused, but there was no doubt in Sean's mind that this was Gary. He felt tears behind his eyes, he was so glad to see him. Gary looked even more sad, tried to say something but was apparently having trouble putting his message into words or sounds, whatever it would be.

Then like a puff of smoke, the image drifted away, leaving behind the faint scent of cigarette smoke. No one stood on the sidewalk as Sean stared, the bug idling roughly, as it always did. If it had been Gary, he was long gone now…in fact, he could never have been there.

Thinking as little as possible, Sean got into the bug and drove off in search of the nearest ramp for Highway 51, the road for home.

‖

He had always lived in apartments, but when Sean arrived home at 1:30 to the sounds of a loud, drunken party next door, he wondered if maybe it was time to buy a house. Tired as he was though, he had no trouble falling asleep.

His dreams were filled with Gary, Gary on the street, Gary in bed, Gary walking around his trashy little apartment with an open beer can, wearing nothing but a smile. In spite of being a street kid, he had always managed to stay clean, and usually smelled of soap, touched with a hint of his own musk. Given a choice, Gary would probably never wear clothes. He seemed perfectly comfortable without them.

But the dreams became dark and urgent, as if something terrible was about to happen.

Sean, you've got to let me in, Gary had said. He was holding the old skeleton key that went to their room at the Ambassador. *I don't know what's going on…what's happened to me. You're the only one who can talk to me.*

Sean didn't know what he was talking about, but knew this was a dream. He might make this a lucid dream; he'd been practicing. Gary was standing there, naked. It had been so long, and he still loved him….

But they were not in the same world. Gary was reaching across a gulf, from somewhere *else*.

It keeps going in circles, Gary pleaded. *Sometimes I know, sometimes I don't.* His words carried fear, and Sean had never seen him afraid, of anything. *Where am I…?*

Sean sat straight up in bed, glistening with sweat, his blood pounding in his temples.

Someone's in the apartment. He was certain of it, even though he knew he had locked and chained the door. The party raged on next door. Maybe one of the drunks had wandered in by accident.

He got up to check things out, the street light casting enough illumination through the open bedroom window to see by. The door was still locked, the flimsy gold chain hanging, intact. He smelled a cigarette, though, and caught the faint trail of smoke rising from one of his ashtrays.

Shit, did I leave that burning? he thought, but he knew he would have put it out in the sink instead of messing up an ashtray. He checked the kitchen, the closets. No spooks. He picked up the snuffed cigarette, a corner of it still burning, then put it out and went to bed, putting the whole thing out of his mind so he could get some sleep.

He rose at noon, as was his custom, and went into the living room to watch the midday news on Channel 6. The preset coffee pot was ready, and he poured himself a big cup before sitting down.

44

The cigarette butt was still in the ashtray, snuffed, crumpled. Sean picked it up, knowing it could not have been his. It smelled like it had been dipped in something. *Butyl Nitrate*, he thought, sniffing it again. *This thing's been dipped in poppers.*

Poppers had been illegal and unavailable for years, but were popular during the late 70s and early 80s. *Gary dipped his cigarettes in poppers. That's how he got stoned when there was no pot around.*

It occurred to him that he had never learned what happened to Gary. He had just disappeared, and Sean was ashamed to realize he hadn't really tried to find out. Now he wanted to know. *Did he have a criminal record? Probably. The cops were looking for him.*

He called a friend on the police force, Joel, who was Family. Joel was a clerk in old records, and owed Sean a favor.

"Gary Tanner," Sean told him, and gave him a description, approximate date of birth, everything he could think of. There was only one way to spell "Tanner" in the phone book, so they went with that. Joel said it wasn't much, but he would find out what he could.

On the way into his three o'clock shift, he stopped at Joel's office in the police department, to see if he had had any luck. His friend was nearing his forties, with thinning hair and wire frame glasses, and they had accidentally run into each other at a gay watering hole two years before.

He was leaving his office when Sean showed up. "Here," he said, handing him a manila envelope. "He was under the John Does. Filed as 'Gary,' no last name. He was a hustler, wasn't he?"

Sean nodded, slightly embarrassed, and hoped Joel wouldn't ask any more questions.

Joel seemed to understand. "Just remember, I didn't give this to you."

"Thanks. We're even," Sean said.

"You bet we are," Joel said, turning toward the hallway.

Sean had an hour before he had to be at his station, so he stopped in the john and closed himself in a stall. He pulled out the file, and paused. It said "autopsy."

Thinking nothing, feeling nothing, Sean went through the photocopies, still warm from the machine. There was a picture of Gary, face down on a silver table. His back was covered with numerous narrow, clean holes. The report paperclipped to the picture said he had been stabbed forty times in the back with a seven-inch hunting knife, and left face down in an alley near 17th and Boulder. There were other pictures, showing his face. It was Gary, without a doubt, and he'd been murdered. The date confirmed that this had happened shortly after the incident in the alley with the tall redheaded kid, the two rednecks and the baseball bat. Sean's first impression was that one or both of the shitheads had come back and done Gary. However, fifteen years later, the case was still "unsolved."

Sean put the copies back into the file, and went to work. He wanted to grieve, but now was not the time, and with effort he went into his detached, 911 operator trance. He couldn't allow himself to feel anything, at least until his shift was over. Then he would go somewhere and get good and drunk.

Three hours into his shift, and so far the calls had consisted of two kids playing with a telephone and a lady who'd gotten wedged between two bookcases at the downtown library. Monday nights tended to be slow, but tonight was downright comatose. He was still laughing halfheartedly with Sylvia about the stuck woman when he got the first "real" call of the night.

"Operator 911."

"Yeah, I'm downtown, at a pay phone. Two guys in a pickup truck beat the crap out of this kid with a bat." He sounded like a kid himself.

"Where is he?" Sean asked. "We need a location." But already the whole thing was sounding eerily familiar. And the kid. He knew that voice.

"In the alley behind the Fourth National drive-up."

"You mean the Citisquare drive-up?" It hadn't been the Fourth National in years. In 1986 Fourth National went bankrupt.

"It's the only damned drive-up downtown," the kid said, sounding like he was holding back tears. "Send an ambulance! He's hurt real bad."

"Okay, okay…" Sean said. He waved to Sylvia, gave her the note that said, "Alley behind Citisquare drive-up. Police and ambulance."

The kid hung up, and that was the end of the call. "Shit," Sean muttered. "What was he afraid of…?"

He froze at the end of that thought, as he realized who that was, and why the situation was so familiar. The injured kid was tall and red- headed, but would live in spite of some nasty internal injuries inflicted by the bat. But the call was only about fifteen years late.

No, but I have to be sure, Sean thought. He wanted a cigarette but couldn't leave the phone, had to call the police dispatcher to see what had happened. It could happen again. *It could always happen again.*

The call was a prank, he learned when he called the dispatch. The police found the payphone, with the receiver dangling off the hook, no one in sight. Hell, it was downtown. No one's down there at night anymore. The only thing the ambulance crew found in the alley behind the drive-up was a wino asleep in a dumpster.

"Great," Sean whispered after she hung up. "It was Gary."

"Who?" Sylvia asked, but she was yawning.

"Nothing," he said, and noticed the time. Break time. "I'm going to go have a smoke."

III

This time he parked the bug at a meter, just south of Seventh and Main, in front of the old Indian store. Of course, it was closed at this hour. Everything was closed. Next door was a print shop, and next to it, the Citisquare bank drive-up. It seemed a logical place to go, given the nature of tonight's frantic emergency call.

The moment he set foot on pavement, he noticed a change in his perception, as if he'd stepped across a threshold, into another place. But it had always been like that, the fine line between the people who drove the cars, and those who did not, who walked the street in search of a place to stay for the night, or for a quick twenty or fifty dollars, to buy a hamburger and a night's drinking at Tim's, a gay bar some two miles away on Eleventh, and maybe if there was anything left over from all that you could get a dime bag of weed behind the bar. This time the transition was different, more final; he was crossing into another time, when he'd felt the stirrings of first sex and first love, a part of him he had shut off for many years. Part of it was because he knew he would never find another Gary again, as imperfect as he was. Now Sean was embracing it all again, and he wasn't at all certain what he was going to find.

The drive-up entered at a right angle, between the old brick buildings. The drive-up had many advantages to the hustlers who had loitered here late at night. There was a short wall to sit on, and a long planter behind it one could ditch drugs in when necessary. Above on the digital display was the time and temperature, useful information to the whores, who wore no watch, and to the johns, who would have an idea how much free skin they would see that night.

Sean sat on the wall, the meatrack, the billboard, the place Gary and any number of hookers had sat which announced to anyone driving by, *I'm for sale.*

He lit a cigarette and waited. Up the street was a vacant lot the junior college had taken over for parking. A few students just getting out of night classes walked by, but Sean knew he was invisible, in spite of the fluorescent light behind him. They didn't look up to see him. Already they were in another world, another time.

Then Sean saw the long black Cadillac, the 1975 boat he remembered seeing cruising the street several times. One of Gary's regulars. As it pulled hard to port, stopped, and let someone out, he noticed it wasn't entirely solid. The parking meter showed through on the other side. The big black car pulled away, leaving a spectral figure standing on the sidewalk.

Their eyes met, and Sean's breath caught. *Well, this is what I came here for,* he thought frantically as his heart pounded. *If I can keep from running from him…*

On the street, driving by slowly, deliberately, were other cars, vague shadows of what they once were, what Sean remembered. The landscape shifted, and the vacant lot now had an office supply store it in, with ads in the window advertising a special on carbon paper, and other items from before the computer age.

Gary casually pulled out a pack of cigarettes from a hip pocket and started walking toward Sean. In his front pocket was another bulge, probably a roll of twenties from the driver of the Cadillac.

"What're you doing out here?" Gary said, accusingly. He stopped a few feet in front of Sean, wearing his usual attire, ventilated jeans and tonight, no shoes. He seemed so much smaller now, but his chest glistened with summer sweat. Such a tough, meaty little guy, with blond hair and a baby face. *Was I ever that young?* Sean thought.

"You're not hookin', are you?" Gary asked. Sean felt heat emanating from his image, which was translucent, as if projected. His voice sounded distant and distorted, as if he heard it in a long, naked tunnel. As near as Gary stood, Sean knew he was far away.

"No, I'm not," Sean said, wondering how Gary recognized him. He was fifteen years older now, thirty-three for crissakes, with short hair and decent clothes. Not the image Gary knew. "I came out here to see you. Being here, on this particular sidewalk, would get your attention. You've been trying to reach me."

Gary's expression darkened, a strange mix of confusion and sadness.

"Haven't you?" Sean persisted.

"Yes," he replied, sounding different, mature, almost. "I don't know what's going on. I mean, sometimes I know. It goes in circles. Right now, I don't know." He looked to his left, at the parade of cars driving past. "Those guys, this was the only family they knew. This damned street. And then they died, and they had nowhere to go, except here."

Gary's image sharpened, solidified. It made Sean ache to see him in such perfection, the smooth skin, the missing teeth.

"You're still beautiful," Sean said.

Gary looked down and grinned. "That's what they all say. But you always saw more than that. That's why I came back to you."

I'm the closest thing he ever had to a family, Sean realized, choking back a sigh. *He never told me. He never knew how.*

"How can I help you?" Sean asked. The image came into sharp focus, and Gary looked solid, real. But he was afraid to see his back, of what he might find there.

"I'm dead, aren't I?" Gary said, sounding small and fragile. He looked like a little boy, lost, so lost. "I know, now."

"Yes. You were murdered. Stabbed in the back."

Gary brightened. "I figured. Came up behind me. I was a little stoned. But I killed one of them. The asshole's still walking around here somewhere, he's more confused than I am. Kicking his ass on a regular basis keeps me going out here. He thinks he's in hell. And the other one will probably never have kids."

Sean sucked in his breath as Gary suddenly turned his back on him, to regard the traffic a little more directly. Thankfully, his back was smooth and unblemished. "Were they the ones who beat up Red?" Sean asked.

"Yeah, they were the ones," Gary replied, still facing the traffic. He turned to face him, looking concerned. "Is Red okay?"

"He pulled through. He's married, with a little girl."

Gary did not look surprised. "I'm glad. He always wanted a woman." He dragged on the cigarette, which looked as real as he did now. He remembered the butt he found in his ashtray at home. "I'm stuck here, you know," Gary said, defeated. "I can't go on. I've been watching you for a long time, only you don't know it. When you would go out to the bars, looking for sex, I watched the guys who came on to you. I could see whether or not they had Gay Cancer, or anything else that would hurt you. If they did, I could make you change your mind about them. I made you turn them away."

"You what?" Sean sat up. The announcement was sudden, startling, and disturbing. That a spirit, even if it was Gary, had such an influence on his life was not a comfortable thought, no matter how he looked at it. "All this time. That's why..." *That's why I'm still alive*, he thought. *Good God, and I always wondered why. All the things I was doing, before anyone knew how the shit spread.* So many times he encountered hot young men with whom he shared a mutual interest. Very few he actually ended up in bed with...the others slipped through his fingers, and he never knew why, what explained it. He'd kicked himself for freezing up, getting tongue tied, or for saying stupid things that turned them off, unable to explain where the words had come from. Later he would hear they had been diagnosed, were in a hospice somewhere, or at home, or at a hospital, or dead. So many close calls. He never knew why until now.

"Yeah, well hey," Gary said. "Don't get me wrong. I didn't mind you getting laid. I just didn't want you to die. It wasn't your time. Anyway, death sucks."

Sean stepped on the cigarette, and lit another, hoping the gesture would hide the tears in his eyes. Gary saw them anyway.

"Now don't get all pickle faced." Gary said. "You would have done the same for me, wouldn't you?"

Wordlessly, Sean nodded. "Gary. Can you touch me?"

"It changes," he said. "But I think now…" He reached forward, his palm touching Sean's forehead. Warmth, nothing solid, just a heat like an electric blanket. Gary pulled away. "It takes a lot to do that. I don't have the energy right now."

Don't go away yet. "You don't have to watch over me anymore," Sean said, knowing that what he was telling Gary would hurt them both. "I mean, you don't have to be stuck here. You have other places to go now, and it's not right for you to stay here." He looked at the strip, the vague shadows of cars that could not possibly be there. "This is your past. You're buried now, you're in the ground…" The words were coming with a lot more difficulty. *Do I know what the hell I'm talking about? Don't I want him to be around?*

"There are so many of us who are stuck here, you know," Gary said, evidently trying to steer the topic away from his possible destination. "Died young. Died in pain. I'm just one of thousands and thousands…"

"It's *you* that matters," Sean said, forcing himself to go on, knowing he was close to a breakthrough of sorts, and uncertain where his words were coming from. "Forget about the rest of them. Others will take care of them. You came back to me for a reason. Why?"

Sean saw that familiar sneer, a self-confident expression that told the world that he knew fucking everything, and no one had better cross him. "Because you can see me now. You're talking to me now. Who else would do that?"

Sean felt there was more. He waited for him to continue.

"And *because*," Gary continued, looking a little embarrassed, "you took me in and treated me like a person. No one had ever done that. Ever. You loved me and I loved you, that was about all there was to it." He looked away suddenly, acting like he was angry. He was still trying to sound tough, even in death. He could not do this any other way.

"Yeah, I think I can buy that," Sean said, trying to sound skeptical. "So what happens now, do you hang around here for eternity? Watch these guys drive around forever, checking you out, picking you up and treating you like shit? What do you need money for, anyway?"

Gary shrugged. "Not much left to spend it on, is there? Who wants to be the richest whore in some cemetery?"

Their eyes met again, and Gary cracked a smile. He could swear he was standing right there. It was such a Garylike expression, the humor leaking through the pain.

"I need to go," Gary said, looking toward the street.

"No," Sean said, getting to his feet. Gary was showing himself to the traffic again. A Lincoln was slowing down. "Don't let them pick you up. Or else it will just go on forever."

Gary looked uncertain. After all, this was all he ever knew.

"You're right," Gary said. "I've talked to you now, I've said what I had to. You heard me, and you came here to listen some more. If I wait around anymore I'll forget I ever talked to you, I'll walk around here half naked like some fucking idiot and do it all over again." Thunder rumbled somewhere overhead.

"Gary, you've been here long enough," Sean said. "You've helped me, now help yourself."

At the end of Main Street, just before a mall, a single headlight appeared. A motorcycle? They both saw it, watched it in silence.

"I don't know what it is," Gary said. "I've never seen it before."

But already, Sean saw the changes in Gary's spirit. He turned transparent again, and his voice sounded distant. The light turned into a tunnel, and Sean felt it pulling, at Gary, not himself.

"I don't know what it is," Gary said. "If it's heaven or hell. Or what."

"It's neither, but it's better than this," Sean said with conviction. "It's time." Thunder again, closer this time.

Gary held up his hand, and Sean reached for it, feeling the warmth again for a brief moment before it was gone. Gary tried to say something, but already he was dissolving, turning to light, swirls of brightness that folded around the entity that was Gary, who was only light now. Suddenly he was gone, the light was gone, having taken him with it.

Lightning ripped through the sky, and thunder boomed between the buildings. The bank clock flickered. Sidewalk and streets were soaking wet, and junior college students ran for their cars.

But he stayed where he was. Under cover of the downpour he sobbed without restraint. What he would give to hold him, one last time… He looked up at the falling rain, a miniature meteor shower reflected in the streetlight, stinging like small bullets against his face. The sobbing stopped, he had truly spent himself, and he felt cleansed. The rain had washed his pain away, at least for the time being.

Then as abruptly as the storm had begun, it faded into the background, leaving behind a freshly showered street glistening black, and the endless dirge of runoff dripping through a thousand gutters.

I'm changed. I'm never going to be the same again. He felt uplifted by the revelation, not depressed. *Time to get back to work,* he thought, and realized he was soaking wet, as were his cigarettes. Drenched. He tossed the soggy pack in the gutter, where a small river had formed, and started toward the bug.

Halfway to his car, he wasn't feeling nearly as sad. *I had to do that for Gary, that was the best thing I could have done. After all…he did it for me.* He had had a guardian angel all these years, and had not known. Now he was gone. *I love Gary. I have to let him go.*

He sat in his car, smelling the strange plastic-and-motor oil fragrance peculiar to old bugs like this. After touching a part of the universe he never really believed existed, it felt rather mundane to turn the ignition of the Volkswagen.

He drove a few blocks on the wet streets, and marveled at what a privilege it was to be alive.

PRINCE OF THE DARK GREEN SEA

BY

MARK MCLAUGHLIN

e have all grown up with fairy tales in one form
or another. Mark McLaughlin gives us a
reworking of the tale of the Prince of the Dark
Green Sea. In the more familiar version, we
know exactly what the fisherman's wife wanted…but what of her husband?
What did the fisherman want? Did he himself even know? In Mark's telling,
we learn that perhaps we do not always know our own desires until someone
else points the way.

—S. P.

A fisherman and his wife lived by the sea in a shack of rotted boards
and driftwood. Each morning the fisherman cast his net into the dark
green waters, and each afternoon his wife carried his catch to the village
to sell. Each night, she gutted a fish and boiled it in a copper pot for their
dinner. Work and sun and salt air toughened the skin and grizzled the
hair of the fisherman and his wife. What time they spent together was
used to collect grass and sticks for their fire. When they spoke, they spoke
of tides and wind and petty village intrigues. So they lived for many years.

One morning, the fisherman caught a most frightening fish. The vile thing had black scales and filthy needle teeth. He was about to slap the monster against a boulder when he noticed that its eyes were brown and sorrowful and strangely beautiful. The fisherman put the fish back in the water, saying, "Swim away, my sad little friend."

When he returned to the shack, he told his wife about his catch. The old woman smoked a pipeful of dried blue seaweed as she listened.

"Surely I am married to a fool," she said. "That was a magic fish, and you should have made a wish."

"What would I have wished for?" the fisherman asked.

"Such a stupid question. Do you want to live in this worthless hovel forever?" His wife blew a cloud of smoke in his face. "Go back and ask the fish for a fine warm cottage."

"I should like to sleep in such a cottage." With this, the fisherman left the shack. He returned to the boulder and called out, "Swim back, my sad little friend."

The water rippled and the black-scaled creature appeared. The man gazed into its beautiful, melancholy eyes. He then noticed that the fish's mouth had changed. It now had a beautiful mouth, too. The lips were red and the teeth were even and white.

"My wife told me to come and wish for a fine warm cottage." The fisherman held out his hands. "She is a hard worker, my wife. No one deserves happiness more."

"Go home, catcher of fish," said the monster in a low murmur of a voice. "The Prince of the Dark Green Sea is indebted to you. I know what you want and I know what you need. Your wife has her cottage."

The fisherman returned home and found a cottage of pink stone where the shack had been. Around the cottage grew bushes abundant with fragrant pink roses. He lifted the gold latch on the cherrywood door and went inside. His wife smiled at him from the rocking chair by the fireplace. He believed the woman to be content, and returned the smile.

But in a week's time, she again blew pipe-smoke in his eyes. "You gave that miserly fish back his life and how does he repay you? With a paltry cottage. Go now: I desire to be a queen in a castle."

The fisherman nodded wearily and returned to the boulder. "Swim back, my sad little friend," he said.

Again the fish poked its head out of the water. The creature's black scales had turned to beautiful milk-white skin.

"I thank you for the cottage, good fish," the man said. "But my wife must be a queen in a castle. She is a hard worker, my wife. No one deserves happiness more."

"The Prince of the Dark Green Sea is indebted to you." The fish blinked its sorrowful brown eyes. "Your wife has what she wants."

Upon his return, the fisherman saw, instead of the cottage, a castle of silver bricks. The trees and shrubs surrounding the castle were adroitly trimmed to resemble fabulous beasts: harpies, satyrs, rampant griffins and more. A lady-in-waiting led him to his wife's chamber, where the old woman sat before a mirror of polished silver. She ignored him as she styled her stringy gray hair around a glorious silver diadem.

The fisherman's wife drank royal jelly liqueur and pomegranate wine from the castle's mazelike cellars. She ate roast lamb and delicate pastries from the well-stocked larders. She slept on cushions filled with the down of baby swans. And by the end of a month, she considered these luxuries woefully lacking.

"Truly I must become an empress, in a palace befitting my rank," she said. "Take this wish to the magic fish. I am sure that he would think nothing of such a small request."

The fisherman went to the boulder and called for the fish. The Prince of the Dark Green Sea now had long black hair and the face of a beautiful young man.

The old man stared in admiration at the fine features of the Prince. He then made his request. The creature said, "I am indebted to you. Your wife has what she wants. Go now, catcher of fish."

The fisherman walked home. The castle was now an exquisite palace of gold. About the grounds were scattered towering golden statues of the fisherman's wife, all more than flattering. In the sky, guards garbed in golden armor rode roaring bat-winged chimeras.

The fisherman found his wife seated on a golden throne. Around her thin shoulders was draped a robe of spun gold; on her head was a filigreed golden crown, graced with cunningly crafted amber plumes. On plush divans lounged smirking pleasure-boys who regarded the aged fisherman with disdain.

In her callused palm, the fisherman's wife held a box carved from an enormous yellow sapphire. She opened the box and dipped a wee golden spoon into the crystalline powder within. With a languorous moan, she snuffed the sparkling powder up a nostril.

"Ah, the life of an empress…" The woman frowned hugely. "So very *boring*."

"But—" The fisherman's eyes opened wide. "I've only just returned from the shore. I thought you would be happy for at least a year."

"A year? A year of this utter tedium?" She dismissed the notion with a wave of her hand. "You must be mad."

A young handmaiden entered the throne room carrying a tray of beauty ointments. She began to massage a mixture of honey and lily oil on the old woman's sere cheekbones.

"There's no need for that," said the fisherman's wife with a bitter laugh. "You might as well rub your fancy balm onto a chunk of granite."

The handmaiden studied the face of the empress. "If you like, I can brew a clever skin-softening unguent, made from the fetuses of rare albino alpacas."

The old woman pushed the handmaiden away. "The pretty fool has given me a marvelous idea," she cried to her husband. "There is certainly no need for her silly creams. Inform the magic fish that I wish to have control over time. Then I shall turn back the clock and make myself young again." She glanced toward her pleasure-boys and simpered.

The fisherman could not believe his ears. "Control over time?"

"Yes—and space, too. I should like to make my palace larger." She looked up into the far shadows of the throne room's ceiling. "This miserable closet is so close, I can scarcely breathe. Now do as I say, before I summon the guards and have you tossed into an oubliette. I am aging needlessly even as we speak."

The fisherman hurried out of the palace—but gradually his steps slowed to a crawl, for he was reluctant to ask the magic fish for yet another wish so soon. It was twilight by the time he reached the boulder. "Swim back, my sad little friend," he said.

This time, the Prince of the Dark Green Sea walked out of the water. The creature now had a human body, well-formed and desirable. The fisherman was so enthralled that for a moment, he forgot why he had returned. But at last he remembered his errand. "Forgive me, good fish, but my wife desires even more. She must have control over time and space."

"I am indebted to you—indeed I am. I know what you want and I know what you need." The beautiful young man stepped forward and placed his cool palms on the fisherman's chest. "Your wife is now back in the wretched shack. And you shall come with me, catcher of fish. You are a hard worker and no one deserves happiness more."

So saying, the Prince of the Dark Green Sea pulled the fisherman beneath the waves.

WATER SNAKES

BY

HOLLY WADE MATTER

or this story, Holly Wade Matter borrowed elements from her own Arkansas summers: "The sculptures down the street from my grandmother's house; my great-grandmother's oil paintings; the graciousness of dinner at noon; gardens, bamboo, heat." It is with this precise evocation of detail that Matter shows us both the sexual and artistic awakening of young Peggy as she partakes of a mystery more complex than she or her wild cousin Jeff ever expected; one that only she will comprehend.
— N.G.

My cousin Jeff crouched down, pressed his ear to the sidewalk like an Indian in a Western movie, and listened for the thud-thud-thud of Miz Wilkes and the creak-scrape-creak of Miz Hicks. I sat in the prickly grass, in the shade of Grandma Estelle's magnolia, watching Jeff's flushed, freckled face, scratching the chigger welts on my legs. Aunt Sue lived in the country, and Grandma Estelle lived in town. During my Arkansas summer, Jeff and I split our time between them. The country had terrapin to tease, and water moccasins to harrow us, to dare us and set our hearts pounding. Town had Elephant and Cane.

Elephant and Cane didn't go to church. They never visited, either, or let anybody visit them. Graying paint peeled from their old house, and their yard was full of weeds and pecan hulls and rotting, worm-holed crab apples. Aunt Sue said they hadn't even opened their tacky blinds in years.

"Lord knows, I've done my best to convince them they don't need to be alone," Grandma Estelle said that morning, when Aunt Sue dropped us off. "But they're proud, private ladies, and they don't want anybody chipping away at their independence, even if it means letting that house fall apart around them."

"I've always said that house was too big for a couple of old maids," Aunt Sue replied. "I expect the college will buy it and turn it into a fraternity house, once they die."

"Yes," said Grandma Estelle dryly. "I expect they will."

Aunt Sue shivered. "It's spooky, thinking of two old maids holed up in that house all their lives. I'd bet you money they're a couple of—"

"Jeff, Peggy, you just scoot out of here!" Grandma Estelle said, sharply interrupting Aunt Sue (something only grown-ups were allowed to do). She did this every time Aunt Sue tried to talk about the divorce and what Uncle Boss had done to deserve it. Used to it, we scooted; once we were outside, Jeff grabbed my arm and whispered, "I knew it!"

I tugged my arm free. "Knew what?"

"They're *witches!*"

"Who is?"

"Elephant and Cane. Didn't you hear Mama? She was about to say it, you heard her."

I breathed out noisily through my nose. "There's no such thing as witches, you dummy."

"Then how come Mama says that peace symbol of yours is a witch symbol?"

I made a mouth and shrugged.

"And how come Elephant and Cane don't let nobody near their tacky old house? 'Cos it's full of skeletons and black slimy kettles and spiders and poisons, that's why."

"That's stupid. Only a dumb Arkie like you would believe in—*ow!*"

As I massaged my punched arm, he hissed, "Maybe they don't have witches in Seattle, but they have 'em here. I been knowing it a long time now. And I'm gonna prove it to you."

I sniffed. "How?"

"We'll show 'em your peace symbol. If it really is a witch symbol, like Mama says, then Elephant and Cane'll go crazy when they see it, like those murderers on Perry Mason."

"If they don't," I said, "you gotta buy me a Coke every day for a week."

"If they do, you gotta buy me. Deal?"

"Deal."

So now I lay on the lawn, watching and waiting, even though Grandma Estelle had told us over and over, "Don't you bother Miz Wilkes and Miz Hicks. Just leave them alone. God Almighty didn't give you life so you could be a nuisance to old ladies."

"Here they come," Jeff whispered.

He waited until the last minute to get back. He threw himself on the grass beside me and grabbed my arm. "Don't you run away, now."

"You're the one's scared, not me."

He squinted and tapped those crooked front teeth of his, the way he always did when he was nervous. "I'm not scared. Sh! Here they come."

I heard them: the thud of Miz Wilkes' footsteps, big and soft and heavy as the body that ballooned her flowered cotton dress; and the creak and scrape of Miz Hicks' false leg, hard and wooden as her rubber-tipped cane. They walked every morning at 9:00, before the heat set on. Back and forth, back and forth, three times the length of Magazine Avenue between Live Oak and Seviere.

"Let go my arm," I said. "You're gonna leave a big bruise."

"Shut up!"

Their shadows crossed the sidewalk. Jeff pinched my arm so hard that I smacked him. Then Elephant and Cane appeared.

Once upon a time, Grandma Estelle told me, Miz Wilkes taught ballet, and Miz Hicks gave piano lessons. Try as I might, I just couldn't picture Elephant in a leotard, though it was easy to imagine Cane giving her students a whack across the knuckles if their fingers flattened out. But Grandma Estelle said she didn't need the cane back then.

"Morning, Miz Wilkes. Morning, Miz Hicks," Jeff said in his Sunday School voice. Elephant, who walked nearest the yard and eclipsed all but Cane's gray knob head, glanced down at him through red slits of eyes. She puffed like a train, though she hadn't walked but the length of three houses, and nodded in reply.

Jeff got up and yanked me to my feet. "This is my cousin Peggy from Seattle, Washington. You remember Peggy, don't ya, Miz Wilkes? Her mama and daddy let her fly down all by herself this year."

"I'm eleven years old," I said, to show them I wasn't a baby.

"She brought me these wings, see?" He tugged at the chest of his T-shirt to show off the silver pin, then dug around in his pocket and pulled out the tube of Vicks. "And this, too. You stick it in your nose and smell it, to keep your ears from hurting when the airplane lands. You wanna smell, Miz Wilkes?"

Miz Wilkes shook her head from side to side, heavily.

"And look what she got! Show 'em, Peggy. It's a charm. A real magic charm, from a fortune-teller."

That was a lie. I got it out of a gum machine in Safeway. But when I hung back, he reached down my T-shirt and pulled out the peace symbol, jerking me forward by the chain.

"It's real powerful, Miz Wilkes. Peggy'll let you wear it, if you want."

Miz Hicks was the one who spoke, in a voice that scraped my ear like a carrot grater. "You should be ashamed of yourself, Jefferson Doty. Taking stock in heathen nonsense."

"Don't ya just want to touch it?"

"I do not."

"But Peggy said the fortune-teller said it granted every wish."

I blushed right down to the tips of my braids, embarrassed to be included in Jeff's stupid lying, but something like loyalty kept me quiet.

"Then perhaps," said Miz Hicks, "it will spare your mother the expense of braces."

They continued their slow stroll down Magazine without another word.

Jeff watched them go, his eyes narrowed, his face red, his fists knotted as though he were trying to squeeze two fireflies to death. His crooked teeth were his sore spot. He said they'd gotten knocked crooked by a twelve-point buck that charged him last hunting season, but even I wasn't citified enough to believe something like that. I thought maybe Uncle Boss had something to do with it.

Jeff's teeth weren't going to straighten out any time soon—Aunt Sue just didn't have the extra money for braces. Miz Hicks was mean to tease him about it.

"*Damn* them."

"Jeff!" I couldn't believe he'd said that word. It was the worst word you could say.

"They're so damn mean, they gotta be witches."

"But they didn't go crazy when they saw the charm," I said, wondering if I ought to tell Grandma Estelle that Jeff used a swear word.

"They wouldn't touch it, either!" he yelled. "Because if they did, they'd probably grow horns and tails and get even damn uglier!"

He stomped back to Grandma Estelle's yard, swinging his fists, kicking the crewcut lawn; flopped down in the magnolia's shade, picked off one of the broad white blossoms, and shredded it. Grandma Estelle had told me never to touch the blossoms, since even the lightest touch would leave a bruise on the petals.

"You shouldn't do that," I said.

"Shut up."

I came over and sat down beside him and rested my chin in my hands. Across the street, Professor Broussard's green Hermes statue, dressed only in a fig leaf and a pointy helmet, watched us as if he had something important to say.

"*Well?*"

Jeff ignored me, staring down Magazine at the slowly walking old women.

"*Well?*"

"Well what?"

"You owe me a Coke every day for a week, remember?"

"Do not. That didn't prove nothin'. But just you wait, Peggy Webster. I'm gonna prove they're witches if it takes all summer."

Dinner was our big meal, and we ate it at noon. Every day at a quarter to noon, Grandma Estelle sent me out to the back garden to pick mint leaves, and told me to make up the iced tea. I got the jar of instant from the pantry, where our height marks were written up in red pencil. Grandma Estelle's pantry smelled of angle food cake, of vanilla and farina and warmth.

Jeff always teased me when I made the tea and set the table and helped Grandma Estelle carry in the chicken-fried steak and mashed potatoes, the black-eyed peas and the cornbread. Grandma Estelle never made him help, because he was a boy. But when the time came to take out the trash, or to mow the lawn, it was my turn to laugh. I'd sit out on the front steps, pretending to read one of Jeff's Archie comic books. When Jeff got too hot, he'd strip off his T-shirt and hang it on one of the hedges. I couldn't do that any more. My nipples had turned into bumps, and before I flew down, Mom had taken all my undershirts away and given me my first bra. When Jeff found out, he snapped my bra strap through my shirt every chance he got. All I could do in return was make fun of the hundreds of freckles that covered his arms, his back and his chest. It didn't feel like an even trade; Jeff had always had those freckles. I didn't even dare tease him about his teeth.

We ate our dinner in the dining room, using the good china and the silver and the chunky Cape Cod crystal water glasses, even when Grandma Estelle was the only grown-up there. When Mom flew down, she'd argue with Grandma Estelle and insist that she shouldn't go to the trouble of fixing such a big dinner. But I liked it.

66

After Grandma Estelle finished the blessing, she folded out her napkin and fixed Jeff with a stare. "I saw you bothering Miz Wilkes and Miz Hicks today. You too, Miss Peggy."

Jeff and I looked at each other, then back at her.

"We were just offering to help them with their yard and stuff," he said. "Weren't we, Peggy?"

"Those two ladies don't have any money to spare on your kind of help, Jefferson Doty. And if they did, they'd probably give it to you just to keep you out of their hair. Now I told you not to bother them, and I meant it."

"We weren't asking for no money," Jeff muttered.

"Peggy, if you keep pushing your food up against your thumb like that, I'm going to cut it off with a steak knife. Use a piece of bread. Now, Jeff, I don't want to hear another word about those two ladies. Eat your dinner. If you like, I'll take you downtown to see the picture show. 'Where Angels Go, Trouble Follows.' Sounds just like you two."

We finished our dinner in silence. Jeff made faces at me, probably for not backing up his lie, but I ignored him and stared at the oil painting above the sideboard. It was a painting Great Grandmother Geraldine had done, of two young ladies dressed in sheets and gold leaf crowns. One looked like she was dancing. The other sat on a broken column, like the ones on Professor Broussard's front lawn, playing a funny, curlicue harp. In the background, a summer storm was building, all black clouds and streak lightning and heavy rain.

I looked at the ladies, thinking how nice it would be to grow up beautiful, how nice it would be to dance in sheets and not worry about getting wet when the storms came.

"Peggy! For the third time—my heavens, child, you can't stop spying on them, can you?"

"What?" I stared at Grandma Estelle.

"Miz Wilkes and Miz Hicks. You watched them all morning, and now you're staring your way through dinner at them." Grandma Estelle nodded toward the painting, exasperated. "I don't know why you can't get them out of your mind, but—"

"That's Elephant and Cane?" I stared at the painting with new, disbelieving interest. Jeff got up and stood right in front of it, blocking my view.

"Peggy, what did I tell you about name-calling?" Grandma Estelle said. "That's Miz Wilkes and Miz Hicks, and don't look so discombobulated about it. I've told you that a dozen times or more."

"No you haven't," I protested, getting up and nudging Jeff aside. "I mean, no, Ma'am."

"Yes, Ma'am! I have, Ma'am! A dozen times or more. You must have been off daydreaming when I told you. Always daydreaming."

"It can't be them," Jeff said. "They're pretty."

Grandma Estelle snorted. "Did you think they were born old?"

"No...I just didn't think anyone that pretty could get so ugly."

"Lord have mercy," Grandma Estelle muttered under her breath. "Imagine what he says about me."

"But Grandma," I said, "if that's really Ele—Miz Wilkes and Miz Hicks, then how come they're dressed like that, I mean, like Romans or something?"

"It was the style," Grandma Estelle said firmly. "Your Great Grandmother painted in the classical style. She wanted to paint a picture of Terpsichore and Euterpe, and she used Miz Wilkes and Miz Hicks as models."

"Who?"

"Terpsichore and Euterpe. They were Muses. Euterpe was the Muse of music, and Terpsichore was the Muse of dance. Don't they teach Greek mythology in the schools any more?"

"Were the Muses witches?" Jeff asked hopefully.

"No, they were not. Now finish your dinner, and I'll take you down to the picture show."

But neither of us wanted to see the movie. We sat in the sticky velvet seats and whispered until the gang of teenage girls the next row up turned and started throwing their popcorn at us.

"D'you suppose Elephant and Cane are really Terp—those Muse ladies?" Jeff whispered.

"No. Shut up."

"You shut up." He pinched me, hard, the same spot he'd pinched me that morning. I howled. The teenage girls turned around as one and glared at me.

"If you all don't keep quiet, I'm getting the usher!" one of them said menacingly.

"Okay, okay." Jeff waved them away. Then he bent next to my ear and said, in a damp whisper, "We're gonna get in that house if it kills us. We're gonna get in that house *tonight*."

I just stared at him, wide-eyed. He stared back.

"Why?" I said at last.

"Because I *say* we're gonna. Now shut up."

And I did, not even saying a word as Grandma Estelle drove us back home.

"How was the show?" she asked.

"Stupid. Girl stuff. And a bunch of nuns, too."

"I'm glad you enjoyed it," Grandma Estelle said dryly. "Why, Peggy, you're awfully quiet. Did you eat too many Jujifruits?"

I shook my head, though the dread did lie in my stomach like too much candy. Jeff kept at me with that purposeful stare, reminding me without a word of what he—what we—were going to do that night. I was sure that Jeff would get in that house, as sure as I was that it would kill him. But I didn't understand why he had to drag me along.

I begged off supper that night, but Grandma Estelle poured me a big glass of 7-Up for my stomach. Then she washed up the dishes and disappeared into the parlor to read.

"What's wrong with you?" Jeff whispered the minute she left.

"I'm not going in that house, Jeff, and you can't make me."

"Baby."

"Creep."

"Scaredy-cat."

"Bucky beaver."

I covered my own mouth the instant after I said it. Jeff colored, and smacked me hard. "You just shut up. I mean it, Peggy. And I don't want you to come along tonight. I don't want to do anything with you ever again, 'cos you're just a stupid girl and you ruin everything."

"I do not!"

"Yes you do. And you know what else? You know what else? You're gonna miss something really big. I'm gonna solve a mystery, and you're gonna miss it. Sure as shootin', because you're too much of a baby to do anything."

"Oh, yeah?" I was mad now, so mad that I almost wasn't scared anymore.

"Yeah!" He sat back, triumph and anger in his face.

"I hope you get killed."

"I hope you get just like Elephant and Cane."

I glared at him, huffed out my breath, and said, "I'm coming!"

Outside, the air was thick, growing thicker as the evening grew darker. There was a storm coming; the smell of waiting lightning surrounded us. Jeff jittered with excitement; a storm would make everything that much better. But my stomach twitched; for me, it would be that much worse.

Fireflies glinted before us, flashing their light bulb tails nearby, then again twenty feet past us. The cicadas' rasp rose and fell in the dusk, and dog-bark echoes ricocheted past our ears down the long, still street. The whip of a lawn-sprinkler suddenly cut off, as if sensing the storm. Hermes seemed to take a step across Professor Broussard's lawn, then stop, as if listening for thunder.

"Here's the plan," Jeff whispered as we huddled down the sidewalk. "We sneak around the back of the house. They got a low balcony back there full of pots and broken chairs and stuff. You gotta boost me up, and once I'm on the balcony, I'll pull you up behind me. Okay?"

"Okay," I whispered, glancing over my shoulder and across the street. I could have sworn that Hermes had taken another step.

It has never taken me so long, before or since, to walk the length of three houses. But it seemed to be hours from the time we snuck out of Grandma Estelle's house to the time we crouched behind the pecan tree in Miz Wilkes' and Miz Hicks' front yard. The wind, hot as the air from a

WATER SNAKES

hair-dryer, had risen, stirring the branches surrounding the old house. All the lights were out. Elephant and Cane must have gone to bed early.

I glanced over my shoulder again. Hermes' left foot now hovered over the sidewalk, copper wings holding up copper weight.

"Jeff, let's go home," I whispered.

"No! Now, come on, Peggy. We have to get in there before—before something happens!" Exasperated, he jerked me through the thick of overgrown camellia bushes to the back of the house.

There was the low balcony, drooping under the weight of old junk, just as Jeff had described it. A gold glow—a night-light?—glimmered through the panes of the French doors. Jeff dragged me beneath the balcony.

"They're up there," I said. "We're gonna get caught!"

"Baby, baby, ba-by," Jeff mouthed. "Gimme a boost up."

I cemented myself against the side of the house and hooked my fingers together. Jeff set a foot in the cradle of my hands, threw his weight up on that foot, and caught the balcony post. He pulled himself up until his belly rested on the rail, then shimmied over. Something crashed, and I froze, my heart hiccoughing against my ribs. For a moment I thought to run away, just run and leave Jeff there; then I remembered Hermes, the walking statue. He was probably in front of Elephant and Cane's house right now. That was probably him rustling through the camellia bushes, coming for me. I wasn't about to run smack into him, not by myself. So when Jeff peered over the balcony at me, I jumped like I'd never jumped before to catch his downstretched hand.

He pulled me as far as he could. I caught hold of the rail with my other hand and grasped my way up and over. Jeff broke my fall.

"God dog, I wish you'd stop making so much noise!" he whispered.

I was too scared to be mad. "Whadda we do now?"

"We look through the doors, stupid!"

We waded as silently as we could through the pots and chair legs, and crouched down by the French doors. The panes were so grimy that we couldn't see anything but the faint golden glow. Jeff grabbed the bottom of his T-shirt and smeared a porthole in the dirty glass. I grabbed the bottom of mine and did the same.

Lightning struck.

It was near, so near that the streak of white fire and the god-gun crash happened as one. It was so near that everything, the peeling paint, the broken junk around us, and our own frightened reflections in the portholes of glass, flared back at us.

"Whoo-whee!" Jeff whistled. "Right in the Taggart's back yard!"

"Please, Jeff, let's just go home!"

"Uh-uh. I'm lookin', and after I look, I'm goin' in."

"Why?" I cried, as the hot-bottled rain poured down.

"Because, ugly, I'm gonna prove Elephant and Cane are witches. And once I prove it, I'm gonna make them do something for me."

He reached up to tap his teeth, almost as if in a daydream. When he caught me staring, he snarled and punched me.

"Stop staring, you baby!"

I started to cry. Jeff gave me a disgusted look, then turned and peered into his porthole.

"Damn. I can't see a—" He whistled, long and low.

"What?" When he didn't answer, I hunkered down by my own porthole and pushed the wet bangs out of my eyes. At first, all I saw was the golden glow, brighter now, and the hazy outline of gryphon-clawed chair legs. "I don't see nothin'!"

"Lookit that!"

"Jeff, I can't see—" And then I could.

At first it was just a flash of slender, fair legs moving gracefully under white cloth. Then the rest of her danced into view, danced like a swan on purple water, like the snowflakes in "The Nutcracker," like the lady in the painting—the lady, Terpsichore, Miz Wilkes, Elephant.

Elephant, shed of her flesh burden, shed of the degenerating years, pared down to birch grace as she danced across the velvet carpet. She was beautiful, more beautiful than the painting had allowed her to be. I watched her, letting my breath drain away like Grandma Estelle said ghost-cats sucked it away.

For the first time, I heard the music over the roar of rain. And I saw Cane without her cane, without her tree-knot knuckles and her doorknob head. She followed Elephant gracefully, also in a draped sheet, and stroked a golden, glowing harp. It was the harp that shone in the room. And the sweeter she played, the warmer it glowed, until it seemed she held a heart-shaped sun in the crook of her arm.

Cane was as beautiful as Elephant. And it seemed to me that they knew each other's beauty and loved it, smiled because of it and with the joy of it.

Then the door to their room swung open, and a pair of copper legs, and copper feet, and copper wings on the heels of those feet, came in.

"I don't believe it!"

"He knows we're here!" I whispered to Jeff, tugging at his arm. "He followed us. I saw him. We have to get out of here!"

"Him?" He looked at me like I was crazy. "There ain't no him in there."

"The—" I stared back, not believing Jeff hadn't seen him. "The statue! Hermes!"

"Peggy, shut up. This ain't no time to be telling me stories." He ducked his head back down and peered through the porthole.

"They've stopped dancing," he said.

I looked quickly. Hermes spoke to them, nodding toward the French doors. Toward us.

"He's telling them about us! Telling them we're here!" I shook with a mouse-trap scream ready to be set off by the first leaf or firefly that touched me.

"There ain't no man in there, Peggy. Ain't no man anywhere around here but me."

I shook my head. "He's leaving now. He's coming to get us."

"I knew I shouldn't have let you come. I knew all you'd do was...was...." Jeff sucked in his breath, then let out a long, shaky sigh. I pressed my face against my porthole.

Terpsichore and Euterpe stood before each other, smiling, still smiling, but with a different kind of smile. And Terpsichore was naked, her sheet drifting over her feet.

For a brief moment, they seemed to glance at me, right at me, with the sudden here-and-gone of lightning. Then Terpsichore reached out, loosened Euterpe's sheet, and let it fall to the floor. Euterpe stroked Terpsichore's face. She drew the dancer to her, and kissed her on the mouth. They pressed together, naked, beautiful, kissing each other the way only men and women did in the movies.

Jeff made a strangling sound, and the next thing I knew, he'd shot past me and scrambled over the balcony railing. I heard the deep, wet thud as his feet hit the rain-pocked dirt.

"Come on, Peggy!" he shouted.

Though I knew he couldn't see me, I shook my head.

"Peggy, get your butt down from there and come *on*!"

I leaned closer to the window, until my forehead rested against it.

"If you don't come on now, I'm leaving you!"

"Go," I said.

He swore. I heard him run from the yard, through the camellias, to the sidewalk. But I sat as if hypnotized, not scared any more. I don't know how long I watched them, their bodies moving like water snakes through the golden light. But when they turned again, and smiled at me, and nodded to me, I knew it was time to go.

When I reached the sidewalk, I found Hermes waiting. It seemed like the most natural thing in the world. Silently, he took my fingers in his warm copper hand, and silently, he walked me home. In front of the yard, I thanked him, and slipped my hand out of his. I reached the front porch and looked back in time to see him freeze into his old position on Professor Broussard's lawn.

"Lord have mercy, what ails you two? Come tearing in here like a bat out of pneumonia, and soaking wet on top of it!"

Grandma Estelle caught my arm and tugged me into the kitchen. The fresh storm smells came through the back screen door.

"First Jeff, bawling like a snake bit him, and now you! What on earth have you been doing?"

"Nothing, Grandma," I stuttered, shivering all over. I couldn't look her in the eye, or she'd know. She'd know right away.

"Well, it must have been something, or Jeff wouldn't be hiding under the dining room table!"

"Ghosts," I said finally.

"Whats?"

I started to cry, not because I was afraid, but because suddenly my inside felt too grown up for my outside.

"Ghosts. We were walking on Magazine and we saw ghosts."

Grandma Estelle snorted. "Ghosts. On Magazine."

"Yes."

"For heaven's sake! You probably just caught sight of old Professor Broussard's naked statue in the lightning."

"Yes," I said. "That's what it was. We—we were telling ghost stories before. In—in the movie."

"No wonder you had an upset stomach. Now just you march yourself into the bathroom and dry off. Change into your nightgown. You've been scared half to death tonight, you might as well not die of cold, too."

I slouched into the bathroom and stripped off my wet jeans and T-shirt, my panties and my hateful bra. But when I glanced in the mirror, I didn't see my body, an eleven-year-old's body, with the nubs of new breasts and the curls of scratchy new hair, but the bodies of Euterpe and Terpsichore twined like two water lilies, dancing like two water snakes.

"Oh, no!"

I started back from the mirror and wrapped a towel around me.

"Jefferson Doty, get in here right now!" Grandma's voice sounded frightened and angry and grieving at the same time. I ran to the dining room and found her, pale and trembling, before the shredded remains of Great-Grandmother Geraldine's painting. The carving knife lay on the floor where Jeff had dropped it.

Grandma grabbed me to her in a strong hug. "My mama's painting. Oh, Peggy—why? Why would he?"

I found him on the back porch, throwing rocks into the wet darkness. His face was sullen. He didn't look at me when I sat down beside him.

"She's calling Aunt Sue to come take you home," I said.

He pitched a rock extra hard.

"She's crying, Jeff."

"So what?"

"That was a terrible thing you did."

He leapt up in a rage, his face red as a balloon beneath the porch light, and shouted, "What about *you*? What about what *you* did?"

"What did I do?"

He glared at me, and at the towel wrapped around me, and spat on the step next to me.

"You *stayed*."

I shrugged. "So?"

He leaned over and hit me on the head. I was up in an instant, breathing hard. I pushed him away. He staggered backward and barely caught himself from falling down. When he came at me, I held up both fists.

"Don't you ever touch me again, Jeff Doty." I stared him down until his face seemed to crumple and tears rolled down from his squinting eyes.

"You know what, Peggy Ugly Webster?" he shouted, wiping his nose on the back of his hand. "You know what? You're just like them."

I went inside, and waited with Grandma Estelle for Aunt Sue to come.

The next morning I felt tired and bored, the way I did when I was sick. I wandered through the house, touching the books and laces and knickknacks that lay in the slatted shadows of the Venetian blinds. The TV buzzed, forgotten, in Grandma's sewing room. Across the street, Professor Broussard watered his laurel tree. When he noticed me watching him, he took off his hat and bowed. I pulled away from the window and sat on the floor.

The destroyed painting was now in the attic, with the other broken treasures. In its place lay a square of stark white, harsh in the mellow, aged white of the wall.

The rest of the summer was quiet, without Jeff.

I picked mint for our tea, and washed up the dinner dishes. One day at dinner I mentioned wanting to take art classes, and Grandma Estelle smiled. The next morning she went out and bought me my first paints.

While I struggled to make water lilies grow, water snakes coil, from wet paint and paper, Grandma Estelle read to me from her mythology book. She read of the Muses, and of Hermes, the messenger, the traveler's guide. And every morning, from nine to ten, I lay out on the stubble lawn, watching Elephant and Cane make their slow, three-times journey up and down the block. I called out, "Morning, Miz Wilkes. Morning, Miz Hicks."

And they smiled at me.

GESTURES TOO LATE ON A GRAVEL ROAD

BY

MARK W. TIEDEMANN

*M*ark Tiedemann and I have been friends since we met at the Clarion Writers' Workshop at Michigan State University in 1988. He has given us a ghost story where the focus is not the ghost but what and who the ghost has left behind. This is a subtle exploration of friendship and the power of final words. It also echoes a theme that crops up every now and again in Tiedemann's work. This piece, he tells us, is "a comment on the one-dimensionality with which people are judged by those who do not and do not wish to understand them."

— N.G.

※

It was a ridiculously nice day for a funeral. I stood off to one side and watched the mourners as if they were actors in a play and I was the critic. Paul was dead and they didn't know how to act. They had forgotten their lines and their ad-libbing was awful. Paul's mother kept breaking out in brief fits of short-breathed sobs, then recovering to stare straightbacked and resolutely at nothing. His father just looked grim, occasionally resting his hand on his wife's shoulder for several seconds, then awkwardly letting it fall. Paul's brother Alan wouldn't look at me, though he dutifully went from person to person to thank them and offer some comforting sounds. His sister Robin seemed caught in between. She looked at the others with a puzzled expression that might have been close to what I felt, then looked at me with a compassion that I almost resented. My friend was dead and no one else supposedly close to Paul knew how to feel about me. I didn't know how to feel about me, either. Somehow I couldn't find the desperate, bitter resentment to Paul's death that shimmered like a heat mirage from everyone else.

Bright sunshine dappled the gathering through leaves just beginning to turn color. It was too warm for overcoats, but everybody had them, draped over arms. One of Paul's aunts, the one from out-of-state who kept asking everyone in secretive whispers what Paul had died from, hid her hands in the folds of her old dark gray coat to hide the chipped nail polish she had nervously scraped at during the service.

Paul's mother wouldn't shovel any dirt into the grave. His father scowled at her, but said nothing. He took the shovel and troweled up a heap of earth and threw it in. He stared down at the casket for a time until one of the workmen touched his arm. He jerked back, startled, then handed over the spade and turned away.

The group began to disintegrate then, as if on cue. Robin made a decision and crossed over to where I stood. Her eyes were pale blue, which made them stand out even more from the redness.

"Hugh…is there anything I can do?" she asked.

"Robbie," Alan called. He stood on his side of the grave, frowning at us.

I shook my head. "Thanks anyway."

"If you need anything," she said, "even just to talk…"

I nodded. I didn't want to say anything. My objectivity was important to me at the moment and saying something to Robin, recognizing what she was offering in any way, threatened that.

"Robbie, let's go," Alan called again.

Robin grabbed my hand and squeezed, very quickly, and then hurried away. I watched everyone retreat, duty done, back to their cars and their lives. I wondered how they would reconstruct Paul, what he would become to them in time. I remembered once Paul explaining to me how the world worked—one of many theories he had, most of them contradictory. "The thing is, there's what everybody expects. Then there's what everybody has. Then there's what everybody says. If you're lucky, they're all the same."

"And if they're not?" I asked.

"Then you have to figure out what's important all by yourself. Alone."

"Not alone. We have each other."

He shook his head. "No, alone. When everybody else goes away, you have to live with yourself. You'd better be comfortable with that."

"So who's going away?"

At the time I didn't think I would. But I did. My job took me overseas, to Japan, for a long assignment. Paul hadn't taken it well, but he put up a good show. We'd drifted by then anyway, no longer lovers, but he always expected me to be there, best friends. We were proud of the fact that at the end we were still friends. I suppose we'd fulfilled all our expectations of each other. I promised to come back and told him I loved him. I told him he could depend on me.

"Ah," he asked, half-joking, "but will you remember me when I'm gone?"

I stayed and watched the workmen clear away the flowers and the other debris, then sit around and smoke cigarettes and tell jokes. A backhoe would fill the grave in later, but they were paid hourly, union scale, and didn't mind spending time in the company of corpses.

I drove down the road that ran alongside the cemetery, deeper into the wooded country. Gravestones grew sparser up to a line of trees. On the other side of the trees I saw another section of the cemetery, overgrown and unremembered, and wondered how long it would take Paul's plot to be forgotten.

I turned onto a winding blacktop and mashed the accelerator. I wanted to find the edge of the world. If I kept driving maybe I would reach it by nightfall someday, then—tap the gas pedal a little harder, make it impossible to brake—I could fly over the lip into nothing.

My best friend was dead and his family would forget him as soon as it was convenient. I didn't care about them.

Would I remember him when he was gone....

The sun came in bursts through the broken roof of trees. I turned onto another state highway. I had no idea where I was, where I was going. I didn't care about that, either.

Another turn. Maybe I could disappear completely and no one would come looking for me, no one would try to find out what happened. Paul's family wouldn't—I would remind them of Paul. His friends? Of those still alive I was the only one who had shown up at the funeral. The family had made it clear that they—including me, but again I didn't care—were not welcome.

Eighty, ninety miles per hour; I imagined myself in Europe—maybe on the Autobahn, maybe in Italy. The blacktop was narrow and winding, though. Perhaps I was driving along the Great Wall of China, reaching down its serpentine back, squeezing through the narrow sections. Maybe there was a convenient place to drive off, into nothing.

I slammed on the brakes. The car fishtailed and I controlled it. Habit. Often we don't die only because of habit. When we do it comes as a big surprise, at least to those left behind....

Head against the steering wheel, hands on either side with thumbs pressed against my temples, I cried. Soft, salted tears, vibrato inhalations, shuddering exhalations. Careful pain.

"You were supposed to be my friend," I said. "You died. I told you how much you meant to me and you *still* died." I remembered the last time I saw him in the hospital. I'd held his hand and told him I loved him. He had smiled.

When I sat back it was twilight. Gentle insect buzzings played against the shadow of landscape broken by a copper strip of road that led only around another turn. I turned on my headlights and the brush along the roadside burst into definition in the bright light. I drove slowly, exhausted. I had no idea where I was.

Soon the sky was black. An ancient wooden sign advertised in faded letters and pictures a film developing company in a town I'd never heard of. There were no other highway signs.

As I rounded another curve my headlights caught the metal edge of an old private road sign. A chain hung from the post down into the humus along the roadside, then crossed a gravel driveway and disappeared into the brush on the other side. I didn't know exactly where I was and thought vaguely that someone in the house at the end of this road could tell me. I turned onto the gravel, tires popping and crunching.

The road wound a gentle path for about two miles. Then I crested a rise that, in my headlights, resembled the bony spine of some extinct giant, and drove into a clearing that was thigh high in stringy grass. In the center of the clearing was a building: a round concrete structure with a domed skylight.

I drove closer and stopped when the headlights illuminated the entrance. It was a cut in the otherwise featureless face of the concrete that extended back into shadow. On the lintel was inscribed ANNA'S SHRINE DEDICATED A.D. 1972.

I took a flashlight from my glove compartment, shut off the engine, and went up to the cleft. There were double doors set about fifteen feet back. A light switch was set into the wall beside them. I flipped the switch and started when the light came on and a cloud of insects filled the air above the doors.

The doors were stuck but seemed unlocked. I put my shoulder to them and pushed my way in. The air smelled stale. My footsteps echoed on tile. There was a row of lightswitches just inside the door. As I flipped them, one after another, the fluorescent tubes flickered greenly, glaring off glass and tile, square by square down a curving hall. For a moment I thought I saw people staring from the walls across at each other. Then the lights brightened to full and the shadows were erased.

Next to the light switches was a glassed-in newspaper bulletin.

"Entrepreneur Malcolm O. Wynter announced his retirement from Wall Street today. Since the death of his wife, Anna, Mr. Wynter has been consolidating his diversified interests and selling off his holdings. When asked to comment, Mr. Wynter stated 'I have no interest in pursuing investments anymore; I intend to retire to private life for a period of mourning. After that, I have no plans at present.'"

I smiled wryly. The rich can retire to private life to mourn—the rest of us have to content ourselves with less public isolation.

Below that was a newspaper clipping about the shrine under

construction. Then there was one more, dated January of 1978.

"'I have no interests anymore,' former Wall Street moneyman Malcolm Wynter told this reporter. 'My wife was everything to me. After she passed away I found that the most important thing in my life is her memory. I built this shrine in her honor. I think it's the finest thing I've ever done.'"

Beside this was a photograph of a quietly beautiful woman with short brown hair and large, pale eyes. Her flesh seemed translucent—I recognized that quality all too well. I wondered what had killed her, how long it had taken her to die.

The gallery circled the interior. I walked from display case to display case and gazed in at objects that seemed intended to quantify Anna Wynter.

The fifth case had been smashed and the contents strewn across the floor. Letters and torn envelopes mingled with the drawers from empty jewelry boxes.

I clenched my fists. The outrageousness of violating someone's tomb, stealing, ruining the careful arrangements those who had survived had made to preserve her memory, fueled my anger at Paul's family, at the so-called friends who hadn't shown up to remember him. For a moment I imagined catching the vandals and pictured beating them to death, screaming at them for their insensitivity, their vulgar scraping after something they could never own. Then I felt ashamed. I stood in this shrine uninvited, an invader, not much different from the thieves who had come in and destroyed.

I stepped carefully over the letters. A few other cases had been broken into. I ignored them and looked at what was contained in the others.

Studio portraits, both photographs and paintings, of Anna from about age five until her early death.

One case held half a dozen tailored business suits. Another half a dozen evening gowns. Curiously, the one that contained coins and currency from foreign countries, each labeled with the dates of Anna's visits, had not been broken into.

Anna had been published; there was a display of all the magazines for which she'd written, and all her books. Next to this were all her cameras, with cards explaining when she had used them. The transom above all the cases contained her photographs. Mountains, trees, solitary flowers, children playing…

Her entire office was preserved in one case.

I felt increasingly uncomfortable. Evidently Anna Wynter had been a very public figure at one time, but I had never heard of her. I'd read none of her books, seen none of her photographs, hadn't even been aware of her passing.

I went back to the scattered letters and sorted through them. The earliest date I found was 1964. I sat on the floor, my back against an unshattered glass case.

They were letters from Malcolm to Anna when she was at college—Vassar. Some were from Europe to her home in Vermont. Malcolm had often gone to England, France, Germany on business. He rambled on in his correspondence, telling her how he intended to conquer Wall Street. One phrase struck me—"Everyone," Malcolm said, "wants to conquer, whether it is other people, himself, the world, or death."

He proposed to her by mail and she had accepted by mail. They had been married on March 15, 1970.

A year later they discovered that she had leukemia.

I wiped my eyes. Paul had had that finally. I leaned my head back against the cool glass and pushed my hands flat on the floor. He had just grown weaker and weaker. His brave jokes had taken on bitter, pale tones. He had fought it but all he could do in the end was delay it. I shook from bursts of memory. I remembered when I had left for Japan, leaving behind a friend fairly robust and optimistic, and returning almost three years later to find him forty pounds lighter and a century more cynical. He had said nothing about it in his letters to me. What people have and what they say…

I closed my eyes and waited for control to return. Then I looked back at the letters.

Anna's illness had progressed rapidly after its diagnosis. I wondered why it always seemed to work that way. A person could be ill for months or years without knowing what it was, but once the disease was discovered deterioration seemed inhumanly swift, as if it started working overtime to kill.

Anna Wynter had died in December of 1971. Construction had begun in the spring.

Carefully, I began refolding the letters and returning them to the case. I picked up the debris, put the emptied jewelry boxes back together, and did my best to restore the display. I went to the other vandalized cases and did the same.

What Malcolm O. Wynter had done for his wife was very impressive. But something was missing. I walked around the displays again, and then a third time. It was incomplete. I didn't know what specifically I was looking for, but I felt I'd know it when I found it.

I shone my flashlight into a space between two cabinets and found another door. I was surprised that I'd missed it before. The door was locked.

I glanced back over my shoulder, self-conscious, then kicked the door. It was heavy and the frame was solid. My calf ached from the impact. I kicked it a few more times, but it wouldn't give.

"We'll see about that," I muttered and headed back to my car. I paused for a moment and wondered why I was doing this. This is a shrine, I thought. Yes, and everything *else* is out on display. A locked door made no sense.

I grabbed the tire iron from the trunk and went back in to force the door.

It was open.

My heart was suddenly racing. I looked up and down the aisle of displays and swallowed dryly.

Holding the tire iron like a weapon I entered.

The air was even staler. The memory of rot permeated the room. Coughing, I fumbled for a light switch. A single bare bulb winked on, burned for a few seconds, then flared brighter and went out. I turned on my flashlight and picked out details.

A cot; dresser; toilet in the corner; a refrigerator and toaster oven; a cabinet; a desk and chair. It looked like nothing but a prison cell.

Stacks of notepads covered the desk. I picked one up. "I loved you," was written on each line. I flipped the pages. Every sheet was covered with the same line, over and over again. I pulled more pads from the stacks. They were all the same.

I hadn't seen the line in any of the letters he had written to her. I might have found it in some that I hadn't read, but it seemed odd that not even the letter in which he had proposed to her carried the phrase.

I backed out of the musty room.

Other things were missing. I began listing them mentally as I pulled the door closed.

No snapshots of just her face, laughing, smiling, being silly; no manuscripts of her work; no negligees; no postcards or birthday cards or anniversary cards; no stuffed animals; no gaudy mementoes of vacations taken together; and except for their wedding album there were no pictures of them together.

And the most important part was locked away.

I turned from the narrow passage and started back to the entrance. As I rounded the aisle I stopped.

An old man stood before the case with the letters. He was gazing intently at them, his eyes wide and moist. I started to say something, give an explanation, but he turned to me and smiled sadly. I don't believe I have ever seen such hopelessness in a face.

Soundlessly, he mouthed "Thank you," and nodded.

I felt twisted inside, as if he had some claim on me and I owed it to him, now. I was the guest here, after all. It was almost painful and for a moment it seemed I was looking at him—at everything—from a place slightly skewed from reality.

"I won't forget her," I said. It seemed appropriate.

The old man nodded again. He turned back to the case with the letters. He started to reach for them, but before he completed the gesture he faded away and vanished.

Reality snapped back into place for me. I let out my breath and felt dizzy. What people expect, what they have, what they say...but what if it's all there and we don't accept it? Don't say it? Don't notice it? Life goes by, the opportunity fades, and everything becomes another lost chance, an empty gesture.

I went back to the cell and began moving the notepads, stack by stack, into the open displays, propped so that they could be read.

THE FALL OF THE KINGS

BY

ELLEN KUSHNER AND DELIA SHERMAN

*A*ward winners Ellen Kushner and Delia Sherman have teamed up to bring us the longest story in this volume, set in the same world as Swordspoint, but two generations later. We all have people or things we want, need, must have. How does that affect us and our everyday lives? Why does this happen and, when it does, do we have any choice in the matter? How can we hope to deal with what this need does to us? Come join Basil and Theron as they explore these questions on our behalf.

— S. P.

When Basil St. Cloud arrived at the Great Hall an hour before the Master Historian's lecture, it was already aswarm with black robed scholars. The timid were lined three deep below the steps giving access to the deep horseshoe of benches. The more enterprising simply climbed the benches themselves to capture prime seats. It looked as if the whole University had turned out to hear Master Tortua lecture on the subject of his famous book, *Hubris and the Fall of the Kings.*

Master Tortua was the greatest living scholar on the history of the ancient monarchy. He was also Basil's first teacher, his champion before the University Examiners, and his friend. His illness this past year had been a source of grief to his young protégé, and it was with a sense of the world having righted itself at last that Basil settled in his seat opposite a stained-glass window and prepared to be enlightened.

But he was not enlightened. Master Tortua's illness had left him the doddering ghost of the scholar who, barely six years ago, had introduced a young country boy to the dark glories of the city's past. Where once he had developed arguments, Tortua presented rambling anecdotes that sounded more like palace gossip than history; where once he had thundered, he mumbled while the spittle gathered in the corners of his mouth. Some men left; some shaded their eyes; some conferred in shocked whispers. Basil blinked and stared at the high arched window across from him. It was ancient, a thousand years or more, and the figures in the center panel were stiff and formal—a man robed in black and a hart with a collar of gold around its neck. The hart was kneeling to the man, who caressed its head with his outstretched hand. A pool of impossibly blue water sparkled at their feet and a flat, golden sky arced over their heads.

Time passed; Master Tortua mumbled. More men left. The sun moved in the sky and came burning through the colored glass of the window, dyeing the faces below with green and brown and blue. Basil noticed one young man who seemed drenched in gold, the light burnishing his long fall of bronze-dark hair and gilding his pale skin. He was slouched forward in his seat with his ankle on one knee, his elbow on the other, and his chin in his hand, looking very interested and somewhat puzzled. He glanced up, and Basil found himself holding his gaze across the horseshoe. The boy smiled, parted his lips as though he would speak. Basil hastily turned his eyes back to Master Tortua, who was talking about the magical rituals of the ancient court wizards. Basil winced. It was lucky that no one was likely to take him seriously. In the old days, men had been thrown in prison for less.

When at length Master Tortua had meandered away into silence, Basil descended to the podium where the old scholar was wiping his spectacles.

"Welcome back, Master Tortua," he said gently. "How good to see you well."

Tortua blinked at him. "Roger...? No, it's young St. Cloud, isn't it? How did you enjoy the lecture?"

Basil could only say dryly, "You seem to have changed your mind about the court wizards since *The Fall of the Kings*."

The old man drew up all his wrinkles like a pleased tortoise. "Why, yes, Basil, I have. Been reading, you know, while I was ill, and it all started to come clear. The power of the royal blood, the hold the wizards had over the kings—it doesn't make sense if it wasn't founded on something real, don't you see? They must have had true magic. Stands to reason."

"So you said," Basil murmured. "But the law says otherwise."

"The law." The old man was grandly dismissive. "Drafted by a clutch of frightened old women. The law means nothing." He fell silent, munching his jaws. "It's a pity about *the book of the King's Wizard*. If we could find that—"

Basil sighed. "Ah, yes. The notorious book of spells, passed down from one King's Wizard to the next. I'm sure the Council of Lords tossed it immediately into the nearest fire, when they found it, and put an end to that nonsense forever."

The old man shook his head regretfully. "A waste, I call it—a waste of human knowledge."

"A waste indeed," said Basil, and let someone else elbow him out of the way to speak to the old teacher.

Basil St. Cloud lectured on the history of the monarchy five mornings a week. Despite the earliness of the hour, he had something of a following among the city's nobility. Young lords idling a few years in study liked hearing how the last kings fell from honor and strength into decadence. They liked hearing how their own ancestors had saved the country by deposing Gerard the Wicked sensibly and legally. It made them feel the weight of the centuries behind them, to hear their names invoked, their family histories analyzed. Basil, who found the modern aristocracy effete and faddish, hoped by his lectures to sow the seeds of true nobility, the nobility of the ancients, in their much-declined descendants.

The room in which he lectured was no help to him, being dank as a well and redolent of rotting straw and torch smoke. His students were little more than the tops of heads bent earnestly over tablets and a small scratching of pencils. Sometimes he thought it was like lecturing to hens in a yard. They were always attentive—sometimes excessively, when a student became confused between devotion to his subject and devotion to the handsome young master, with his firm mouth, ironic voice, and his demand for precise and well-informed argument. Basil had grown accustomed to such attentions, had even occasionally enjoyed them, when the student was bright and good to look at. He always knew when a student was interested in that particular way, for he would suddenly be overcome by an intense self-consciousness, as though he'd been stripped naked, as he did the morning after Master Tortua's lecture.

Basil stumbled over a phrase and cleared his throat firmly. "Hilary always insisted upon hunting the sacrifice himself and bringing it to the wizards to be prepared. The court wizards approved of King Hilary, even though almost no one else did."

A movement caught his eye: a head nodding slowly, as though in wry understanding; a head covered with bronze-dark hair pulled back in a ribbon. A long head, with slanting cheekbones and a long, arching nose. A familiar head, he thought as he went on, "Hilary went about the kingship with a kind of mad intensity unmatched by…"

Ah. He had it now. The young man from Master Tortua's lecture. The young man who had smiled at him, who was smiling at him again. Basil hurriedly lowered his eyes to his notes and kept them, and his mind, firmly on King Hilary and his peculiarities. Which, in his later years, centered increasingly on beautiful young men and women of no birth and little common sense, one of whom had cut his throat for him. Hilary had been naked save for a fine deer skin, and the young murderer had been discovered weeping over the corpse, his monarch's blood smeared over his face and chest.

"The court wizards questioned him, of course," Basil said, "but they could get nothing out of him save the babblings of madness. He died under the questioning, much irritating Hilary's heir Gerard, who had been looking forward to executing the traitor. Not to be cheated of his revenge, King Gerard commanded that the corpse be drawn, quartered, and burned just as if it had been alive. Gerard was a great believer in following the rules. As we shall see tomorrow, when I will discuss the early years of his reign."

The University bell tolled heavily over his last words, and there was a general rustle and scuffle as the students gathered up their effects. There was little talking, and more than one shocked and troubled face. They'd always known the last kings were corrupt and mad—it was one of the city's truths, like the economic usefulness of the river. But they'd never really thought what *corrupt* and *mad* meant until the story of Hilary's death brought it home to them. Basil had just been reading about it in the letters of a certain Hieronymous, Lord Tielman, uncovered in a clutch of old books and papers he'd bought from Foster Rag-and-Bone. It was a story he'd been unable to resist sharing at once with his students, clearly to good effect.

"Thank you." It was the long-haired young man, standing below the lectern. "That was interesting, about King Hilary and his lover. Can you tell me any more about it?"

Basil brought up his head sharply. "No," he said and forced a smile. "Really, how could I? It was three hundred years ago, and the records are sketchy."

"Just so," said the young man. "All those details, about the deer skin and the slit throat, they aren't in any of the standard histories. I'd be interested to know your sources."

Basil, who intended to amaze the scholarly world with his discovery at his own leisure, looked down his nose. "Quite," he said. "Will you hear some advice, Master…?"

"Campion." The young man swept a courtly bow. "Theron Campion."

"Master Campion. A scholar's facts are a scholar's honor. Question them, and you question his honesty. I was not made a Master of this University for inventing colorful details."

"Of course not, Master St. Cloud." His glance flicked up mischievously. "Your youth precludes those privileges of invention granted to poor Master Tortua. But…how charming of you if you had been!"

His eyes were greenish. Basil found that he was looking into them. Theron Campion smiled engagingly; Basil fought down a disproportionate anger. "Dishonor is hardly a jesting matter," he said. "Good day to you."

❋

Returning to his rooms through the crowded streets of University Town, Basil was jostled by a chattering crowd of students in black gowns, who apologized when they realized who he was. One of them wore his hair long like Theron Campion. It looked better on Campion, Basil thought, and wondered if the young man would turn up again at his lectures. Not that it mattered. Basil had more important things to think about. Like the book he was writing, the book that would make him more famous than Master Tortua; the book that, later that evening, he found himself regarding with the bitterest frustration. Hieronymous was being singularly coy and unhelpful, Basil could no longer remember his own argument, his head ached, and his mouth was as dry as the Twelve-Months' drought. A cup of wine would cure at least part of what ailed him, he thought, and might help him sort out the rest.

The Blackbird's Nest was a noisy, cheerful tavern at the river edge of University Town, popular with students and the younger masters, like Basil. When Basil came in, he saw that a hilarious group of students had colonized the fire, and was shouting and arguing over some point of philosophy. One boy had his foot up on the table, lunging like a swordsman with an accusing finger at his laughing opponent's nose. Basil sat at an empty table and watched them over the edge of his beer. It hadn't been that long since he'd been one of them—no, that wasn't strictly accurate. Basil St. Cloud had never had the time for tavern jests, nor the money for the sort of drunk these boys were on. Basil St. Cloud's assault on scholarship had been single-minded, his rise concomitantly swift. He might be near these students in age, but in rank and learning he far surpassed them, and he thought the bargain a fair one.

For a moment he considered taking part in the discussion. All he'd have to do was raise his voice, and the center would shift to him, a lodestone potent as the pole. But he was sick of company tonight, and attention and even debate. So he turned his back on the students, addressed himself to the fowl pie, which was excellent, and was contemplating another tankard when a student detached himself from the group by the fire and headed toward Basil's corner.

"Master St. Cloud," said the student. "Good evening."

This time, Basil recognized him immediately. "Master Campion, isn't it?" asked Basil. "Good evening to you."

"May I sit down?" The green eyes were a little glassy with drink, the white hand heavy on the table's edge.

"I'd just as soon you didn't."

Campion staggered, catching himself against Basil's shoulder. "Whoops," he said. "Sorry. Just sit here quietly. You won't know I'm here." He eased himself onto the bench next to Basil, thigh to thigh. Basil jumped as though the touch had burned him.

"Sorry," said Campion again, and moved over.

"Don't you think you should go home while you can still walk?" Basil asked.

"I'm not so drunk as all that," said Campion. "I can still say 'Seven seditious swordsmen sailed to exile in Sardinopolis.' Shall I buy you a drink? The wine's not so bad here, if you know what to ask for." He smiled like a cat who knows where the cream is kept. "I know what to ask for."

Basil laughed. "I'll wager you do. No, you shall not buy me wine."

"Brandy, what about brandy? Or beer. Men who drink beer are seldom beautiful, but it's the exception proves the rule, or so 'Long John' Tipton would have us believe."

"'Long John'?" Basil said. "Is that how you refer to Master Tipton? What do you call *me*, then?"

The boy smiled a very creamy smile. "Now, that would be telling. But I should like to call you Basil, if you will permit it."

The question should never have been asked, but having been asked, it hung between them like a challenge. "I can't stop you," Basil said.

"Oh, yes, you can. One hard look from your eyes could turn me to stone. Everyone is afraid of you."

"You exaggerate."

"I do not, sir. I always pay ver-ry particular attention when you speak." An aristocratic drawl was beginning to bleed through his University sharpness. "Though, mostly, I watch your mouth. It is severe. Austere. It bears watching."

"I wasn't aware that you had had much opportunity to watch it before today. You are hardly a regular attendee of my lectures."

"It's a morning lecture," Campion explained apologetically. "I have come before, though. I've watched you talk about the Barley Wars and the rise of the Inner Council and the Ophidian Invasion and the court wizards. You're wrong about the wizards, you know."

He looked so earnestly owlish that Basil smiled. "No, I don't. In fact, I have very good evidence that they believed that the magic they performed was real."

"Nonsense. You have no idea what was going on in their minds; you only think you do."

From a mere student, that was a remarkable piece of rudeness, yet, "What were the court wizards?" the boy went on, cutting off any protest Basil might have made. "What was their function, after all? They were counselors to the kings. They gave advice. All this business about their seeing into men's hearts, binding the kings with chains of gold...it's figurative language. Any poet can tell you that. They were like you, Basil: they sifted the evidence, looking for truth. They were scholars of the heart." Pleased, he repeated it: "Scholars of the heart. And because they were good scholars, they got it right often enough to be credible and thus maintain a reputation for working magic."

The boy spoke earnestly, leaning close enough for Basil to smell the brandy on his breath. His point was sufficiently interesting to give Basil pause. Campion, taking his silence for surrender, sat back on the bench with a complacent smile. "I knew you'd agree, once I'd explained it to you," he said.

Basil recoiled. "Agree? On *that* argument? Master Campion, you

astonish me. Has no one bothered to teach you the principles of debate?"
And he commenced to depress the boy's pretensions in a well-reasoned
and constructed exposition of Theron's rhetorical shortcomings, ending
up, "...and furthermore, Master Campion, you yourself have no more
idea of what the wizards really were than Master Tortua does. You believe
what you want to believe, on no more evidence than your own inability
to extrapolate beyond the known."

"Are you suggesting—*you*, Master St. Cloud—that I try believing in
wizardry to expand my imaginative range? To...let me see now...*to set
about inventing colorful details?*"

Basil gritted his teeth. "I am suggesting that you leave yourself open to
the possibility of evidence as yet uncovered."

"Such as?"

A student reeled past them, or nearly—at the last moment he did a
drunken bounce off the table and into Theron's lap. "Bugger off,
Hammond." Theron dumped him on the ground. Hammond wandered
off in the other direction, with people shouting after him.

"We can't talk here," Basil snapped. "I can barely hear myself think."

"It's cold out," Theron objected.

"My rooms are close by. There's something I want to show you. Will
you come?"

"Certainly," said Theron. "Lead on."

※

The argument continued unabated all the way to Minchin Street. Basil
lived up four pair of stairs in an old stone building that had originally
been a royal archive. Some time shortly after the fall of the kings, it had
been cut up into a warren of more or less cramped rooms for the use of
masters and lecturers. It was furnished with an iron bedstead, a table and
a chair, and scores of books and papers that were piled and drifted on the
floor, against the walls, in the corners, and spread out on the mattress
like an eager lover.

"The scholar's mistress," observed Theron, folding his body down onto the bed. He laid his hand on one closely written sheet. "Is this what you wished me to see?"

On the way from the Nest, Basil had had ample time to regret his impulsive invitation. "No," he said coldly.

"Do you have a mistress?"

Basil, who was poking up the fire, jerked upright, his lips compressed. The young man returned his look gravely, like a curious child. He'd loosed his shirt at the neck, laying open the fine linen to bare the hollow of his throat, which was also fine, and very white. Firelight polished the fold of hair over his shoulder and touched the high curves of his brow and his aquiline nose with a warm light, lending them the look of alabaster or carved ivory. His eyes, shadowed, were blank.

The room spun once around Basil and settled again, realigned around Theron, a figure descended from the marble frieze above the Council Hall and sitting on his bed, the living image of an ancient king. "Majesty," he whispered, bowing his head.

"What?" Theron moved two books on to the floor, clearing a larger space on the bed. "I can't hear you. Come and sit beside me."

The movement had broken the illusion, but not the enchantment. Basil no longer saw one of his beloved kings come again, but rather a king among men, all passion and pride. He wanted that pride, to caress it into full potency and then to break it to his will and his desire. He took one step toward the bed, and then another, holding out his hand for Theron to grasp and pull him down into a long kiss that broke only when Basil pushed Theron back onto a pile of papers.

"Watch out," Theron murmured against Basil's mouth. "She has nails."

"What?"

"Your mistress. She's scratching my back. And this can't be doing her any good. Let's get rid of her."

Basil propped himself up on his elbow and leaned over Theron to scoop papers and books off the end of the bed, lifting him to get at the papers he was lying on, pressing against his belly, working his hands under the tight waistcoat, the fine linen shirt, to the strong, smooth back beneath. The young man's flesh was warm and supple under Basil's hands; his mouth was sweet and firm under Basil's lips. Kissing him, Basil could think of nothing else, but he made no objection when Theron rolled him away, laughing, and helped him disentangle himself from his master's robe and the neat suit of clothes beneath it.

When they were both naked, Basil reached for him, and hesitated, suddenly shy. Theron put his hand to Basil's chest and ruffled the dark hair that crossed it. His fingers were cold. "I've always fancied a fur coverlet," he said. "Come and warm me."

And Basil did warm him, until they threw the blankets on the floor, and they flared and leapt and burned themselves out to lie at last in a smoldering glow of satisfaction.

Basil said sleepily, "Tell me something. Have you in fact been following me? I seemed to see you everywhere."

The young man swept a shimmer of bronze hair from his face. "I seemed to see *you* everywhere. But—yes, it was by design. I noticed you before you noticed me."

"I noticed you at once!"

Basil felt the smile against his skin. "No, you didn't. I attended lectures; I saw you in the Nest surrounded by your students, your particular followers—"

Basil chuckled. "I love the way you say that."

"What?"

"Par-*tic*-u-lar. You sound as though you're picking up something tiny with silver tweezers. Never mind. Go on."

The student shifted uncomfortably, as though he were thinking of protesting. "Well...I studied you until I knew you, or at least the parts of you that were available to me: your learning, your passion, the way your voice slows when you answer a question. I studied your hands, and wondered what they would feel like on me; the clear skin of your face with the beard just coming through. I wondered about all that, and about the rest of you I could not see, and I wanted you to know me. I wanted you to see me. I wanted you to feel my eyes on you like fingers under your robe."

"Have you gotten what you wanted?"

Theron trailed his hand down Basil's breastbone to his belly. "Yes," he said. "I have."

✳

After Theron had gone, Basil hung over the edge of the bed and groped under it for a battered wooden trunk. He released the hasps and opened it upon bundles of yellowed paper tied neatly with tape and a package wrapped in an old linen shirt, which he picked up and settled in his lap. He eased aside the folds of cloth like petals to lay bare a small, thick book bound in brown leather sueded with age and damp. Stamped on the cover was a tall crown, its gilding all worn away save for a few flakes lingering at the tip of one of its sharp points. The leather reminded him of Theron's skin, cool and a little sticky with drying sweat; the crown reminded him of Theron's face, white as marble against his dark hair spread on the pillow. Basil felt his sex swell and press against the book in his lap. Now he owned them both, he thought; the precious book and the precious man.

"I have to go home tonight," Theron had said. "Sophia worries when I don't come home at all."

"Sophia?" A tiny serpent stirred in Basil's chest.

"Lady Campion. My mother."

The serpent quieted. "Your mother. You are certainly a dutiful son."

Theron laughed. "Not in the general way, I'm not."

Campion, Campion, Basil thought…he knew plenty of dead ones. An old family, but fairly minor in the great scheme of things. There was a Bertram Campion who saw King Tybalt slain at Pommerey; a Raymond Campion who was a notable cartographer. But what the Campions had done lately, he had no idea. He'd have to ask someone, but he'd better be careful about it.

✳

The next morning, Basil lectured as always. Theron was not present, which was not really a surprise. Basil was conscious of disappointment nonetheless, and a certain sense of betrayal. By the time he got to the Nest, he'd decided that the young noble and the events of the night were best drowned in something stronger than his usual beer.

The first thing that met his eye was Leonard Rugg, Master of Metaphysics, sitting at the end of a bench, morosely staring into a bowl of snapdragon gone cold. Basil excused himself to his students and approached him. "Good day to you, Master Rugg."

"Sit down, St. Cloud," said the metaphysician. "Have you heard the latest?"

"Probably not."

"You should get out more. Youngster like you." Rugg peered at him over the rim of the bowl. "You look pale. Stir your blood. I'll pass along my mistress if you like—the bitch. Stir anyone's blood." Master Rugg looked contrite. "Begging your pardon. The bitch."

Basil snagged the potboy, ordered brandy, and settled back. "Is that the latest? It sounds old to me."

"Oh, no, no. It's Tremontaine again. Trouble all 'round. Lady Sophia's trying to endow a chair for *women*, if you please—"

"Lady Sophia?" Basil sat up sharply. "Lady Sophia *Campion?*"

"That's the one."

"I suppose young Theron is trouble, too."

"Really?" Rugg looked more cheerful. "Never saw anything wrong with him myself; harmless enough puppy—though I hear that last mistress of his did him some damage. Still, no harm in him. Been coming to classes since he was a lad. One after the other. Can't stick to a subject, loves 'em all: an academic flirt, eh? Still, he probably knows more about history than I do...and more about metaphysics than you do. What kind of trouble's he in?"

"Ah, disappointment to the family?" Basil hazarded.

"Ha!" Leonard Rugg roared. "It would take a lot of work for him to give Campion's family a sleepless night, after what the father put them through."

"Oh?"

Rugg said expansively, "Oh, no one can say the old man wasn't generous to the University. But one can't imagine him as a *husband,* if you catch my drift."

Basil gave up. "Leonard," he said. "Who is Theron Campion's father?"

"Oh, don't you know? He's dead. Something in your line, I'd think, St. Cloud: Tremontaine, the Mad Duke. That one."

Basil said frostily, "I don't do modern history."

His colleague took pity: "A scandal from start to finish. Attended University back before any noble would have been caught dead here. He became a swordsman's paramour. But they let him inherit Tremontaine anyhow. He filled the house with scholars, reprobates, and lovers of all, ah, shapes and sizes. He was finally driven into exile, left the duchy to his niece, and came back years later with a beautiful foreigner in tow, claiming to be his lawful wife, who conveniently produced an heir four months after the Mad Duke's death."

"And that is the Lady Sophia."

"Damned queer woman. But, odds are, the boy will still inherit on his cousin's death."

"Inherit the duchy?"

"So it really doesn't matter what he studies, does it?"

"On the contrary," said Basil shortly. "I think it matters a great deal. If there's one thing ancient history has to teach us, it's the importance of educating the ruling class in the realities of life."

Rugg laughed. "They'll hardly learn that in University, dear boy."

"Oh, I don't know," a voice above them drawled. "Unheated lecture rooms, watered beer, incomprehensible feuds, indiscriminate sex, casual violence, and a general shortage of sleep seems uncommonly like real life to me."

Basil started. He wondered how much of the conversation Theron had overheard. He wondered if Theron were sorry about what had happened the night before. He wondered whether the beating of his heart was visible through the thick stuff of his robe. He thought it might be.

Theron was speaking. "Master St. Cloud, I wonder if I might trouble you for a word in private?" His light voice sounded annoyed, but that just might have been the drawl. Basil turned to look at him. The long mouth was hard and still.

Leonard Rugg punched him on the arm. "New student, eh? Congratulations, St. Cloud. Don't take a copper less than 20 for the term. He can afford it, can't you, my lord?"

Theron smiled tightly. "Yes," he said. "I can."

"Shut up, Leonard," said Basil. "I'm not exactly new at this, you know." He rose and looked around the tavern. "There," he indicated one of the empty tables with his chin.

The walk across the room was a journey across a wasteland. Basil imagined Rugg and the students whispering and snickering. Determined to hold fast to his dignity, Basil lifted his head to see Theron convulsed with silent laughter.

"Was I perfect?" he chortled. Basil stared at him suspiciously. "Well, *Master* St. Cloud?"

"Campion, are you mad?" Basil snapped.

"I'm sorry." The student wiped tears from his eyes. "I'm ruining the effect, aren't I?" He reached across the table, touched Basil's hand lightly. The scholar's insides lit up like fireworks. "Let us discuss fees, then, so as not to disappoint Master Rugg. Tell me—" he leaned forward. Basil smelled his mouth, sweet with mint and the tang of his breath. "How much must I pay for another lesson like last night's?"

His eyes were flecked with gold. Reading nothing in them but a warm and friendly conspiracy, Basil smiled. "I wonder," he said, "if you remember your lesson."

"Perfectly," the boy smiled back. "I paid particular attention. And now I would know more."

"Would you, indeed?"

Basil realized that he was flirting—flirting *after* he'd achieved his conquest—and that it was delightful.

"You are the subject of my study, Master St.—Basil. I desire to understand you thoroughly, to uncover your mysteries, to pass examinations in your history and your tastes."

Basil laughed. "My history is not so interesting as yours, Master Campion."

"Oh?" said Theron, then, in a very different voice: "What has old

Firenose been telling you? That I have a boundless appetite for men, women, and ponies? Or merely that I change lovers as often as I change suits of clothes? Not quite true. I deny the ponies. Are you going to bar me from your classes?"

He looked at once haughty and so wounded that Basil reached out to comfort him. Theron glanced down at Basil's hand, square and dark against his own fair skin, and smiled. "A tutorial," he murmured. "I've an hour free before Thurgood's lecture."

Two hours later, they lay together in a welter of discarded garments and blankets. Theron unwound himself and poked through the tangle until he found a black scholar's robe, which he draped over his shoulders.

"My father," he said, settling back into Basil's embrace, "was a colorful character. I thought, when I was younger, that I would try to be more colorful still. Finding that to be impossible, I settle for pleasing myself. I've nothing to apologize for. A variety of lovers is a family tradition, really."

Basil touched the thin, sensitive lips. "It's an older tradition than that. There's evidence that the kings were encouraged to take many lovers of both sexes. The wizards—"

"Wizards and kings," interrupted Theron. "They're dead, Basil, and beyond all feeling. I'm not."

"That's just the point. You carry their seed—"

"Shut up, Basil." The boy stopped his mouth with lips and tongue. Basil pulled away from his kiss and pinned him flat to the bed with the weight of his body and his hands around his wrists. He gripped him hard enough to feel the long bones under the flesh.

"You don't want to hear me, do you?" hissed Basil. Theron moaned. "I know you've the blood in you, I can smell it on your skin, taste it in your mouth, hear it in your heartbeat."

Theron struggled under him, half-angry, half-laughing, wholly aroused. "You've been studying too hard, Basil," he panted. "I'll have to see to it that you get out more."

"Be silent!"

Theron opened and shut his mouth and began breathing hard through his nose. Basil lowered his head, kissed Theron on each temple, just above the hollow where the bronze-dark hair sprang back from the brow. The boy shivered from head to foot. Basil shifted his grip so that he held Theron stretched taut, and the world narrowed to the damp slide of skin over skin, the unbearable vulnerability of the secret places, the fierce, hot joy of possession, of shooting his seed, his whole being, into his lover's pliant, trembling body. Silently Theron yielded to him, and silently received him until he spent his passion in a high, clear cry like a wounded animal's. Then Basil turned his lover over and laid his head on Theron's breast.

For a time, the only sound in the room was the hushing of the fire and the lovers' slowing breaths. Then Theron said, "I love it when you lose control. It excites me. It frightens me."

"Not so much as it frightens me."

"Why?"

Basil thought of the dark and wordless place Theron's struggling had sent him. His body had been shot through with lightning, burning with infinite power. "I am not myself," he said shortly.

"You are wonderful," said Theron.

※

The days passed in a jumble of lectures, students, and hours in Theron's arms, interrupted by his lover's rushing off to an appointment with his cousin or the theatre with his mother or a ball or a horse-race. In Theron's spotty absences, Basil found himself studying not Hieronymous' letters, but the book stamped with the crown, the book he dared tell no one he possessed. Though the text itself was written in no language he knew, the headings were in an antique dialect, quaint but clear: "A Spelle for Forcynge of the Trutthe of Those Suspect of Treeson"; "A Spelle of Glamour and Hony-tonge." Sometimes he was near to weeping with frustration over the nonsense syllables that followed, which promised so much and delivered so little. What was the use of a piece of history that could not be read, he asked himself, and buried the book in the trunk until curiosity drove him to take it out again.

Thus caught between love and fruitless labor, Basil's teaching suffered. One morning he found himself delivering the same lecture he'd given the week before; one morning he woke to hear the University bells tolling noon and one of his students banging at his door and demanding to know whether he were well or ill.

"Ill indeed, to be awakened so rudely," Basil shouted through the door. "Go away, Justis. I'll be there tomorrow."

He slapped the lump that was Theron snickering under the blankets. When the student's footsteps were gone into the ringing of the bells, Basil pulled the boy out from under them, almost angrily unweaving the wild web of hair from his sleep-thick face, entering his mouth with kisses until he felt his body's yielding. When Theron lay, a warm and satisfied heap across him, he breathed in their mingled scent and felt perfectly happy. He could hear the smile in Theron's voice as he said, "I wish I spoke a hundred languages, to tell you how much I love you."

The pleasure of the moment snapped. Basil laid his finger across Theron's lips, sealing them shut. "Don't say that. Don't say you love me."

Theron kissed his fingertip. "Why not?"

"Because that is something that should not be said between your father's son and mine."

"My dear," Theron purred in amusement. "I've told you: my father was a notorious libertine."

"And you're doing your best to follow in his footsteps."

"God!" Theron swore, and flopped back on the pillow. "I get enough of that from the Duchess! I don't need it from you, too. My mother thinks he was a saint; my duchess cousin thinks he was a satyr. And, I might add, they both wonder what I'm doing spending all my free time down here with you. Or, rather, they do not wonder—which is almost worse. I am what I am—no more, no less—and I would very much appreciate it if you could all stop measuring me against dead dukes I've never even met!"

Basil said, "I've offended you. I'm sorry."

Theron was silent a while. Then, trying for a lighter tone, he offered: "When you ask a girl to dance three times at a single ball, it means you're serious about her. It's the same with this: you can't make love with someone three times and not fall in love."

Basil shifted uncomfortably. "You make it sound like a magic spell: three times and you're caught."

"It would depend on the timing, I suppose." Campion gave the question his full attention. "Three times in one year would be safe, but three times in one week, and you can't help falling in love."

Basil said indulgently, "You're confusing the body with the heart."

"People do, you know." Theron raised himself on one elbow. "But I'm willing to entertain the notion that you have them neatly divided. Maybe for you it takes something more direct." His fingers made an elaborate pass over Basil's face.

Before he could complete it, Basil caught his wrist and pulled him down into his arms. "Don't, Theron. It's not something to joke about."

"Are you going to cry me to the Council for practicing magic? Even though my spells never work?"

"You've no need of spells, my lord."

"It's you who are magical, Basil. Who could resist the enchantment of your eyes, your neck, your broad chest and narrow hips, your—"

"Stop!" Basil was laughing as Theron kissed each beloved feature, struggling to get away. Then the bell rang again.

Theron yelped, jumped out of bed, and began diving for his scattered clothes. "My tailor! I've stood him up twice already, and he's fitting my coat for the Montague ball next week."

Basil found Theron's stockings and his belt. "Be at my lecture tomorrow?"

"Without fail. I am particularly keen to hear your opinion of Hilary's walrus-oil treaty with Arkenvelt."

⬚

In his warm room in his mother's house, Theron Campion stood still while a servant dressed him for the Montague ball. Fine linen against his skin, followed by layers of more linen, stiff with embroidery, then brocaded silk, rounded with collar and cuffs of lace. A wide gold chain was laid across his chest. His long hair was brushed and oiled and bound with a velvet ribbon. He had eaten nothing for hours; come rushing home from Basil's just in time to change. His consequent pallor, and the unusual hair, gave him an antique air that his lover would have approved of.

The ball was already crowded when he got there; he bowed and swam his way through well-dressed women of every age and size until a hand at his elbow stopped him: "Young Campion! Pried you away from your books, have we?"

He was in a knot of men he knew. They wanted to talk about politics and the latest fashion in lovers, which did not seem to include dark and brilliant university masters. He said nothing; he couldn't bear their inevitable sly pleasantries. Of course he could not escape the usual jokes about his father, the mad, bad old duke. Theron smiled mechanically and took a glass of wine from a passing tray. He began to feel much better after he'd downed it.

A fragile-looking girl with dark hair came into view just past the swirl of pattern in the tailored shoulders around him. Her hair was severely upswept, exposing delicate ears. The few tendrils that escaped onto her neck served to enhance its frailty.

One of his companions followed Theron's look. "Ah!" he said archly. "The true purpose for our sojourn in these parts: the flowers in the garden of maidenhood, ripe for the plucking."

"Harris!" a young man expostulated. "I hope you do not mean my sister!"

"Plucking," explained Harris smoothly, "is a very considerable enterprise, involving ladders of contracts, baskets of jewels, and volumes of vows."

"*Is* it your sister?" Theron asked.

"*It's* not the cat, you rogue!"

But he achieved his introduction. Lady Genevieve Randall smiled shyly. Her skin was fine and flawless, with a ripe-peach glow; Theron had to stop himself from reaching out to touch it, just to feel it under his fingers. Even her shoulders, rising from a calyx of lace, glowed faintly golden in the flattering candlelight.

But he might take her hand if he asked her to dance, and so he did. They trod the measures of a slow *pas*, and he was careful to exert no pressure of the fingers that might alarm a young girl fresh from the schoolroom. He could not help looking, though, at the wisps of hair at the nape of her neck as the two of them moved back and forth, gravely dipping and bobbing. A sheen of moisture appeared on her upper lip; he wished he might bend down and lick it off.

Genevieve's mother met them as they came off the dance floor. Lady Randall inquired after the health of his mother, into his studies, and after his cousin the Duchess. Theron took pains not to say anything particularly original. He'd learned long ago that it put people off; they admired his intellect from a distance and tolerated his eccentricities as long as he did not ask them to participate.

He was able to dance once again with Genevieve Randall, carefully avoiding the third time by taking several other partners. While getting a cooling drink, he was cornered by a politically active noble who wanted to know where he stood on the proposed new corn levy, filling out Theron's professed indifference with a full set of opinions of his own. By the time Theron returned to the floor, the Randalls, mother, daughter, and son, had gone. No longer hungry or thirsty, Theron suddenly longed for bed, the closest bed he could find, which was in a small room on Minchin Street.

❋

From experience, Basil knew that his lover was unlikely to come to him until well past midnight, leaving him hours to devote to scholarship. He knew he should work on his book—he'd not so much as looked at a page since the night he'd met Theron. He opened the trunk to get out Hieronymous' papers, found himself holding the book of spells instead, opened to the "Spelle for Summonynge of a Absente Mann." His eyes scanned the incomprehensible words, then he shut the book with a decided snap, folded it in its cloth, took up the letters, sat himself at his table, and began to sort through papers.

Gradually, he began to reconstruct the elements of his argument. The last time he'd looked, it had seemed impossible. Now, it was obvious that he'd gone off-track in his discussion of Petronius' *Chronicles*. He picked up a pen, uncapped the ink-well, and some hours later, was happily engaged when a perfumed gentleman appeared in the shadows at his door.

"Am I disturbing you?"

"No." Basil closed the ink-well and rubbed his cramped fingers. "No. I was just winding down. Are you cold? Come in by the fire."

"There isn't any fire. You've let it go out."

"So I have, so I have." Basil peered in the woodbasket; it was empty. "Sit down and take some brandy while I fetch up some wood. Here," snagging the quilt from the bed, "wrap this around your legs. I won't be a moment. This wizard business is fascinating, fascinating. There's a way in which it explains everything about us—the Council, the fall of the kings, even the swordsmen."

"I don't want to hear it just now," said Theron petulantly.

For the first time, Basil looked straight at him. "Oh, my dear," he said. The boy looked like a doll, white face and glittering eyes above an elaborate costume.

"I'm tired," he said. "Please let me lie down."

"Are you all right?"

"Yes—but never mind the fire. Just come and warm me."

Basil undressed him, save for his chain and rings, and covered them both with every blanket he possessed, as well as both his scholar's gowns and Theron's rich cloak. "There," he said when the boy stopped shivering. "Better?"

"Yes. I'm sorry—I should not have disturbed your work. But I'm cold and weary and my cheeks ache from smiling. All I want is to rest quiet and warm."

But Theron seemed disinclined to sleep. He responded to Basil's kisses as if he would lose himself in them; and in some measure, he did, until at last they both were lost and found again.

Basil licked sweat from his lover's throat. "Why do you go to these parties if they upset you so?"

"I must. It wouldn't do for me to disappear into University, however much I want to. Someday I must take my place among the nobles of this city. They have to know me. My mother put up with a great deal of nonsense from these people over my birth and my inheritance—I owe it to her, and to my family, to do the thing properly."

"You speak as though you were not one of 'them.'"

Theron gave an embarrassed shrug. "I am, by birth. Someday I shall take my seat in Council...."

"But you don't look forward to it."

"There is so much I want to study first!"

"But, Theron..." Basil fingered the chain whose precious links had left its mark on both men's chests. "Theron, you are no scholar."

"*What?*"

"Not a real one," Basil went on gently. "Not by temperament. You must know that."

Theron turned away from him, but Basil kept on. "Why can't you be proud of what you are? A great noble, from the seed of kings..."

"*Damn* your kings! Sometimes I think you take me only because Hilary's not available!"

"Hush." Basil gave the chain a tweak. "I am trying to tell you something important. The kings no longer rule. You nobles have taken their place, and must strive to be better than they were."

Theron sighed, burying his face in Basil's chest. "I know. I do know. But it is hard, being two people all the time. I wish I could...hire someone else to go to parties for me—to remember people's names and families, and to be charming when I don't feel like it."

"You mean like a wife?"

Basil meant it ironically, but the young nobleman answered candidly, "Yes. I will have to marry someday, for the title and the lineage and all. Already they are circling, the mamas with eligible daughters. I don't know what I will do! Marry, I suppose, and get it over with."

"The kings didn't need wives," said Basil. "They had their wizards."

"Oh, really? How did they reproduce?"

"The wizards chose their women for them. From what I've been able to gather, the king was a stag, both monarch and prey. When he was crowned, he hunted and killed a deer, and when his end came, he took a deer's form and was killed in his turn, whether by the wizard or the next king, I don't know. What I do know is that he begot as many children as he could while he reigned."

Theron murmured, "What an extraordinary amount you do know. And in the end, did the wizards corrupt the kings, or was it the kings corrupted the wizards?"

Basil opened his mouth to give him the standard answer, and realized that he knew better now. There were things no book could teach. "Love," said Basil, "allows for no corruption. It is a fire that burns away all impurity. As I love you, mind, body, and soul."

"I know," Theron whispered. His fingers in Basil's hair were at once soothing and tantalizing. He turned Basil over, looked tenderly down into his face. The chain brushed Basil's chest. Basil felt that he might melt, whether into tears or honey he was not sure. Salt or sweet, it made no difference.

"We're even now," the nobleman said. "Love for love." And he laid the chain around the scholar's neck.

There was a pause, full of breath and waiting. Theron grinned. "Have you ever loved anyone else?"

It was not what Basil had wanted him to say. "No," he said, rather sharply. "Never."

"Never?" Theron tweaked the chain. "Not very experienced, are you?"

"I never pretended to be. I've had other lovers, of course."

"Really? How many?"

Basil tabulated his actual conquests, added the ones he might have had if he had cared to try for them, and answered, "Eight. Or so."

"Eight. Or so. And you never told one you loved him?"

"It was of the body only. You're different; the way I feel about you is like nothing I've ever known." Basil stopped and smoothed the chain, warm and heavy across his breast.

"I'm glad," said Theron. "It's always better when heart and body agree. Come kiss me, and see."

When he next encountered Genevieve Randall, Theron knew she was the answer to all his problems. They were at the theatre, he with his cousins in the Tremontaine box, and she in the Randall box, accompanied by suitable chaperones. He couldn't take his eyes off her: her slim neck, her bright eyes, the way her hand flew to her mouth at the comic bits, the careful way she always turned her head to reply to others' comments, the air of propriety that breathed from her like perfume. He quickly bought some flowers, and gained access to her box at intermission. Lady Genevieve seemed pleased; her mother, Lady Randall, seemed very pleased.

Lord Theron regretted that he couldn't offer to escort them to their carriage after the play, but, he explained, "There is a lecture I must attend." The girl's eyes widened; boldly he went on, "I am so often at University. You will think me very dull."

"Oh, no," said Lady Genevieve. "It must be very exciting."

"It is exciting," he said, and took his leave.

And there it was, a neat solution. He hoped Basil would approve, but he feared that he might misunderstand unless Theron explained it all very carefully. Basil could be a bit dense about the modern world and its demands; sometimes Theron envied him the simplicity of his concerns. Perhaps if he couched it all in terms of ancient kings, a dynastic necessity—that there would be a social fuss, a legal ceremony, and then it would be over, and everything back to where it was for them…. He'd just have to go carefully, that's all. And then he could have everything he desired.

✖

The Blackbird's Nest was filled with black robes, smoke, the smell of beer, and the hard, quick rattle of scholarly debate. Basil was happily arguing the relative antiquity of the three ducal houses with two of his best students. It wasn't until the tavern emptied as students scrambled for afternoon lectures that he realized Theron was not among them. Which was odd, as Basil was sure Theron had said this morning, as they kissed and parted, that he would be. Basil waited a little longer, and was rewarded for his patience by the sight of his lover arriving, breathless, as the University bell tolled twice.

Theron flung himself onto the nearest bench. "Sorry! Beer? No, wait— it's two already—I must get to Tipton's Mathematics—"

"Theron, what is it you're wearing?" The young noble's black robe was crookedly buttoned over a pair of tight-fitting yellow striped breeches and an embroidered waistcoat.

"Sorry—had to go see the lawyer this morning, no time to change—"

"Here." Basil redid the buttons. "Cover them up, and maybe no one will laugh at you. Lawyer, eh? Nothing's wrong, I hope?"

"Oh, no. I think it will all be fine. Thanks, Basil, I'm off—"

"Wait." The black whirlwind froze. "Theron, wait. Tell me if you're coming to Minchin Street tonight."

"Will you be there?"

"Will you?"

"Yes."

"Then so will I."

※

But he was not there, though Basil started at every rattle of the street door, every step on the stair. Theron stuck to no fixed schedule; Theron was often late. At last Basil fell asleep in his chair with a book in his lap, and woke up, cramped and cold and miserably weary, as dawn was silvering the city.

Theron appeared at his lecture that morning, neat and well-rested and very late. Basil could say nothing, but from the low murmurs it was clear his other students were saying it for him. Basil found his place again, and went on about the ceremonial duties of the later kings, pointedly never meeting the one pair of eyes he felt burning on him. Afterward, he ignored Theron and allowed Justis Blake to monopolize him all the way back to the Blackbird's Nest. Justis was in heaven; Basil hoped Theron was in hell, but was prepared to forgive him at the slightest sign of penitence.

But Theron had disappeared as soon as he stepped through the door into a crowd of black-robed young nobles who were slapping him on the back as if he'd done something heroic. No doubt he'd hear about it later. Basil turned away, but was intercepted by a well-dressed young man who stuck out his ringed hand to shake.

"I'm Clarence Randall. I—that is, my mother—I mean, I wondered if I might attend your lectures? On the kings? If it isn't too late?"

Basil forced himself to smile. He couldn't afford to turn away paying students, not if he wanted to keep brilliant but impoverished ones, like Justis. "Well, Lord Clarence, the term is almost over and the kings totter on the brink. But if you'd rather not wait until next year, read the Tortua *Hubris*, and perhaps we can arrange a tutorial."

Lord Clarence nodded, grinning. "I'll get the book from Campion," he said, and pushed off shouting, "Campion! Hey, Campion!" Basil, following close in his wake, came up in time to hear him say, "Thank you, Theron. I'll return it, I promise. Oh, yes. You'll be at the Godwin ball tonight, won't you? My sister asked me."

Basil caught his lover's gaze past Randall's head, saw his eyes widen, shift, veil themselves under the heavy oval lids as Theron turned away to put his arm around the young nobleman's shoulders. "Not the place to be talking of balls, my dear," he said, and then they were out of Basil's hearing.

Simple bewilderment rooted Basil to the spot, followed close upon by rage. Someone, Justis, was plucking at his sleeve, repeating his name; he shook him off roughly and strode blindly through the crowd, paying no more heed to what they might be saying than the cawing of so many crows. Theron was hiding something from him. Was he ashamed of Basil after all? Did he have another lover?

Basil's antidote to everything was work. All that long afternoon and evening, he wrote and crossed out sentence after sentence, wrote and crumpled page after page, until at last he found himself sitting among a snowdrift of spoiled sheets, unable to think of anything but Theron's face turning from him. Whatever was going on, he would lie about it, try to charm or kiss his way out of a confrontation. Basil thought he could bear anything better than Theron's false protestations of love and innocence. He rose and went to the bed, and opened the wizards' book.

The text had been written by several hands. The earliest spells were all of rule and dominion, scrying and sooth-saying: practical spells to ease the difficulties of ruling. But later spells had no purpose that Basil could see but control and revenge. They had titles like "A Spelle for the Drynge of a Mann's Seede" and "A Spelle to Turne Men into Beastes." They were written in a thick, brownish ink that Basil suspected to be blood.

Basil went back a few pages, a few hundred years. He hesitated over "A Spelle for the Un-covring of Hidden Trothe," then began to read it aloud as he had read it silently a hundred times before. The nonsense syllables clashed and slid in his mouth like rough pebbles. When he came to an end, he looked around the room, half-expecting to see the candle burn black or an evil and shapeless shadow seething in the corner. But all looked as it always had, homely, cluttered, shabby, and prosaic. Basil sighed, shut the book, and was swaddling it once more in its soft cerements when the door opened behind him.

"I've been having the most excruciating evening," Theron announced. "I've been conversing with debutantes, flattering dowagers, and listening to politically minded nobles discourse upon the salt tax. Comfort me, my dear, before I explode from an excess of respectability."

He wore full ball-dress. His hair was oiled and pulled back into a glossy club held by a jeweled clip. Rings weighed down his hands and a pearl hung from the lobe of one ear. He was flushed and a little unsteady and obviously quite excited. He held out a hand to Basil, who ignored it.

"Aren't you glad to see me?" Theron asked plaintively.

Basil laid the book on the table. "I did not expect you tonight. I was working. You interrupted me."

"You've never minded being interrupted before." Theron closed the door behind him and stepped into the room, stripping off his cloak and tossing it into a corner. "And you won't mind it this time, either." He came up behind Basil and put his arms around his chest. He smelled sweet and complicated, of perfumed oil and red wine and desire. He leaned over Basil's shoulder and rubbed his face like a great cat. The pearl in his ear brushed against Basil's cheek, smooth and hard as glass.

116

THE FALL OF THE KINGS

Basil shook him off. "That earring." The pearl had seared his cheek like a torch, ice and fire at once; as he spoke, he knew his words were truth. "That earring is a woman's jewel. She gave it to you tonight, from her own ear as you begged it."

The flushed face turned pale. "Nonsense, Basil."

"Nonsense, indeed. It does not become you, my lord, to lie."

Now two spots of color, like red bites, stained Theron's cheeks. "There we have it. So if I were no lord, but just a common man, might I lie with your good will?"

"But you're not one, are you? You think you may do what you like, with whom you like, to whom you like—"

"That isn't true!"

"Isn't it?" Basil asked icily. "You say that you reject the blood of kings, yet you reveal it with your every action. Arrogant, careless…"

"But that's what you want from me, isn't it?" Theron drew away to lounge provokingly by the fire. "What is it that you so love in me, if not that?"

Basil clenched his hands, words flashing through his mind like shooting stars, disconnected, unrecoverable. "I thought you were of the true blood," he said at last. "I thought that you were pure."

"And now you realize your mistake." The slow voice was harsh with anger. "You wanted an ancient king, and all you got was me. Only Theron. I am so sorry that I disappoint you."

A dark joy flooded through Basil. Theron's pain called to him like desire. He had never touched his lover so deeply, even when he spoke of love. He said, "Come here, Theron. You do not disappoint me."

But Theron turned away. "I thought you knew me. I thought you loved me. But you never looked at me; you never saw me—just the image of what you wanted me to be."

"I do know you. Come here." The nobleman shrugged his brocaded shoulders. His proud head was low; the earring hung like a tag of ownership. "Come," Basil coaxed. "Let me see your new pearl. Tell me about your conquest."

"Ah," Theron rallied with mock gallantry. "The hunt is on." He turned to face his inquisitor, very pale, still holding back, as if he were afraid to let Basil touch him. "I don't know how you guessed where this came from, but it's just a flirtation." He laughed mirthlessly. "What do you think I *do* at these balls, after all? Mathematical proofs?"

Basil held out his hand. "Come tell me about it."

Theron shook his head. "No." The earring danced.

Basil smiled. "What did you have to do to get it? Did you tell her you loved her, too?"

"Stop it."

"I do know you, you see. You may not be the true scholar you'd like to be, but you are a scholar of the heart."

"Shut up!"

"I'm sorry if I offend you, my lord."

"That is enough." Theron could barely bite the words out for anger. He flung himself to the door and fumbled at the latch, which rattled with his trembling.

Basil gathered up the rich cloak, dusted it down with his hand. "Your cloak, my lord?"

"*Damn* you!" Theron snatched the cloak from him and was gone.

Basil sighed with satisfaction. Knowledge was sweet, and power was sweeter. With something approaching awe, he wrapped the book back up in its cloth. "Un-covring of Hidden Trothe" indeed.

✳

The Blackbird's Nest was jammed with drunken boys. Someone had been liberal, and the liberality had included Master Rugg.

"Looking for your true love?" the drunken master asked as Basil surveyed the mess. "You've just missed him. He stood it as long as he could, but it seems his mind is nicer than his judgment."

"Stood what?" asked Basil.

"Listen," said Rugg.

A voice raised itself above the general roar: "I've got one, I've got one! To Campion: May his rod never falter!"

118

"Good one, Reynold, good. How about this? To Campion: May his bride's maidenhead prove as tight as his lover's arsehole!"

There was a brief, shocked silence. "Hammond, you fool," said someone, and "Oh, bugger," said Hammond, catching sight of Basil standing at Rugg's elbow.

Basil surveyed the crowd: flushed faces turned up to him or down to their cups and tankards, bearded, clean-shaven, round, hollow-cheeked, young as he'd never felt himself, waiting for him to react.

"Just a joke," rumbled Rugg uncomfortably. "High spirits, eh? Youth."

"It's traditional," said Basil evenly, "to toast a man on the occasion of his betrothal." He took the cup from Rugg's lax hand and lifted it to the room. "To Campion. May his dedication to his name and lineage not go unrewarded." He put the cup to his lips and drained it, unsurprised to find it an excellent red wine. Hadn't Campion said the Nest kept good wine if you knew how to ask for it?

Silent bewilderment greeted his toast, and silence followed him as he turned on his heel and strode out of the tavern into a bright, cold afternoon. Basil felt no anger as he walked through the narrow streets, just a slow bleeding away of mind and spirit that could only be stanched by the sight of Theron Campion on his knees before him, weeping.

When he reached his room on Minchin Street, Basil closed the door and locked it, sat at his table and laid his hand upon the cover of the Book of Spells.

He turned through the book, searching for the spell he needed, hesitated over "A Spelle to Entrappe the Spirrit" and "A Spelle to In-Force Love," rejected them; came to "A Spelle to Turne Men into Beastes." He read it once and then again, his mind filling with images of green leaves and still waters, of a kneeling stag and a collar of gold and a black-robed man. The third time, he read aloud.

✳

Conversing in a gilded drawing room on the Hill, Lord Theron Campion felt the green leaves of the wood close around him. He lifted his head and gave a peculiar, belling cry.

"My dear, what is it?" Lady Randall stood over him, trying to reach beyond her corsets to help him to his feet. Theron's body felt heavy, his sex was a weight between his legs. For once, he had no words to answer. Lady Genevieve hurried to his side in a rustle of skirts.

"No!" he cried hoarsely, arm upraised to fend her off. "Don't—"

The girl's scent filled his nostrils. He stumbled to his feet while his hands still sought the floor. The scent of woman overpowered him. "I must go." He lowered his head and ran, kicking aside the presents he had brought her, moving, not to the door, but to the window, the fresh air. The glass baffled him for a moment, but it gave way to his battering and fell in a glittering rain onto the patterned carpet. Then he leapt through the window and fled through the garden, head high, nostrils flared to catch the scent of the hunt.

❊

Basil sat with the book between his hands. Under his scholar's robe, he was naked and barefoot. The night had grown chilly, but he felt no cold, all his being concentrated on listening for the king's arrival. Knowledge burned through his palms. He was coming; he was close. There was a clattering on the stairs as of booted feet or hooves, and then the door shook under a powerful, rhythmic pounding. He was come.

Basil rose, took up his candle, and opened the door. Theron lifted his head and looked at him, wild-eyed. There was blood on his forehead; his unbound hair was spangled with blood and broken glass. His sides were heaving with the force of his panting. His fawn-colored coat was torn and streaked with mud and wet leaves.

"My lord," said Basil, and stepped back. Theron stumbled after him to the bare middle of the chamber, where he stood trembling, just beyond Basil's reach.

Basil felt in the long sleeve of his robe and drew forth the chain Theron had given him. The heavy links lay heaped in his hand, glowing in the candlelight, burning his fingers like ice.

"Come," said Basil.

Theron stood stiff-legged, his head raised unnaturally high, his fine-carved nostrils flared.

"Come," said Basil again, and held the chain out over his outstretched palms, a golden garland.

Theron swung his head and cried out, an animal's sound in a man's throat.

"Come," said Basil a third time, and Theron fell awkwardly to his hands and knees before him. Basil bent to lay the gold chain gently around his neck and caressed his head, heedless of glass. The blood from his hand ran between Theron's eyes, tinging the tears that streaked Theron's cheeks as he murmured, "My king, my lord, my love, my own."

CLOUDMAKER

BY

CHARLEE JACOB

C harlee Jacob read Fort's The Book of the Damned when she was sixteen. This story, she says, comes from the dream that resulted from reading that book and watching Arthur C. Clarke on A&E talk about objects falling from the sky.

The cloudmaker's raw feelings remind me of the great yawing emotions we experience when we first fall in love: joy; the initial terror of making the inevitable error that will lead the beloved to realize we are less than perfect; the urge to remake the world to please her. Unlike thoughtlessness between mortal lovers, though, the Cloudmaker's mistake will last forever.

— N.G.

✳

"A procession of the damned...
...The power that has said to all these things that they are damned, is Dogmatic Science.
But they'll march."

— Charles Fort
The Book Of The Damned

There was a crowd of people gathered in a Kansan cornfield. They were a rural lot in muddy overalls and boots, polyester house dresses and tennis shoes. A sick child flailed in the center. He'd been laid upon a frayed cotton blanket which his mother had spread on the ground as if for a picnic. The boy was covered with open sores and his pitiful cries rose to reach my ears like the thin skree of a wounded sparrow.

A teenage girl knelt beside him. She was chanting in a more melodic voice than the child-sparrow's. More of a cross between nightingales and whippoorwills with a soft mourning dove thrown in for good measure. From on high I could actually see the sores as they developed and expanded, reproducing. They were quite literally devouring him in fast inches, eating him alive.

The crowd was tense, very silent as they watched. The girl's fingers ran over his wounds, touching him lightly here, there. She didn't seem to be bothered by the fact that putrid gum from these lesions would pull free of him to cling to her own skin. Her fingers just moved, pattering not unlike gentle rain. They began to glow.

I concentrated so that I might hear what she was saying.

"Up from mother earth, I draw. From our mother who is love. And with this love I heal you."

The lesions on the child's flesh ceased their carnivorous growth. They jiggled wetly, then shrank as his skin reknitted. The wounds closed and some actually vanished.

The crowd cheered. They took the child and left.

I shrugged. A faith healer, so what? I almost turned away as I had my own work to do. The girl began to dance in the cornfield and for some reason I couldn't stop watching her. The storms that needed doing would simply have to wait.

There is a beauty in watching things fall from heaven, be they inanimate objects or living creatures such as the humans below perceive 'living' to be.

There is a marvelous power in causing them to fall, a sense of personal embodiment that is a sort of creation.

How they land once they reach the ground is another thing altogether. It can be ruinous to those directly in the path. It can be bloody and horrible if those that fall have ever breathed.

But on high, I seldom saw that result clearly. Or perhaps I never gave it much thought, being chiefly concerned with clouds, not earth.

The shatter of bones and stones has little importance from thirty thousand feet and up. The gore of splattered flesh and more is but an extension of carnage in the history of an already sanguine planet.

Lo! What the author Charles Fort never knew of his procession of the damned as they fell from the bountiful sky: fishes and frogs and hazelnuts. Angels frozen in space are the Milky Way according to him, and their celestial praises in song that leak from the glacial chattering of their lips is the mystery radio that human scientists lend their ears to. It is seraphim static.

I have to laugh, knowing what I know that Mr. Fort did not.

"Look!" I cried out to Ariel as I showed her my skies for the first time. She had been badly frightened when I flew down to scoop her up from that cornfield, my wings beating hard to lay the stalks of corn down in circles and arcs. I do give her credit for not screaming at the sight of a goddess when many mortals would. Perhaps it's because her affinity for that other—earthbound—spirit kept her mind more open. That more worldly lady and I are supposed to be distant kin but we were ever miles apart.

Ariel watched the ground recede as I carried her against my breasts. She asked me who I was.

I replied, "I am the cloudmaker."

I demonstrated once we were in the upper realm of atmosphere. I blew some substantive bubbles and some more spindly tendrils from my cloudblower's reed. It was fragile stuff for these shrewd lips, phantoms of virtue and rain, monsoon ogres, aerie queens voluptuous with trains of tears.

"See? I breathe them out as the glassblower does her water shapes.

Hers are a menagerie that swells vitreous and hard. Unlike my gentle vapors."

She watched, her eyes growing round with wonder. She lost most of her fear in that moment, as any intelligent creature will, when the desire to know overrides the need to flee.

"I've always been told that clouds formed as water on the ground evaporated," Ariel said.

I laughed heartily and this made her jump in nervous surprise. She windmilled her arms in panic but she was in no danger of falling. I held her safely with a thought, as sure a net as any woven from my blue hair. I told her, "Now you know the truth."

I touched her hair, so unlike mine. It was the same color as the kernels of corn in the field where I had noticed her, softer than cornsilk. She let me touch it, responding with a shudder of pleasure. I touched her shoulders, tracing the bones that didn't bear wings.

"Your fingers are both cool and warm," she said in a marvel. She turned as I gently blew her clothes off. "I like your breath most of all."

Why had I never brought a human up here before? Perhaps because I had never seen one such as Ariel before, dancing on the flat farmland round and round like a cyclone. She'd been pirouetting for joy at having saved the child's life. Her head had been tilted back, hair across both shoulders and down to her waist.

Her face was upturned to taste rain she sensed was coming. (What she'd sensed was my interest.)

Somehow I looked when I never had before.

Now I showed her things no mortal had ever seen. Indeed, none of the others of my kind, those I can only guess exist because I hear their names shouted by worshippers into the winds. I blew Ariel a gray rose that swelled petals into tempest and thunderstone.

"Gorgeous!" she exclaimed with delight. She pressed her mouth to me. Her breath was nothing like mine. It was hot, full of cloudless sunlight. This was the kiss that poets spoke of. I nearly melted under it, wondering how it was even possible to have never kissed before. She showed me my face reflected in her eyes. "You're so beautiful," she said, unblinking, letting me use her as a mirror. "Surely you have had hundreds of lovers in an eternity."

Looking into her eyes, I saw only clouds. This made me a little sad but I covered it by blowing her a cirrocumulus galleon that raced across heaven to end a drought in the Swaziland. I blew her an opal castle filled with birds singing "Swanee River."

I enchanted her with muted bells in nimbus. With cartoon xylophones played upon the bones of a mackerel sky. With crows that buzzed ceremoniously like black flies along the contrived wisp of a mare's tail. These things scudded from my magical reed which I took from my mouth only long enough to embrace her, to melt a little under her warmth.

※

Ariel grew bored after a while. Had it been days or years?

I saw her in a restless mood and asked her, "Darling, have you ever read Charles Fort?"

She had her dimpled chin propped on a dainty fist. "Who is that?"

"He wrote *The Book Of The Damned* about the falling of all manner of things from the sky."

"I've never heard of him. But I've heard about stones falling. About rains of frogs and fish," she said.

"That too," I replied, smiling. At least she was familiar with the concept. "Fort did a treatise on the whole subject. We are similar, he and I, in that he didn't think much of the excuses of science. But he never guessed that I was the cause of it all."

Her cornflower blue eyes sparkled with interest. "You cause those things to happen?" she asked. "How do you do it? By scooping up bunches of stones and frogs like you picked me up from the farm?"

I rustled a breezy arm around her shoulders as I whispered in confidence, "Actually, I only need one pebble, one amphibian."

I pulled an object from her pocket to show her how it was done. It was—what else?—a golden nub of corn. I took my reed and blew against it, pronouncing, "I toss it into the bloating moisture of my exhalation and watch what happens!"

How it reproduced. The single nub multiplied into thousands as the cloud stretched into cotton lakes and fuzzy cat mountains. The cloud swept the kernels aloft in continental polarity of gentle rain and fomenting light.

Ariel blinked against the brilliance of lightning, against the reflecting of it off the golden corn that poured.

I boasted, "I've done it forever. The peasants look up as showers of objects which ought never to fall from the sky descend. I've loosed corks, broadbeans, and shoes, locusts shocked from their senses, and slagheaps of steel. I've dropped bolts of silk rippling rainbows like Chinese flags. I've let fall barrels of sugar sparkling grains snowy and sweet.

"Some eggshell-skulled scientists have suggested that the masses of fish were swept up from the ocean in hurricane force winds. That they were then dumped thousands of miles away in a sudden downdraft. Ridiculous," I added with a huff of contempt that made my breasts heave and my wings shake out a few feathers.

I held a single digit in front of her face to distract her from the steady drizzle of golden corn and back to my narrative. "*One* fish in my fingers is given to the folds of the wind. I release it from my reed with this single fish slightly resonating, gills opening and closing. *One* fish."

Ariel gasped. "But how does it become so many?"

I shrugged. "I am the cloudmaker. Clouds are the font of all genesis. Do you like it?"

She twirled in the same sunwise dance I'd seen her do in the cornfield, laughing with the splendid joy I found so infectious. A healer she was indeed! When she turned again to face me, I thought I glimpsed something in her eyes, something that also had eyes and a full-lipped mouth. Was that me?

She begged me to show her more. I clapped my hands and sang "Pennies From Heaven." I did the hokey pokey. Should I make it rain cats and dogs and buckets of green-eyed frogs?

I wanted to be romantic. I was the cloudmaker. I put my reed to my lips.

Red rose petals fell in a torrent over Glastonbury.

Chocolate-covered cherries dropped on Dallas. Unfortunately they fell at a hundred miles an hour to splat against the streets like so much organ meat. (I really used guts once. They unroped from a shower onto a village in Argentina until the inhabitants thought Hell had gone either bulemic or ballistic. But that was long before Ariel's time. Entrails were hardly poetic.)

Little lace-trimmed valentines fluttered to settle on the lily domes of the Taj Mahal.

Diamonds fell on Capetown as the frozen angels of this galaxy thawed a bit in their profusion. These Milky Way angels whispered her name through the transmitters that scientists aimed at space. They clearly lilted, "Ariel?"

"*Ariel.*"

To completely thrill her, it took only one red rose, a single Godiva sweet, a sappy Hallmark card, a flawless gem plucked from a dancer's navel in Constantinople.

Ariel swirled. Her skin was as clear as a cloudless sky, as translucent as winter's first ice. When she kissed me in gratitude for this display, her lips were April rain. Her healing touch was witchcraft. I might never have known I was lonely until she cured me of it. I would never have known what I looked like if I hadn't seen my face in her eyes.

"Look at those crazy Texans," she said, laughing as they tried to lick the chocolate off their lampposts. They made dog-day summer love in the mud of it that melted in the streets downtown.

She smiled as Africans gathered up handfuls of diamonds.

"More, Cloudmaker!"

I made the clouds pour champagne on Sydney. The Aussies ran outside and opened their mouths.

"They're getting drunk!" she cheered as she hugged me. "More!"

I blew a great cloud in the shape of a jacaranda tree. I placed one quivering, silver-throated nightingale within the flowers of fog. Hundreds of them fell on Paris at 2 A.M. The moon had reached a glorious yellow apex. Lovers were clasped together on honeysuckled balconies.

What came as the birds smacked feathered bullets onto rooftops and disintegrated in piles along the Champs Elysees wasn't song, weren't sighs. What came as their bodies whistled through the air between raindrops I had scented with vanilla weren't frigorific angels warm and ardent in the Milky Way chanting, "Ariel?"

"*Ariel.*"

She watched, horrified. She no longer danced. She was shaking with outrage. I hadn't done it deliberately. Sometimes I forget how fragile living things are. They are as delicate as the glassblower's creatures.

I am not a monster; I am the cloudmaker. Charles Fort and his data of the damned didn't know about me, but he was right in that their quasi-souls march. Even a cloudmaker may take her place in such a doomed parade.

Ariel's lovely lips downturned into a grimace. Her hands balled into fists. Tears ran down her cheeks for those stupid squashed nightingales. "How could you?"

In her eyes my reflection had become only clouds again. Where was the face she'd given me? Seeing myself disappear there made me feel strangely empty. I have never been afraid, so I couldn't identify this loss of myself with terror.

I did grab her by her yellow hair, holding her with one hand as I picked up my reed with the other so tightly that the tube squeaked. I placed it to my pouting mouth and blew the most vicious cloud I had ever made.

It was the sort of gale that pulverized cities. It was the squall that changes shorelines forever by swallowing beaches like strings of taffy. It was the whipping vortex that drove survivors into years of making dire religious predictions and carrying out pogroms on each other.

Looking into her eyes I saw lightning. I threw her into the cloud I had made.

One slip of a girl, fragile as a dragonfly.

I blew and blew until battalions of tornados helped pummel my thunderheads across the earth. There I let it storm her out again into tailor-made wastelands.

Ariel fell screaming, hundreds of her plummeting through the hard rain. She landed in sand, in beaten dust, in canyons where flood waters shrieked over rocks. She fell on cliffs that were striated in reds and blacks, that had been hollowed out by ancient tribes and later abandoned. I watched with a slow realization of my stupidity. I tried to think if there was a way to call it all back. But storms are never recalled; they cannot be stopped. I even tried to fly down to catch her, any one of her, but the lightning forced me back. I scratched at my breasts with my nails and tore out feathers from my wings by the fistfuls. I beat at my face that I had seen for such a short time in her eyes. I ripped at my blue hair which vanished into the clouds as if it were nothing.

Some of Ariel died, imprinted flat as Nazca's etchings. Some incinerated in the lightning. Some survived miraculously but were crippled. These lay for days in the desert, hands paralyzed in pools left by the storm. Nomads scuttled out from wind-beaten tents, rescuing some of her. They wrapped her in the oily bandages of their burnooses. Other Ariels crawled into caves, minds turning mad or holy.

I wept, cursing myself, watching as the storm turned red with my blood. I limped along in the procession of the damned with everything that becomes lost. I even marched with the many animals and the flotsam that fell from my clouds to be postulated as excommunicated from the Sargasso Sea.

The lightning stopped and the red rains stopped falling. I went down to earth, hoping to find at least one of my Ariels uninjured.

I took each one I could locate into my arms. I apologized to twisted limbs. I touched strands of limp cornsilk hair. I kissed the darling faces that had adored the fall of roses and diamonds.

"I'm sorry," I whispered, brushing her cheek with cool/warm fingers, hoping she would once again love my breath most of all.

One or two of her would open an eye that was as cracked as a fried marble. One parted her lips but no sound came out. Another tried to move her arm, and it popped like the wing of one of the nightingales that had broken on Paris.

Had she been trying to hug me with that arm or strike me?

The forefinger on the hand extended slowly. It faintly glowed, the light from a candle going out. She managed to lift the shattered arm. She touched my cheek and managed to speak across the broken teeth. I hato lean very close to hear it.

"Up from mother earth, I draw. From our mother who is love. Andwith this love I heal you."

In her eyes the clouds parted and I saw my face. It was bruised and cutwhere I had damaged myself but this was going away. I waited to see if she would heal herself but she didn't.

Ariel was destroyed, one of the glassblower's fantasies, too brittle to be touched. I threw my head back and cried out, a long painful howl.

I saw a woman standing in a pool of the red water that had stormed. The blood was going clear, all traces of the raw and the deadly disappearing. I could see my face in her eyes, in her sparkling teeth, in her fingernails, in each of the beads that made up her dress.

I noticed the terrible devastation I had made of the world. I had done this before, never being concerned with it. But I had never seen it from ground level before.

This woman saw what I felt and said, "It always recovers to begin new cycles of life."

But there was no place left that resembled the field I had first seen Ariel dancing in. I had thought then it was dreary. Just flat Kansas.

"I can't leave her here," I told the woman. She nodded, and I saw her dress turn green, then red and gold, finally white. When it turned green again, I understood that it was all right.

I took all of the Ariels I could find and placed them among the frozen angels. She was a handful of wounded stars seeping a bare but crystalline light.

It was cold there among the nebula wings. My Ariels stiffened, frosted to the eyelashes. I could look out and see her there, mad and holy.

Our galaxy is a white cloud dancing in the night, and she is part of it. If I could turn around my magic and make it rain that way, I would shower her with corn flowers.

The human scientists who ran to survive my storm now sit by their machines, pointed out to where they believe there are other worlds. They call it alien radio and get very excited. They listen as a new voice sings through the static of chattering angel teeth and trembling bitter bones. It murmurs, "Cloudmaker?"

"*Cloudmaker.*"

MAGICKED TRICKS

BY

K. L. BERAC

*ew people can write a good fantasy mystery; fewer still can do it at novelette length. This story has everything a mystery fan needs: a dead body, suspicious circumstances, and an innocent character of low morals. Add to this the basic elements of fantasy—wizards and magic—and you have a delightful and wickedly fun read. Join Nikki and his friend Kev as they try to help out Nikki's roommate, Silky, when she finds herself in difficult circumstances.*

—S. P.

I know it sounds incredibly shallow, but the thing that bothered me most about the whole affair was it happened on the first good night I'd had in *weeks*.

I was sitting in Tam Gilvris' after-hours club, working my way through a third mug of surprisingly good ale and indulging in some heavy-duty eye contact with the exquisitely athletic-looking black-haired boy Tam had tending bar that night. Tam isn't *vash'k'ante* himself—he has three ex-wives and a near-infinite number of girlfriends who will attest to that—

but his male bartenders always are. He says it's the one way he can be sure the hired help won't run off with his girlfriends. That's fine with me. Not only has he let me tend bar on occasion when times were tight, but most of the men he hires look like walking wet dreams. I think he does *that* to test the *girlfriends*.

Anyway, like I said, I was having a good night. Every client I'd had had paid well, and none of them had even wanted anything particularly strenuous. I'd made my share of the rent in the first hour, and enough after that to buy food, put money aside to get my *own* place at the end of the month, and still be able to indulge myself with a few ales and an eighth of *sahr* I was hoping to smoke with my ebon-haired object of lust later. I was done hustling for the night; this boy I wanted purely for fun.

The crowd ordering drinks had just cleared and I was about to go strike up a conversation when I saw Silky making a beeline for me. She didn't look happy.

"Nikki, thank the gods you're here!" She plopped down in the chair across from me and took a drink of my ale, ignoring the annoyed glare I gave her.

"Where else would I be? You told me to stay away tonight 'cause you had some important client coming over. I hope you know you're fucking *ruining* my chances of picking up the most gorgeous thing to ever pour an ale right now." Okay, so maybe I was being overly cross with her, but her timing *sucked*. I could see an attractive little redhead moving in on him already. Silky's arrival also reminded me of my unsatisfactory living arrangements. While I appreciated her help while I waited for my place to become vacant, paying Silky for the privilege of sleeping on her couch and getting kicked out every time she had a trick over was wearing on my nerves.

She rolled her eyes at me. "Sorry to interrupt your busy social life, but this is important. You gotta come back to the apartment with me."

"Why? It turns out he likes boys too?" I took my ale back from her and finished it. "Forget it. I'm done for the night. I want to have fun now."

"Don't be such a bitch, Nik," she sighed. "I'm *serious*. I think I'm in real trouble. *Please* come with me."

Great. She was in trouble. I should've known it was too good to last. I glanced up at the bar. Sure enough, the redhead was in animated conversation with my prospective bed partner. There was definitely some god up there with a sick sense of humor. Disgruntled, I went with Silky.

⚹

All the way back to the apartment, I tried to find out what sort of mess she'd gotten herself into, but she just kept telling me I had to see it. Sometimes Silky's sense of the dramatic is damned annoying.

When we finally got there, she unlocked the door and led me straight to the bedroom, which was dimly lit by a single oil lamp. Before I'd even made it through the doorway, she had planted herself in the middle of the room and was gesturing wildly toward the bed.

"Look! What the hells am I supposed to do?"

"Look at what?" I asked.

"That!" She made another grand gesture at the foot of the bed. I looked down this time. "That" was a naked middle-aged man lying crumpled on the floor. "What's wrong with him?"

She gaped at me like I'd just asked her to bear my children. "What's *wrong* with him? He's fucking *dead*, you idiot!"

I glared at her indignantly. "Look, sweetheart, if you're going to be insulting, I'll be more than happy to fuck off and let you deal with this on your own." I turned like I was going to leave.

"Nikki, no!" In a flash she raced across the room and locked my arm in a death grip. "I'm sorry. I didn't mean it. I'm just scared, okay? Just *please* help me. I'll owe you a *big* favor if you do."

"Damn right you will." Point made, I relented. "So are you sure he's dead?"

She let go of my arm, her relief visible. "Yes, I'm sure. He was just getting into it when he stiffened all up and made this weird little noise and then thud!, I'm under a hundred *chot* of dead guy. It was awful."

"I thought this sort of thing only happened in tales," I said.

"Tell that to him." Silky made another theatrical gesture at her former client.

I walked over and poked at him with the toe of my boot. His head listed slightly so it looked like he was staring up at me. He looked surprised, in a deceased sort of way. "He's dead all right. What're you gonna do with him?"

" 'What am I gonna do with him?' I thought I'd have him stuffed and keep him as a souvenir hat rack. Gods!"

Okay, so it was a stupid question. Disposing of dead bodies doesn't fall within my field of expertise. I tried to come up with something more useful. "Well, I take it calling the City Guard is out of the question…" Of course it was. The Guard would either say it's not their problem or blame us for his murder. "…So why don't we just throw his clothes back on him and dump him in an alley somewhere. Let someone else find him."

Silky shook her head. "Sorry, but it's not that easy. Do you know who this is?"

"You mean aside from your important client who is now ruining my night? No. Enlighten me."

She pointed at the corpse. "That is Mage-Lord Alveron M'karesh."

"Horseshit." I poked at the thing with my boot again. "It may look a bit like him, but come on, Silky. Why the fuck would one of the most powerful mages in the country bother coming downtown to boff a common hooker? He was feeding you a line of shit and you fell for it."

She glared at me mulishly. "I know it sounds insane, Nik, but it's true. I don't know why he was coming down here. Maybe that's how he got his kicks. It wouldn't be the first time someone from Lords Hill came down to sample the street trash, you know."

Well, that was certainly true. I'd had a few highborn types myself in the four years I'd been hustling. But still…"You expect me to believe he came down here, picked you up at random, and *told* you who he was when he could just as easily stay up on the Hill and magick up anything he wants?"

"No, of course not." She sat down on the edge of the bed. "This isn't the first time he's come down here. I just didn't remember who he was 'til he was dead. I'm pretty sure he put some kind of spell on me so I wouldn't. Don't you remember—you told me just last week I Felt weird."

That's my Talent, you see. I can Sense magick; when it's being used and what it's being used on. When I came to the city at age 15, I was absolutely convinced that I'd be able to march up to the doors of the mage school, show them my incredible gift, and they'd fall all over themselves in their haste to admit me. I'd played out the scene so many times in my head since my Talent manifested that I'd come up with several charmingly witty comments to make as they escorted me with excited pride and the tiniest hint of envy to meet the senior instructors and launch me on my life of wealth, glamor and excitement. It was my Destiny.

Well. No such luck. Turns out magick-sniffers are relatively common, and my gift isn't even a particularly strong one. In short, they didn't want me. Obviously I was underwhelmed, but I wasn't about to go back home—the people where I grew up, my parents included, think *vash'k'ante* are a lower form of life than rabid rats. There wasn't much else to distinguish me from a thousand other youths but my looks, so I turned to hustling. Not as noble a profession as magecraft, admittedly, but it pays the rent. It can even be damn enjoyable, depending on the client.

In any case, Silky was right. I had Felt something strange about her. I had simply dismissed it as unimportant. That alone wasn't enough to convince me, though.

"So maybe he was a mage, but a forget-spell doesn't prove he was Lord Alveron," I argued. "He could've just said that to impress you."

"Why would he care about impressing a whore?" she said, throwing my own logic back at me. "Besides, how do you explain this." Grimacing slightly, she knelt beside the body and yanked the stiffening left arm up so I could see its hand.

"*Shit!*" She was telling me the truth. It was him. The ring on his second finger was—if you'll pardon the expression—a dead giveaway. It was a snake made of white gold, ruby and sapphire, coiling three times around the finger, grasping its tail in its mouth. There was only one like it, and everyone knew it belonged to Alveron.

Each of the four ruling Mage-Lords has a ring unique to them, fashioned by magick and coveted by every damn thief in the country. And covet is all they can do; the ring goes on when the Mage-Lord takes the oath of office and is spelled to never leave the finger, even in death. I've heard tales of grave-robbers making their fortunes through removal of skeletal digits of Lords long-dead, but no one seems to actually know one of the lucky thieves.

I looked from the ring to Silky. "You do know what this means, don't you?"

She dropped the arm. "Yeah. It means we can't just dump it in an alley. They'll use everything they have to find out how he died and *where* and with *whom*." Her eyes widened in horror. "Goddess! They'll do a read-back of the last thing he saw and it'll be *my face!*"

I couldn't help it; I snickered. "Look at it this way—it'll make your reputation. The whore so hot she killed a Mage-Lord. See if you can handle what Alveron couldn't!"

"Nikki, this is *not* funny! What if they think I *did* kill him?" She sat on the bed again.

I sat down beside her. I was getting tired of his Lordship staring at me with that blankly surprised look. "Settle down, okay? More than likely his heart just gave out. I think we should just get his clothes on him and dump him anyways. Even if they do find out he was with you, what can they really do? They're not going to tell the public how he died. The most they'd probably do is hit you with another forget-spell so you don't know you ever *met* him."

"If they find out you helped me, they'll probably spell you too," she said.

I shrugged. "So? I wouldn't count this as a cherished memory anyways. If they erase everything from the point you came into Tam's, at least I'll *think* I had a good night. Now help me with his clothes." Silently she complied.

I was wrestling to get his tunic on him when I found it. My hand brushed the back of his neck and I Felt a jolt of magick so strong I thought at first that something had stung me. Cursing, I told Silky to stop attempting to force his shoes on for a minute and hold him steady. I parted the graying brown hair and, now that I was sensitized to it, soon spotted the cause of the magickal shock. A small, odd-looking black dart was embedded in his neck just below the hairline, and it was pumping a huge amount of magickal energy into the corpse. That's where my Talent as a magick-sniffer falls short: I had no idea what the thing was doing or how it could do anything in the first place. I was reasonably sure, however, that it wasn't good.

I sat on the floor, feeling a bit overwhelmed, as Silky demanded to know what the problem was. I told her what I'd found, but she didn't seem to get it.

"Think about it," I told her. "That dart got in his neck somehow, and it's still doing some high-powered magickal shit. Do you really want to move him without knowing what's going on? I don't know *what* that thing's doing and I'd really rather not fuck with him 'til I do."

She scuttled away from the body like it was going to wake up and attack any second, leaving Alveron to crumple back into a boneless heap. "So what are we supposed to do *now?*" she squeaked.

"I don't know," I admitted. "I think we need help."

⚹

What we needed, I figured, was a mage. Since we couldn't exactly go looking for one on Lords Hill, we did the next best thing—went back to Tam's. If he couldn't help us, we'd have to dump the body and take our chances. That's the other side of Tam's business, you see—he finds shit. Things, people, information, whatever you want. It was something of a long shot to hope he'd know of a handy mage floating around, but I didn't know what else to do.

When we entered the club my spirits immediately lifted. Not only was Tam holding court at a table in the back of the room, but my black-haired beauty was still tending bar and the redhead was nowhere to be seen.

I ordered us a couple of ales, giving him my best "I'm Beautiful, Don't You Want To Fuck Me?" look. He handed them to me with a grin I hoped signified interest rather than amusement and went off to deal with another customer. I would have hung around waiting for him to finish, but Silky was hovering next to me like a morose little storm cloud, so once again I reluctantly put my potential love life on hold and led her over to Tam.

He was sitting with his current girlfriend and a couple of tough-looking mercenary types like himself, one of whom was relating a story about some sort of disastrous campaign he'd been on up north in Dashiren. I waited for him to finish, then got Tam's attention. He'd been pleased with my last stint at bartending, so he was happy to talk with me now.

I pulled him away from his tablemates and, without going into detail, explained that we had a potentially nasty magickal problem and needed to find someone who could tell us what we were dealing with. Tam nodded thoughtfully then, telling us to have a seat, waded off into the crowd.

"Does this mean he can help us?" Silky asked, fidgeting nervously.

"I hope so." I took a drink of ale. " 'Course, he might've just had to take a piss. Do me a favor, Silk—don't have any more high-born clients over 'til after I move out."

She raked a hand through her short blond hair and sighed. "Nik, right now I don't want another high-born trick as long as I *live*. I'm sorry I dragged you into this; I really will make it up to you. For one thing, forget about paying me any rent. I'll—"

"Don't worry about it right now," I said, waving her to silence. Tam was coming back, and trailing behind him was none other than my object of lust.

He reached our table and said, "I think Kevaris here is the person you're looking for. He was close to getting Adept status when he and his school had an unfortunate parting of ways. I can let him go for the rest of the night, so go ahead and tell him your problem." He gave me a bone-jarring clap on the back and returned to his friends.

Kevaris, huh? And he was a mage, too. Maybe this night wasn't a total write-off.

We introduced ourselves and invited him to have a seat. He did so, regarding us curiously, and I took advantage of the moment to get my first really close look at him. His eyes were such a deep shade of brown they almost looked black. Nice. Along with his hair it made a striking contrast to his fair complexion. I wondered if I could dare to hope that his personality was as good as his looks.

He cleared his throat. "So Tam said you have some sort of magickal problem?"

"That's putting it mildly," Silky muttered. I kicked her ankle. We couldn't afford to scare him off with premature doomsaying.

"We don't exactly know if it's a problem," I said. "The magickal part, anyways. We were hoping you'd be willing to take a look at it. It's some kind of spell, I think, but I don't know what it's doing or if it's dangerous, and it's sitting in the middle of her apartment."

He looked a bit confused. "The *spell* is sitting in her apartment?"

"It's a long story." I downed the rest of my ale. "Would you just have a look at it, Kevaris? It's not something I really know how to explain."

"Kev. Just call me Kev. Only my relatives and authority figures call me Kevaris." He studied us for a few moments; I was pleased to note his eyes lingered on me much longer than Silky. Finally he said, "All right, I'll have a look. You've got me curious. Besides, it gets me out of tending bar." He grinned charmingly.

Silky was out of her chair like a shot. "Fantastic! Thank you! Can we *please* go?" As if we had a choice.

We followed her out of the club and down the street, not even trying to match her pace. I didn't really blame her—it was *her* trick who was sitting in *her* apartment with *her* face embedded in whatever was left of his memory—but personally I wasn't eager to start dealing with it again. Maybe we'd get lucky and the dart would've dissolved the body and itself while we were out.

"So tell me, Nikki," Kev said quietly, "when you were in the bar earlier, was that all you looking for—a mage to help you with this problem of yours?"

"Fuck no," I snorted. "I didn't even know there *was* a problem. Believe me, I had something *far* more enjoyable in mind." I looked him in the eyes, smiling suggestively.

"Hmm. I was hoping that was the case. When we get a few moments, we should discuss that in more detail. I had a few thoughts of my own on the subject." His baritone purr was just as suggestive and my groin was responding accordingly. I inconspicuously adjusted my breeches, now *really* hoping bloody Alveron had been reduced to a small pile of dust or something. His expression grew serious. "Hey, I'm not going to find myself in the middle of something between you and Silky, am I? No offense, but if you two are in some kind of relationship, I'm not interested."

I laughed and hurriedly explained to him that I was just camping on her couch for a month, we're just friends, I'm definitely exclusively vash and even if I wasn't she wouldn't be my type. He relaxed, but still looked a bit worried, so I added one final bit of proof—I told him I know Tam 'cause I tend bar for him on occasion. At that he relaxed completely, and once again I mentally praised Tam's hiring policies.

All too soon we reached the apartment and Silky, who was bouncing impatiently in front of the door.

"Maia's *tits*, can't you two save the get-acquainted games for *later?*"

"You could've gone in ahead of us."

"Oh sure, and get eaten or zapped into goo or something. No thank you."

She unlocked the door, but before she got it open Kev said, "Just a moment. Would you mind explaining 'get eaten or zapped into goo'? Exactly what do you have in there?"

"You mean Nik didn't *tell* you?" Silky looked at me accusingly.

"I was going to, but you were rushing me and it fucked me up." I tried to sound wounded. "Besides, it's probably perfectly safe."

"What is?" Kev demanded.

"Well..." Silky licked her lips, "It's sort of a dead guy..."

"With a weird dart in his neck," I continued. "It's pumping magickal energy into the corpse something fierce."

Silky took over again. "See, Nik can *sense* magick, but he can't tell what it's doing. That's why we need a mage—so we know if it's safe to get rid of it without, like, reanimating it or getting blasted by a spell."

Kev nodded slowly. "Is the dart what killed him?"

Silky shrugged. "Most likely. I don't think it was in his neck before he died. I know I touched him there an' didn't feel anything. I don't know how it got there." She brightened slightly. "Hey—is there any chance you could just blast *him* into goo? Then we wouldn't have to worry about it."

"Sorry—I haven't gotten quite that far in my studies," Kev smiled.

144

"Might as well have a look at him. I'll Shield us before we go in, just in case." He concentrated briefly and I Felt a tingle of magick around us, then Kev opened the door.

When no shambling ex-Mage-Lord who had suddenly developed a taste for human flesh confronted us, we proceeded in a slightly nervous little cluster to the bedroom. Alveron was still lying in the same awkwardly boneless heap by the foot of the bed. It seemed rather anticlimactic of him, but I wasn't going to complain.

"Is that him?" Kev asked.

Silky gave a put-upon sigh. "Well, I just don't know. With all the *hundreds* in my collection it's hard to tell."

"It's him," I interpreted. It was nice to know I wasn't the only one to ask stupid questions when confronted with a dead body. "The dart's in his neck, right at the base of the skull."

"Let's see what it's up to then. I was always good at spell reading." He knelt next to the body, then looked up at us. "You may as well have a seat; this might take awhile, and it's not very interesting to watch."

Well, *he* was interesting to watch, but I could do that just as easily sitting down. I'd already had a pretty athletically demanding night, and chances were I'd still have to help dispose of a dead Mage-Lord. At the rate things were going, even if I *did* get a chance to explore Kev's delicious body in detail, I'd drop from exhaustion before I could get it up.

As if to confirm my depressing prediction, he said, "Oh, if I start behaving strangely or stay in trance for more than an hour, snap me out of it, would you? It might mean I'm in some sort of trouble." He bent over the body and went silent. I Felt a tingle of magick and sighed. More than an hour in dead silence? I could easily fall asleep in that amount of time.

Beside me, Silky yawned, setting me off too. "Does he have any idea what he's asking for?" she whispered.

"I doubt it. Remember—he hasn't been working since early this evening. If I have to just sit here for a fucking hour I'm gonna pass out."

"Me too." She opened her nightstand drawer and pulled out a carved wooden box. "Guess it's time for these." The box contained about half a dozen *tak* cigarettes. I could've kissed her. I know *tak*'s fairly mild as stimulants go, but at least it would keep us awake and coherent, something my eighth of *sahr* wouldn't do. If I'd smoked any of that at this point, I would probably have lain there getting off on fantasizing about Kev and playing with my nipple rings 'til I drifted off to sleep. Not a good efficiency drug, *sahr*.

So for the next hour we sat and smoked while Kev communed with the dart. We were just wondering if we should shake him back to reality when he came out of it himself, all blinking and wide-eyed. I gave him a drag off my smoke. It seemed to help him some. He lost the unfocused look, but he was definitely agitated and his first words came out in a sort of panicked gasp.

"Great bloody *gods*, do you know who this *is?*"

We nodded serenely, having been through this before.

"Now you see why we said we have a problem," I commented.

"This is *Alveron*," he answered himself.

"The one and only," I confirmed helpfully.

"What's he *doing* here?"

"Not much, anymore," Silky said dryly. "But I can assure you he wasn't paying me to help him pick out carpet swatches."

"But why would…" Kev trailed off awkwardly.

"We don't know. At this point it's not important; he's in no shape to tell us." I knelt in front of him and put a hand on each shoulder, effectively forcing him to look me in the eyes. "Kevaris, what's *important* is what that dart is doing. Did you find anything out?"

He blinked and finally lost that look of confused panic completely. "Oh. Yes. The dart. Gods. Help me up, would you? My leg's gone dead from sitting like this so long. Is there anything to drink around here?"

I gave him a boost and, while he limped in little circles around the bedroom, I went out to the living room where I had my things stashed and retrieved a bottle of whiskey I'd been saving for times of need. Returning to the bedroom, I uncorked it, took a drink and handed it to Kev, who was now sitting next to Silky on the bed. I sat next to him as he took his own drink and passed the bottle to Silky.

Kev sighed. "That's better. Now—the dart. First of all, you don't have to worry about him reanimating or exploding or anything. It's not doing anything like that. I can't believe what it *is* doing."

"And that is…" Silky prompted him, passing the bottle back to me.

"It's literally changing his mind. I don't know how; I didn't even know such a thing was possible. It's…you know the final memory patterns the mages replay in post-death read-back. It's supposed to be a foolproof method of seeing the victim's final moments, because any magickal tampering has always been obvious. I don't quite understand the science of it, but it's taken as Holy Writ that final memory patterns are untouchable. Well, this thing is doing it. It's altering those patterns magickally, and from what I can see, when it's done you won't be able to tell those aren't his original memory-patterns."

"Couldn't they tell something was funny by looking at the dart itself?" I handed him the bottle. "I mean, that's a lot of magick it's pumping out."

"Huh-uh." Kev shook his head and swallowed. "It was *loaded* with the spell somehow. Once the spell's finished, it'll look like a typical assassin's dart. Any magickal residue could just as easily have come from Alveron himself."

"Why would anyone go to all that trouble?" Silky asked. "I know a lot of people probably wanted him dead, but isn't the way he really died bad enough?"

A thought occurred to me. "Not if you wanted to implicate someone else. Someone who would never actually kill him, or someone they wanted to take down along with Alveron. Think about it—you know damn well he probably didn't tell anyone about his little downtown adventures, or at least not the real reason he was coming here. So he's trying to be anonymous, no one really knows what the fuck he's up to, he's way less protected than up on Lords Hill, and some assassin finally manages to nail him. You could put all sorts of shit in his head that would make him or the country or other countries or whatever look bad."

"Nikki, that's brilliant!" Kev exclaimed, giving me a warm rush of pleasure. I've been called a lot of things, but brilliant isn't usually one of them.

His expression darkened. "And all too probable. Do you realize the implications?"

"Can't you just read what it's doing and find out if Nik's right?" Silky asked.

"I wish," Kev frowned. "Unfortunately, it doesn't seem to want anyone peeking before it's done. I had to totally tiptoe around the damn spell just to find out what I did. Thing's got more booby traps than the Labyrinth of An'koreth."

"I guess this means we can't just dump him in an alley," she said glumly.

"That's probably what they were counting on," I theorized, feeling I was on a roll now. "I mean, if you dumped him, the spell would've had plenty of time to do its job before he was discovered and taken to someone who can do read-backs. Assuming the bad guys knew about you since he was darted here, they figured you'd panic and dump the body just like we were going to. How could they know that I'm a magick-sniffer or that Tam would have a mage working for him?" I was really wondering what Kev had done to wind up tending bar for Tam, but he hadn't volunteered the information and it didn't seem like the time to ask. I'd briefly entertained the horrible thought that the school might have kicked him out for doing blood magick, but he didn't Feel like he was into that, and Tam's too sharp to let that sort of sickness get past him.

"So what the hells are we supposed to do with the cursed thing?" Silky said, glaring daggers in the direction of the body.

"Take it to Lords Hill," Kev replied.

Silky leapt to her feet. "Oh, *right*. We'll just *waltz* up there and say, 'Excuse us, but have you lost a Mage-Lord? 'Cause we have one. He's a little worse for the wear, but at least he's still in one piece.' I'm *sure* they'll be happy to usher us in and *shower* us with gifts and kisses, no questions asked. Get *real*, rich-boy."

I was inclined to agree with her. Gutter trash like us simply are *not* welcome on the Hill, regardless of how charming or well-spoken we might be. I said, "Even supposing we are able to get him up there, who are we supposed to give him to? We don't know who did this to him in the first place, except that to do that sort of spell they'd have to be pretty damn smart and powerful. And what if the spell finishes its dirty work before we get him up there? We'd be fucked."

"Why? Nobody *here* killed him. This has to be brought to the attention of the authorities," Kev said stubbornly.

"The *authorities* don't *like* us," Silky snapped.

"They will if we show them this kind of magick can and is being done," Kev argued.

Silky snorted derisively. "They'll probably accuse us of being in on it."

"No, they won't," Kev insisted. "I know what to do when we get there. I *did* live there 'til recently."

"Well, pardon *me*, O Great One." She made an exaggerated bow. "Your *brilliant* impersonation of a lowly bartender made me think you were one of *us*."

"That's not what I—" Kev spluttered.

I downed the last of the whiskey and cut him off. "Silky, give it a rest. Kev—do you really know what to do once we get him up there?" He nodded. "Okay. It's gonna get light out in a few hours and that dart's going to finish its job at some point, so let's just do it and get it over with *now*. I'm sick of Alveron and everything connected with him," I said crossly. This whole night was giving me a headache and the two of them sounded like they could keep arguing forever. *Anything* was preferable to that.

Half an hour later we were skulking down the dark and empty streets, heading to Lords Hill. Well, Silky was skulking. Kev and I were hauling Alveron between us, hoping anyone seeing us would assume he was drunk. Kev had put something he called a stasis spell on the Mage-Lord; apparently it slowed or froze the spelled item in time for as long as the spell lasted. Which, he told us, would be just over an hour. After that the dart would return to its task, which had to be nearly done. At the moment I was wishing he'd said to the fifth hell with the dart and put a levitation spell on the old boy instead. How could one slightly portly middle-aged man manage to weigh as much as a draft horse (not that I've ever *carried* a draft horse)?

Suddenly Kev cursed as he tripped over something and lost his grip on the Mage-Lord. Alveron immediately listed violently in his direction, causing me to lose my grip, and as Kev leapt out of the way, he landed in an ignominious heap in the pile of rubbish that had tripped Kev in the first place. We both stared at him in exhausted dismay. "I swear, the old bastard is trying to make this difficult," Kev grumbled.

I nodded in agreement, trying to suppress the urge to give Alveron a swift, hard kick.

Silky materialized out of the darkness. "Gods, do you think you can get him the rest of the way to Lords Hill without *breaking* him?" she complained.

"You think we're doing such a lousy job, you try carrying him," I retorted.

She looked at me smugly. "I can't. I'm too short. He wouldn't balance right. You both said so—remember?"

"Funny how you only agree with any assessment of your shortcomings when it involves something you don't want to do."

She stuck her tongue out at me and crouched down to investigate the current condition of the corpse. "Eeew! I don't know what you dropped him in, but it *reeks*."

Kev groaned and, concentrating briefly, magicked up a small, blue light to hover over Alveron. We followed her lead and crouched to assess the damage. He'd landed in a pile of refuse somebody had thoughtfully left at the side of the road. Among the more identifiable bits were some horse dung, a dead rat and a half-eaten sausage roll. Kev muttered something under his breath; since I didn't Feel any magick along with it, I assumed he was simply cursing again.

"Are you sure you still want to take him to Lords Hill?" I asked.

Kev gave Alveron a look that, if he weren't already dead, would have killed him on the spot. "We have to. This is too important for us to simply abandon it."

I was afraid he'd say that. If he wasn't so damn gorgeous I would've told him he was more than welcome to finish this task of civic responsibility on his own while I went off to down enough *sahr* and ale to forget this night ever happened, but...lust has been known to make me do stupid things. So I settled on pointing out that it was his side that had landed point-blank in the refuse, and if he was so dead set on seeing this through then he'd better not expect me to switch with him.

As Kev sighed, Silky spoke up again. "Well, we'd better get this slop cleaned off him somehow. At this rate we won't have to worry about anyone seeing us; they'll be able to smell us coming." She turned to Kev. "Isn't there some way you can magick it off him?"

He drew himself up and glared at her in perfect outrage. "I will have you know that I was being trained as a *combat* mage. I am nearly Adept level. My skills are in combat, defense, and strategy."

She looked at him blandly. "So?"

"So—" his voice shook with wounded dignity, "I DO NOT do DRY CLEANING!"

Silky shrugged. "In other words, all your fancy training is of no practical use whatsoever." For all that she deals most intimately with the public, Silky can be incredibly obtuse when it comes to reading people. Kev flushed furiously, the blue mage-light coloring him an unflattering shade of purple. I figured it was time to step in before he demonstrated one of those combat spells on her.

"Silk," I smacked her lightly on the back of the head, "Don't be a bitch. If it weren't for Kev, fat-boy would still be sitting in your apartment with you afraid he was going to jump up and bite you, and the use of your couch isn't so precious to me that I might not've left you to deal with him yourself. Now why don't you make nice and help us find something to clean him up with."

"You're just sticking up for him because you want to fuck him," she hissed petulantly. I shrugged and smiled sweetly at her. She glared back. "Sometimes you really suck, Nik."

I grinned. "So do you, sweetheart. It's part of the job description."

She huffed in exasperation and flounced off, practically radiating righteous indignation. I wasn't worried about her actually abandoning us; Silky's happiest when she has something to complain about.

By the time Kev and I had levered Alveron out of the muck, she was back, announcing that she'd found a rain barrel nearby. We tore some strips off his tunic—after all, it wasn't like he was going to care—soaked them, and scrubbed furiously 'til the old boy wasn't quite so fragrant. In a short time we were on our way again.

We reached Lords Hill with no further problems, but as we approached the Mages' complex we discovered an insurmountable one.

Kev's "plan" was for us to haul Alveron—who was definitely the worse for the wear now—right up to the front gates, demand to see some instructor he swore was trustworthy, and *explain* it all to him.

Silky stopped dead and gaped at him. "Are you *nuts*?!" She turned to me. "He's nuts. I've had it, Nik. You seem to think there's something in that pretty head of his besides a lot of air, some useless spells and a happy little picture of this world that *most* people lose by the time they're six, so *you* explain it to him."

I sighed. "Let's set fat-boy down a minute. Now, lemme ask you a question, Kev. Why are you tending bar at Tam's instead of finishing your final year or whatever at mage school?"

He looked at the ground and said sullenly, "I was sort of kicked out."

"Is that like being sort of pregnant?" Silky remarked.

I ignored her and bulled ahead. "Well, if they kicked you out, that would suggest that they don't much *like* you, right? To get *kicked* out you'd have to be considered either a major problem or a major embarrassment or *both*, yes?"

He nodded, looking like he was going to burst into tears. I sympathized; hells, I don't generally let this be known 'cause it's too damn embarrassing to admit I was ever that naive, but when the mages said they had no use for *me* I went around feeling like I'd been kicked in the guts for *weeks*, and I hadn't even made it in the doors. But no matter how much I wanted to, this was no time to give him a comforting hug and let him off the hook. I had to keep pressing. If I could talk him out of this suicidal idiocy there'd be plenty of time for comforting later.

"Now I'm guessing that the main reason you're so hot to announce this new spell thing in person is that maybe they'll be so fucking grateful to you that they'll let you back into the school." I raised an eyebrow at him.

"I—I guess that might have crossed my mind," he admitted guiltily.

Mm hmm. I pushed my hair back over my shoulders, hoping it would help make me look dead serious rather than dead tired, and closed in for the kill. "*Think*, Kev. Odds are it's not gonna work like you want it to; there's too many strikes against you. One—they are *not* happy with you. Two—you *don't* know who can be trusted. What if this instructor guy's in on it? You can rename yourself Dead Meat if he is. *If* they even fetch him, 'cause Three—it's late, we're *not* the most respectable looking bunch, and what are we doing with a dead Mage-Lord. They're more likely to toss us in a cell for questioning at a more civilized hour regardless of what we tell them. And Four—that stasis spell of yours is gonna die pretty quick, and you *know* the dart's nearly done with *its* spell. What if it finishes before you can get anyone qualified to come down and look at it? You can't prove anything then, and it's very likely to happen. All they'll see at *best* is some disgraced ex-student trying to weasel his way back into the school by delivering Alveron's body along with some impossible, unprovable story to try to make himself look good. You'd be lucky if they didn't tell a couple of Guardsmen to kick the shit out of you and drop you in an alley downtown to teach you your place. And it will be just you, 'cause Silky and I are *not* going to do it. That's just too much to ask us to risk, and if you have any sense you'll leave with us. *Now*."

He sat down with a thud. "You really think that's what will happen?"

"Absolutely," I said, Silky nodding in agreement beside me.

"And you honestly won't help me take him in there?" he asked plaintively.

"Not for all the money in the world," Silky stated. "It's not our fault the old fool got himself dead. We didn't know you had such an utterly harebrained plan for getting him to the authorities."

"If we had, I never would've knocked myself out dragging him up here," I added.

He tried one last time. "But you agreed the political implications of this kind of magick existing are *dreadful*...."

"So the government's overthrown," Silky shrugged. "What've they ever done for us? Mine and Nik's lives aren't likely to change no matter how many political big shots bite it. Our services are in demand no matter *who's* in power."

"For that matter, what've they done for you except ruin your chances for any kind of decent life in your chosen craft? Uncertified mages don't get any work higher up than our part of town," I pointed out. I was still wildly curious about what he'd done to get himself kicked out, but he wasn't taking the hint to expand on the subject.

Instead, Kev sighed gustily and rubbed his eyes. "You're probably right. It's insane to think we could just walk up and demand to see someone important, even if we *weren't* out of time. But…I have to do *something*."

I sat down next to him and put an arm around his shoulders. He snuggled in closer to me and rested a hand on my thigh, squeezing it lightly then settling into a slow, rhythmic stroking that sent little electric tingles running straight to my groin. As he was looking at the ground, I took the opportunity to flash a giddily triumphant grin at Silky.

She rolled her eyes and gave me a patient smirk, knowing I have a tendency to react overenthusiastically to fairly insignificant things when I'm exhausted and horny. Clearing her throat, she said, "Look, Kev, we're all dead tired and it's going to start getting light any time now. If you have to do something, why don't we just write a note explaining what happened and stick it on him. We can dump him by the front gates; somebody'll find him there soon."

He looked up at her, brightening. "That might work. But what are we going to write it with?"

As Silky pulled a stick of kohl out of her pocket with a flourish, I said, "Tear off a piece of his shirt; it's nearly white. Just *please* don't sign it."

We scratched out a fairly legible and straightforward note (I thought Kev expressed a truly inordinate amount of surprise that I knew how to read and write), then hustled Alveron to a spot near the front gates of the Mages' Complex. We affixed the note to the front of his tunic as securely as possible and beat a hasty retreat back toward downtown, Silky complaining all the way that she was dying of thirst and her feet hurt.

In retrospect, sticking a note on the old boy was probably a dumb idea, but we were all pretty punchy and it made Kev happy.

I was just happy to see the last of the Mage-Lord, and even happier when a now-mollified Kevaris suggested that rather than return to Silky's couch, I grab my belongings and come home with him. It was undoubtedly the most shit I'd ever gone through to get a date, but as his hand gave my ass a proprietary squeeze, I was inclined to think it might've been worth it.

✳

Now, if this were a child's tale or some Bard's song, the story would end right there. Brave, Misunderstood, and Above All Modest, Heroes Save the Land From Evil and Live Happily Ever After. Unfortunately, life in the real world seldom lends itself to such neatly pretty conclusions.

Don't get me wrong—some things are going well. Kev and I have more or less reached Relationship status. We enjoy each other both in and out of bed (by the by—there are some perfectly fascinating things you can do with the aid of a levitation spell), and so far we haven't found anything we disagree about too violently.

Still, I have moved into my own apartment. His flat above Tam's club was just too damn small and we both have an overwhelming need for privacy at times. Also, he's one of those people who's all cheerful and likes to talk when he first wakes up, whereas I'm doing well if I can spit out two words in a vaguely civil tone, and that drives him crazy. He drives me crazy with his ever-more-frequent suggestions that I quit hustling and find a "respectable" job. Like I could make the money I do at anything "respectable." I will quit someday, but for now—I'm good at it, I enjoy it (well, most of the time), and it pays well. I get myself checked by a Healer every fortnight or so, and he knows my clients don't mean anything to me, so what's he worried about?

But I digress. (I've always wanted to say that.)

See, they found Alveron the next morning just like we figured they would; the news was all over the city long before we ever crawled out of bed. By hanging around Tam's most of the night we got as detailed a report on what happened after that as anyone outside of Lords Hill had, and guess what—no mention of the old bastard's final memory-patterns being magickally altered. Our note either fell off him, was disregarded, or was disposed of before the right people could read it. It would be nice to think they're just pretending they don't know to flush the bad guys out, but things have gone too crazy for me to believe that.

In a startling display of efficiency, they did Alveron's read-back within hours of discovering the body (maybe because he's a Mage-Lord, but I can't help wondering if his little tumble in the refuse earlier gave them the impression he was getting dangerously ripe).

The read-back apparently shows Alveron in a nondescript room accepting some sort of package from a member of the Me'Kesht embassy and giving her some very sensitive information in return. In the middle of a brief but damning conversation, the assassin's dart hits its mark. As Alveron lays dying, the last thing he sees is the Me'Keshti bending over to take her package back while someone standing just behind her tells him smugly that someone will be along to dispose of his body shortly.

The only thing no one seems to agree on is the identity of the second person. The most popular choices are another Mage-Lord, a top-ranking noble or government official, or a Dashiren national. There's also considerable speculation about the one who dumped the body—was he selling out on the conspirators or just plain incompetent? Of course, none of it matters.

What matters is they all believed the read-back unquestioningly, and in the last few weeks heads have literally rolled on Lords Hill. There's been increasingly serious talk of war with Me'Kesht and half the city seems to be operating in a constant state of paranoia. Gods only know what else has been going on that the public doesn't know about.

And here are me, Kev and Silky—the only three people in the whole fucking country who know this whole situation is based on a lie…aside from whoever set it up in the first place. We talked about that last night.

Kev already tried to tell a few people the truth (without mentioning our involvement—I told him I'd kill him if he blabbed that), and not one of them believed him. Even Tam just laughed. So of *course* he thinks *we* have to do something to find and expose the real culprits. His opinion is: if their first try caused this much chaos, what kind of damage will their second one do?

156

Silky still thinks we should let the whole world go to the seventh hell rather than get involved.

And me? I think we'd be complete fools to pursue this; it's *way* out of our league. Problem is—and I can't decide whether I'm becoming a masochist, suffering from delusions of grandeur, falling in love or merely developing a conscience—I think I'm foolish enough to agree we have to try.

THE SOUND OF ANGELS

BY

LISA S. SILVERTHORNE

*T*hose who have heard the songs of whales, especially the
sound of the orca's song, know the true sound of magic
and joy. Traveling to the San Juan Islands may not be
possible for you, however. With "The Sound of Angels"
Lisa Silverthorne has provided us with the next best thing. Saying goodbye to
a loved one is always hard, but sometimes there is joy to be found inside our
pain and sorrow, if only we have the courage to look.

— S. P.

Carrie leaned against the boat railing, Ellen's neuro-crosslink in her
ear; Ellen had wanted Carrie to be with her when she died today. Carrie
gripped the edges of her teal windbreaker. Haro Strait in May was nippy,
making her shiver.

The doctors had pinpointed Ellen's bodily functions to begin shutting
down by 3 P.M., with the moment of death arriving at 4 P.M.. Ah, the
wonders of modern medicine, Carrie thought. No scientific breakthroughs
for curing cancer, but a new process to estimate the time of death.

Over the months, Ellen's condition had deteriorated, rendering her practically comatose. If it hadn't been for the neuro-crosslinks that Ellen had demanded be installed between them, Carrie wouldn't be able to be with Ellen now. She was a thousand miles away in a hospital bed while Carrie was out in the Puget Sound on a whale watching boat. Ellen had jokingly referred to the crosslink as a cellular phone.

'Buck up, love,' Ellen thought. 'You've been with me this long. Stay with me an hour more.'

A cold blackness hung inside Carrie, warmed only by the presence of Ellen's thoughts and feelings transmitted via satellite. Morphine-fogged images of their lakeside cottage fed into Carrie's already overloaded cortex.

'Why couldn't I stay with you, Ellen? In twelve years, this is the longest we've ever been apart. Why now?'

Ellen's tired voice whispered through her head as the cool breeze off the Strait pressed against her face. 'This will be the toughest hour of our relationship, kiddo. Stay with me, okay?'

Carrie fought down a sob and nodded. She watched the horizon, the blue blurring to green and back again. Cedars and firs framed the edge of the dark teal water. The hum of the boat resonated through her arms and into her chest. The air tasted of salt. It calmed her. There were less than a dozen people on this cruise, all of them keeping mostly to themselves. Off season was a good time to be here.

'Can you see the Sound, Ellen?'

Ellen had grown up here—on San Juan Island, near Friday Harbor—and hadn't been back in twelve years.

'When I was a kid—' Ellen paused and in a moment, pain rippled through Carrie, minimized for her by an endorphin filter. 'This water murmured peace and the dockboards echoed laughter,' Ellen continued. 'They still do—to anyone who'll listen. Are you listening?'

"I'm listening," Carrie whispered into the wind.

'I feel the motion of the boat. It's soothing. I'll miss boats.'

Carrie bit her lip, imagining Ellen's faraway smile, framed by honey-colored curls that were always too tight around her angular face. And her hazel eyes that conveyed so much more than her words. A tear streaked down Carrie's face and she quickly wiped it away. Her windbreaker rustled.

160

'No tears, kiddo. Not this trip.'

'Why won't you tell me why I'm out here? Tell me why I need to be here when I should be with you, Ellen!'

'I've already told you. To find the orcas. J-Pod.' Ellen paused. 'I feel the wind in my hair—' Another wave of pain. Carrie jerked, bumping the elbow of the woman next to her.

"I'm sorry."

"No harm done," the woman answered with a smile. She gripped a pair of binoculars and her floppy straw hat shadowed her face and glasses. "Is this your first time to see the whales?"

Carrie nodded. "Do you always see whales on these cruises?"

The woman shook her head and pushed the brim of her hat out of her eyes, revealing graying dark hair. "Not always, but I heard the Captain telling one of the crew that a pod of orcas was spotted near Stuart Island. That's where he's headed."

'Orcas, kiddo! Looks like my final wish has been granted.'

Tears trickled down Carrie's face again and she wiped them away. The woman squinted at her.

"Are you all right?"

"Fine."

The woman let the binoculars rest against her blue slicker. "It's okay. Lots of people get emotional on these trips. There's something special about orcas."

'Summer '78,' Ellen thought. 'Lime Kiln Point. My sister and I were sleeping on the warm rocks like a couple of lizards when I felt them in the water.'

'You're making that up,' Carrie thought.

She waited for Ellen's response. When none came, panic spiraled through her body, colder and tighter. 'Ellen?' She tapped frantically at the transmitter in her ear. 'Ellen? Don't leave me! Dear God, Ellen!'

Pain gouged her middle, even through the endorphin filter. Hunching over, she held onto the railing until it subsided.

"Maybe you'd better sit down," said the woman, a hand on Carrie's arm. "Until you're used to the boat."

Carrie nodded and allowed the woman to help her over to the bench. "My name's Donna, Donna Ketcham."

"Carrie Brunner," she mumbled, her arms folded against her middle. 'I'm—here.'

'Ellen!' Carrie pinched her eyes closed. 'I'm sorry. I never realized how much pain you were in until now. Are you all right?'

'Fraid not, kiddo. It's 3:15. They say my kidneys are shutting down. I might not make 4 o'clock.'

Carrie rocked against the anguish mangling her heart.

'Be strong and listen. I want you to keep your eyes on the Sound. No matter what. For the next forty-five minutes, you take in as much of the islands as you can. This is my last visit. Promise me.'

Carrie fought back the tears. 'I promise.'

'Good girl. I'll stay with you as long as I can. We had twelve good years, didn't we?'

'All of them!'

'Now, get back to that railing and watch for the whales.'

"I'm feeling better now," Carrie said to Donna. She rose from the bench and walked back to the railing.

Donna followed.

The water sparkled with sunlight as Carrie turned to the south to catch a glimpse of the Olympic Mountains. Mountain-framed islands with fir trees seemed unreal; the mist that hung over the islands at sunrise and sunset made them magical. On one of the smaller islands, a pair of Harbor seals sunned themselves on the rocks, their bulbous bodies oozing across the shoreline. The seals seemed unconcerned by the boat slipping past.

Slowly, Stuart Island drifted toward the boat. That's when she felt it. A soft, static electricity that brushed across her arms and down her spine. She moved to the front of the boat and leaned out. 'I feel something.'

'I know.' Carrie pictured Ellen's smirk and the wink in those mischievous hazel eyes. 'Listen to the water.'

A satiny black fin broke surface and a slick body arced through the dark teal water, a hint of white at its back. Carrie heard a soft, clear call, a mixture of melancholy and joy.

"They're so loud," said Carrie.

"Who's so loud?" Donna asked.

"The orcas," she answered. "See? Out there." She pointed, her windbreaker rasping.

Donna squinted. "I don't see anything. Much less hear anything."

Another fin, much larger than the first one, broke surface, joined immediately by two smaller fins. The droning sound deepened as the orcas rose and submerged again. They called a second time, haunting the water with pain and bliss.

Other people moved to the front of the boat.

'Stay with me, Ellen,' Carrie stared at her watch. 3:38. 'Please stay with me.'

'Listen, kiddo. Listen.'

'Ellen, please…tell me why I'm here.'

'Soon enough, love. Listen.'

"Somebody said J-Pod was spotted very near here," Donna said and raised her binoculars.

'The others won't see them yet.'

"There are three pods in this area: J, K and L. K-Pod is the smallest. J-Pod lost one of their adult males recently. The Captain said they've been acting funny ever since." Donna panned the horizon. "I can't see a thing."

Carrie stood motionless, riveted by the orca calls and the fins slicing through the water.

"Wait, I think I see something!" Donna bounced up and down in her deck shoes. "I see fins. Three of them! Right where you said, Carrie! Look!"

Carrie felt Ellen's life ticking away as the boat moved toward J-Pod.

'Look, kiddo. And listen.'

Slowly, the boat drew near the orcas and when Carrie saw five or six of them, their sleek bodies humming through the water, the tears welled in her eyes. Joy washed over her, like that snow-covered midnight when she had stepped into her first candlelit Mass on Christmas Eve and swore she could hear the angels singing in the rafters. The orcas' song echoed in her ears, and she felt it, understood it: mourning, acceptance, memory.

They had accepted the death of a loved one and, honoring him, they went on, singing of him to anyone who listened.

Suddenly, their song widened, enfolding Carrie. They sang to her of Ellen, of her childhood, the pain they had carried since she had left them. And now their song soared with new joy: Ellen was back. Back through Carrie and the cross link, if only for a little while. Carrie did not understand this closeness between the pod and Ellen, but she felt it, and was glad to be included, if only peripherally.

Two of the orcas rose from the water, the white of their bellies showing as they seemed to almost stand straight up.

"Look, they're spyhopping!" Donna shouted.

Cameras clicked and people pointed. The orcas' faces held such fellowship that Carrie began to see the emotion reflected around her in the other passengers' faces. She watched the pod of passengers sharing binoculars and huddling together beside the railing. She felt herself drawing closer to these people and allowing them better views than she had for herself.

'Twelve years was a long time without them. I've missed them for so long.'

'Twelve years?'

'That's when I fell in love with you and left here. Listen.'

One of the orcas breached, black and white streaking out of the water. That set off a string of clicks and gasps. A lady moved out of the way so a toddler could see the whales. J-pod moved within six feet of the boat, veered around the bow and headed north toward Canada.

Carrie watched them disappear on the horizon, but she heard their whisper long after the fins had faded from view.

She felt the loss immediately, like her body was hollow. It was more than letting go of the whales. She looked down at her watch. 4:04 P.M..

'Ellen?'

She waited. Water hummed against the boat. A pair of gulls called.

'Ellen?'

Wind whispered over the hull. A sandy-haired toddler giggled. Ellen was gone. Ellen with her special gift, the link with the orcas. A gift she'd had since childhood—that she'd given up without a word.

Carrie closed her eyes.

At last she understood why Ellen had sent her out here. It hadn't been for Ellen; it had been for her. Ellen had only wanted one last look at the place where she'd grown up and loved. The orcas had been for Carrie. The whisper of orcas and Ellen's voice undulated across the water.

Her tears welled. The trip hadn't been about letting go; it was about holding on. She had the courage to do that now. The orcas' song hung in her ears and for the first time in many, many months, she felt peace. She wasn't alone either. Ellen had made sure of that. She had passed on her link with the orcas and now, their communal presence lingered.

Slipping the transmitter out of her ear, she kissed the top.

"Goodbye, my love," she said and cast it into the Sound.

Scattering Ellen's memories instead of her ashes, Carrie thought. She could call them back by listening to the whispers on the waves, the laughter in the dockboards. She knew now why they called it the Sound.

THE KING'S FOLLY

BY

JAMES A. MOORE

*T*his is a love story set in the traditional milieu of castles and ogres and dragons, but it is not a romance. It does not look at how people fall in love or win the love they seek. Its gaze is more concerned with what happens after one of the lovers starts having second thoughts. Moore asks which is the wisest: One who gets rid of a spouse when bored? One who torments him- or herself by watching their spouse with another beloved? Or one who takes direct action to retrieve the lost love?

—N.G.

※

Morlis stared at his monarch. Eldan the Second stood atop the watchtower gazing down on the land he had ruled for the last fifteen years. His mane of red hair blew in the wind, and his noble features were locked in an expression of deep concern.

Morlis stood behind him, as he stared down into the masses gathered below the castle. No doubt, the king wondered how much longer he would rule. Fifteen years of peace was something to be proud of, certainly, but with the rising of the morning sun that peace would end. Eldan's face spoke volumes to his Advisor, who had watched the king grow from infant to leader and, eventually, to monarch. Unless Eldan could find a solution to the puzzle facing him, the serenity and safety of his people would end, crushed under the boot of a woman who had sworn revenge against him five years ago. Morlis could see every moment of worry etched into the man's handsome face.

"The hour is late, Lord Eldan." Morlis' voice was soft, scarcely even a whisper in the late night air. "Might I suggest that you continue this need to stare at your enemies in the morning? You'll have a better view. I assure you their faces will be much clearer from the back of a steed than they will be from a height such as this." He knew the monarch strained to hear his words. In all of his years in the palace, he had never spoken above a whisper. He rather liked making the ruler of Kastenwar work for the advice he gave.

"You have absolutely no sympathy for me, do you, Morlis?"

"None whatsoever. It was not me who insulted the Queen of Tannamoc. I would never have considered creating such a foolish law."

"I had no choice!" Eldan's voice was hoarse. "The damned witches were creating havoc wherever they went!"

"No. That is a lie. You know it now and you knew it then. You simply took offense at the Sorcerer Guild's refusal to pay more in taxes." Beneath his dark blue tunic and the red mantle he wore against the night's chill, Morlis shrugged his shoulders. "Besides which, if you were actually going to kill all of the 'witches,' you'd have had to kill me as well. You just felt the need to have more control over the lands than you already had."

"Morlis, you try my patience." He could tell that Eldan desperately wanted to strike him down for his arrogance, but could not. Not because of his chiding tone of voice, but because he was right. "Have you nothing better to do than to mock me in my time of need?"

"I could remind you that this entire war is unnecessary."

"And I told you before, damn your eyes, that I don't know who it is I supposedly killed!" His voice was like thunder, and many people in the land feared the rage of Eldan the Second, slayer of armies and self-proclaimed giant-killer. Morlis was unaffected. He'd seen twenty-three generations of rulers rise to power and die within the castle where they awaited the morning. Eldan was hardly the best of them. "The stupid cow simply sent a message and told me that my life was forfeit unless I returned her people's corpses!"

"And yet you never bothered to send a messenger to find out how you'd offended Sithian. Instead you ignored her threats."

"Well, come on, man! Tannamoc was hardly the size of my stables back then! How was I to know she'd actually gather a fighting force worth seeing?"

"The fall of Lan Fromach should have given you a hint, Eldan. The destruction of Ellis Nar should have made the point painfully obvious."

"You should have given me a hint! You're my Advisor! I trusted you to give me good advice!"

"Yes. And I trusted you to listen to me when I gave my opinion. 'Beware, my Lord. The Queen of Tannamoc raises an army of the Sidhe to stand beside her.' And 'My Liege, the Fae themselves aided Sithian in crushing your allies to the West.' These are warnings, Eldan. You simply chose to ignore them."

"Not that again, Morlis. I told you before, I thought you were growing senile."

"I have served the rulers of this land for seven-hundred and ninety-three years. In that time I have watched men and women rule and then fall into ruin or die of old age." His voice did not rise, but Eldan blanched. "Never, in all that time, have I been accused of senility."

"Never in all that time did you claim that the Fae were gathering together in a force to fight against the kingdom, either. No one has seen a member of the Sidhe in a thousand years, and you expected me to believe you when you said they were coming to do me battle?"

"You make the same foolish mistake that everyone else makes." He sighed. Mortal arrogance was always cause for depression.

"What mistake, Morlis? What mistake am I making, aside from ignoring that stupid whore's threats?"

"Simply because you could not see them, you assumed the Sidhe were gone."

"Well it seemed a bloody solid idea at the time, now didn't it!" Eldan's voice cracked on that last note, and he turned away once again.

Morlis moved to the edge of the castle's balustrade. In the valley below, the armies of Sithian stood, silently watching. For as far as he could see, strange creatures stared back, inhuman eyes glittering with dark amusement. Amid the dark masses, small as ants from where he stood, several man-sized figures towered. They looked close enough to touch, though he knew of no arrow that could strike them from this range.

Beside him, Eldan spoke in an awestruck voice. "By all that is sacred, they've giants with them."

The wind died down, and Morlis could hear the rapid beating of Eldan's heart. Beneath his cowl, he smiled. "Aye. That they do. They also have ogres, and a few hundred of the border goblins." He pointed with a long finger to a spot in the far distance where a bonfire flickered. "And that, Lord Eldan, is a dragon."

"That cannot be. The dragons are all long dead. It's only a campfire."

"To be sure. It must be a campfire. And all of the creatures standing below us are merely humans dressed in disguises. Surely those giants in the distance are no more than a hundred men standing upon each other's shoulders. Why, the swords they carry are likely little more than wood and a few skins dipped in the stage paint from some traveling minstrel show." Morlis patted the king's shoulder and moved back from the edge of the tower. "Keep telling yourself that in the morning, Eldan. Perhaps you can make yourself believe it as you lead your soldiers to their deaths."

"How am I to escape this madness, Morlis? How can I save my people?"

"The most obvious choice is to throw yourself on the mercy of Queen Sithian. Perhaps she has more sympathy for the lives of your people than you had for the lives of hers."

"I did not know they were her people! I only knew they broke the laws!"

"The gifts they brought you in her name should have served as announcement enough."

"Where were you when they came to court, Morlis! Why were you not there to council me!"

Morlis sighed: Desperation made Eldan's voice shrill. He almost sounded like the old queen. In her last days, after her mind had started wandering. "I cannot watch over you all the time, Lord Eldan. I have my own affairs to handle."

"You always go on and on about your 'affairs.' Yet I have never seen proof that you go anywhere."

"I do not have to leave the castle to handle my business. I merely need to have solitude."

"I imagine you get that in abundance," Eldan retorted. "You've a full wing of the castle you call your own."

"That I do. As per the agreement I made with you and with every other ruler of this land."

"For all the good that agreement has done me." Eldan swept his hand across the horizon. "Look where my charity has led my kingdom."

"It was not my advice to kill the ambassadors from Tannamoc. Nor was it I who felt the need to have his way with the women they brought with them." He'd heard of the king's twisted pleasures with the women of Tannamoc.

Eldan cast a defiant glare his way. "I was young and foolish."

"You were bored and tired of your wife."

"I loved Moirenna."

"No doubt. What a pity that you found her guilty of witchery a fortnight before the Tannamoc ambassadors came into your lands."

"How is it that you always know what to say in order to make me face my own flaws, Morlis?"

"My sworn duty to you and the other rulers of this land has always been to advise you. How could I accomplish this task if I did not know what secrets lay hidden in your heart?"

"I'm afraid, Morlis."

"Yes. And you have every reason."

"What shall I do, Morlis? How can I hope to make amends?"

"There is only one way. You must forfeit your own life." Morlis watched dispassionately as Eldan's face went white.

"I cannot do that!"

"Perhaps if you hadn't burned the bodies of her ambassadors you could have lived beyond the dawn. But Sithian is not a woman who forgives those who tread upon her people. In that, she is much like you."

"She said to return their bodies." Sudden hope lit the monarch's face. "Do you suppose their ashes would do as well?"

"Did you not scatter their ashes, my Liege?"

"No. I placed the ashes of each into an urn. They are all together in a storage room I had set aside for holding their remains."

"That is not what your own laws dictated, Eldan."

"I'm the king, Morlis. One can bend the laws when one makes them."

Morlis contemplated the ruler of Kastenwar. Still so stupid, arrogant and self-righteous. "Why did you keep the ashes, Eldan?"

He may as well not have spoken. "Well, what do you say? Is there a chance the ashes would be accepted?"

The whelp had kept them because he reveled in having their remains nearby. No doubt he ran his fingers through their ashes to spur his memories of those nights with the women of Tannamoc. "There is no reason why the ashes would not suffice. I don't believe the people of Tannamoc have any taboos against burning the dead."

"Then there is still a hope of saving the kingdom?"

Morlis looked over the edge of the watchtower again. He stared long and hard at the forces gathered below. "There has always been the hope that the kingdom would survive, Eldan. The question now is whether or not you are too late to save yourself."

For the first time since he'd heard of the advancing army, Eldan felt hope. There was a chance that he could still save his people. Perhaps he could even save himself. While he was not a coward, the monarch of Kastenwar preferred the idea of dying an old man to that of being killed in battle.

At the advice of Morlis, Eldan moved swiftly to finish the task he'd decided to take on. Several of his sturdiest soldiers were roused from their sleep or taken from their posts, and used both as guards and mules to gather the large ceramic crocks carrying the remains of Tannamoc's ambassadors. Each of the soldiers was sworn to secrecy and promised great rewards, should the task be accomplished. Failure would mean certain death at the hands of the enemy, which was almost expected anyway.

One look into the darkness beyond the stronghold's walls was enough to remind anyone of that simple fact.

Over one hundred urns waited in the storage room he'd set aside for the burnt remains of the witches he'd had executed. Only twelve carried the remains they actually needed.

Eldan replaced his typical finery with a far more practical leather tunic and breeches; his slippers fell to the side, supplanted by heavy horseman's boots. Instead of a helmet he wore a thick hooded cloak. The ornamental scepter he'd carried for the last five peaceful years was replaced by the trusty weight of his father's sword, a finely crafted weapon he'd hoped never to carry again. Were this to be his last night among the living, he would take as many of his enemies as he could before he fell.

Morlis stood at the gate. "Morlis, there is no need for you to accompany us. You should remain here to protect the castle in my absence."

"Your attempt at chivalry is appreciated, my Lord. However, the keep will hold in my absence. My place is to advise you and to keep you from assuring the destruction of the kingdom."

"I'm capable of negotiating for my life, Morlis."

"You have never dealt with the Fae. I have. What you would deem an insult is to them a compliment. What would seem praise to you is enough to ensure that the ogres feast on your bones. Ogres, by the way, prefer their meat alive and screaming."

Eldan dry-swallowed the massive fist that had crept into his throat, and nodded his thanks to the man. "Let's be off, then. The dawn will come soon enough. We should do our best to meet with Sithian before it is truly too late for this gesture to make a difference."

"You have gathered all of the bodies, King Eldan?" There was an undertone in his advisor's voice that Eldan did not like.

"Of course. I am not fool enough to sacrifice myself for nothing."

"Good."

At Eldan's signal, the doors to the gate were opened and he and his procession of soldiers walked away from the safety of their keep and into the night. Into the darkness, where the Fae waited. With a final weary sigh, Morlis followed.

From afar they had seemed almost human. But even the darkness could not hide the alien nature of the Fae as King Eldan and his entourage moved toward the distant fires where the queen of Tannamoc waited. In a thousand nameless ways they were different from the awkward forms of mere mortals. Though some appeared strong enough to tear a man asunder and wide enough to block the massive gates of the castle, they also moved with a liquid grace that was unsettling. Females moved past with no clothes upon their bodies, and their eyes promised a hundred delights to the man who dared try to catch them. More than once, Eldan was tempted to try.

Whenever the temptation became too much, when he felt certain that he'd flee from the monsters or leap toward one of the women, Morlis was there to prevent his being too foolish. An enormous brute, easily seven feet in height, stood before the entourage and lifted arms as wide as Eldan's chest into the air. It bellowed, a thunderclap of noise, and looked as if it would charge. Then Morlis lifted one hand and made a very small gesture. The creature scurried away as swiftly as a frightened mouse.

"What in the name of all the gods was that!" Eldan's voice cracked as he spoke, but he found he no longer cared. His men murmured among themselves in voices equally fractured.

Morlis replied in a calm voice, "That was an ogre, my Lord. Nothing to be afraid of, really. He was a mere child. Be glad I could scare him away. Had you injured the lad his father would surely have come over."

"His father?"

Morlis pointed to a creature in the distance. Even from where they stood almost a hundred yards away, the beast seemed impossibly tall and wide. The shapes surrounding them in the night made mocking sounds and hissed laughter from all directions as the color drained from Eldan's face. Morlis' face appeared unmoved. The monarch found comfort in the idea that nothing could possibly scare his Advisor.

"You would do well, my Lord, to remember that the Fae are not foes to be taken lightly."

"Rest assured, Morlis."

"And might I recommend you keep the title 'giant-killer' to yourself when the introductions are made?"

Looking to where the first giant crested the horizon, Eldan nodded vigorously and proceeded onward.

Throughout the journey, Morlis answered his questions, giving him a comfort no member of his family had ever provided. Morlis understood him. That was more than even his father could have claimed in life. What started as a nightmare soon blurred into little more than an expedition to see new sights. Morlis made the going easier. Just as he always had.

The travel from then on was uneventful. Whenever another of the monstrosities came too close, Morlis made one of his gestures and sent the creatures scurrying away. Within another hour, they were finally in sight of the bonfire where the queen and her entourage were camped. The area had been a forest the night before and now was a grassy field. There were no mounded piles of uprooted trees, and the fire, while large, was hardly substantial enough to explain the disappearance. But as Eldan was opening his mouth to ask Morlis what could have made the ancient oaks of the area vanish, arrows sailed from every direction, buzzing past Eldan's head and landing in the center of the king's shadow.

"Stay your place or lose your hearts," a deep voice warned from the darkness.

Before Eldan could speak, Morlis' voice rang out in an unknown language. The words were musical and nuanced, enough to make a minstrel wish for an instrument as versatile. Whatever he said, the results were immediate. A dozen or more of Tannamoc's soldiers stepped forth from the shadows and surrounded the entourage.

A hot rage soared through the monarch. "Have you betrayed me, Morlis?" His voice was a hiss. His hand moved toward the hilt of his sword.

"I have killed men and kings alike for comments like that, Eldan. I have simply announced us." The frost in the old man's voice was evident. "Might I suggest you leave your weapon be? They won't take a bared blade as a sign of peaceful intentions."

The deep-voiced figure, now revealed to be a large but apparently mortal man, demanded that they drop their weapons. Much as it pained him,

Eldan did as required. As Morlis had said, there was more at stake than his own life. There was the kingdom to consider.

Within a few minutes of their arrival, the soldiers and Eldan were without weapons. The idea of being at the mercy of someone else was still unfamiliar to the king, and he found very quickly that he did not like it. Years of being in complete control had long since stripped away the fear of others—all save Morlis, at least. Now, for the first time since his ascension to the throne, he was powerless. Beside him, Morlis smiled enigmatically. He relaxed a little. If Morlis could remain calm in their current situation then so could he.

The apparent leader of the soldiers spoke to Morlis in the musical language so unfamiliar to Eldan's ears. The Advisor spoke back, his tones fast and furious, yet oddly as sedate as ever. Eldan would have sacrificed a thousand pieces of gold to understand the words flying between the two like silvered arrows. He listened, but never recognized so much as a single word. After almost five continuous minutes of discussion, the soldier nodded once and walked across the campground to the largest of the tents.

"What did he say, Morlis?"

"He wanted to know why we are here."

A beat of silence. "Well? What did you tell him?"

"I told him the truth. That we are here to barter for your life and for the freedom of your kingdom."

"What did he say to that?"

"He made several comments about the dubious nature of your heritage and then told me he would bring Queen Sithian to speak with you, if she feels so inclined."

"What did he say of my ancestry?" Eldan's voice became a low rumble.

"Nothing that hasn't been said before. Despite an amazing knowledge of the Fair Tongue, he lacks originality in his insults."

"No one speaks of me like that! No one!"

"Incorrect. No one speaks of you like that to your face. Moreover, you should do well to remember that you are powerless here. While I can defend you to a certain extent, I cannot fight an entire army." He looked around. "At least not without the benefit of a few hours to prepare."

"You've had those hours, why did you not use them properly?"

"I did. I convinced you to do your best to avoid a war you would surely lose."

Eldan was preparing a retort when the curtains leading into the main tent opened. For the first time, he saw his enemy.

Sithian, Queen of Tannamoc, had the face of an angel. She was, by far, the most beautiful woman he'd ever seen. He could only imagine what the rest of her looked like, as she was dressed in a full suit of armor, prepared for war. She walked toward him, and Eldan's heart beat savagely. Her full, perfect lips parted slightly as she opened her mouth to speak, and the thought of kissing her nearly drove him to his knees. She moved past him, pausing before Morlis. For the first time in his life, he saw the Advisor to generations of kings avert his eyes. The Queen of Tannamoc smiled and spoke softly in the Fair Tongue. Morlis responded in like, sounding almost vulgar in comparison.

Sithian gestured, and the soldiers around them moved in, taking the heavy loads that the brave souls had carried from the castle. Every man among them looked ready to run or fight or both. They also managed to stare at Sithian with lustful eyes between struggling with their emotions. If he survived this night, Eldan decided, he'd have them flogged on general principle.

After several minutes of listening to the Queen of Tannamoc's voice weave together with that of Morlis in a verbal symphony, Eldan's patience was rewarded. She turned away from the King's Advisor and moved to face Eldan himself. Her striking features did not move into a smile. Instead, her face contorted into a quiet look of consternation. Eldan could have wept. The very idea that he had offended the woman was almost enough to make his knees turn watery all over again.

When she spoke again, he could understand her. "For three years, Eldan of Kastenwar, I tried to retrieve the bodies of my people from you. For two more years, I made threats and demands. Now, as I stand at the gates of your castle, you can finally manage to deliver them. Do you think that is enough?" Her eyes burned into his very soul.

"Milady, as I have already told my Advisor, I was not certain their condition was appropriate for your people. They were tried as witches.

By the law of my land, they were burned at the stake. I did not wish to cause additional offense." Sithian of Tannamoc laughed, a tinkling of crystal bells on a bitter cold day. Something in Eldan's being stirred at that moment. The laughter hurt his pride, and that was one pain he hated to suffer above all else. "I have returned their bodies to you, Sithian. What else do you require before you will be satisfied?"

"Morlis, who serves you for reasons I do not understand, has already agreed to aid me in their resurrection."

Eldan forced himself to look away from the beauty before him and stared into the eyes of the Advisor to the Throne. "You can do this, Morlis?" A chill ran through him as he looked upon the man.

Morlis stared back, his face as set as a mask carved of stone. "It is within my power, my Liege."

"Yet you never let me know of this?" Eldan felt his anger begin to blossom.

"I am your Advisor, Eldan. I am not your court magician. What I can and cannot do is entirely my own affair."

"You could have brought Moirenna back from the dead. You could have revived both my father and my brother."

"Witchery is against the laws of your land, Eldan. I would have brought none of them back to life in any case."

"Why then? Did they not treat you well?"

"You father was a wise man. He would not have wanted to serve the land in a second life. Your brother was an arrogant fool. He did not deserve the gift of life a second time. And Moirenna…. Moirenna deserved better than she received at your hands. I would gladly have given her life again, despite the cost to me, if only her husband had truly cared for her."

"I did care!"

"You had her killed. It was only later you decided that you wanted her at your side."

"Lies!" The rage moving through Eldan was as irrational as it was monumental. The thought that Morlis could have spared him so much grief, so much anguish, and decided not to was almost more than he could stomach. "She toyed with forbidden powers. How could I be a ruler to my people if I did not enforce my own laws?"

"Enough of your anger, Eldan. I grow tired of this charade. You would see me punished for your own shortcomings. I will not tolerate any reprimand you cast my way. I am here to save the kingdom from your folly. Perhaps Sithian will be gracious enough to let the people of Kastenwar alone if I do this thing. Perhaps not. Either way, I am forced to use magics I would rather avoid. Either way, this incident is a result of your arrogance." The calm face of Morlis broke, and his features were made ugly by the rage that boiled just beneath the surface. "I will not tolerate insolence from you, Eldan. I will do this task and then you will forget you ever saw the deed accomplished. Or I will most surely destroy you, body and soul alike."

Eldan went cold remembering suddenly how his brother had pushed the old man too far and died a day later. Far too young and strong a man to die from heart-failure. "I—I am sorry, Morlis. I overstep my bounds."

Morlis simply stared, and the cold that had breached Eldan's soul grew. "Morlis?" But still he said nothing, and Eldan finally understood: Morlis felt only contempt for him. He had always felt contempt. Eldan was alone in the camp of the fae with no one to call friend. His eyes began to sting. He blinked rapidly. He turned away, feeling alone and small, and found himself looking straight into the face of Sithian. His enemy, and the source of all his grief. But he said nothing. Could say nothing.

Morlis walked past him, shoulders set and eyes only for the Queen of Tannamoc. "Come, Queen Sithian. Let this task be done."

"My gratitude, Morlis." She spoke to the wizard, but her eyes still looked at Eldan. For the second time that night, he found he could not hold the gaze of another.

The urns bearing the remains of Sithian's people were taken into the massive, gilded tent where the queen resided, and Morlis was escorted inside. Eldan and his soldiers were not permitted to join them. To the East, the first hints of dawn were beginning to light the sky a rich crimson. A storm was coming. No matter how powerful the tempest might be, it could not compare to the chaos in his heart.

Sithian stared at Morlis for several moments after they had entered the tent. He loathed the inquisitive expression on her face. Almost as much as he hated what he was about to do for her. Surely she knew what the cost to him would be, and yet she asked this of him just the same.

He would not look at her. He turned away without a single word, save a command to one of the guards to bring him the material ingredients he needed to cast his magics. He pried the lid from the first of the urns, running his fingers through the greasy ashes.

"Will you bring them all back to life?" Her voice sent shivers through him, made him remember vows made and broken.

His tones, when he spoke, were tired and bitter. "Is that what you wish, Queen Sithian?"

Silence reigned for a moment before she answered. "If you can, Morlis. I know the pain this causes you, and I am grateful."

The laughter that spilled past his lips was dark with the promise of violence. He broke the seal of another cask, holding a handful of ashes up for her to see. "Doubtless, you will want Ellonwie back first." He spilled the ashes across a marble table large enough to hold the body of even an ogre. Sithian nodded, he could see her pulse slamming into the curves of her delicate throat. "Very well, Queen Sithian. You shall have your people back. All of them. Even your precious consort."

"You have my gratitude, Morlis."

"Your gratitude is not enough, Queen Sithian. I expect you to keep your part of our bargain. Kastenwar is to be left in peace."

"And what of Eldan, the 'Giant-slayer?' Do you care what happens to him?"

Morlis poured the rest of the ashes from the urn, careful to avoid spilling even a single grain of the fine powder. "I do not care. Whatever you decide is what will happen. You are the one he slighted."

"I thank you again, Morlis."

He grunted as he reached for the herbs that a fearful guard placed on a smaller table beside him. "You should leave this area. You are distracting me, and I do not wish to make an error with this particular magic." Morlis looked away from the powdered remains of Ellonwie, forcing himself to look at the Queen of Tannamoc. "The results would not be pleasant."

Sithian nodded again, bowed, and was gone from his presence. He

180

took a deep breath and prepared to work his magics. Within minutes, the screaming began.

Not long after the sun began its plunge toward the ground, Morlis left the tent behind, drawn and bitter. "Did all go well, Morlis?"

"I am beyond weary, my Liege. The blood in my veins is cold with the touch of death. They are alive again. They will speak with Sithian of what befell them, and then she will decide the fate of Kastenwar." The old man sat slowly, coming to rest in the dirt, not far from where Eldan lay. Eldan tried to study the features of his Advisor, but was thwarted when the man turned to face another direction.

"Do you think she will spare the kingdom, Morlis?"

"I do not know. I believe her people will decide for her." The men were silent for a time. Then Morlis spoke again. "I should pray that the people of Tannamoc are more forgiving than you, Eldan. Or all is lost."

The silence stretched out for a very long time. Eldan wanted to speak, to ask forgiveness of the man who had raised him well. Raised him better than he'd allowed himself to become. In the end he held his tongue. Morlis looked exhausted. More importantly, he feared the man might turn away from him again, and that was more than the King of Kastenwar could bear. Before long, Morlis' breathing grew steady and soft. He knew the man was asleep. The shadows grew longer, and the air lost much of its heat as the hours passed and still the king did not sleep. Eldan sat by the fire, wishing he could go back into his own past and figure out exactly when his world began to fall apart. At some point, sheer exhaustion sent him tumbling into a dreamless slumber.

Eldan awoke to the smell of roasting meat. The night had returned while he rested. His stomach roared indignantly at the scent of food, and his traitorous mouth salivated like that of a dog. Beside him, Morlis was just standing, dusting himself and gazing toward the opening of the tent. As Eldan rose, the Queen of Tannamoc left her tent, followed by people he had not seen alive in half a decade.

"Eldan of Kastenwar, your kingdom is spared." Eldan breathed a massive sigh, and opened his mouth to offer his thanks. He was stopped by her continued speech. "Your life, however, is forfeit. By your hand my love died, and so I shall have revenge."

"I killed no one!" he protested. "All died by the fire after their trials."

"Do not degrade yourself by lying to me, King of Kastenwar. Ellonwie died at your hand after you forced yourself upon her. I shall not allow that violation to go unpunished." With a gesture, two of Sithian's people stepped forward. They were both women, and Eldan recognized them well enough. He had found pleasure in them both before sending them to burn with their associates. But one of them had attempted to fight back on the third day and he'd been forced to defend himself. Well he remembered carrying her lifeless body to the courtyard where the stakes had waited. Well he remembered tying her lifeless form to the third stake. She too burned that day, but when she burned she did not scream. The dead do not make protests. "You had your way with my woman, Eldan of Kastenwar. I will have my revenge or I shall see your kingdom in ruins. The choice is yours."

Within an hour the stake was placed in the ground and stacked high with seasoned wood. Eldan was offered a last meal but refused. Morlis did not speak with him, save to say that his son would be a wise ruler and well protected. Unlike Ellonwie, King Eldan the Second of Kastenwar screamed when he burned. He screamed for a very long time.

As the night drew to a close, and the morning began to move across the land again, Morlis prepared to leave the Queen of Tannamoc and her people. Before he could go, Sithian demanded a moment of his time in private. With no one else around them, her regal features softened at last and she spoke her mind. "Morlis, I cannot hope to repay you for what you have done this day."

Morlis looked at the face of his wife and sighed. "A kiss then, for what we once had?"

Sithian nodded and moved into his arms. After a time she pulled away from his strong embrace, and kissed him gently. "You are a special man, Morlis, to forgive me when I have hurt you so."

"No, Sithian, I am merely a man who would rather see you happy than make you endure what you cannot stand."

"I do love you, Morlis. I have never lied to you about that."

"I know. But the love you feel is not the love of man and wife. It is the love of friendship. They are as different from each other as summer from winter."

"I love Ellonwie as a friend as well."

"Aye. And as a mate."

"Will you come back to us, Morlis? Back to the Land of the Moon?"

"Someday, perhaps. But not now. A thousand years has not taken away the sting of seeing you with another." He turned away, hoping to hold the sorrow he felt inside. With every sight of her, his heart broke anew. "Be well, my love. I shall be here should you need me." He hated the coarse sound of his voice, the betrayal of his normally stoic exterior.

"Morlis, did I do the right thing?"

"By killing Eldan? Yes. He was a fool, and would have brought this land to ruin. His son, I think, will do a far better job of ruling the land."

"Did you know that he had kept the bodies?"

"I suspected as much. I did not know for certain until last night."

"Why did you never look for them?"

"Because I am still a man, Sithian. For all that I love you, I still resented that you chose Ellonwie over me."

"Will you be well, Morlis?"

"No, my wife, I will not. I will sit here in this vulgar land and I will wait for the day when you have need of me. And while I wait, I will ponder upon all that I have lost and stew in my own sour thoughts."

"I wish it could be different, Morlis. I truly do."

"I know. That is why I allow myself to be a fool for you, Sithian. That is why I brought your one true love back from the dead. I would rather you be happy."

"I would wish the same for you."

"You must live with your decisions, Sithian, and I with mine. I will be at your command should you call." With that, the King of Tannamoc and the ruler of the Fae left the side of his wife and moved back toward the castle he called home. Throughout the journey, the soldiers heard him say the same words a thousand times. "Damn me for a fool," he'd whisper. And as he said these words, the Sidhe army waiting before the gates of Kastenwar parted to let him pass.

BESIDE THE WELL

BY

LESLIE WHAT

o matter how bad life gets, there is always a choice—even if the choice is whether or not to fight for survival. Those who live at different times in different parts of the world may not have the same choices we have today; or if so, they may perceive them differently. Their decisions might not be our decisions. There are many different paths to empowerment.

—N.G.

Lo Yi could barely walk through the rooms of her house without finding at least one small tribute left out for First Wife. Her mother-in-law, Kim Hyung-pun, constantly hid things like jeweled brooches and perfumed oils, carefully arranged in Lo Yi's sewing basket, or in her empty rice bowl, or even sometimes tucked away in the toes of her shoes. Places Lo Yi would be sure to notice. There was no attempt at keeping the task of appeasing First Wife a secret. The whole arrangement was driving Lo Yi mad.

That afternoon she had found a saved lock of First Wife's black hair in the muslin bag where the apples ripened. It made her sick to her stomach, seeing the dead woman's hair mixed in with the food as if it meant nothing. It was obvious Kim Hyung-pun had placed the lock there to remind Lo Yi that First Wife still lived with them, at least in spirit. As if Lo Yi needed any more reminders that she—a girl so stubborn and distrustful of men she had remained unmarried until turning fifteen—did not truly belong in that house with Kim Hyung-pun and her beloved only son.

Lo Yi despised them both. Kim Hyung-pun was an ugly old woman, nearly twice Lo Yi's age. She had lost her husband back when the Japanese swept through Korea on their way to Manchuria, and had turned bitter as old almonds. And Husband…. Husband was little more than a hairless fat pig masquerading as a man.

When Husband came in from the fields at dusk he called for Lo Yi to assist in bathing him. He did not use her name—he simply clapped his hands, and she hurried to help him, as she had been taught she must do to avoid a beating. She kept her eyes averted, and tried not to flinch as his rough hands, still filthy from harvesting potatoes, caught on the silk of her sleeve.

Later that night, when Lo Yi spilled a drop of soup as she served their dinner, Kim Hyung-pun said, "Girl!" fairly spitting out the word. She refused to say Lo Yi's name, refused to call her "Second Wife."

Kim Hyung-pun pointed to Lo Yi's waist and shook her head in warning. "There is something very wrong that this *girl* does not yet carry my son's child," she said. "Perhaps it is her clumsiness that has angered First Wife. Perhaps First Wife's spirit has come back to punish us and deny us an heir."

From the way Husband frowned Lo Yi knew that he would again try to prove himself a man with her that night. Lying beneath him was something she could barely stomach. Maybe it would be different if she were in love, but Lo Yi imagined that love was rather like fog, something she could barely see, and only vaguely feel. Something that hid in the safety of the horizon. The melancholy feeling that had started only a few weeks before got the better of her, and she said without thinking, "Perhaps First Wife died on purpose. Perhaps it was her only way to leave this house."

186

Kim Hyung-pun let out a strangled cry. She pushed away her food and stood, then limped away like a wounded old dog. Husband ran after his mother and begged her to return to dinner. When she did not answer he rushed back to Lo Yi and slapped her face, hard. "You must never to speak to us of First Wife in this disrespectful manner," he said. Lo Yi bowed her head, praying that the Buddha might spare her pain just this one night. She had the feeling that what Husband really meant to tell her was that she should never speak at all, about anything, or in any manner. She nodded and thankfully he let her be.

※

"You have made First Wife feel unloved since you came to this house," said Kim Hyung-pun, who was always the first to arise. "Only evil can come of it." With her face puckered up the skin looked like wrinkled silk. While Husband nodded solemnly, Kim Hyung-pun asked her, more like *bade* her to take rose petals out to the well and assuage First Wife's spirit.

Lo Yi agreed at once, always anxious for the chance to walk outside into the courtyard. The day was warm, with so much moisture in the air that she sensed it might soon rain. How she loved the rain in summer. Steam would rise from the sun-hot stones and make them look like a pathway to the world of spirits.

Lo Yi cranked up the wooden bucket and fished out a few black beetles from the water. She set the bucket at the bricks on the edge of the well, and tossed the beetles into the flower garden, where those who still lived could scurry away, and those who had succumbed could return to the earth. Next, she picked from its bush a rose so red and dark its color was almost black, then crushed its petals in her hand. She smelled their sweet fragrance. It was wonderful the way roses kept their essence, even long after the flowers had died. Maybe spirits did the same thing. Maybe part of her would stay behind on this earth when finally she died.

She sprinkled the petals over the water and lowered the pail until she could no longer see any part of it except the rim. But as she stared she saw something else, something that looked like a face seen through glass, only pale and beautiful as the moon. "Thank you, most kind and lovely one," said a voice and Lo Yi knew at once this was the spirit of First Wife, whose voice rushed out to cover Lo Yi's face in a cool breeze.

She had not heard such kind words in the six months she had lived in this house. The kindness warmed her heart so, that soon she found herself standing there like a fool, crying, more like sobbing, more like blubbering, more like raining a lifetime of salty tears that spilled like soup into the water.

A cool mist sprayed her face and made her tears disappear within it. She felt herself leave the earth and begin to float cloudlike in First Wife's strong embrace. First Wife smoothed her hair with a most patient touch. And then as quickly as it had begun it ended, and Lo Yi stood alone in the courtyard.

She tried to walk into the house unnoticed, but Kim Hyung-pun waited for her behind the door. She grabbed Lo Yi's arm and shook it roughly. "Have you done as you were told?" she asked.

"Yes," Lo Yi said.

"And what happened?"

Her cheeks warmed and despite herself, she smiled. "I saw First Wife's true spirit," she said.

When her mother-in-law squeezed Lo Yi's arm the thick nails dug into her skin and drew blood. Lo Yi cried out, but Kim Hyung-pun only tightened her grip. She screamed for her son, who interrupted his labors on the chamber pot to join them. "The girl has seen her!" she said. "First Wife, who has now become emboldened enough she dares to flaunt herself to the one who has replaced her!"

"No!" Lo Yi protested. "That is not how it is at all. First Wife is lovely and very gracious. She showed herself to thank me for my kindness at bringing her a remembrance."

Kim Hyung-pun grimaced. "I will call for the *mudang* at once. Perhaps in my innocence I was wrong to let this problem linger for so long. Perhaps the reason First Wife keeps this girl from having a child is because she harbors hatred toward me."

Lo Yi kept herself from smiling, though she felt secretly pleased to be ignored for once, while First Wife took the brunt of Kim Hyung-pun's scorn.

"What will the mudang do?" she asked.

Husband waved his hand to shush her, but Kim Hyung-pun paused as if considering whether to answer. "She is the shaman," she said. "She will perform the *kut*, a ceremony to drive First Wife from the well and out of our lives. I see now, that we can never live happily in this house until First Wife has been banished."

Husband snorted and turned to leave. Lo Yi backed away to let him pass, gloating at the trouble she had caused. All these months she had believed Kim Hyung-pun had praised and honored First Wife out of respect. Instead, it was nothing less than fear that had determined the old woman's actions.

"We must prepare," said Kim Hyung-pun. "I will market and bargain with the mudang. Husband will invite our friends in the village to be our honored guests. The girl," she said pointing to Lo Yi, "will clean the house to prepare it for our company."

Lo Yi excused herself to attend to her chores. When she'd finished sweeping the floor she allowed herself a short bath. She listened to the melody of the water as she poured it from her pitcher into the bucket. As she plunged her hands into the water and washed her face, Lo Yi remembered First Wife's gentle voice. A shudder passed through her. If the mudang managed to send away First Wife, Lo Yi vowed to follow her. If First Wife left, Lo Yi would find a way to leave this house.

That night, while Kim Hyung-pun slept, Lo Yi crept from the house and into the courtyard. She placed her hands on the rim of the well and felt the coolness of the sweating bricks. "First Wife," she called. "I have brought you no present but myself and my love. I hope that is enough to please you."

The scent of rose petals and warm bricks after a rain rose from the water. Then before she knew it, First Wife stood beside the well, reaching to her with delicate pale arms. Lo Yi felt First Wife's hands caressing her and bathing her face in cool water. First Wife's lips, soft as rose petals, pressed against Lo's cheek. Lo Yi turned her face to kiss First Wife on those soft lips. She lingered there, and as she tasted the velvety sweetness of First Wife's tongue, Lo Yi knew that for the first time ever she understood about love and why a woman might require it. First Wife tasted both salty and sweet, like bean cake. Lo Yi stroked First Wife's back. Her skin was smooth and fluid as water. "Kim Hyung-pun has called for the mudang," Lo Yi said. "She hopes to send you away."

"The shaman can come but she will not drive away my spirit," said First Wife. Her laughter gurgled like a stream. "My mother-in-law has tried that once before—when she learned about what I was, and then after, when I had killed myself."

"After…you…killed yourself?" said Lo Yi.

"Only the spirits of the damned choose to stay where they are not wanted," said First Wife, and she laughed bitterly.

Though she knew that to be true, Lo Yi said, "But *I* want you to stay."

First Wife sighed. "Perhaps things may yet change for the better."

✳

At dawn Kim Hyung-pun woke Lo Yi to tell her she must prepare the courtyard and bring out barrel tables and sitting mats for their honored guests. Lo Yi turned to look at Husband, his fat face red with sleep. He looked like an ugly baby, one so vile only a mother could feel love for him.

"It is time!" said Kim Hyung-pun, pulling off her blanket.

Reluctantly, Lo Yi stood and watched Kim Hyung-pun replace the covers on the still-sleeping Husband. She dressed and set to work. There was a chill in the morning air that made her long for hot tea, but she knew better than to ask Kim Hyung-pun for nourishment until completing her chores. She weeded the garden and swept dust from the bricks. She dragged the sisal mats into the courtyard and unrolled them in a U-shaped configuration around the edges of the courtyard.

At last the tables were set out and covered in white lace. Kim Hyung-pun covered it with dishes filled with fruits, glazed rice cakes, rice, kimch'i, and pickled ginger meats. "Make sure you do not eat," she said, "until the honored guests have had their fill. Now go and change."

190

Kim Hyung-pun had already set out a royal blue hanbok for her to wear, with matching flat silk shoes. The clothing was beautiful, but impractical. The heavy fabric clung to her moist skin and weighed her down. She hoped she would not stain it with her sweat.

In a while the guests started to arrive and Kim Hyung-pun showed them to their places in the courtyard. The air was filled with laughter and talk. The mudang made her entrance, dressed in a flowing white gown with full sleeves and a matching square hat. Over the gown she had tied a red silk apron and a wide belt that anchored a long embroidered scarf that wound around her neck and reached all the way to her hem. She carried a large tied sack, which she set on the ground. When she removed her shoes there was silence.

Kim Hyung-pun brought out two knife blades from the sack and set them on the ground, sharp side up, so that their tips met at an angle like a steeply pitched roof. She brought the mudang a drum and stick, bowing in supplication until the mudang took the instrument and nodded for Kim Hyung-pun to back away. The mudang banged her drum and started to sing in a loud warble. She rolled up her eyes, leaving only the whites to stare out at her audience. She walked a circle around the knives and then lifted one foot, followed by another until she was perched on top of them. She stood, the whole of her body supported by the sharp edge of the knives, but did not draw one drop of blood. She banged her drum and cried out in some foreign tongue. She shrieked and laughed and butterflies flew from her sleeves.

The old ladies oohed and ahhed and the men laughed after, when the mudang bowed and crossed through the courtyard to the barrels, where she sliced through a melon to display the sharpness of her knives. She left the knives in place. Kim Hyung-pun looked around until she spotted Lo Yi. She pointed to the melon, then clapped her hands. Lo Yi hurried over to take her place cutting up the fruit for their guests.

The mudang danced and sang and called for everyone to get up and join her. Someone grabbed Lo Yi and spun her around until she felt dizzy. Next, Kim Hyung-pun brought out a long knotted piece of cloth. The mudang explained that the cloth symbolized emotional wounds suffered by First Wife while alive. She sang and in a trancelike state, untied the knots. "Your suffering shall now be untied," she said.

Her hanbok trapped the heat like a windowless room. Perhaps because she had not yet eaten, Lo Yi felt somewhat faint. She saw herself slump to the ground while at the same time, another part of herself turned to mist and evaporated from the ground.

First Wife was waiting for her beside the well. She floated across the courtyard to slide her arms around Lo Yi and draw her close. "I fear you are with child," said First Wife, stroking Lo Yi's belly.

Lo Yi groaned. "Why must you fear this?" she asked. "Husband says it is my purpose."

"I fear it only because you shall bear a girl child, and she has no chance but to inherit all that is yours."

"No," said Lo Yi, horrified. "No." She felt herself becoming smaller than a drop of water and as that drop splashed to the ground she awoke to see Kim Hyung-pun glowering above her.

"Lazy girl!" said Kim Hyung-pun with a kick to Lo Yi's flank. "Get up!"

Lo Yi turned her head to the side and heaved the juices in her stomach.

"You shame me before all my honored guests!" said Kim Hyung-pun. "Get up!"

Lo Yi rose up onto her elbows. She eyed the tables set with delicacies, but she did not long for the meats or fruits or sticky cakes. She looked determinedly at Kim Hyung-pun. The old woman could not stop her if she acted quickly.

Like a cresting wave she rose and became stronger and felt her way back to the barrel and the mudang's sharpened knife. She felt a sharp pain as she plunged the silver into her belly up to the hilt, but that might have been a cramp from her happiness, for surely she laughed to hear the astonished screams of Kim Hyung-pun, Husband, and all the honored guests.

✳

On nights when there is no moon Lo Yi and First Wife scream with pleasure, knowing how their passion haunts Husband and Kim Hyung-pun. Their love has grown so strong no mudang lives who is powerful enough to drive them apart.

On those black nights, Husband berates his mother and orders her to hold blankets against the door in a vain attempt at keeping out the noise. Kim Hyung-pun forces herself to remain awake throughout the night. She begs the Buddha to forgive the many mistakes she has made over her short life. Perhaps she was a little harsh, she thinks, in her treatment of the girls. But even so, she doubts she is deserving of the life they have left her with.

Kim Hyung-pun listens to the ruckus in the courtyard and forces herself to close out their joy. She feels the same dull anger she has always felt—but never dared direct—toward the room where her lazy son sleeps. She will not admit to herself that she is jealous of the spirits. Jealous that they have found a way out of this life, and selfishly left her alone to care for their Husband.

THE HOME TOWN BOY

BY

B. J. THROWER

*H*aving graduated college with a dual major, sociology and social work, I was really interested in "The Home Town Boy." What is it like to be called back to your home town—after running away when it would not accept your being gay—because it suddenly needs you? Do you really want to save it? Sociologist Dr. Bob Murdoch must face these questions and more when he returns to Baker, OK to find out that the townspeople are beginning to—change.

— S. P.

Standing in the doorway of Freda's Diner, Dr. Bob Murdoch had to admit he was spooked. Every booth inside was crammed with overlapping bodies. Six chairs were pulled up to tables meant for four. People stood sandwiched between the speckled cherry-red and white stools at the long mahogany counter. They sat in nooks and crannies, the heartiest or unluckiest on the floor gorging themselves, bent eagerly over plates in their laps or balanced precariously on the mounds of their knees.

Bob had an unwelcome glimpse of the top of an elderly lady's support hose—which were barely managing the task of suppressing her purpled network of varicose veins as she took her repast on the dusty floorboards. Clumps of cream gravy and bits of biscuit were welded to her chin like wads of bubble gum. Neatness was not a prerequisite for dining at Freda's. Bob got a distinctly queer feeling in the pit of his stomach—since these people were under the impression they were becoming immortal, and all.

Outside, the orderly line stretched from the glass door of the maroon brick diner along the dawn-warmed sidewalk of Madison Street, the main thoroughfare of downtown Baker, Oklahoma. The people angled north toward the intersection at Okmulgee Avenue where they curved around the block, disappearing from view. To the west, the courthouse square with its symmetrical rows of familiar shops was deserted.

Sheriff Jeffry Drummond, a lumberjack of a man, said in Bob's ear, "Crazy. The place is weird. It's the Restaurant of No Return. Ya'll come to Baker, ya'll'll live forever. 'Cept it's not a damn bit funny."

Bob recalled the sheriff's frantic phone call of last night: *Help me, Bobby! My town's changing, and I don't know why*— Baker was both men's home town, but while Bob had found greener pastures as a sociology professor at the University of Tulsa, Drummond had stayed put.

Bob agreed. "Right. It's crazy and weird, but fascinating, too. What does the fire marshal say about this many people in a business establishment of this size?"

Drummond snorted. "Fire marshal's in here chowing down. He recommended a special dispensation for Freda's, unanimously approved by the city council. Hell, the owner of Freda's, Alfie Leaps-the-Brook— you remember him—well, he's got Alzheimer's. The place was sagging at the seams until the past week. I figured the county health department would close it down, but now the kitchen's immaculate, the diner's run strictly by county health codes. It's a legal operation, unfortunately."

Bob asked, "What about unlawful assembly?"

"Are you kidding, this ain't a demonstration. Should I haul her off to jail?" The sheriff nodded toward the elderly lady wearing support hose. "Besides, I'm not sure what they'd do if I shut it down. It just seems hopeless, as if nobody's gonna stop this…miracle-in-the-making. God curse all fools!"

There was minimal conversation, but lots of pronounced chomping, chewing, swallowing and slurping. Four harried teenaged waitresses squeezed through the mass of humanity, tip pockets bulging. *Jing-ching*; melody of the cash register. A young deputy posted by the door—the only crowd control Drummond thought necessary—dutifully moved them in and out like a wrangler with a strange herd of cattle. The rich odors were redolent of scratch cooking and summer sweat, and an underlying hint of livestock manure.

Drummond was glum. "I guess I still have the authority to commandeer stools at the counter. Follow me."

The sheriff used his considerable hips and elbows to scrunch between the back-to-back chairs and tables. Bob almost collided with a waitress carrying a tray of clean silverware over her head, and another tray of condiments at shoulder level. He ducked, but she was already gone, more adept at negotiating the surreal and crooked paths inside Freda's. When he reached the counter, Drummond offered him a stool.

He sagged on it gratefully, abruptly seized by swarming vertigo. He shut his eyes, gasping for air and feeling disoriented, convinced he was about to faint.

"Don't wimp out on me, Murdoch."

Bob's face gushed oily sweat. He tore open the knot in his tie, grinned weakly at Drummond. "Hot! Air conditioning's inadequate. Funny, I'm not normally claustrophobic."

But he knew it was much more than that. *Strange to be in Baker in broad daylight*, he thought. Because of his home town reputation, it was Bob's habit to *sneak* into Baker at night to have holiday dinners with Aunt Bess, his only living relative. She'd taken him in when he was fourteen, after his parents were killed in a car wreck. Bess was witty, but bound to home by an agoraphobic umbilical cord Bob never could quite fathom.

"And? What's your professional opinion of the people in here?" demanded the sheriff.

"Well, they appear to be a group crowd, which is caused by a shared emotion. It will probably be a social phenomenon of short-term duration.

They haven't evolved into an integrated, organized group, this isn't some type of social revolution or mob mentality. It's not anarchy."

"It isn't?" Drummond sounded skeptical.

"No...Jeffry, people develop mutual expectations for each other's behavior, which over time crystallize into customs and traditions collectively called the culture of our society.

"There are rewards for conformity to the expectations of others in society, such as respect and material benefits. And then there are punishments for failure to conform, from deprivation of human warmth to formal imprisonment.

"Sure, they've been reforming these crowds at Freda's for, what, six days? But then they go about the daily routine, work, shopping, constructive activities, right?"

"Until the next meal."

"They're not blowing their brains out with the handy deer rifle, or setting fire to the neighbor's house."

"So?"

"So, what isn't applicable here is Durkein's Concept of Anomie: social and personal disorganization in accord with the common values—as values are perceived in Baker, anyway...Miss, may I have a glass of water?"

Drummond cursed softly. "Dammit, I'm warning you, Murdoch, don't eat or drink in this place!"

Bob paused, then shrugged unhappily. "It's only tap water."

"Shit. There's Jack Merrill, that fat-ass banker from Concord. The gospel's spreading, the miracle talk. It's not only the folks in Baker who believe now."

"A mass delusion?" Bob said, parched and mystified.

"Or a helluva advertising gimmick." The sheriff cocked back the brim of his pale green, Dudley Doright hat, tiredly shaking his head. "A reporter from the *Oklahoma Eagle* called. The press is coming, Murdoch. What'm I gonna do?"

"These people are waiting in line to eat breakfast. I doubt that makes for much of a news story. Anyway, maybe they're just hungry." Although he didn't believe that himself, not anymore.

Drummond grasped Bob's elbow. "That's a lame-brain thing to say!"

Bob yanked his arm free, the ancient dislike for Drummond swelling in his chest. Even now he could vividly picture Jeffry Drummond's big werewolf fists plunging at him, punching on the last syllable for emphasis, "Sis-sy! Sis-sy!"

Drummond added, "I have a bad problem here."

"And you were so desperate you called me." Bob glared at his childhood nemesis, suddenly awash in a flood of pathetic anger.

"What do you want to hear, Bob? That I'm sor-ry I used to kick your ass when we were kids? Sure, okay, I'm sorry."

"Very sincere, Sheriff. That wipes the slate clean."

"Hell, what did you expect? Your type isn't popular in this town."

Bob laughed bitterly. "Oh, yes. In Baker you can be a good ol' boy wife-beater, a drunk, a God-forbid Catholic, even an Indian—just barely—before you can be, to quote my mother, 'an effeminate child.' I hate this lousy town, and I hate you, for that matter." He fumbled for his keys, executing an about-face on the stool toward his Lexus, parked in Drummond's own slot at the sheriff's invitation. Why kid himself, he'd never been happy here. "I don't know what I thought I'd find, but I don't give a damn, Jeffry. This was obviously a mistake."

"Wait. Please—come on, Bob, listen, I didn't mean that.... You are interested in what's happening, aren't you?" He looked sad, afraid, weak. A curiously rewarding role reversal, because Bob was certain that's exactly how he'd always appeared to Drummond.

Bob paused. "Yes. I am."

"Then stick around, will ya? For Christ's sake, none of this makes sense. When Freda died a year ago, the diner died. Until now."

"Freda..." Bob whispered.

✖

In the cluttered alley the ten-year-old boy climbed two concrete steps and rapped hesitantly on a wooden screen door, the rear entrance of the only cafe in Baker. He thrust his hands moodily in the pockets of his red-checked jacket, wishing he'd chosen a warmer shirt than the short-sleeved cotton madras. He scuffed his brown penny loafers, loathing the white crew socks his mother forced him to wear, waiting with a lost expression for Freda Leaps-the-Brook.

She did not disappoint him. With a lovely smile she opened the squeaking door wide. Freda had an exotic Kiowa face, but he liked her eyes best, which were sparkling, slate-gray. He would have been shocked to learn that she was forty, since from his perspective, forty was pretty ancient.

"Hullo, Bobby Murdoch," she said, beaming at him with undisguised friendship. "You want some cookies?"

"Yes, ma'am."

Her slender copper-colored finger stroked his cheek with a gentle yet electric touch. Bobby was sporting a vicious black eye—because he was different. With sympathy, Freda asked, "Jeff Drummond again?" He nodded, miserable, but proud he wasn't weeping for once. "Your Pa oughta teach you to fight."

"Pa don't fight much, I guess." His dad was a wraith of a man who barely knew Bobby was alive. This harsh reality had only recently occurred to Bobby, and he felt awfully guilty about it, because of course, it must be his fault.

Freda said cheerfully, "I'm mighty grateful to you."

Bobby was amazed. "Me?"

"You didn't forget me. Somebody real mean started a rumor I bake my cookies with rat poison."

"Oh, I never believed that, not for a second!"

" 'Course you didn't, it's a damn lie. Lots of bigots in this town, including Alfie." Her husband was a known child hater, particularly of white children who weren't paying customers like Bobby. "I won't make excuses for him, though—"

An irascible man's voice came from inside. "Back in a jiffy, Bobby."

He stood there, listening to the idle clink of china, the pumping spray of hot water. To be polite he never showed up for free cookies on Saturdays unless it was between the breakfast crowd and the lunch rush, though "rush" was an overstatement. Business at Freda's Diner in later 1962 was steady, but never brisk.

She came back and thrust three large, chocolate chip cookies wrapped in wax paper at him, a hurried variation of routine that hurt him until she glanced furtively over her shoulder. "Alfie's here, I can't invite you in the kitchen this time."

"Oh." Bobby thought it was strange she married a guy like Alfie, because she liked kids.

She yawned. "Come to the county fairgrounds tonight."

"You mean, f-for the powwow?"

"Sure. You can be my special guest. Don't cost nuthin'."

"I...okay!"

Bob felt his own rather nondescript face cracking with a goofy smile. Remembering Freda always made him emotional. If she hadn't been here— He stopped smiling when he saw the sheriff's bleak expression.

"Bobby, Leslie threw me out."

Bob was secretly amused by the news. Leslie Drummond was a former high school homecoming queen, who had been especially cruel to Bob in that homecoming-queen way.

"It's because she eats at Freda's," Drummond said. "She claims she can't live with me anymore, unless I become immortal with her and the kids. Does that qualify as a violation of personal social disorganization, Mister Hotshot P-H-D?"

It was bewildering. "Actually, it would."

Bob had left primarily because this small society wouldn't change for him. But that was life; there were no guarantees of happiness or acceptance. Yet he understood that what was taking place here was unnatural, inexplicable, but apparently spreading to nearby communities.

From an ethical standpoint, it's already too big for me to handle alone, he tried to tell himself. Instead, he told Drummond, "All right, I'll stay for awhile."

The sheriff exhaled explosively. "Thanks." He stared at Bob. "What was the name of that sci-fi book you dragged around? About the guy from Mars?"

Wary of ridicule, Bob said, "*Stranger in a Strange Land?*"

"Yeah. Well, that's me. I've been so scared I've been buying out the deli at Price Mart. I feel like I don't dare set foot in Freda's unless I'm bloated with food. What if it's some weird kind of poison, but not like that stupid rumor about poison in Freda's cookies? What if it's real this time?"

"Well, I doubt that—"

"Here's your water, sugar." A waitress, thumping a glass down in front of Bob as she rushed by behind the counter.

He hesitated, then gulped half the glassful. As he drank, he noted they ran the gamut, from suits and ties, to dusters and coveralls. Business people, grammies, farmers, whites and Indians and a few blacks, average Americans in this neck of the woods, from every socioeconomic background. *No discrimination in this li'l ol' line based on age, race, creed, sex or religion!* he thought.

A specific stimulus was definitely present—and the food at Freda's had always been good—but irresistible to this degree? Maybe, if served with an extra helping of eternal life, the whipped cream equivalent of no-more-worries, no-more-woes.

"Bob Murdoch, you handsome devil!" From the head of the line in the door, a flabby white arm waved at him. Wanda Dallas, an old friend of Aunt Bess'. Wanda Dallas, who despised him, who usually wouldn't condescend to speak to him. He waved back, stunned and uncomfortable. He wasn't certain he was even welcome here, yet it was sort of nifty to come back and find himself suddenly transformed into a "handsome devil." But didn't Wanda remember how much she hated him…?

On a hunch he called, "What's on the menu today, Wanda?"

She said dreamily, "Why, I'm sure I don't know. Doesn't matter what you eat at Freda's, long as you eat enough of it."

The four donuts Jeffry force-fed Bob in the sheriff's office rushed a film of sugary acid up his throat into his mouth.

The young deputy escorted Wanda inside, and slipped through the crowd toward them. "Howdy there, Dr. Murdoch."

"Hi, yourself. How did you know my name?" Did Bob's personal reputation filter into the next generation too?

"Oh, heck, I guess just about everyone in Baker knows who you are. You're the home town boy who made good, sir."

"Ah," Bob said, awkward from the compliment, absurdly pleased too. Disconcerting to discover how much he'd actually yearned to be accepted in Baker, never facing it until now because his memories were so painful.

"I'm Lonny MacIntosh," the youngster said, sticking his hand out while Drummond glared at him.

"Do you eat in Freda's, Deputy?" Bob asked, shaking with him.

MacIntosh patted his stomach. "Ho, I'm stuffed to the gills on the Sheriff's donuts." He lowered his voice. "It's a job requirement these days." A titter passed down the counter like a friendly breeze. Whatever the implications of the situation were, Baker had accepted them wholeheartedly. Baker had never accepted *anything* offbeat before, not in Bob's dismal experience.

"No one's relieved you!" Drummond barked. Lonny swiftly reassumed his post.

A bell tinkled merrily. *Jing-ching!* The cash register. Bob mopped his damp face with a handkerchief, and froze: "Dollar fifty-five," the cashier said in a monotone. Alfie Leaps-the-Brook, Alzheimer's Victim. *Jing-ching.* Except there wasn't anyone paying a bill. It was just Alfie with emaciated silver braids, perched on a stool pressing function keys, watching the cash drawer pop out and remembering to shove it back in. A roll of receipt tape looped across Alfie's bony knees to the floor, where it was callously trampled by the hungry horde. On to the next imaginary sale, speaking to nobody: "Dollar fifty-five."

Bob said, "Shouldn't Alfie be in a nursing home? Why isn't he in a nurs—?"

A sincerely cheery voice interrupted, "What can I get for you?" Startled, Bob swiveled on his seat. Yet another waitress had materialized from behind the tubs of orange soda and pink lemonade. She smiled, fussing with a napkin dispenser.

"Er, nothing." He was suddenly and deeply frightened by the idea of eating here, like Drummond.

"Holy crow, if you ain't gonna eat you oughta make room for those who will," the waitress complained with a telling glance at Drummond, who ignored her. She was heavyset, neither young nor old. "Business is boomin', case you hadn't noticed."

"I—noticed," Bob said. Gripping the edge of the counter for support, he asked, "What *are* you serving?"

"Eternal life! Oh, we knew it was a big decision, but most of us decided to accept the offer. I mean, it's better than friggin' dyin', ain't it?"

Fear ran up his spine like cold wire. He squinted at the waitress' blouse, where SUZY was stitched in pink thread script. "Suzy, I may be dense, but how are you serving immortality?"

"We gotta great cook!" Suzy said with genuine enthusiasm. "But you eat every meal here for seven days straight if it's to work proper, that's the cook's rule...I mean, I guess it's Cook's idea. Don't actually recall now."

"What is this, Jeff, a con game? Have you met the cook?"

"No!" Drummond said hoarsely. "I've been back to the kitchen fifty times, but I only find pots simmering and grills frying, like someone just stepped out."

Two heaped plates rattled into the serving window between the kitchen and counter area with a customer's order of buckwheat pancakes. Suzy shuffled away to fetch them, calling, "Anything you like, we'll cook it. You see, it's on the house. Us girls'll accept tips and there's a donation jar for Alfie's medical expenses, but that's fair, ain't it?"

"Dollar fifty-five," said Alfie.

Bob jumped off the stool and charged the swinging kitchen doors, determined to introduce himself to the chef responsible for this macabre, insane feast. He banged into a modern kitchen gleaming from antiseptic, so clean it was almost holy.

A lean, lithe, dark-haired woman who reminded Bob so strongly of Freda he assumed she was a relative, stood before the red-hot double grills....

The boy Bobby tramped through the chill evening air inside the rickety board fence at the fairgrounds, toward flickering campfires encircled by gyrating ghost-people. The yipping human voices might be mistaken for coyotes from a distance. Trying to be inconspicuous, he inched closer to the biggest fire. Freda hip-hopped gracefully in a ring of costumed dancers to the steady beat of the buckskin ceremonial drums.

She was dressed in full, splendid tribal regalia; her soft white leather dress with fringe slapping at her golden shins, a colorful handmade blanket draped around her shoulders, beaded moccasins, a streak of red paint drawn precisely in a line down the part of her hair, and two bouncing braids decorated with her prized eagle feathers.

Bobby was suddenly afraid, because she seemed to be a stranger to him, as alien as an Amazon from Venus. Until she winked at him with one smoke-gray eye as she danced by...

The woman flipped fatty strips of bacon with her bare fingers. Grease sizzled like a rush of warm rainfall on dry leaves.

He cried, "Doesn't that hurt?"

She looked at him. Freda Leaps-the-Brook, and she hadn't aged a day! No, that wasn't quite right, there were wrinkles at the corners of her piercing, cloud-gray eyes. The calm tolerance on her wonderful face was just the same as it had been when Bob was a boy. She seemed incredibly shrunken, until he realized that he was six feet tall now and not seeing her as a child...

"You've grown up, Bobby." Had she read his mind? "Figured you would, though you had a tough time of it. Bess is mighty proud of you. We're deliverin' her meals, on account of she's so shy." She smiled at him with perfect teeth, hand magically working the bacon.

"You're dead," he said flatly. "I sent flowers to your funeral. You can't be here."

"Can't I? But I'm doin' a bit more cookin' for my beloved home town. Alfie, he's kind of a jerk, but he needs the money. Besides, good food cures the aches and pains and worse of this bitter world, I always say. An apple a day...you know."

He was nonplused. "Don't you realize that the people you're feeding believe they're becoming immortal?" *And why shouldn't they?* Baker had buried this woman a year ago, and she had risen from the grave to feed them—for free.

"Well, bein' immortal *is* packin' them in. Weren't my idea, though. I just showed up to cook and someone got too excited."

He whispered, "Why are you cooking here, Freda?"

She shrugged. "Why not?" He felt hypnotized by her fingers moving beneath coughing exhaust fans which sucked up the burning smoke.

"Stop!" *The kitchen was dreadfully empty.* The alley door opened. "No, that can't be it, Freda, *wait!*"

Bob lunged after her but tripped on a mop handle, overcompensated and crashed sideways into a tower of cardboard boxes. As he fell he heard the door sighing shut and the outside screen slapping backward.

He struggled among the boxes, one of which was dumping about five hundred paper napkins in his lap. He fought the boxes and himself, trapped in a dreamlike, rubber room suspension of time...He'd gotten to his feet and now he burst out the door, plummeting down the steps because he'd actually forgotten them. He stumbled into brilliant summer sunshine, the air so heavy with humidity it seemed to drip. Then Freda Leaps-the-Brook plucked napkins from his waistband with cool, *dead* hands. Bob screamed shrilly.

Now she was younger than he'd ever seen her when she was alive, wearing her white buckskin dress, eyes solemn, her beads so bright he ached. She said gently, "You're a sweet boy, Bobby Murdoch." She hugged him, and unable to resist he hugged her too. Fierce light reflecting off silver garbage cans assaulted his retinas. Half-blinded, he reeled in the dead woman's arms, staggering against her solid body.

He kissed her, thinking stupidly, *I can't be doing this because I'm gay, it's the reason why I left Baker, fled from Baker, I failed to conform to the rules of this society, but there aren't any rules now and I'm kissing a lovely dead woman!* Pressing his lips deep in the texture of her thick raven hair, he confessed, "I've loved you all my life."

"I know it." She moved strong square hands up from his waist to his shoulder blades. "Just hold me, Bobby, it's all right. You can hold me." He did, as closely as he dared, as if he thought he could squeeze the love he craved from her.

Pulling him over to sit on the steps, she kissed his cheek. "I need your help, Bobby. I don't have much time left."

He gasped. "You're not leaving! You can't." He folded her in his arms. "Tell me the truth. Why are you here, Freda?"

"To finish what I started—bring a gift of light to Baker."

"This one-horse town doesn't deserve a gift from you."

"Who needs it more? Ahh, you're thinkin' Alfie don't deserve no favors, neither. But Alfie grew up here, just like you did. You been lucky, you threw off the yoke of this place, you made something of your life. Alfie would've been a fine person except for what Baker did to him. Why do you think your Aunt Bess spends her whole life hidin' in her house? Because there's a poison in Baker, Bobby, but it weren't in my cookies like they claimed. It's in the dark heart of this town.

"When I was alive there was always someone to say, 'Who do that Indian woman think she is, givin' our kids cookies, acting like we need her charity?' Whenever I tried to change people, *lighten* them, it didn't work. But it's workin' now, they have to pay attention. I'm changin' that darkness, the old poison of hate while I can. You've already felt somethin', haven't you, Bobby?"

He thought of Wanda Dallas and Lonny MacIntosh, and nodded.

"Would you like to help me in the kitchen, Bobby? Would you like to feed the people who done you wrong?"

He grinned. "Me? I burn water, Freda."

"You won't in my kitchen. Your cookin' will be a marvelous thing."

"Okay...sure, why not?"

Wind chimes. It was her, laughing with joy. "No reason."

They linked arms and climbed the steps. When she passed through the doors her buckskin dress dimmed. She became the older woman Bob had seen earlier, dressed in jeans, a T-shirt, hightops, a linen apron.

She gave him his own apron. "Time's a wastin'."

Smiling like an escapee from a lunatic asylum, Bob tied the apron strings. He had never been so happy in his life as he was at this crowning, lunatic moment.

※

The storm arrived at the presunset hour on Sunday, battering Madison Street with a wall cloud of salmon-colored lightning and an alarming deluge of hail the size of golf balls. After the hail, rain fell from the low, sullen sky in straight hard sheets of water. Thankfully, it lasted no more than five minutes. But as the electricity faltered within the diner, Freda Leaps-the-Brook dissolved.

✳

Bob trailed the subdued crowd outdoors. Stepping on the rain-freshened sidewalk, he realized he hadn't left the diner since yesterday morning when he'd talked with her in the alley. Oh, the delicious meals he'd eaten, especially the Salisbury steak smothered in mouth-watering brown gravy, swimming in tomato bits, carrot curls and onions! Freda prepared it for him while he labored over the steaming stoves, his catharsis, his own act of love.

People around him were moaning or quietly sobbing with disappointment and grief, clutching each other in a physical need for moral support. There seemed to be no traffic, as if automobiles didn't exist. Bob roamed to the middle of Madison, contemplating the melting hailstones surrounding his shoes.

"So, it's over." Drummond, sounding relieved and miserable. "Nobody's going to live forever." He looked perplexed. "Was it real? Was she real?"

Bob kicked some hailstones. "The storm was real, these are here. Yes, Freda was real, too."

"I feel like an idiot now, that I finally ate in there."

"You were supposed to eat, supposed to relish the miracle of Freda being back and remember the way she lived, the example she set—change the way you think, the bad old Baker way. You were too much of a horse's ass to realize it, Jeffry."

"Meaning I'm not a horse's ass now, because I did?" Drummond's earnest attitude pleased Bob tremendously.

"Something like that."

"How long can it last? People are people."

Bob smiled. "Yes, people are people, and what's a town but the people in it? I think it will last. These folks will be proud of the change in Baker. They'll grow accustomed to the idea: Baker, The Friendliest Town In Oklahoma. The Chamber of Commerce can order signs and install them on the city limits, heck, all over town. You can live up to the ideal on signs like that because it's a better way to live."

"Jeffry?" Leslie Drummond, with two tired teenaged children.

Drummond smiled at his family. Distracted, he thrust out a beefy hand. "Thank you for coming, er—"

Bob shook with him. "You're welcome, Sheriff." He watched the man go to his wife, who embraced him. When Leslie looked up and waved to him like a dear old friend, Bob lifted his hand in greeting as if it were the most natural thing in the world.

Alfie emerged from Freda's. He and Lonny MacIntosh clutched pickled egg jars full of cash. Lonny grinned. "I'm taking him back to the nursing home. So long, Dr. Murdoch."

Alfie stared with an innocent gaze. "So long, so long."

"Take care, boys." Bob noticed the power was still out in the diner, realized it was permanent. But it was okay. Freda's Diner should be closed now, in honor of the incredible week the cook had returned to start a new beginning for the town she'd loved, the town incapable of loving her until now.

Deciding to leave his Lexus parked downtown, Bob strolled north in the wet street, through the intersection, toward the hill by Washington Park. He felt the urge to take a long walk this evening, and it would be quite a nice hike to Bess' house.

The sun broke through the bluish remnant storm clouds above the western horizon, shining in a spectacular display of slanted, rainbow-colored beams. In the park, birds began to warble and sing; their final song before the velvet night cradled them in their nests.

He noticed he was still wearing the apron Freda had given him. It had cranberry and gravy stains splashed on it.

I'll wash it, he thought, but I'll keep it—to remember.

A small, delicate, white-haired woman appeared at the crest of the hill, walking briskly. She was calling to him, "Bobby! Bobby!" He smiled, because it was Bess, come out of her house, at last.

Moving swiftly uphill toward her, Bob Murdoch reflected that for the first time in his life, it was good to be home.

EXPRESSION OF DESIRE

BY

DOMINICK CANCILLA

epending on when and where one is brought up, some things are more shameful than others. The world may change, but often our interior landscape does not keep up.

Dominick Cancilla introduces us to Kisa, who lives in a closet within a closet. To herself at least it seems that Kisa can acknowledge one part of who she is—she knows what she needs, she acts to get it—but that other part makes her too uncomfortable to ever admit its existence.

—N.G.

It had been seven months since Kisa last fed, and her every waking moment was a morass of pain and need. Only the knowledge that satisfaction was finally within reach kept her from being completely overwhelmed.

Once Caroline arrived, it would be at most a matter of hours before Kisa could sate whatever demon it was that kept life in her limbs and fire behind her eyes. After two weeks of work, the painting for which Caroline was being paid to pose was almost done, and with that completed, Kisa would have no more need of her model.

211

Seven o'clock, seven ten—the minutes seemed to lengthen as they approached the hour. Even when Kisa had been among the mortal she'd been unable to handle the mixed emotions of anticipation. Six hundred years had done nothing to teach her patience; she paced the wooden floor of her windowless loft with heavy, rhythmic steps.

Often, Kisa avoided boredom and nervousness by exercising her arcane powers—shifting through forms, watching objects burn in her invulnerable hand, spreading herself across the floor as a mist. But as Kisa's hunger progressed, her powers waned. She had not the strength to alter her body, and escaping injury now brought pain. There was nothing but the mundane reality of existence to distract her.

Twenty minutes before the hour, Kisa did what little she had to do to prepare her work. The easel stood in the northwestern corner of what she thought of as her studio—bordered on one side by the back of a long couch and on the other by the line where wooden flooring became the tile of a little-used kitchen. The cloth covering easel and canvas was stiff with spattered paint. It crackled when she pulled it free and folded it onto its resting place on the floor.

The easel faced away from the door; Caroline would not be able to see it when she came in. Surprise deepened emotions, so Kisa never let her subjects see a painting until it was finished. Joy over the work they inspired sweetened the blood, and blunted the sting of death. The intermingling of creation, christening, feeding, and death brought Kisa rapture beyond anything she had found in mortal life. Her tongue tingled, and her feed teeth slid a little lower in their sockets.

Trying to focus herself on the present, Kisa took in her work. It was beautiful, graceful, full of all the things that Kisa most craved in her second life. The painful process of creation was almost over; she would treasure it like a child when it was finished. And it never would have lived had it not been for Caroline.

Across the room, the grandfather clock, standing in an eccentric six-sided cabinet, struck the hour. The sound of its chimes was mixed with the heavy rumble of the building's old freight elevator climbing toward Kisa's floor.

Kisa sighed at her foolishness; Caroline was arriving and in her agitated state she had forgotten to mix her colors. Not that there were many to mix with the painting so close to completion.

Kisa crossed the room to the front door; she opened it just as Caroline was raising her fist to knock.

Caroline laughed and smiled. "You got me again."

"It's easy when you're so prompt." Had she said that the last time? She couldn't remember.

Kisa closed and locked the door as Caroline took off her overcoat and tossed it on the couch. "You don't have to rush," Kisa said, knowing that Caroline expected her to be impatient. "I've still got to mix my paints."

"That's fine," said Caroline, kicking off her shoes and unbuttoning her blouse. "It'll give me a minute to stretch out."

The artist within Kisa couldn't help but watch Caroline undress. The woman was a perfect model—wonderfully proportioned, smooth skinned, patient, pleasant.

There were dozens of tubes of paint in the box next to the easel, and Kisa's practiced hands selected those few she would need. Four colors to mix Caroline's tan skin, two for her long, gold hair, one for her sky-blue eyes.

Once her clothes were all neatly folded on the couch, Caroline circled into the studio and climbed lithely onto the large, carpet-covered block that served as her pedestal. She stretched and twisted the tension from her muscles in preparation for long periods of immobility. Kisa watched and blended colors. She had mixed them so often in thought and deed that they quickly matched their model.

"I'm ready for you." Kisa took one of the brushes from the rack at her side.

Caroline turned onto her left side facing Kisa and rested on her elbow. Her left hand lay on the carpeting palm up, and after spreading her hair across her shoulders and breasts, the right hand took its place draped across her slightly curved stomach. Her face assumed the look of wonder and joy that Kisa had spent so long coaxing from her on the first day.

Comparing canvas to model, Kisa could see almost no difference.

Caroline was a consummate professional, not needing the constant prodding and coaching that some of Kisa's past models had required. It pained Kisa that she would not be able to paint Caroline from life a second time.

With small, delicate strokes, she transferred paint from palette to canvas. Hers was a painfully slow and exacting method, learned from a woman in

Paris so long ago that Kisa could no longer remember the year, but the results were the stuff of dreams and Kisa had nothing but time.

Once she was well into the rhythm of her work, Kisa could feel the ache of her hunger becoming sublimated by her love of creation. In her state, she could live for years without sustenance if need be, but if she were forced to abandon her art, the pain of frustration would quickly become more unbearable than that of starvation.

"I won't be able to come tomorrow," Caroline said, the soft sound of her voice blending with the smooth motion of Kisa's hand, causing no disruption.

Kisa didn't mind her model speaking—at least not this one. "That's fine. I should be finished in an hour or so in any case."

"Really!" Caroline's excitement pulled her from position for a moment and drew a stern, correcting glance from Kisa.

"Just bear with me and I'll let you see it before you leave." She did her best to hide her own excitement, lest it interfere with her work. "Tell me, why wouldn't you have been able to sit tomorrow?"

"Oh, just a date. Nothing important but, you know."

"Of course." Kisa's brush wandered, dragging a trail of flesh from Caroline's lip to her eye like a scar. She scolded herself for letting impatience get to her. A few more mistakes like that and the painting would require another night's work.

"Do you think you could use me again?" Caroline asked.

"I would like to." Kisa tried to sound noncommittal, but was so absorbed in repairing the damage that her voice came out cold.

"It's just, you pay better than the agency. And you don't hassle me." They were silent for a moment. "Sometimes guys will call for a model but that's not what they really want. You know. They figure that if a woman will pose nude—"

"I understand," Kisa interrupted. "We'll see."

A few touches to the eyes and Caroline's face was finished. Kisa's exacting eye searched it for flaw and found none—perfection. All that was left were a few spots on the girl's torso where the veil effect of hair across breasts was not quite perfect. But such delicate work took a great deal of time.

"If we do work again, do you think we could start our sessions a little earlier?" Caroline asked.

"Why would you want to do that?"

"It's not that I mind the late hours." She paused as if looking for the correct turn of phrase. "It's just this neighborhood. This building. They kind of get to me at night, you know?"

Kisa nodded but said nothing. With hands more steady than those of any creature with a pulse, she painstakingly formed each hair of her subject's only raiment.

"Even if we just started a few hours earlier, that would be good. It's just—"

"I don't think so," Kisa snapped, and then felt embarrassed. Her concentration was broken. She sighed. "Why don't you take ten."

She rinsed her brushes and remixed the color of Caroline's hair, not because she needed to but to get back into the rhythm of her work.

There was no way to tell Caroline that she could not work before sundown, and no way to express her dislike for being reminded of that fact. Hiding from the light, not being able to join others for meals, her extreme discomfort around those things considered sacred—they emphasized Kisa's separation from the rest of society. And the fact that she was no longer a part of humanity only made the truth that much more bitter.

There was a certain irony in her feelings, Kisa realized; in a way it had been her inability to fit in with others that brought her immortality in the first place.

Over the centuries, Kisa had forgotten enough for scores of lifetimes, but painful memories clung like burrs. One of the worst was the horrified looks from her parents when at sixteen she had refused to go through with the marriage they'd arranged with the butcher's son. Their pleading fell on uncaring ears; their worry about embarrassment, public humiliation meant nothing. Kisa had entertained thoughts of breaking from the restraints that life in an isolated village placed on her. She fantasized about escaping inland over the hills, perhaps joining with others like herself to rewrite the rules of society. They had been the dreams of an idealistic fool.

On the night before Kisa was to go before the count's envoy and have her fate decided, the stillness of her family's cottage was disturbed by a shadow-clad figure whose shape and soft voice tempted her in a way that no husband ever could. When she was offered power and eternal life at the cost of her soul, she paid the price and reveled in the experience.

Her innocence and spark of mortal life were wrenched away with one deliciously horrible penetrating kiss. For a moment her moans were blended with a scream, and through it all her family slept undisturbed.

The transformation was swift and complete. Even with the wounds in her throat still moist, she felt doubt and paralysis where her confidence and sense of self had been. Unrestrained, her many hungers increased a thousandfold to fill the hollow left by her soul.

With the power to change lives finally within her grasp, Kisa no longer had the urge to do so. Instead, she left bloodstained sheets to say her goodbyes and set off to search the world for some way to regain the inner being that she had once treasured. It took her twenty years to discover that only in art might she find some glimmer of her lost self.

Behind the easel, Kisa was a god. Her thoughts, her unfulfilled desires, became real in two dimensions. Study and endless nights of practice brought her skill to fruition, and experimentation defined her range.

Still lives, abstracts, pastorals—Kisa tried her hand at them all. In time, she settled upon portraits, using her subjects to reflect upon the mortal woman dead within her; innocence, life, frustration, and need frozen in time and preserved forever.

Caught up in her thoughts, Kisa had taken longer fiddling with her materials than she'd meant to. Caroline was sitting in silence on the edge of her platform, probably still too upset by being snapped at to say the first word.

"I'm ready," said Kisa. Caroline returned to her pose.

Thinking about her progress had relaxed Kisa a great deal. Color flowed easily from her brush.

"I'm sorry I lost my temper," Kisa said.

"That's all right. It's an artist thing, right?"

Kisa smiled at that. "I suppose so." She chose another brush and squeezed a little green onto her pallet. Kisa set to work on the background, but let Caroline stay in pose as her motivation.

"You are really quite inspiring," said Kisa.

"Thanks. That's nice of you to say." The same self-comfort which allowed Caroline to pose unabashedly in the nude protected her from being embarrassed by Kisa's remark.

"This is turning out quite well. I think you've earned yourself a bonus."

"Thanks!" Caroline didn't move a muscle but her pleasure was obvious. "I could use it."

"I understand how it is to be on your own."

"Oh, sure. I've got friends and stuff, but, you know."

"I do." Through Kisa's brush a blade of grass reached up to caress Caroline's thigh.

Soon, Kisa was painting on automatic, doing nothing more than retouching areas which were already in a state of perfection. The painting was finished.

She stepped back to take it in in its entirety with Caroline in the background. It was a masterpiece, if she did say so herself.

"It's finished," she said, putting her pallet and brushes aside.

Caroline hopped up from the pedestal. "Great! Can I see it?" She was moving around the easel even before she had an answer.

The gentle sway of Caroline's hips, the curve of her bare neck reminded Kisa of the hungry ache within her. In moments, she would finally be sated. But first, there were artistic matters to take care of.

Kisa stopped Caroline with a raised hand. "Just a moment. Before you look, you have to promise me something."

"Sure."

"You have to close your eyes and not look until I tell you to. Then, you have to say exactly what comes into your mind."

Obviously pleased by the game, Caroline closed her eyes. "Okay."

Kisa took her model by the hand and led her to a spot in front of the canvas. There she turned the girl with gentle pressure on her shoulders. They had never been this close before, and Kisa found Caroline's smooth skin pleasant to the touch, the smell of her hair fresh and clean. Her temptation to run her fingertips down the woman's spine to the dimples which sat on her hips was strong but she resisted; at the moment, only vicarious pleasure through Caroline's reaction to the painting mattered.

For what would have been a dozen heartbeats, Kisa stood behind Caroline, drinking in the sensation of her presence. Kisa's body ached with emptiness and she could almost feel the soft flesh giving way beneath her lips, the warm juices flowing against her tongue. Such a shame for one so beautiful to have to die, but Kisa's hunger was strong within her.

It seemed a cruel trick to use Caroline so thoroughly—first by living through her emotions, then by draining her flesh—when she had been so cooperative. With that in mind, Kisa made a decision. The painting was perfection, and if Caroline had the vision to see that, then she would live. Otherwise, she would die in Kisa's embrace, staring into that which she had inspired.

"Can I look?" Caroline asked, a little confused by the long delay.

"Certainly," Kisa said.

Caroline opened her eyes; Kisa waited for the response.

Kisa tried to imagine the thoughts going through Caroline's mind. At first, she would be surprised to see what appeared to be a landscape as opposed to a more traditional portrait. Then she would be taken in by the beauty of it all, the gentle low hills, the soft grass, the wide river leading to a lake in the distance. Perhaps she would notice the hint of a dark wood across the river, and then her eyes would be drawn to the reclining figure at the edge of the water. Caroline herself, beautiful, perfectly reproduced, lying on the grass with a peach in her hand.

"I'm so small," Caroline said. "That took you two weeks?"

Kisa was surprised by the tone of Caroline's response and frustrated that what she needed was not being given her. "You're everywhere in the painting, Caroline, not just in the single figure."

"What do you mean?" Caroline sounded dubious.

"Look at the sunlight, the way it plays on the water and brightens the land. Look at the sky, how blue it is, how the trees seem to be reaching for it. In the distance, on the edge of the lake, is a small cottage, a place of security and comfort. And all of it is centered around you." She made no mention of the gaunt figure barely visible within the shadows of the woods, staring across the river at the reclining nude with an expression of desire.

"Oh," said Caroline, and nothing more.

Frustrated like a starving man faced with an apple encased in glass, Kisa grabbed the girl's arm and spun her around. "What is the matter with you?" she asked, as Caroline, thrown off balance by Kisa's unrestrained use of force, fell against her.

Their gazes locked, one surprised and shocked, the other manic with need.

Glaring down into Caroline's wide, moist eyes, something in the back of Kisa's mind clicked. The energies of her undead body surged within her, calling forth what power they could. In her half-starved state, Kisa could ill afford to expend the effort of invoking the supernatural, but her hunger, her desire demanded it.

Kisa's eyes irised wide and their colors began to swirl. Caroline was taken in immediately, and the cry which was forming on her lips became a soft outbreath which stirred Kisa's hair.

"It's wonderful," whispered Kisa, staring down at Caroline. "Tell me you love it."

"I…I love it," Caroline stuttered. "It's wonderful. So beautiful. A work of art."

The words had the form if not the feel of sincerity, and in her mind Kisa gave them the meaning she needed them to have. They would be enough, for now.

When the moment was gone, Kisa let go of Caroline's arm and stepped back, breaking the link between them. "I suppose you had better be going," she said, motioning Caroline toward her folded clothes. "I'll mail you that bonus I talked about."

Caroline seemed to be waking from a daydream. "Oh, yes," she said. When she turned, the painting caught her eye. "It's beautiful. Wonderful."

"Yes," was all Kisa could think to say.

※

When Caroline was gone, Kisa went through the motions of cleaning up her work area. The painting pained her now, just as she knew it would. Contentment was always fleeting.

She penned a quick letter to the newspaper, asking them to reinstate her "Model wanted" ad. Perhaps the next one would prove to be more satisfying.

In a day or two, when the paint was dry and she had tired of the sight of her work, Kisa would seal the canvas in paper and take it to the loft next to hers. There it would find a place among the other paintings, some on canvas, some on wood, some on paper or tile. Soon it would be nothing more than one picture of the unreachable among more than ten thousand.

THERE ARE THINGS WHICH ARE HIDDEN FROM THE EYES OF THE EVERYDAY

BY

SIMON SHEPPARD

*S*imon Sheppard *writes about sex: as transgression, as performance, as a means to transformation. We are always searching for something: the meaning of life, why peace eludes us, where did that damn sock go? Most of us are so caught up with the taboos of sex that we never think of it as a tool in that search. Thank goodness for writers like Simon who are not afraid and offer us a chance to look at ourselves in a new mirror.*

— S. P.

�֎

Please, take your time. Finish your mint tea. Perhaps you'd like another of these baklava? No? Well then, I'll have the last of them. I'm afraid I can't resist temptation.

My friend, there's a story I'd like to tell you. A story that may shed some light on what we've been discussing tonight. Perhaps it will help you deal with your...desires.

Long ago, when the Great War ended, a man found himself in Gibraltar, aimless and alone. (He'd lost whatever small family he'd had, whatever small faith had remained.) It was then that he first heard rumors of the

Magicians of Fez. A stranger in a café, a man he'd met on a train, a friend of a wartime acquaintance, each had mentioned a secret circle of miracle workers whose identities were unknown to any but one another. In clandestine workshops—some versions of the tale had them located under the winding streets of the city—they pursued investigations into the fabric of the universe.

Depending on who was telling the story, the Magicians of Fez were said to have power to transmute base metals into gold, or to read the thoughts of another, or to reshape matter in such a way that it was possible to walk through solid walls. Where they gathered, it was said, the night sky burned with the light of the sun. Some even whispered that these sorcerers had gained power over the very workings of life and death.

An elderly man he'd met in Tangiers had pulled out a yellowed newspaper clipping and, claiming to translate from the Arabic, recounted the story of one Mohammed al-Nasser, a dyer of leather who had fallen to his death from a rooftop in Fez, but who, through the intercession of an unnamed passer-by, had subsequently risen from the dusty street and walked off with no more than a scratch.

So, though not without mishap and misadventure, he made his way to the Imperial City of Fez in search of this underground cabal. It was not that rationality had failed him. He fully suspected that his myth-mongering would prove futile. But, rootless as he was, he knew that even the wildest of fancies might distract him from bleak memories of combat and loss. As is often the case with those who think they have given up all hope, he set himself on a quest which would have been meaningless if hope were truly gone.

He began to make inquiries wherever he went, follow every lead, no matter how unpromising. Always, he would soon enough come to a blank wall. Like the endless horizon, the spectre of the brotherhood fled before him. The shoemaker knew nothing, but told him to ask the school teacher; the school teacher knew the name of a certain brassworker who'd know the truth of the matter; the brassworker, when found, professed ignorance but recommended making inquiries of the shoemaker.

However, it did not take him long to understand that, as a white man, an attractive young man with money, he might find all sorts of things in

THERE ARE THINGS WHICH ARE HIDDEN FROM THE EYES OF THE EVERYDAY

Fez, even if the Magicians eluded him. One afternoon (he'd only been in town a few days), a teenaged boy guiding him through the sun-washed souk pulled him into a blind alleyway and pressed his young body up against him. Though his only previous experience of sex had been with his late wife, with half-a-dozen loose women during the War, and with a miscellany of neighbor-children long, long ago, he felt an undeniable, unsettling attraction to this brown young man.

Part of him was quite naturally appalled, but the boy's dark-eyed glance seemed to conquer his will. And the guide's hand quickly found stiffening evidence of his response. He leaned against a whitewashed wall, eyes closed, allowing his fly to be unbuttoned, feeling not danger, but a strange kind of safety as his hardness was exposed. The feeling of the young man's mouth on him was a delicious shock. His wife had never done this. One of the whores had, but her mouth was nowhere near as expert as this brown boy's.

He opened his eyes, looked down, watched his spit-slick, veiny cock being licked, swallowed down again and again by this ragged young stranger. As the guide took him all the way down his wet, warm throat, he closed his eyes and with a sharp cry shot deep into the boy. He leaned against the rough wall for a moment, eyes still closed, dreading the inevitable haggling over the dirhams that would be demanded in payment for this pleasure. But when he opened his eyes, the boy had silently vanished.

Whatever guilt he came to feel after that was overwhelmed by a greed, a longing to find the boy and once again thrust himself down the beautiful young man's warm throat. In the mornings, wakened by the muezzin's cry, he would dress, gulp down a glass of syrupy mint tea, and go off to wander the streets of the city. He told himself he was on the trail of the secret magical brotherhood, but he knew he was always keeping watch for the boy with the beautiful face.

Evenings often found him in a dimly lit café where Berber men would pass around smoldering pipes of sweet-smelling kif. One such evening, he was invited to a table where three elderly men sat, sipping lemonade from greasy, chipped glasses. The oldest of the three stared at him with his one good eye and told him the following story:

SIMON SHEPPARD

In the name of the Prophet, this story is true (he began) for I have indeed been its witness. Once, not so very long ago, there were born twin boys. Abdallah was the eldest by just minutes, but he and Yakub grew up in very different ways. They both became sorcerers, but while Abdallah worked his magic for the forces of light, Yakub followed the left-hand path. While Abdallah became part of the holy fraternity of magicians, Yakub worked his dark magic in solitude. As the years passed, they became strangers one to another.

Then one day, Yakub appeared at the threshold of his brother's house. On the very brink of collapse, he barely managed to tell Abdallah what had befallen him. He had, in the course of his workings, conjured up an evil djinn which had turned on him, attacking the very roots of his soul. "And now I am truly damned": with those words he fell down dead.

Leaving his twin brother where he lay in the dusty street, Abdallah rushed inside and returned with a scrap of parchment on which he had inscribed Yakub's name and a magical incantation. He placed the incantation between his brother's lips. His brother stirred, his eyelids fluttered. Abdallah drove a brand-new nail into the ground where his near-lifeless twin brother lay. This nail, you see, would nail down the djinn and keep him from repossessing Yakub's body and soul.

Abdallah bent over Yakub's prostrate form and kissed him on the lips. The parchment lay between the two brothers' mouths. As Yakub returned fully to life, Abdallah grasped the parchment spell between his own teeth and withdrew it from Yakub's lips.

With amazement, Yakub returned from the land beyond death. But he did not shower his brother with gratitude. Rather, he asked, then begged, then demanded of his brother the parchment that contained the wondrous spell holding power over Death itself.

At this, Abdallah held the parchment out before him and a dove swooped down and plucked it from his hand. Yakub became enraged. "How dare you so dispose of that which your own brother has asked of you?" And with threat and imprecation, he demanded that Abdallah call the dove back to him.

"Oh my brother," said Abdallah, "you still do not understand. The wondrous power you seek is truly all around you." He pointed toward the sky. And in the bright blue expanse there flew not one dove but dozens, then hundreds, then thousands, until the sun itself was hidden from view. "But, since you insist," Abdallah continued, "I shall do as you ask." And he held out his arm. From the airborne thousands, a single dove swooped down and perched on his hand. It held the parchment in its beak. Abdallah took the parchment and held it toward his brother.

"Here is what you seek," said Abdallah. Yakub lunged and grabbed the parchment from his brother. It was blank.

The one-eyed man, having completed the tale, chuckled softly and sipped his lemonade. Despite repeated questions, he refused to say any more about the remarkable story he'd told. Eventually though, as the kif pipe made its rounds and the night grew deeper, the three elderly men consulted among themselves and then proffered an invitation. They would like to take him to a special sort of place, one they felt he might enjoy.

Following the three strangers through the twisting alleyways of the souk, he had to fight back waves of fear and suspicion, for it seemed they were passing the same corners, the same painted doorways, time after time. Would he be robbed and left for dead? Or were his suspicions the clouded workings of an intoxicated mind? Furtively, he slipped his wallet from the pocket of his trousers and hid it inside the waistband of his underclothes.

Just when his suspicions had reached fever pitch, his guides turned a corner and brought him to an unremarkable blue-painted door.

"Is this," he asked aloud, "where I can find the Magicians of Fez?"

He was told: "You'll have to decide that for yourself."

In response to an elaborate coded knock, the door swung open and they stepped inside. It was quite apparently a male brothel. A single leather hassock, decorated in gold, stood against a tiled wall of the dimly lit room. A middle-aged man, eyes ringed in kohl, hair tinted with henna, entered through the archway carrying a brass tray holding a hookah and glasses of mint tea. The man served the visitors, clapped his hands, and was gone.

He took a sip of the sweet, hot tea. He felt not at all at ease. From the adjoining room, another hand-clap, then another, then a rhythmic beat. Two young men, naked and lean, came through the archway and started to dance. Slowly at first, then picking up speed, they whirled before him to the hypnotic beat. They came so close to him he could smell their bodies. He wanted to reach out to them. He wanted to get up and run away, forget about the Magicians of Fez, go back to the place that he once had called home. He wanted to find peace.

The clapping ceased. The young men stood still, very close to him, so close he could see the sheen of sweat on their dark pubic hair. He looked to either side; the three old men were gone. He was all alone in a tiled room in a far-off land, alone with two beautiful, naked men.

One of the dancers reached out and stroked his face. He tensed. The boy leaned over and gently kissed his tight-shut lips. The naked men were both upon him then, unbuttoning his clothes, stroking his chest, rubbing up against his stiffening crotch. He realized with a shock that his wallet, precariously hidden in his underclothes, had dropped out and been lost to him somewhere in the winding streets. Money, papers of identity he'd tried to protect were gone. But it mattered not. For all at once, he knew he had no choice but to give himself over to pleasure, more pleasure than ever he'd felt before. Two mouths found their way to his nipples, lips and teeth expertly stroking and nipping, till he felt so hot he knew he must surely be blushing.

He was naked. He was floating. He was on his back, being caressed by wet lips and warm fingers. He looked down. A naked stranger was straddling him, positioning himself over his hard cock, sliding down and up and down again. The other dancer kissed him, tongue pushing his moans back in his mouth. He didn't want to, not yet, but he exploded, exploded in the hot, soft ass of the young Moroccan. And went into a dead faint.

He awoke fully dressed on the bed of his hotel room. The morning sunlight was yellow as a lemon upon the whitewashed walls. And somehow, his wallet had found its way to the bedside table, all contents intact. It was as if the night before had never happened. When he went to open the door, it was locked from the inside.

He found his memories of the previous night troubling, not so much because what had happened was so unnatural, but because he had received so much pleasure. Never again, he resolved, would the seductive indolence of the tropics corrupt his soul. It was time, past time, to go home.

He soon found himself at the railway office, counting out a portion of his meager funds for the passage he'd booked. As fate would have it, though, an offhand reference he made regarding his failed quest brought an unexpected reply from the railway agent. If he truly sought the wonder-workers of Fez, the agent said, it was necessary only to go that night to a certain tent on the outskirts of the medina. The agent drew a map for him. The unbought ticket remained on the counter.

When the burning sun had retreated, and the Muslims had said their evening prayers, he took map in hand and made his way to the tent. This tent turned out to be a shabby, unpromising affair. In Arabic and several Western tongues, a sign hung above its doorway read "The Melting Girl." A primitively painted picture showed a beautiful, near-naked woman, part of her body flowing into thin air. Could this possibly be the place he sought?

As if in answer to his thought, a man neither old nor young, neither handsome nor homely, came to the door of the tent and silently beckoned him inside. There beneath the canvas, a single chair sat facing a curtained stage.

The nondescript man demanded what seemed an exorbitant amount of money. He tried to haggle.

"Do you wish to find what you seek, or will you let the matter of a few dirhams determine your fate?"

He reluctantly paid and took his seat.

The nondescript man vanished behind the stage. For several minutes nothing happened, nothing at all. He found his thoughts wandering back to the night before, to the touch of the naked men. His cock began to swell.

The tent went dark. A single lamp above the stage began to glow feebly. The curtains parted. A girl, probably no older than twelve but with a garishly painted face, sat in a chair, facing straight ahead. An unknown instrument played a sinuous tune. Bit by bit, the face of the seated girl turned into a skeleton, a grinning skull.

He was outraged. It was a cheap conjuror's trick. He had come all this way, paid all this money, to see a threadbare "miracle" produced by mirrors and shifting lights. He stood up abruptly. His chair collapsed noisily. The stage curtains clapped shut as the lights in the tent were lit.

"I demand my money back, all of it!" His cry went unanswered. He tried again, this time in heavily accented Arabic.

The nondescript Moroccan appeared from behind the stage. "Something troubles you?" he asked.

"You're damned right. I paid to witness real magic, not this shabby charlatan's trick."

"Ah, and you believe that you can find true magic simply by spending your dirhams?"

He was silent for a long moment. Then, calmed and crestfallen, he said, "No, of course not. I was a fool. I'm sorry to have troubled you. Good evening."

He knew then that it was a dead loss, that there were no men who could walk through walls, and that even if there were, he would never find them, ever. And that he would never be free of what he'd come to Morocco to lose, which was, after all, himself. He was defeated. It was time to go home.

He was nearly out the door when the nondescript man called him back. "Wait a moment. I believe that I can show you something else that will perhaps satisfy your needs. No additional payment will be required. Please, this way."

Having come this far, he could see no harm in doing as the Moroccan asked.

He followed him behind the stage. From there, he could clearly see the mirrors and paper maché skeleton which had created "The Melting Girl." The ageless Moroccan drew aside a curtain and led him into a courtyard lit by lanterns of filigree brass. Beautiful carpets covered the ground.

Three men stepped from the shadows. They were naked, their cocks erect. Startled, he recognized them: the guide who had sucked him in an alleyway, the two dancers from the night before.

THERE ARE THINGS WHICH ARE HIDDEN FROM THE EYES OF THE EVERYDAY

He knew then what he needed to do. He removed every bit of his clothing and stood naked before the three. He was giving up every claim he had to his own misery.

The young guide walked over to him. He felt the boy's hands run down his torso, down to his cock, at first half-hard, then throbbing. The boy's hand grasped it tightly, squeezed hard. It was a beautiful sort of pain. He threw his head back, closed his eyes. The guide's thumb worked the head of his cock until fluid seeped from the slit.

Eyes still closed, he felt other hands on his buttocks, stroking and kneading his trembling flesh. Fingers made their way into his cleft, to a place no one was permitted to touch. But someone did.

Wordlessly, he lowered himself to the carpet-covered ground, crouching on all fours. He felt the moisture lubricating his hole, felt a finger loosening the tight ring of muscle, felt a cockhead pressing against him, firmly, insistently, until he let it in.

The slight pain passed quickly. He backed onto the shaft until it was all the way inside him. He'd never felt anything like it. Suddenly he was opened out, vulnerable, and as the hard cock began its long, slow strokes inside him, he felt the peace that had always eluded him. This was where he was meant to be, giving himself up to another man. In the alleyway, at the brothel, he'd allowed others to pleasure him, but had remained closed off still, his self-imposed barriers rigidly in place. Now at last, as he gave of his body, allowed another into his most secret place, his soul became open, free as air.

All his life, he now saw, had been built upon oppositions, lines of demarcation. Himself or others. Pleasure or pain. What men did or what women did. His army or the enemy's. Now, at one mighty stroke the barricades were broken. He'd crossed over into no man's land. And rather than finding a wasteland there, he found a world that was somehow whole. His burden of pain was so tiny beneath the infinite sky.

He opened his eyes. The colorful patterns on the carpet were moving, twisting, dancing before him. Arabesques. Dizzying arabesques.

He was wide open now, relaxed, all resistance gone. When one man had come inside him, another took his place. He knew there were three of them, but identities seemed meaningless as he lost himself in the dance of flesh. He shut his eyes again, and kept them closed.

At some point, he was on his back, ramrod strokes making his body shudder, when he shot all over himself, hot, sticky, running down his sides. He screamed. It was a scream of joy.

He felt a kiss upon his closed eyelids. He opened his eyes. It was the man who was neither young nor old.

"Perhaps the time has come. Look around you," the Moroccan said.

He looked around the lamplit courtyard. There were others there. Not just the three naked men who stood over him, smiling. There were many of those whom he had met in his search for the Magicians. The shoemaker, the brassworker, the teacher. The elderly man from Tangiers who'd read him the newspaper clipping. The railway station agent. There, in the corner—could it be?—the man from whom he'd first heard the rumors of the secret brotherhood. And the two old companions of the one-eyed man. And amidst them was "The Melting Girl," who, head scarf removed and stripped to the waist, proved to be a young man of surpassing beauty, smiling the smile of an angel. All standing in the courtyard. All looking at him as he lay there, his own juices running down his body.

"What are they all doing here?"

"Can you not guess? No? Then perhaps I should show you who I am?" With that, the nondescript man passed his hand before his face. His features became fluid, shifted, resolved themselves into the face of the one-eyed man. "You understand now, don't you? At last you see the truth. It is we whom you have been looking for. We who are men like you."

The one-eyed man continued, saying to him (as I now say to you), "Oh nobly born, this world is but a dance and we are merely dancers. Any meaning discovered in this dance, once grasped at, once written down on parchment, is doomed to vanish before our eyes. Thus mankind is fated to forever search for magic, and insofar as we search, we become that which we seek. True wisdom lies in knowing that the journey and the goal are one. Do you understand?"

"I think I do," he said. And perhaps he did.

The one-eyed man continued, "For truth is not our joy and truth is not our sorrow. It is merely a secret which we already know, though we may keep it hidden even from ourselves. But we shall never taste of truth till we let ourselves become that which we are, and indeed always have been, from the moment of creation. Though we are not this flesh, yet our flesh is all we have in this world. And so from the center of your being, come join us in the sweetly whirling dance of life."

"And the story of the brothers that you told me?"

"It is all the truth. It all took place about a century ago. I did, however, omit one small detail. The evil brother, Yakub? That man who died and came to life, that man was I. Only when I surrendered my greed for immortality did I begin to live. I allowed the world to be what it is, no more, no less. And with time I truly learned, as you now also see, that there is a wondrous power all around us, if we are open to it, if we but have the open eyes to see." The one-eyed man looked toward the heavens.

He, too, looked up, following the one-eyed man's gaze. (Or rather, *I* looked up. For as you must by now suspect, that naked man in the long-ago courtyard, that man who found what he'd long sought, that man was I.)

And the full moon, rising, filled the sky with its light. And there against the starry firmament, the form of one dove, then dozens, then hundreds, filled the nighttime sky.

A single bird swooped down, alighting on my heaving, naked chest. It had a parchment in its beak. I took the parchment. On it was written a single sentence: "Welcome to the brotherhood, O blessed one." And the dove flew up, rejoined its brothers, and the sky above Fez was filled with blinding light.

FULL MOON AND EMPTY ARMS

BY

M. W. KEIPER

hy is it that jilted lovers often take it out on the new paramour rather than the original object of their affection—especially when the jilted lover, for whatever reason, feels, well, unmanned? M.W. Keiper's narrator is a wry vet who comes across something utterly unexpected and struggles to regain his equilibrium while going through an education. Fortunately, neither of the antagonists get hurt by the other...or at least not too badly. The one who really suffers brings it upon herself.

—N.G.

Joanie named the cat Tiger Lilly. For the month and a half I'd had her (the cat, not Joanie; I hadn't had Joanie at all at that point) she had been known as either "Here, Kitty!" or "Get Down From There!" Joanie chucked her under the chin a few times, gave her a skritch behind the ears and pronounced her Tiger Lilly.

I had found the tiny creature rummaging in the garbage cans behind my garage. In response to my extended hand she ran up my arm and perched on my shoulder, purring loudly with a definite undertone of desperation. She is sleek, beautiful, wildly affectionate when it suits her, possessive of what is hers and vicious when thwarted. She once bit a friend of mine hard enough to draw blood.

"Reminds me quite a lot of Carol," he mused, while wrapping a napkin around his savaged index finger. Carol, my third and (please, God) last ex-wife. It was an astute observation on his part and it came to me then that all my exes and principal girlfriends ran to type. A bit of insight and self knowledge that would have been a hell of a lot more useful at twenty-three than forty-three.

That Joanie's gentle charm and low-key wit provided such a contrast to these women was perhaps the reason I didn't make the serious efforts I should have to fend her off when her intentions became obvious. A 19-year-old would-be hippie earth-mother who affected sixties drag of tie-dye T-shirts, peasant skirts and bare feet and who was, worse yet, one of my students. My initial efforts at discouraging her were, I admit, half-hearted.

"Hon, I got opinions older than you."

This got me a small laugh and a comradely shoulder butt that nonetheless managed to rub both taut breasts across my arm. She had an unfashionably full figure tending to a slight heaviness in the hips and thighs that, I suspected, partly accounted for her fondness for the retro-look skirts.

Only a few minutes after they first met, the newly dubbed Tiger Lilly began to purr approvingly and rub against Joanie's legs while exploring the perimeter of the floor-length skirt. Nosing her way under the garment, Tiger Lilly became intrigued with the lace trim of Joanie's panties.

The resulting ensnarement of claws and lace resulted in a leaping dervish dance to which Tiger Lilly's howls and Joanie's screams combined to provide a musical accompaniment not unlike a demon-possessed bagpipe. Centrifugal force ended the dance and Tiger Lilly streaked to a place of refuge under the bed.

Joanie ended up on the couch sipping a medicinal Jim Beam and branch water (heavy on the branch water) with her skirt bunched around her waist while I dabbed, alternately, tissues and iodine on the four seeping red streaks high on the inside of her right thigh.

"Give it to me straight, Doc. Will it have to come off?"

"To soon to tell. We'll have to keep you under close observation for a while."

"Kiss it and make it better?"

"Not a proven therapy."

"We'll take notes," she said, putting her arms around my neck and drawing me down to the couch, "It'll be our contribution to the research." The rest of the afternoon disappeared in a warm silver haze of Joanie and bourbon.

※

Joanie envied me the sixties. I got as many cool-points for lying about being at Woodstock as I did for actually being a semi-Indian, although that came to intrigue her even more. One Sunday afternoon we were lounging together in the oversize hammock in my backyard. I was reading term papers while Joanie peered intently at the space just over my head trying to "Read your aura."

"What kind of name is Walker?" she asked abruptly. "Your vibes are…odd."

"It's the white-eye's version of my real name, the one my grandfather gave me; He Who Walks In Peace With His Spirit Brother The Wolf. At the Catholic mission school, it was John Wolfwalker. When I went in the Army I shortened it to Walker, in anticipation of the mature sense of humor of my fellow recruits." She looked at me in amazement. "That may be old Lobo you're picking up on," I teased. I tried to go back to work, but there was no putting her off after that. She badgered me until I put aside the papers and gave her the whole story.

"I'm probably one-eighth, or less, Lakota; but grandpa was full-blooded. Generations of despair, poverty, alcoholism and all that goes with it left mom about one-quarter. She came back to grandpa's ranch pregnant twice before I came along. My oldest brother was stillborn. The other died of pneumonia and complications due to severe fetal alcohol syndrome when he was less than two months old.

"Grandpa locked her up and dried her out. She had begged him to help her get straight. For months she was hardly out of his sight, wasn't allowed off the place alone. One night she slipped out. Grandpa found her the next day passed out in the parking lot of some roadhouse. My father was two truck drivers, a traveling salesman and a guy with a red Jaguar convertible who said he was on his way to Hollywood. He gave her a ride back to the bar, the others left her at the motel. I suspect he might have been a writer. They know what it's like to get screwed for short money.

"Anyway, when she realized she was pregnant again, she tried to slash her wrists. She was all of seventeen. She told Grandpa she couldn't live with what she had done to her babies. He took her back into the hills to see an old hermit who made medicine. The hermit built a fire in a circle of sacred stones. He chanted and sprinkled magic powders over the fire for hours. At midnight the full moon stood overhead and the fire had burned down to a mound of glowing red coals. Out of the darkness came a white wolf with one eye of silver and the other of turquoise.

"The hermit told her this was the last wolf in the territory, and that he carried the spirit of his lost people. If she would agree to let the wolf spirit enter her unborn child, the wolf would lend her the strength to bear the child safely. When she agreed, the hermit told her to go to the wolf and lift her shirt. The wolf licked her belly three times, then loped off into the dark.

"Well, mom was a changed woman. She took care of herself and got almost healthy. She even started to smile from time to time and you couldn't give her dope or booze as a present. Of course, it might have helped some that Grandpa shot one of her old boyfriends who tried. In any case, I was born a healthy, blond, blue-eyed baby who was, nonetheless, technically an Indian. When I was three months old mom disappeared. She died a year later in Fargo; acute alcoholic insult to the brain."

"Wow," her voice breathy with wonder, "Is that true?"

"That's my story, and I'm sticking to it."

"No, really! About the wolf spirit?"

"Well, in Ranger school they were just delighted with me. The top-kick who was my escape and evade instructor said, 'Kid, you're a fuckin' ghost! Charlie won't know whether to shit or go blind!' Me, I was delighted with the G.I. Bill, which I planned to ride out of poverty. About halfway

FULL MOON AND EMPTY ARMS

through my tour somebody finally figured out I was using my talents to avoid ever running into the Cong, and the army wasn't nearly as pleased with me anymore. But then, Brother Wolf didn't get to be the last of his kind by going looking for trouble."

✼

I held for her the attraction that amusement parks always hold for children. A mature lover can offer a plethora of intriguing rides and exhibits. There's the voyeuristic excitement of a tour through the life experiences of someone who's been around a bit. The heady thrill of the aura of instant sophistication acquired by sleeping with an older man who's also your history professor. To say nothing of the mysteries to be explored with a lover who's experienced enough to be concerned with your pleasure, too—a quality rare to the point of myth in someone her own age.

We agreed almost immediately to a physical monogamy; it being embarrassingly early in our relationship to speak of an emotional one. But we agreed we wouldn't expose the other to the risks of a new sex partner without due notice. We got blood tested together and were able to dispense with unromantic chemical solutions and latex. Joanie liked that. A good deal of her sixties fascination had to do with fantasies of free love and impulsive sex. She was forever trying to coax anecdotes on the subject out of me. I obliged with tales both lurid and, I believe, strangely credible. I began to think I might have squandered my talents with nonfiction tomes on the history of the American Southwest when I might have had a notable career as a pornographer.

I didn't inquire about her past involvements. In the first place, given her age and what I knew about her background, I figured I could guess with a reasonable degree of accuracy. More importantly, I've come to realize that if people don't want to tell you something you can't make them; at least not with the amount of force I'm prepared to use. On the other hand, if they do want to tell you something, no matter how coy or "don't ask me about it" they get, you can't stop them with a gun.

Perhaps she took my lack of inquisitiveness as lack of interest; something her still soft-shelled ego found wounding. She began a subtle campaign of casual hints and allusions designed to pique my interest. A heartfelt sigh and "That song used to mean something special to me," to a ballad on the radio. "I went out for cheerleader," this while we cuddled on the couch watching Monday Night Football, "just so I could meet this guy." Now that did interest me. I'd finally balled a cheerleader.

I should have played along. I realize now that I was hurting her. Making it easy for a lover to share their past is an integral part of respecting their dignity as a person. Avoid someone who won't.

Then one day something slipped through the banter that hit like a missile.

We were at a house warming party given by some friends of mine. It was one of those party conversations a group of couples have, full of innuendo and double entendre. We were both laughing, and a little drunk, when she let slip with, "It's not as though you're my first prof."

I didn't visibly react. Inscrutable, us injuns.

But, two days later, after my one o'clock class, I went back to my office and took a bottle of Jim Beam out of the bottom desk drawer. It had a good layer of dust on it. I took a long pull and put my feet up on the desk. You've got to watch out for ol' Jim Beam. He's killed more Indians than the U.S. Cavalry.

I knew she didn't have any more classes that afternoon, so I called her dorm. She was glad to hear from me. Over her objections, I'd enforced certain casual rules of conduct for our relationship. No more than three nights a week, hardly ever two nights in a row. Too many students flunk out in their sophomore year. And, although we weren't breaking any written rules, I felt I needed to maintain at least some degree of separation.

I proposed dinner and a movie.

"Between my senior citizen's discount and your child's half-price ticket, the whole shebang shouldn't cost me more than five bucks."

"I dunno, it's a school night."

"If you're one minute late I'm leaving without you."

"You do and I'll write 'John Walker is a fabulous lay!' on the wall of every women's room on campus."

"Why not 'John Walker is a lousy lay!'"

"You know me, not a dishonest bone in my body."

"Oh, really, then just who was your first prof?"

"What do you...Oh!" and a big laugh. "I can't believe you took that seriously! How sweet! Are you actually jealous? I love you for that."

"Indian revenge can be a terrible thing. His scalp may yet decorate my lodge pole."

"Just wait 'til I get done with your lodge pole. Bye!"

It was the first time she'd lied to me.

Early on in our involvement there had been some unexplained crying and absences; some brief, red-eyed moroseness and telephone conversations that ended when I entered the room. I never asked any questions and these episodes had faded away. However, there had been some reoccurrences of late.

I took another substantial hit of bourbon. Somewhere, a white wolf raised his hackles and gave a long, low growl deep in his throat. Old Lobo didn't go looking for fights, but he hadn't survived so long by losing many either.

I hate moments of epiphany. I've never learned anything from one that I really wanted to know.

From the beginning I told myself that these things have a short half-life; and I truly thought I had been listening. But I hadn't. Not a bit. I'd been counting on at least the rest of the academic year, and fantasizing about more.

The best one was about a sabbatical year in Mexico working on a novel set during the first Indian revolt against the Spanish. A thatch and bamboo beach house on an isolated part of the Quintana Roo. I'm at my typewriter on the porch and Joanie emerges naked and laughing from the surf, the gentle curve of her belly showing the early stages of pregnancy. Yeah, I had it that bad.

I thought about how ridiculous it would be to have my heart broken for the first time at my age. It's true, I'd never been left by a woman that I had wanted to stay—if you don't count mom. The prospect left me ill and shaken in a way I hadn't experienced before.

Lobo, you dumb son-of-a-bitch, do something! Help me out here! He ducks his shaggy head and whines, wagging his tail apologetically. Never mind, old pal, not your fault. I'm sorry. Just keep guarding my back.

I'll handle it.

※

I got into the habit of eating cold lunches at the faculty dinning room. They didn't start out cold, but I'd fall into this speculative study of the male faces around me and…. I was sitting there, a forkful of now tepid casserole suspended above my plate, staring across the room at this new guy from the English Department, when Lois Bradford sat down uninvited across from me.

I knew her only slightly and disliked her to about the same degree. She was a P.E. instructor and coach of the women's volleyball team. A tall, sinewy blonde in her late twenties, she had the well defined muscularity and hard compact breasts of a female body builder. She was active in a number of politically correct causes around campus and had that air of barely contained impatience typical of such people.

I nodded politely and she gave me a warm smile in return—which immediately put me on my guard. She ignored her food and sat regarding me with that same smile. I decided I should break the ice with some insightful observation or quip.

"What?"

"You're very well thought of around here," she said, never losing the smile. "I've been talking to people. Your students adore you, the administration considers you an ornament to the profession and your publication record is impressive by any standard. You're clearly not one of those drones whose principal attraction to the job is ready access to teenage pussy. Joan Clarke appears to be your first."

I was completely taken by surprise and had no idea what my attitude or response was supposed to be. Rather than stare blankly, I broke the glass and hit the emergency arrogant/assertive button as a first line of defense.

"Jealous?" I inquired in a distinctly snide manner. She went all white around the mouth and her jaw muscles flexed visibly. Twin spots of an almost purple red glowed on her high, fine cheekbones. I've mentioned how much I hate moments of epiphany, haven't I?

"Christ on a stick. It's you, isn't it?" She took a glass of iced tea from her tray and drained half of it in one long swallow. Then she put it down and pushed the tray away, leaning forearms on the table and interlocking her fingers.

"Look," she said. "Let me tell you a few things about the way she acts with you, and you can tell me if I'm at all right."

"And there would be some point to this? It's not that you want to compare notes just for fun? I've never been into locker room talk."

"Bear with me a moment and I think you'll see. To start with, she's extremely sexual. You can hardly touch her without ending up in the sack. She's very willing to experiment, but it's always your suggestions she wants to act out, she never has any of her own. She's always ready to quit when you are but, afterward, she conveys a deep desire to be excessively complimented. She clearly yearns for you to do so and is restless and distressed if you don't."

Bingo.

It must have shown. So much for inscrutable. The enigmatic smile was back now. She continued.

"If you're honest with yourself, you will admit that the object of her lovemaking is to totally accommodate you, and to be praised and reassured for it. What it is, is that she's in a state of panic and denial about her true sexual identity. In you, she's found the perfect all-approving, all-accepting daddy figure to take refuge in. You're not doing her any favors by helping her delude herself."

"As fascinating as this has been, I'm afraid I'm going to have to adjourn this meeting of the 'I Humped Joanie Club.' Hope to see you all at the national convention." I made a move to rise. A surprisingly strong hand pinned my forearm to the table. She leaned toward me.

"One more thing. Sometimes, when she thinks you're asleep, she gets out of bed and goes into another room and cries. You know this because you've either followed her and heard, or you've noticed that she's still red-eyed and sniffling when she comes back."

Again, dammit, bingo. Then she answered my unspoken question.

"I was a little younger than her, but I acted out in much the same way. I ended up going through a series of guys who treated me like trash, and eventually, an overdose of pills before I got my head right. I'd like to see her skip as much of that as possible."

"You're a regular Mother Theresa, you are. You do volunteer work at the battered women's shelter, don't you?" I didn't give her a chance to answer. "With all those women, certainly sick of men just then and eager for a strong shoulder to cry on, can't you find enough playmates?" She slowly and deliberately moved her hand away from my arm.

"You're not ready to talk yet," she said as she stood up and stepped away from the table. "Feel free to call me when you are."

"Stay away from Joanie," I said smiling back at her. "Or I'll break your fucking neck." She turned and walked away, still with that goddamn smile on her face. Some small part of me was trying to get my attention; trying to make me realize how horrible I'd been—but all I could hear was the howling.

Joanie was sitting on my front porch steps when I got home that night. She had a bag of groceries between her feet and announced her intention of cooking dinner for me. It was some sort of quiche—I think. Joanie tasted hers, then reached out for my fork hand as I steeled myself to take a second bite.

"That's okay, Lancelot wouldn't take a second bite of this for Guinevere."

I thought a change of subject might lighten the mood a little.

"Say, hon. I ran into an old friend of yours today, Lois…" But she was already out of the room in a crash of crockery and silverware. I heard her pound up the stairs and slam the bedroom door. "…Bradford."

She lay face down on the far side of the bed, rhythmically pounding the pillow with her fist. I lay down on my back next to her, crossing my feet and putting my hands behind my head.

"Give it a whack for me, I hate pillows too." She gave a short, snorting laugh that turned into a hiccup. That started a series of hiccups and giggles until she turned over and threw herself at me, burying her face in my chest. I held her and stroked her hair.

"That was inexcusable of me and I am truly sorry," I said. She wound up and gave me a punch to the shoulder that she pulled at the last moment.

"It really was, you know," she mumbled into my shirt.

So we lay there and talked for hours; Yin and Yang, I'm okay with what you're okay with, everybody has components of both genders to their psyche, plenty of time to work through it all and, I think, my most salient insight.

"Look at it this way. You, a female, are in bed with a male, a normal heterosexual sort of thing to do. I, on the other hand, could be willingly and knowingly in bed with a lesbian; you see?"

"What's your point?"

"I could still turn out to be the pervert in this relationship."

"I don't know about that," she grinned. "But there's no doubt in my mind that you're a dangerously disturbed person."

"Come on. I'll whip us up some pemmican and fried eggs."

"Pemmican. That's Indian stuff?"

"Yep." I rattled the pots and pans while she cleared up the damage in the dining room. When I slid her plate in front of her, she gazed at it with suspicion.

"This pemmican smells like fried corned beef hash."

"Uh huh."

"This pemmican looks like corned beef hash."

"So it does."

"Tastes like it too."

"What's your point?"

"That this is the best pemmican I've ever had."

⁂

We were okay. You might say things got a little better. Joanie was more relaxed and seemed less compulsive about our relationship.

A month after our little crisis she tentatively asked me how I'd feel if she rejoined the judo club—coached by Lois Bradford. They'd originally met in the three-week women's self defense course Lois gave each semester. If I had the least objection, she wouldn't think of it. But she was all squared away with Lois now, no problem, and she really wanted to pursue the sport; she'd been getting pretty good.

What was I going to do, ride shotgun on her from now on? No, I'm fine with it. Go ahead, dear, I'm cool.

That night Brother Wolf led me into the dreamtime. I did not want to go, but I could not resist him. His great fangs closed on my wrist and I felt the irresistible pull of his spirit in the depths of my marrow. He took me to the Blue Mesa where shamen go to seek visions—looking over their right shoulders at the past, their left to gaze a upon the future.

I looked over my right shoulder and saw Joanie and Lois lying together on a couch. I averted my eyes and stubbornly stared straight ahead. Lobo bit down insistently on my wrist. Slowly, reluctantly, I turned my head and looked over my left shoulder. I saw Joanie and Lois strolling hand in hand along a sun-drenched beach.

There are no tears in the dreamtime, but when I awoke my pillow was soaked with them.

※

It was a week before spring break and I was crouched in the front hall lacing up my running shoes, getting ready for an evening jog. Joanie was at judo practice. She'd said she'd be coming by afterward. There was a brief, rapid hammering at my front door, then the sound of running footsteps on the porch. I opened the door to find a folded piece of three-ring notebook paper taped next to the knocker. In a delicate script, in pink ink, it read, "Joan is going to Florida for break with Lois. I'm so sorry. I thought you should know."

Ya gotta have friends.

I'd offered to take Joanie to the islands for a week, but she'd said that she had better put in some time with her folks as she and I had been kicking around plans to spend the summer together.

I did my warm-ups, then set off down the street at a slow trot. After a few minutes I moved into an easy lope. The evening air was alive with the scents and sounds of life and movement. I opened my mouth slightly the better to taste the night on my tongue. The street lights were too bright so I turned off into the shadowed places, clearing backyard fences and small obstacles with almost soundless bounds. No hint of alarm followed my passage.

I stood just outside the fan of light from the propped-open main doors of the gym and watched. Lois ran a dozen or so kids dressed in white cotton judo outfits through a warm-up routine of falling drills and basic throws. For a judo player her footwork was mediocre; balance carried too far forward on the balls of her feet.

I know about things like that because I spent the last twelve months of my hitch in the service guarding an empty warehouse on Okinawa. It's a humbling place for a Y.M.C.A.-trained martial artist, as the average twelve-year-old there is better than you can ever hope to be. I spent three nights a week studying with a bandy little farmer who seemed to take an almost spiritual delight in smacking us big-nosed, butter-stinkers around—for money yet.

When Lois called a five minute break I strolled in, stopping and standing just a little too close to her. Joanie ran over and put her hand on my arm.

"Please, John."

I turned my head toward her and she looked into my eyes, then recoiled; snatching away her hand and clutching it to her breast. I know what she saw.

Silver and turquoise.

Then I suddenly understood about Lois' bad footwork; for a ju-jitsu master it did not matter. The spear hand she fired into my left short-ribs was expertly delivered. It sent slivers of black ice into my heart and teleported most of the air out of my lungs.

Forget about all those chop-sockey movies. A real fight between martial artists rarely goes past one exchange. Before she could draw back for another blow, and while I could still stay on my feet, I stepped in close, bringing my right arm straight up between us and pivoting to catch her hard under the chin with the two inches of bone just below the elbow joint. Following through I extended my arm straight overhead, then pistoned it almost straight down catching her on the left cheek with the corresponding two inches of bone just above the elbow. She dropped to her knees and, somehow, managed to stay there, swaying slightly. She should have been laid out. She should have been half dead.

I took two steps back on wobbling knees, still trying to locate the forwarding address of my missing breath. Lois' left eye was already swelling shut and blood was running from her nose and one corner of her mouth. Staring me in the face, she spoke in a gasping, thick-tongued voice.

"But you haven't really won, have you?" and fell over backward, unconscious. She lay there making faint, wet, choking sounds. About then the air started to filter back into my lungs, but I was still afraid to try taking another step. I shouted at the tableau around me.

"Get her up, she's aspirating blood!" A couple of kids moved toward her. "Don't let her head loll around, support her neck. Fold up a towel lengthwise and wrap it around for a brace. Keep her leaning slightly forward so the blood doesn't run down into her lungs. Tell the EMTs she was struck a severe martial arts blow to the face at a downward angle. Tell them to check for fractured neck vertebrae first, not to waste time looking for a concussion. She wasn't hit in the upper skull." I looked around for Joanie. She wasn't there.

I didn't hear from her for six years.

※

I went home that night and waited for the police. They never came. Apparently, since Lois was wearing the judo costume, the people at the hospital assumed it was a training accident. She never made an official complaint.

Lois turned up after spring break wearing a neck brace, the left side of her face purple and yellow and a surgical dressing under her ear where they had gone in to pin the cheekbone back together. I felt a pang of guilt at seeing her injuries, but then my ribs were still taped and every deep breath reminded me that two of them were cracked.

I couldn't honestly say who was really to blame for that night. God knows, there was plenty to go around. I don't know—let whoever is without sin throw the first punch: or something like that.

Lois and I have become friends and sometimes drinking buddies. I help her out with the self-defense class by wearing a heavily padded suit and helmet and letting the women take turns pummeling me while they scream "NO!" This never fails to make old Lobo rock back on his haunches and laugh like a coyote. I can live with that, I just wish Lois would quit introducing me to the class as the campus "hand-to-hand combat mixed-singles champ."

FULL MOON AND EMPTY ARMS

We're like old soldiers of once opposing armies; veterans of the same campaigns. We have more in common with each other than with the civilians who stayed home. She even came to my wedding, although she refused my invitation to be best man.

My bride was a 38-year-old former Wall Street MBA who came back to school to get her Ph.D. I met her at an off-campus party where she asked me why men of my "vintage" felt compelled to lie about being at Woodstock.

"You think you're pretty clever," I replied.

"If Boesky had listened to me he'd still be swindling widows and orphans with impunity."

How could I not fall for her; that and "vintage?" She's sleek, beautiful, wildly affectionate when it suits her, possessive of what's hers and vicious when thwarted. She hasn't bitten any of my friends—yet. She and a mature, but still spry, Tiger Lilly are thick as thieves. We just found out she's pregnant again. My wife, not Tiger Lilly.

Today I got a letter from Joanie. It was three pages that distilled down to "Sorry, wish you well." She lives in a little place called Cassagada, Florida where she and her husband are "new age channelers." There was also a Polaroid and a folded brochure. The photo is of Joanie, her two little girls and her husband; a tall balding man. He has the same look in his eye as those people on talk shows who can hardly wait to explain how good the shock therapy really was for them. Joanie looks to have put on about sixty pounds. In the brochure it says that Joanie's spirit guide is an ancient Indian medicine man named Wolfwalker who always appears to her in the company of a white wolf.

"Spirit guide." I just love that.

I'm not prepared to say much else about love with any certainty at all. It seems to be something you are exposed to in its season and sometimes you catch it. When you do, there's nothing for it but to bundle up warm and drink plenty of fluids.

I recommend bourbon.

MAHU

BY

JEFF VERONA

"*I* come from a generation that lacks a defining moment like Vietnam, the Kennedy assassinations, or a World War. Yet I've seen people whose lives were so transfixed by a single event that all the years since never changed the essential person within," states Jeff Verona when asked the question all writers dread: Where did you get your idea? Couple that with his belief "that the choice of coming out is probably the most important decision a person can make," and you have the setting for the following thought-provoking piece.

—S. P.

✄

"Mahu."

Sammy Retseck lowered his paper and squinted against the glare of sunlight off the ocean. "Did you say something?"

"Mahu." A man stood ten feet from him, his skin the color of the dark wood in the tourist shops. His chest was a wall of brown muscle, and below his long-cut shorts were legs solid as tree trunks.

"My who? What?" Sammy shook his head. "Do you speak English?"

A grin, wide and white, split the man's face. Warm brown eyes shone above the smile, and he turned and trotted away toward the water, back muscles flexing and twisting. Just as he reached the ocean he turned back, still grinning, and waved. Then he strode out waist-deep before diving like a dolphin into the surf.

It must be the heat, Sammy thought. He pulled off his cap and fanned himself with it, staring at the globe-and-anchor insignia embroidered on the bill. *Did he mean 'veteran'? Sure are enough of us here.* Sammy had joined a group of them from Duluth to get a break on the airfare, but after hearing them carry on about the Navy and practical jokes from half a century ago he was glad that he hadn't decided to share their hotel as well.

But he sure looked like a native. Just like the old days. Never really learned any Hawaiian then, though. He fumbled the hat back into place, fingers clumsy and stiff, then tried to refold the paper. His hands cramped and stung, useless as clubs, and he trembled in frustration while the spasms died down. *Sammy, you're a damn fool, sitting out on the beach in the heat of the day.* With a grunt, he lifted himself from the little half-chair he'd brought from the rental apartment, then used it as a brace to stand up. Sand trickled through his loafers, slipped through a hole in his right sock, grated against the dry skin within. He glanced back toward the ocean, but there was no sign of the stranger, just a wiry Filipino boy jogging past.

He tucked the chair under his arm and walked slowly to where the sand turned to grass before striking off toward the concrete edge of beachfront Waikiki, where crowds jostled and flowed past restaurants, hotels, and shops. His apartment beckoned, promising cool shade and a nap, but Sammy paused as he neared the glittering bazaar. A man sat in a canvas chair next to a pushcart of trinkets, a man with iron-gray hair and tanned, weathered skin. *He looks native. Maybe he knows, or maybe he's got a phrase book.*

"Excuse me," Sammy said. The man glanced up. "Do you have a Hawaiian phrase book? A man on the beach said something to me, a native man, and I didn't understand him."

"Speak Hawaiian, bradah. What he say to you?"

"It was 'something-who.' 'My who', perhaps? Something like that?" The man frowned and shook his head, so Sammy pointed to his left. "It was over there, on the beach, by the jetty."

"The beach? Kapiolani Beach?" Suddenly, the man's face cleared. "Oh, *mahu*. Kapiolani Beach, that a *mahu* beach."

"*Mahu*." Laughing brown eyes flashed. "Yes, that's it. *Mahu*. But what does it mean?"

"*Mahu*? That mean gay, brah, you know, homosexual? Down there by the jetty, that a *mahu* beach."

A cold finger slid up Sammy's spine. His mouth worked soundlessly.

"You okay, brah?"

Sammy licked his lips. "Fine, I'm fine. It's the heat. I'll be okay." He bobbed his head at the vendor. "Thank you."

"*Aloha*."

Got to lie down. Sammy bumped past a crowd of Japanese tourists and made his uncertain way to the bus stop. A young couple offered him their spot on the bench, and he waited for ten minutes and two buses before his ride appeared. He dug up a fistful of change, but then his hands balked, and he was forced to ask the driver to pick out two quarters and a dime and drop them in the box. The bus rumbled, buildings slid by, and Sammy's mind whirled. Kapiolani Beach. *Mahu*. The handsome native grinning at him, eyes full of joy and secrets.

"Wiliwili Street." The doors groaned open, and with a start Sammy looked out to see his apartment building. Leaving the bus, he fumbled for his key, then wrapped his fingers around it and used two hands to guide it into the lock. The door swung open.

Inside was cool and dark. He stepped out of his loafers, stripped down to his T-shirt and boxers, and eased himself onto the bed. He stared at his stockinged feet, then muttered and swung them up level. *It's the heat. I'm too tired.* The pillow cradled his head, and he dropped into sleep.

✳

"Hey, Rusty, chow time!"

The pair of legs poking out from under the number two piston shifted slightly, but the only reply was the cranking of a ratchet. Sammy leaned over and jogged one of Rusty's feet. "Hey, I said 'chow time.'"

The foot jerked back. "Shit! You want me to crack my skull in here?" Though muffled, Rusty's tenor still held a hard edge. "Do that again, short-timer, and I'll kick your butt back to the States."

"I told you to stop calling me that." Sammy crouched down and craned his neck, but all he could see was Rusty's arm working the wrench back and forth. "Just because you've got three months on me—"

"Four." The arm stopped, shifted, resumed its work. "And don't you forget it, short-timer."

Sammy straightened back up. "Man, I had enough of that crap in boot camp."

"Welcome to the Navy, son. Your drill sergeant was like your mommy, out here it's the real thing." The feet crabbed sideways. "What that means, short-timer, is that I'm staying here until I get this right. Now are you going to help me or are you going to go eat?"

"I'll help."

"Good. This bearing's stuck. Get me a hammer." Suddenly, Rusty's legs kicked. "Aaah! Jesus! Shit, shit, shit!"

"Rusty, you okay? You okay, man?"

"Christ!" Rusty wiggled out from under the engine housing. "What a mess!" Fresh bearing grease caked his shirt, and a splotch of it covered one cheek, green-black against the shocking white of his skin and the carrot-colored hair that had given him his nickname.

"What happened?" Sammy's nose wrinkled at the burnt-metal smell of old grease.

"Some clown left metal shavings in there when he repacked the bearings. One of them froze up the works, and when it came free…" Rusty gestured at his face and shirt.

"You better get that off. That stuff soaks in, they'll think you're a native."

"Yeah, right. Get me a rag, would you, Sammy?"

"Sure." Sammy hesitated for a second as Rusty pulled the grimy shirt up over his head. His stomach and torso rippled, white as seafoam, and his nipples were twin carnations. Sammy quickly snatched up a few rags and handed them over.

"Thanks." Rusty wiped his chest, then proceeded to scrub the side of his face. He glared at the engine, then turned to Sammy and grinned. "Guess that's all for today."

"Guess so." Rusty stretched and twisted his head left and right, and Sammy winced as he heard the other man's neck crackle and pop. "Man, you'll hurt yourself some day doing that."

Rusty laughed. He walked over to a crate, lifted it up to reveal six dark bottles. He snagged two, tossed one toward Sammy. "Heads up!"

Sammy grabbed the bottle as Rusty dropped the crate and sat. He wedged the cap in his back teeth and popped it open, gagging briefly on the gust of foam that sprayed out. Then he took a swig of the beer.

"I wish I could do that trick." Rusty fumbled in his pocket for a church key and opened his own bottle.

"Maybe I'll teach you sometime."

Rusty took a pull on his bottle. "Well, you've certainly loosened up," he said. "First time I showed you a beer, you wouldn't even look at it. You thought the CPO was waiting in the engine housing to jump out and put us on report."

Sammy laughed and drained the bottle. "Yeah, I guess I was kind of green then."

"'Was?'" Rusty echoed. "Eighteen years old, son, you're still green."

"Like one year makes such a big difference."

"There's times in a man's life, Sammy, one year makes a world of difference." Rusty laid the empty on the floor. "You want another?"

"Sure."

"Okay." Rusty shifted the crate. "But this time, I want to see that trick of yours up close."

Sammy walked over to the crate, suddenly shy as Rusty's clear blue eyes met his. "Well, you hold the bottle so—"

"Like this?"

"Not quite. Here." Sammy fitted his hand over Rusty's, gently shifted the other's grip. "That's it. Now, watch close so you can get the angle right."

"I feel like a dentist." Rusty leaned forward until his bare chest brushed lightly against Sammy's arm. "Okay, go ahead."

Sammy fitted the bottlecap into the notch on his molar, bit down lightly, then tightened his jaw and snapped his wrist up. Beer dribbled onto his shoulder as he spat the cap away. "Got it?"

"Maybe." Rusty opened his mouth and set the bottle in place. He closed his teeth on the cap, paused for a heartbeat, then shook his head and took the bottle out. "No, I'll cut my gum or something. You open it for me."

Sammy accepted the bottle and peeled the cap off. "Here you go."

"Thanks." Their faces were close, almost touching. Sammy could see the spray of freckles along Rusty's nose, smell clean sweat under an edge of oil and grease. "I owe you one, Sammy. What do you want?"

"What?"

"What do you want?" Rusty's lips curved upward. "You must want something from me."

"I don't know." Sammy pushed beer past a sudden lump in his throat. "I'm not sure."

"I know." Rusty leaned forward and pressed their mouths together.

For an instant, Sammy's entire body froze. His mind blanked. Then, as Rusty stroked his tongue along Sammy's lips his own tongue darted out to meet him. He heard a distant crash as the bottle slipped through his nerveless fingers. His arms wrapped along Rusty's smooth sides while the other man's hands rose up between them, tearing at the buttons of his shirt. Rusty's tongue probed, darted, and slipped out to trail across his cheek. Sammy groaned as he felt the blunt tip slide gently along his ear.

"One year makes a world of difference," Rusty whispered.

�֎

He shuddered awake, gasping, an unfamiliar erection straining between his thighs. Sitting up, he hugged himself until the shaking stopped and the sweat on his face and chest cooled. An image floated across his mind: Rusty's face, the hollow of his throat, the shining edge of his collarbone. The pain, the ache, the *need* was like a punch in the gut, shocking and swift. Tears mingled with the sweat on Sammy's cheeks. *Dear God, am I going mad?* His chest heaved. *Slowly, now. Slowly. One thing at a time. Get a drink of water.* He swung his legs off the bed and padded over to the sink, filled a glass and gulped the water down. *Good. Now wash your face.* Sammy worked the taps, and while the basin filled he stripped off his T-shirt. He breathed deeply, calmly, emptying his mind of everything but the steam rising off the water as he plunged the washcloth into the sink and swabbed his face. He scrubbed neck, chest, and underarms, then pressed his face against a soft white towel.

"*Mahu.*"

The towel slipped through Sammy's fingers; automatically, he snatched it out of midair and whirled around. "Who's there?"

Gauze curtains rippled in the afternoon breeze.

Now I'm hearing voices. Sammy glanced at his pale reflection in the mirror and tried to smile. It didn't help. He stared at the towel, clenched in a death-grip between his fingers. *Clenched* between his fingers, fingers that for the past six years had been as responsive as sausages. He laid the towel on the counter, spread his hand open. Closed it. Spread it again. His fingers stood long and strong, no shaking, no pain. He placed his hands palm to palm. *Here's the church, here's the steeple, open the door—* His fingers wiggled up at him. *Here's all the people.*

He dropped his hands, walked back to the bed, sat heavily. *This is not possible. Not possible!* He caught himself. *Stop it.* Clothes hung in the closet, and he stared at them for a few moments before rising and mechanically dressing himself. If he could only get out of the room, go into the street, then he wouldn't think about his hands, wouldn't think about...Rusty. *No.* He closed his mind against that name.

Sammy walked through the late afternoon to the raucous strip of Waikiki. He stared at cars and street signs, waving occasionally at people who smiled and waved back. He crossed a canal and headed east along a wide boulevard, trying to pronounce the names on the signs. *KaLAlmoku.*

KalaiMOku? He shook his head. *Launiu. Kaiolu.* He turned right on Kaiolu, toward the ocean.

The next sign announced Kuhio Avenue, and neon signs glowed in the approaching dusk. The Hotel Honolulu beckoned, and a sudden rumble in his stomach prompted him to go inside.

When he stepped back out onto the street, night had descended. Sammy idled up Kuhio, pausing before a bar with the incongruous name of Hamburger Mary's, then continuing his leisurely stroll. The dinner hour was in full swing now, and a steady stream of people glided across the sidewalks, together or alone.

Lots of couples tonight. Sammy glanced at a pair that passed by, hands twined together, chattering and smiling. *Good-looking young men there.* Men? He stopped. Come to think of it, there were a lot of men on the street, talking and joking. Eyes shone with happiness, smoldered with desire or despair. A fair-haired man wrapped an arm around the neck of his blond companion, and something shifted in Sammy's chest, something composed of loss and jealousy. Uneasy, he turned up Kalakaua Street and headed for the canal and an apartment that suddenly seemed less threatening.

"This is crazy," Sammy hissed.

"We've got to work on that attitude of yours, short-timer." Rusty kept his voice low. "Remember, I do the talking. Act natural, a little bored if you can."

Sammy nodded, reaching up to scratch behind the collar of his dress uniform.

"And stop fidgeting." Rusty shook his head. "Jeez, I feel like your mother."

Caps tucked smartly under their arms, the two men strolled up to the doorman of the Moana Hotel. Rusty turned an intense smile on him. "Nice night, isn't it?" No response. "Say, buddy, can I bum a light off you?" The doorman stared Rusty full in the face, then slowly reached into a pocket and pulled out a Zippo. "Thanks." Sammy caught a glimpse of paper in Rusty's palm as he reached for the lighter. He flipped a cigarette into his mouth one-handed, lit it, and passed the lighter back to the doorman, who accepted it and swung the hotel door open. A faint suggestion of a smile shadowed the man's face as Sammy passed him and entered the building.

Rusty puffed a smoke ring. "Just like money in the bank."

Sammy stared at the dark wood, the thick carpet. Marble and brass gleamed in a golden light that seemed to emanate from everywhere. The sound of a jazz trumpet, high and clear, floated over a mix of talk and laughter from an outside patio.

"Yo, Sammy." Rusty touched his arm. "Bar's this way."

The bar was a slab of dark polished wood trimmed with chrome. Rusty dropped onto a stool and tossed his cap on the bartop. "Got an ashtray, my man?" The bartender, a thin native man with graying hair, set a crystal square before him.

"What is your pleasure, gentlemen?"

"Gin," Rusty said. Sammy opened his mouth to protest, but Rusty cut him off. "Not a word from you. You want to be a Navy man? Fine. You drink gin." He glanced back at the bartender. "Make that two martinis. Let's be civilized."

"Two martinis," murmured the bartender.

"I still can't believe we pulled this off," Sammy said, as the bartender moved away. "I thought this place was for officers only."

"Naw. You just got to know how to carry yourself." Rusty grinned all the way up to his eyes. "My daddy always said a smile will get you a long way in this world, and where a smile can't get you, money will." The bartender set napkins and drinks on the counter. "Thank you, my man. Can you run a tab for us?" The bartender nodded and shuffled off.

They raised thin, triangular glasses. "Here's mud in your eye," Rusty said.

Sammy sipped at the clear liquid, winced. "Tastes like paint thinner."

"There you go, talking like a short-timer again." Rusty closed his eyes, tilted back his glass. His throat bobbed. "That's good. Well, go on, drink up."

Sammy finished the rest of the tongue-curling liquor. "Now how about a beer?" he gasped.

Rusty smiled again, shaking his head. "Son, you're a slow learner. Two more," he called to the bartender.

The second martini eased something in Sammy's chest, and the third went down quite smoothly. He gulped down the fourth with a smile as wide as Rusty's. "I guess you were right about this after all."

"Was there ever any doubt?" Rusty checked his watch with exaggerated caution. "How about one for the road?"

"I'm game." The gin and the opulence around him made Sammy feel as if he were floating. The feeling ebbed slightly as he saw Rusty flip bills onto the counter to pay the tab. "That's almost a week's pay!"

"So what?" Rusty shrugged and tossed down a hefty tip. "It's only money." He picked up his cap. "How about a walk on the beach?"

"I'd like that." They wound their way back through the lobby and out onto the patio, where the jazz quartet Sammy had heard earlier was swinging through "Rock-a-bye Basie." Steps led down from the patio to a smooth stretch of beach. Barely fifty feet away, the ocean hissed and rolled.

All was quiet and still. Off to the west, Sammy could make out a scattering of lights. "That Pearl?"

"Sand Island," Rusty said. "Come on." He gave Sammy a tug in the opposite direction, then started jogging off. "Come on!"

"Hey, where are you going?"

"Going to race you to Diamond Head!" Rusty kicked into a full sprint.

"Oh, yeah?" Sammy lowered his head and launched himself after him. His shoes slid out from under him, and he fell. Rusty's laughter echoed back as the lean redhead raced on down the beach.

"That's right, keep laughing!" Sammy yanked off his shoes, rolled up to his feet, and took off after Rusty, who was now several hundred feet ahead of him. Legs pistoning smoothly, he whittled away the distance between them. Then, as Rusty began to flag, he closed the gap quickly. "Heads up!"

Sammy plowed into Rusty and the two men went down, rolling,

spinning, and laughing. Sammy sat up and shook sand from his hair while Rusty spat grit. Then he stood and began to unbutton his shirt.

"Hey, what are you doing?"

"Thought I'd go for a swim. Want to join me?"

Sammy glanced up the beach. The lights of the Moana were a distant flash in the darkness. "Sure." He peeled off his socks, loosened his belt.

"Well, hurry up." In the dim wash of starlight, Rusty's skin was burnished ivory. Sammy's breath caught as he stared at the lean slabs of muscle, the tufts of red at armpit, belly, and crotch. Rusty's eyes danced. "Last one in's a rotten egg!"

Sammy slipped out of the rest of his clothes and trotted down to the edge of the water. Rusty was already in to his waist, and his back flexed as he porpoise-dived into an oncoming wave. His pale face bobbed up further out. "Come on, short-timer," he sang over the heave of the surf.

The shock of the water flushed away the film the gin had left in Sammy's mind. He whipped spray from his hair, gasping, then struck out to where Rusty floated in the water. Just before he arrived, a wave swelled around them, and when Sammy passed into its trough Rusty had vanished. "Rusty? Rusty, you there?"

Something grabbed at Sammy's leg, yanking him down. He rolled in the water, peeled Rusty's arm away, touched bottom and kicked back up. Together they rose, whooping. Rusty circled his arms around Sammy, pulled him tight until chilled flesh pressed against chilled flesh. Their hearts thudded like twin drums. Sammy pressed his lips forward, tasted salt as the sea rocked them up and down, up and down.

✺

"It's about a fifteen-minute walk from here, sir, and the road's pretty steep," the young ensign said. "Can you make that okay?"

"I think so." The bus rumbled away as Sammy studied his brochure. He smiled at his impromptu guide, an impossibly young blond woman who nevertheless wore her uniform with a certain rightness. "I'm sure you know how far it is. Let's go."

"I try to come out to the Punchbowl once a month." Her heels rang smartly against the pavement.

"You have relatives buried there?"

She nodded. "We're a military family. Four generations. What about you?"

"I was in the big one in the Pacific."

"Really?" She stared at him. "You sure don't look that old."

"I've been lucky." There'd been stubble on his cheeks in the morning, *dark* stubble, and the loose flesh on his arms was thicker, fuller. His pot belly appeared to be melting away as well.

They walked in silence. The sky was purest gold and deepest blue, and as the road wound before them Sammy occasionally glimpsed the skyscrapers of Honolulu, the immense presence of the ocean beyond. A wall sprang up beside the road, and farther ahead stood a gate.

"We're here," she said.

The gate guard nodded at them as they passed. She squeezed his hand, said "Goodbye, sir," and walked off. Sammy drifted past the flags, past the plaque which read "National Memorial Cemetery of the Pacific," and toward eight long walls of marble. People moved quietly between them, some pausing to touch fingers to the cold surface of the stone. As Sammy drew nearer, he could distinguish sharp lines on the marble, lines which resolved themselves into words, then into names. An inscription ran along the top of the nearest wall. *The names of the missing,* he thought. He took a step closer, hesitated. *No.* Sammy walked past the silent stones to the grassy areas beyond, precisely cut, each dotted with neat rows of flat granite slabs.

It seemed that the armies of the dead marched on forever. As Sammy walked between the graves, he found himself passing back through time: *1974. 1967. 1952.* And then, finally, *1945.* He studied the tombstones. Some had names and dates, but many—too many—simply read "Unknown." *But I know them.* He stopped at familiar dates, each ringed with the nameless dead, the memories sudden and sharp as a lash. *Corregidor. Guadalcanal. Coral Sea.* His eyes burned. *Where are you, Mark? Hank? I know you're here, man. Somewhere.*

He turned down a new row. The date on the nearest grave transfixed him: *December 7, 1941.* He stopped. *He's here. Right down here.* The twin line of stones beckoned, like a passageway to a foreign and fantastic land where the whims of time would be undone, where the despairing would find joy, where the lost could be found. He took a half-step forward, hesitated, his foot shaking in the air. *I can't. Not now. It's too many years.* Sammy backed away from the graves, blindly, and staggered toward a bench. His heart thudded as all around the dead pressed against him, a silent chorus, waiting. *Not now. Not yet.* Sudden anger flared through him. *"Don't you know how much I wanted to?"* he raged, silently, at the empty eyes, the tongueless heads. *"We didn't want to live, but we did, we did."* His thoughts turned pleading. *"Just leave me alone."*

By slow degrees, his heartbeat calmed. Walking stiffly, he made his way out of the Punchbowl and back to the point where the bus had dropped him off. Most of the seats were empty on his ride back, but the dead continued to press up against him, names and faces untouched by half a century of forgetting, of trying to forget. They whirled around him as Sammy made his way back to his apartment and weighed him down as he sat on his bed. He wasn't tired, he didn't want to sleep, and he knew, he *knew*, what the dreams would bring. But the silent eyes begged him, the lifeless hands plucked, and there was no way to escape. He leaned his head back. His eyes closed.

✳

"Son of a *bitch!*" Sammy gritted his teeth and shook his left hand until the edge of the pain dulled. He stared at the wrench in his right hand, tossed it on the catwalk next to him before glaring up into the clutch he'd been working on. *Okay, so the bolt is definitely frozen. Get some lube for it.* He worked his injured knuckles slowly, hissing slightly against the little jolts of pain, then relaxed. *At least nothing's broken.* He walked on his knees to the ladder and began working his way down it.

The clutch assembly of the USS *Shaw* rose around him and he felt a sense of strangeness, of unreality, at seeing such an ordinary object blown up to such a gargantuan size. The silence further unnerved him; the only sound was the scuffing of his shoes against the metal rungs of the ladder. *Of course it's quiet,* he chided himself. *You know where everybody else is. The game.*

"What do you mean, you're going to the game?" Sammy had asked when Rusty came by in the morning.

"Just what I said. Buddy of mine, Dave Tyler, he's from Oregon, and there's a team from Oregon playing today at Honolulu Stadium. He managed to wrangle some tickets, and last night he asked me to come along. So I'm going." Rusty frowned. "What, something wrong with that?"

"I thought we were going to catch the surf on the North Shore," Sammy said.

Rusty's eyes widened. "Shit, Sammy, you're right! Oh, man, I'm sorry. I guess I forgot."

"Yeah, well I had to bust my tail to get out of duty shift for today. It cost me both weekends before Christmas. So you better tell Dave that you had a change of plans."

"I can't, I'm supposed to meet him in ten minutes." Rusty turned the full force of his blue-eyed grin on Sammy. "Hey, it's no big deal, okay? We can go after New Years'. The surf will still be there."

"You're really gonna go to this game?" Sammy looked away for an instant, then his eyes snapped back, angry. "Dammit, Rusty, we've been planning this for weeks! Then some guy shows up with football tickets last night and you forget all about it? I don't believe it."

"Well you better believe it, because it's going to happen." Rusty's eyes hardened. "You do what you want. Dave asked me to the game, I'm going to the game, and you can go surf with yourself."

"Fine. Maybe I will." Sammy turned his back to Rusty and stalked out of the PX. He nearly collided with a colonel, bit back a sharp response, and saluted, his hand trembling with anger and shame. *I've got to do something. Before I hit somebody.*

So that's why he was crawling around the bowels of the *Shaw,* looking to unfreeze a jammed bolt. He found a row of storage lockers, flipped them open. *Nothing. Nothing.* The metal shutters slammed back in disgust. *Nothing. Wait a minute.* He swung the door wider and smiled at the stacked rows of solvents and oils. *Bingo.*

His watch read 1645 as he returned to his station with two cans of fluid and a bigger wrench. He set to work, his mind blissfully empty of everything except his tools and the task at hand, and when he paused again the time was 1810. *Better get some chow before it closes.* But on the way out, his feet led him to the duty officer's station. "Hey, you got a cot or something back here?"

A sandy-haired man looked up from his magazine and nodded. "Yeah. You want to use it?"

"Can I borrow it tonight? I'm making some progress on that clutch reline, and I may just crash here later."

The man stared at Sammy. "You want to give up your Saturday night to fix a clutch?" He nodded back, and the man shrugged. "Fine by me, buddy. Cot's in there." He hooked a thumb over his shoulder at the office behind him.

"Thanks."

※

Waking was as sudden as the flipping of a switch, and it took him an instant to sense a looseness in his mouth, a taste of copper. He reached for his partial plate, and when he pulled the piece of plastic out it trailed ropes of saliva and blood. He swabbed fingers inside his mouth, and they came back sticky and red. Sammy leapt to his feet and raced to the sink. He swirled a mouthful of water, spat crimson. Then he pried his lips apart and held his face close to the mirror. Stumps of white bone pushed up from his gums in the place where his partial had been. He tested them lightly with his finger. They itched.

He rinsed his mouth until the water ran clear, then splashed his face and ran wet fingers through his hair. He studied the face in the mirror carefully. A slightly worried, decades-younger version of himself stared back. His hair was thick and black, and lines of muscle defined his arms and chest. His cheeks were full, and a smile revealed dimples, as well as a mouthful of shining white teeth.

It was impossible. Insane. But the only thing more insane would be trying to explain it to someone else. *"You see, doc, I'm really seventy-three years old. I'm here for the V-J Day reunion. Then some guy on the beach said the word 'mahu' to me, and this happened."* He snorted. *And then I spend the rest of my vacation in a rubber room.*

Hunger tickled his belly, and he snatched up a shirt and thrust an arm into it. The fabric caught on his bicep, then tore. He stared at the ruined sleeve. *Wonderful. Looks like I get to buy some clothes, too.* A search of his wardrobe turned up a loose T-shirt (no longer loose) and a pair of pants he could belt enough that they would stay around his waist. Embarrassed, he headed out to eat.

Hours later he returned, fed and clothed. He stowed away the small bag of extra clothes, then turned to the bed. Something new prowled within him, a restless thing that had cut through fifty years of isolation like solvent through grease, and he was afraid. *This is going to hurt more than a wrench across the knuckles. And after that...* His mind was completely blank. There was absolutely no way to know what would come next.

His hands moved. He undressed himself and lay down, his mind spinning. *I'm never going to be able to get to sleep.* But his eyes closed, and a dark tide welled up and pulled him down.

✖

Sammy woke to the drone of distant bees, blinked away the disorientation of his unfamiliar surroundings. His watch read nearly 0800. *Must've been at it later than I thought.* Yawning and blinking, he scratched his chin and narrowed his eyes against the light streaming through the slats of the window blinds. The bees droned louder, nearer, and then he heard a new sound, a sharp and high-pitched whistle. *Wait a minute. Those aren't bees*—Then the room groaned and shuddered around him.

He dove for the blinds and jerked them open onto a scene from hell. Across the bay from him, the battleships lined up alongside Ford Island erupted into fire. A plane flashed low overhead, and Sammy saw the water kick up as a torpedo dropped down and lanced toward its target. Then, amid the scream of engines and the rattle of small-arms fire, came a deep-throated bellow that went on and on. A massive fireball rose up, bright as a thousand Fourth of Julys, and the window before him shattered.

The blinds absorbed most of the glass, but a few shards nicked his arms as he raised them, instinctively, to shield his face.

Men were screaming. Bombs whistled and ships died. Sammy stared, mesmerized, until some primitive part of his mind forced an idea up over the chaos: *What if they started bombing the drydock?* He glanced at the *Shaw*, an immobile and inviting target looming beside him, then tore out of the room, out of the building, away from the wrath of the bombs.

But they were everywhere. Ford Island had vanished under thick black clouds, and great pools of fire burned on the surface of the harbor. The *Arizona* had listed and was sinking, and Sammy felt his chest freeze as he thought of the hundreds of men trapped in their bunks belowdecks. Far, far above, the attacking planes were shiny gnats wheeling against a blue Sunday sky.

Time seemed to slow as the planes dived, and for a horrifying moment Sammy thought it had stopped entirely, that the attack would continue forever with no escape, no release. Then out in the harbor he saw puffs of smoke, ridiculously tiny in the distance, and small black clouds blossomed overhead. The antiaircraft guns of the *West Virginia* had opened fire. *We're fighting back*, he thought, with a growing sense of excitement. He turned to his right and saw fires burning at scattered points around the navy reservation and Hickam Air Force Base. *I've got to help.* He headed out to fight the fire.

The next half-hour was confused, hopeful, terrifying, and swift. He found a crew and pitched in, stopping only when a soldier pricked up his ears as they finished dousing a burning B-17. "Hey, what's that noise?" he said. It was silence. They stared up at the clear sky, now empty of planes, and a ragged cheer rose up. "Don't get all excited yet," somebody warned. "There could be another wave of bombers on the way."

The men quieted. Then one of them, a shirtless corporal perched on the still-smoking remains of one of the bombers, called out "I see a ship moving!"

Sammy scrambled up beside him. "Where?"

The other pointed out toward the harbor. "Just past the drydock. See?"

Sure enough, one of great battleships was slowly creeping out toward the channel that led to the open sea. "It's the *Nevada*," Sammy said.

"The *West Virginia* was firing earlier, and the *Nevada* was docked next to her. Now that space is empty, see?"

"Hot damn! The Japs didn't get them all." The man grinned and punched Sammy on the arm.

"The *Nevada*." Something tickled the edge of Sammy's memory, then his stomach clenched tightly as the realization hit. *Rusty was stationed on the* Nevada! Sammy stared at the giant ship, desperate, fearful. "Please make it," he whispered. "Sweet Jesus, please let her make it out." He dropped to the tarmac and took a hesitant step in the direction of the dock.

"Hey, where you going?"

"Back to my duty station," Sammy said. "They're gonna need repair crews." He waved to the men and started back toward the *Shaw*, fighting against the urge to run. *He's already out there, you can't do anything for him. Save your energy. You're going to need it.*

As he cleared the edge of the tank farm something prompted him to look up, and far overhead he saw a broken line of steel wings glittering in the morning sun. An arc of the line slipped free and fell toward his position. Sammy did a quick inventory. The *Shaw* was in drydock, and nearby the *Cassin*, *Downs*, and *Pennsylvania* were in for repairs as well. None of them had been hit in the first assault, but now, with almost all of Battleship Row damaged or destroyed, the immobile ships would be too tempting to pass up. He gazed first at the *Nevada*, nearly across the channel now and ready to head out to sea, then up at the wave of planes as they descended. Then, as the first of the bombs whistled and slammed home, he dove into a ditch and covered his head.

For five minutes Sammy counted every beat of his heart, every shallow and ragged breath, as the air thundered around him and the earth shook. He heard the dull clap of the bombs, the deeper rumble of magazines as the ammunition inside them exploded, the solid boom of erupting fuel tanks. As the bombs started to fade in the distance, he stood cautiously and stared out to sea.

A black pillar rose from the dock where the *Shaw* was housed. The clutch he had labored over so lovingly the night before was nothing but twisted metal now. To his right, a cloud of smoke and flames marked the pyre of the two destroyers and the battleship beside them. Then he looked toward the channel.

The *Nevada* was afloat, and the Stars and Stripes stood up tall on her stern rail. But the front half of the battleship burned from bridge to bow. And Rusty was somewhere inside that inferno.

Sammy was on his feet, running, searching for an undamaged patch of dock, for a harbor boat that had somehow made it to safety. Several of those small boats were out on the water, desperately trying to pick up survivors who had fallen into the harbor or to gather men from the battleships before they capsized. Then he was aboard one, clinging to a rail as they made their way through blazing lakes of oil, leaning out to pick up men floating in the water. Burned men. Dead men. He lifted and carried and hoped and prayed that they would make it to the *Nevada*, that he would push through the haze and fire and find Rusty.

He found him in late afternoon. Not on the *Nevada*, though, nor even at Tripler Hospital, where the wounded shrieked and cursed and every nurse and doctor was a hero. No, he found him in the nurses' quarters. Abandoned a week earlier to make room for a drydock expansion, they now served as a morgue. Bodies were laid out with as much dignity as the catastrophe would allow, and grim corpsmen moved among them with clipboards, jotting down names and numbers when they could find dog tags that hadn't melted in the intense heat. Sammy stopped one of the men as he made his silent rounds. "I'm looking for someone." The man stared at him with haunted eyes, listened to the name, flipped a few pages, pointed. Then he continued on his methodical way.

No. This can't be him. The body was sere and blasted, black and wet like charcoal left in the rain. In places the skin had peeled away like cheap plaster, exposing yellowish fat and charred hunks of muscle. The face was a grinning horror. Sammy started to shake. *This isn't Rusty.* But the few remaining threads of hair shone vivid red. He reached out his hand slowly, willing it to touch nothing but the metal of the dog tags, and lifted them with trembling fingers. The thin metal had warped and blistered, but there was enough of it left to read the name. Rusty's voice rang in his ears: *"If you were named Thaddeus Clyde Petersen, you'd go by 'Rusty', too."* He read the words, reread them. He was still reading them when the silent corpsman returned and led him back to the hospital.

✳

He awoke, chest heaving, with the reek of burnt flesh in his nostrils. For an instant he thought his fingers were still coated with the greasy slickness of boiled skin, and he scrubbed them fiercely against the sheets before realizing that it was just sweat. A glance out the window revealed gray predawn. Still shivering, he walked over to the sink and flipped on the light.

Except for the fear in his eyes, he was the double of his enlistment photo. His skin was taut and healthy, showing the faintly luminous quality of true youth. Outside and inside, he was the same man he had been the instant he'd found Rusty's body.

He wet a rag and slowly washed himself. *Fifty years gone, as if I'd never lived them.* The rag traveled across his cheek, his throat, the back of his neck. *But I never did live them, not really.* After the shock of Pearl Harbor, the war had engulfed him. The frantic months working the drydocks, miraculously resurrecting half-destroyed ships; the agonizing hours as he lay in his bunk at sea, sleepless, waiting for the drone of the planes; the ceaseless days of work, where sleeping, eating, and repairing merged into an indistinct fog—these were his substitute for grief. He remembered the hero's welcome in Duluth, which some deep part of him knew to be a lie, and the tired procession of years in the machine shop, where loneliness grew into a second skin. Oh, he had spent his time at the VFW post, an unchanging raft drifting across the decades, but each year he saw fewer familiar faces, and the eyes of the men who had fought in later wars were too knowing.

All gone, now. He reached for a towel and dried himself, then fished shorts and a shirt from the dresser. Outside, the air held a faint edge of coolness, and the breeze was a whisper dying out in the face of the approaching dawn. He broke into a trot and headed for the ocean, feeling the blood pound strongly in his limbs as he passed the shuttered shops of Waikiki. The sky blushed pink as he hit the strip of Kuhio Beach, and he continued on, jogging smoothly past the zoo to where the land widened out into Kapiolani Park.

Light filtered in, first a wash of bronze, then gold. He shaded his eyes and looked out toward the surf, where a figure raised an arm and waved. He stepped closer, saw it was a man whose wide white grin stood out against familiar brown skin. The native stepped aside, revealing another man behind him, his skin like milk in the dawn light. Copper hair gleamed as he, too, waved an arm in welcome. Sammy laughed and ran down the beach to join them.

THE STARS ARE TEARS

ROBIN WAYNE BAILEY

*T*he last time we were with Dismas and Gestus in Sanctuary, better known as Thieves World, was in late 1989. Since then I have often wondered what happened to Lady Chenaya's two exceptional gladiators. Here, they are—as usual—in a bit of trouble, except that this time their love for and trust in each other may not be enough to get them through. (Note: I have known Robin Bailey for a decade or so, if he ever asks you if you want a "personalized" autograph, answer "yes" at your own risk.)

— S. P.

✺

"If the last star falls from the heavens tonight, I won't fear the darkness with you beside me."

Dismas didn't respond. Stretched out on a low hillock just above the point where the Red Foal River flowed into the sea, he dismissed Gestus' romantic clap-trap, and watched a dazzling star shoot across the night sky. An instant later, another star streaked after the first, slicing the blackness, trailing smoke. With a small gasp of appreciation, he sat up, thrust his hand out, pointing, and followed it with his gaze right down to the watery horizon.

For three nights the stars above ancient Sanctuary had plunged from their orbits, creating a spectacular—and to some, a frightening—show. Behind the high city walls, priests shivered and prayed in their temples, and astrologers sweated feverishly over their charts to determine what it all meant, while Sanctuary's citizens watched nervously from the privacy of their rooftops or in awed throngs from the wharves.

Far beyond those walls, well outside the city itself, Dismas lay back again, watchfully alert for the next fireball or smoker.

Gestus turned his head, his gaze trailing slowly down the sky to take in Dismas' profile. "Is this the end of us?" he whispered. His roughened fingers brushed gently against Dismas' hand.

Dismas frowned. "It's just a few shooting stars," he answered. Pulling his hand away, he folded his arms to cushion his head. A blue-white ball flared above and winked out. Afterward, the sky appeared still for a few moments. Dismas watched and waited with quiet anticipation.

Yet in those few moments, his thoughts returned to Gestus. *Is this the end of us?* He pursed his lips and tried not to think, yet the words echoed in his head. His lover's softly spoken question hadn't referred to the apparent collapse of the heavens.

I don't know, he admitted to himself. He didn't want to deal with such questions now. He wanted only to lie in the grass in the warm darkness, to stare into the unfathomable depths of night and count the falling of the stars. Still, he slipped one hand from under his head and reached down for Gestus' hand on the grass between them.

Neither of them spoke again for some time. The shower of stars continued. The river purled gently into the sea, the surf sighed with a constant weariness, and a salty breeze blew with a subtle susurrus. Far beyond the beach, a lost gull cried.

Dismas thought it the loneliest sound he'd ever heard.

THE STARS ARE TEARS

The faint light of a rising half-moon shone on Gestus when he rose and stretched. Bits of grass clung to his bare, powerful shoulders; he brushed them away and rubbed the back of his neck. The wind stirred the folds of the brief white chiton he wore. "We're due on the training machines at dawn," he said. Bending, he recovered a broad leather belt and a scabbarded short sword from the grass.

Dismas fought his way up from a half-dream state. With a sigh, he sat forward and reached for his own belt and sword. Far over the sea a bright orange star streaked earthward. As it perished, he extended a hand and let Gestus pull him to his feet.

Just beyond the shore, the moonlight fell on something pale that bobbed in the silvery water. For an instant it vanished as the surf swept over it, then it reappeared again.

"What's that?" Dismas asked curiously, catching Gestus' arm.

It might have been a jelly fish or a man-o-war the way it appeared to spread upon the sea, but it seemed to glow with an eerie luminescence. The waves washed over it again, submerging it, and again it rose.

"A piece of sail blown loose from some passing ship," Gestus said. So it might have been, and the fading luminance some chance trick of the moonlight. Still, Dismas stared, his brow furrowing.

Yet again the white-capped surf curled over it, and the sea tried to suck the mystery back into its watery maw. A grasping hand thrust up through the foam.

"It's a man!" Dismas shouted. "He's drowning!"

"Your eyes are dazzled from too much stargazing," Gestus said.

Dismas ran across the grass, his gaze locked on the struggling unfortunate. Grass turned to sand, which crunched under his sandaled feet and slowed his speed. The surf pushed the man down yet again. Dismas marked the spot. Casting his sword aside, he dove into the water and swam.

The moonlight glimmered on the waves. Pausing, treading water, Dismas brushed droplets from his eyes and desperately looked around. Near the horizon another star fell, but he barely noticed. "Where are you?" he called, twisting in the water. "Cry out so I'll know where you are!"

No answer, nor any sight of the man.

Dismas dived. With wide eyes he tried to penetrate the stygian depths, hoping for any hint of whiteness, a hand or face or bit of garment in the impenetrable gloom. A powerful current resisted him, then seized him. He fought free. Gasping for air, he broke the surface to find himself facing the shore.

"Dismas!"

He started at the sound of his name, but could not tell from where it came.

Something closed about his ankle. A cry of fearful surprise bubbled from his lips as he felt himself pulled under. Water filled his mouth. Heart hammering, he kicked, kicked again, and surged upward. Glorious air rushed into his lungs.

"Dismas!" He heard his name again, and this time recognized the sound of Gestus' voice. It came not from the shore, but from some distance to his left. Before he could answer, a cold and slimy grip closed about his ankle and pulled him under once again.

This time, with sufficient breath in his body, he reached down to grasp whatever grasped him, and when he stared through the inky water, lambent eyes stared back. A chill shivered up his spine as he encountered that strange, nearly lifeless gaze, and a sense of horror and panic filled him.

Yet he fought down his fear. With a determined effort, he felt for the hand that gripped his ankle and pried loose icy, viselike fingers. His own fingers locked around a wrist. Those eyes floated nearer. In the murky waters, Dismas could barely make out a bloated face, a roundly gaping, lipless mouth.

His lungs began to burn. With a powerful kick, dragging the drowning man with him, he strove upward toward fresh air. The weight of the other held him down. He struggled for a better grip on the limp form. Slipping his arm about a narrow chest, he battled to the surface.

Sputtering, gasping, he cradled a dark-haired head on his shoulder. Dimly, he heard Gestus calling his name, but for the moment he lacked the strength and breath to answer. He paddled his feet furiously, attempting to tread water for two. A wave washed mercilessly over his head. With eyes full of water, he looked for the shore. For a heart-stopping instant he failed to spot it. Adrift in a tossing, white-foamed ocean, he couldn't find the land!

A form cleaved suddenly through the water, swimming with grace and speed. Before Dismas could react yet another wave swept over him, filling his mouth and nose. A powerful current threatened to push him deeper; it tried to tear the unconscious burden from his arms, but he clung tighter and managed once more to win the surface.

Strong hands closed about his shoulders, buoying him up. Coughing, spitting, he strained to speak. "Gestus!" he sputtered.

His grim-faced lover said nothing, though his eyes flamed with worry. With anguished and unyielding strength, he fought the sea, towing them all through wave after glittering wave toward the shore.

At last Dismas felt sand under his feet. He grasped one of the stranger's arms, and Gestus grabbed the other. Together they dragged the man onto the beach and collapsed beside him. The stranger coughed weakly; one hand twitched, brushing Dismas' thigh.

Overhead, the stars continued to fall.

The lamps burned low in the halls of the great estate called Land's End. The Lady Chenaya slipped quietly through the doorway of a small second-floor guest room. Her blond hair flowed loosely about her shoulders, and the white linen robe she wore stirred in the draft from the open window. Dismas and Gestus both turned as she entered.

Chenaya ignored them. Frowning, she bent over the bedside where the stranger lay half-covered by a white sheet. An older man in nightclothes sat on the edge of the mattress. An array of tiny vials containing scented oils stood arranged on a small table close by, and the pungent odor of cinnamon hung in the air. "How is he, Rashan?"

"Very lucky, I'd say," the old priest/physician answered. "He's swallowed a lot of water, and he's suffering from exposure. No telling how long he was adrift."

Dismas drew near to the bed. "He looks starved," he said, noting how the stranger's ribs showed through the pale, almost translucent skin. There was an odd beauty there, too—a delicateness in the finely boned face, the shell-like ears, the shock of ebon hair that curled over one closed eye. He was young, almost boyish. Cleaned up and dressed properly, he would be quite handsome.

"I don't like strangers in my house," Chenaya said, snapping him out of his reverie. "Tensions are too high between Sanctuary and the Rankan Empire. Spies lurk behind every bush and tree…."

Dismas dared to interrupt. "He was drowning, my lady. I hardly think…"

Chenaya's eyes flashed as she cut him off. "Heed me, gladiator," she said. "Get him well and on his feet. Then get him out of here."

The stranger stirred suddenly on the bed. His eyes remained closed, yet as if with some unerring sense, he reached out a thin arm and caught Dismas' hand. Startled, Dismas glanced down, observing a softening around the stranger's mouth, almost a smile.

"If it will allay my lady's concern," he said, "I'll watch him every minute."

Gestus spoke up. "We have training duty in the morning," he said with a note of irritation. "Net and trident techniques."

Chenaya fixed Dismas with a stern glare. "Your mind hasn't been on your assignments lately," she said. "Change that. Rashan can keep an eye on him for now. The two of you get to bed."

Gestus bowed and moved toward the door, but the stranger's grip on Dismas' hand tightened. Carefully, even tenderly, Dismas pried the fingers loose. That the boy, even in sleep, wished him to stay lit a quiet fire of pleasure in his heart. Bowing to Chenaya, he bid Rashan goodnight and followed Gestus out.

As a reward for longtime service to Chenaya, they shared a room on the estate's lower level instead of billeting in the barracks with most of the gladiators and recruits at Land's End. With scant hours remaining before dawn, they shed their still-damp clothes and climbed into bed. Gestus curled around Dismas, and the two settled into the familiar depressions their bodies had long ago made in the mattress.

But sleep eluded Dismas. He lay in his lover's arms, listening to the soft whispers of their breathing. His thoughts, though, were mostly on the room upstairs.

"You want him," Gestus murmured suddenly with only a hint of weary accusation. "I saw it in your eyes when you looked at him."

Dismas shifted uneasily beneath the sheets, drawing his body a little apart from Gestus. "What do you want me to say?" he said finally.

Gestus' hand brushed lightly through Dismas' hair. "Nothing," he answered in the barest whisper. "I've felt you drawing away from me for some time." His hand trailed down over Dismas' shoulder, then pulled back. No other word passed between them. Gestus turned over and withdrew to the farthest edge of the bed. Eventually, he slept.

Dismas lay trembling, alone and frightened, his mind in turmoil. He and Gestus had been together for years, since their first master had purchased them, little more than boys, from a Bhaktar prison and entered them in the arena as a matched pair. Virtually twins, they resembled each other—same height and musculature, same blue eyes and sandy hair. They wore close beards similarly. Frequently they dressed alike. They even fought alike.

A tear rolled silently from the corner of his eye as he remembered. He felt his past, all that he held secure, slipping through his fingers like grains of salt, and he didn't know why.

After a restless time, he rose. For a long while he stood naked beside the bed, staring at Gestus, wanting to touch him, but not daring to do so. Guilt gnawed at him, because he kept thinking of the handsome youth he had pulled from the sea.

Though he fought to deny it, the seed of a dark passion grew within him. Slipping a cloak around his shoulders, he crept into the hallway and upstairs.

Rashan had retired with his oils to his own rooms. The boy reclined unconscious on the bed. The sheet lay about his hips. His bare chest rose and fell softly, and the amber lamplight gleaming on his skin highlighted the dark, tantalizing circles of his nipples.

Drawing his cloak closer about himself, Dismas sat on the edge of the bed and studied the sleeping face. "I'm here," he whispered, touching a pale cheek. Once he had thought that mouth almost lipless, but in the faint light it proved full and red.

Once again, the sleeper reached out and grasped his hand. Lids fluttered tremorously open to reveal dark, moist eyes. The lips parted. "Uloi," he breathed, and though Dismas couldn't explain how, he knew it was a name. The eyes closed again.

Freeing his hand, Dismas left the bed and drew a chair close. The lamp's wick sputtered nervously, causing the shadows in the room to quiver and stir. Dismas paid no attention. He watched the boy, fascinated, until sleep finally stole his senses.

※

Deep in the chasm of his dreams vaguely perceived shadows performed plays with themes beyond his comprehension. Voices speaking no known language whispered lines with poetic rhythms that, for all their lyric beauty, filled him with an apprehensive dread. Some figure at the bottom of that chasm beckoned.

He heard his name.

His eyes snapped open. The Lady Chenaya stood in the doorway, hands on her hips, eyes flashing with anger. Gone were the soft garments of a woman. She wore the accoutrements of a gladiator—the *manica* on her left arm, greaves on her legs, a short-bladed sword strapped around her waist.

"The sun is long up, and you're not on the field." She made a gesture of imperious scorn. "What am I to make of this?"

Dismas blushed at her scolding, but more so to discover that Uloi had slipped from his bed sometime in the night to curl upon the floor at Dismas' feet. He lay there now, a tangle of sheets covering his frail loins, one hand hanging lightly upon his rescuer's thigh.

Dismas pushed the hand away and stood up. Uloi stirred sleepily, then noting Chenaya's presence, roused himself, gathered the sheet closer, and struggled to sit up.

"I only came to check on him," Dismas said, sounding unconvincing even to himself. "I fell asleep in the chair...."

"No excuses, gladiator," Chenaya interrupted. Her stony gaze turned to Uloi. "Are you strong enough to get back in bed?"

Without thinking, Dismas bent to help the young man rise. Gently, he placed him on the mattress, eased Uloi's thin legs into a comfortable position, and smoothed the sheet. "Rest," he murmured. "I'll return later." Then, avoiding his mistress' withering stare, he headed for the door to take up his duties.

Chenaya caught his arm with an unladylike strength. "I'm disappointed in you, my friend," she said, lowering her voice. "I'm not blind. I know something's been troubling you lately. But don't let this sick puppy-dog come between you and Gestus."

Refusing to compound his shame with weak-sounding protestations, or worse, lies, Dismas kept an embarrassed silence.

Chenaya shrugged. She looked back toward Uloi, who watched them wordlessly from the pillow. "Odd," she whispered, half to herself. "Last night in the lamplight I thought his hair was black."

"It is," Dismas said, but he turned also, and a puzzled frown turned down the corners of his mouth. Uloi's hair was sandy blond. And though Chenaya failed to notice, he spied another difference. Those eyes, seemingly dark before, were blue. "I must have been mistaken," he said.

"Well, I'm not mistaken about this," Chenaya answered. "You're overdue on the field. I'll have Rashan bring some food for this one, but you've forfeited breakfast. Move out."

The day crawled from hour to excruciating hour. The Rankan sun burned hotter than usual. Sweat streamed from Dismas's pores, and his sleep-deprived body ached. Throughout the morning he worked with a group of twelve green fighters, but he found it difficult to concentrate on the drills. Uloi filled his thoughts, and Gestus distracted him endlessly with wounded glances. For the rest of the afternoon, though it pained him, he worked carefully and deliberately to avoid his lover, unable to endure those looks, yet unable to apologize when he saw nothing for which an apology was needed.

By sundown, however, his mood had softened. After the evening meal, when they were alone in the room they shared, he touched Gestus' shoulder. "Are we going down to the Red Foal to watch the starfall again tonight?"

Gestus' eyes reflected a poignant sadness. "I promised Chenaya I'd escort her into Sanctuary. She wants to pray at the Temple of Sabellia."

"The Moon Goddess?" he said, arching an eyebrow in surprise. Chenaya worshipped the sun.

Gestus squeezed his lips into a fine line and looked away. He let go a sigh before he spoke again. "Do you know that some people at this end of the empire believe the stars are Sabellia's tears? They wonder these last few nights why She's weeping."

Without another word, his twin and lover picked up a cloak and walked away, leaving Dismas to stare at the empty doorway in hurt confusion. Finally, he sank down on the bed. Picking up a volume of Ilsig poetry from a bedside table, he found his place marker and tried to lose himself in its pages.

Perhaps it was the lush romanticism he found in those verses. Or maybe it was the strangely haunting echoes of refrains half-remembered from his previous night's dream. Uloi stole into his thoughts. He tried to concentrate on his book.

> From the sky or from the sea
> She comes in ancient pageantry
> With eyes that speak of mystery
> And lips that taste of tragedy.

In every poem some detail, some image, emerged to remind him of the boy/man. The words of the Ilsig poets rose off the page to take song in a chorus of muted shadowy voices. His senses swam, and the hand that held the book trembled. He heard his name and glanced up nervously at the door, but Chenaya wasn't there, nor was Gestus. He turned the page.

> *Who would not risk hell's hottest fire*
> *For one night of passion and supreme desire,*
> *To fill the heavens with celestial moans,*
> *For love that sucks the marrow from our bones?*

Dismas closed his book. Perspiration trickled down his face. He burned as with a fever. A sectarius of Bhaktaran wine rested on the surface of a small cabinet across the room. Rising from the bed, he seized the soft-skinned vessel, unstoppered it, and squirted a dark red stream into his mouth.

Setting the sectarius aside, he leaned on the cabinet and fought a momentary dizziness as he swallowed the bitterly delicious liquor. He spun toward the door.

Silence greeted him as he stumbled into the corridor. The light of a single cresset, suspended by a chain from the ceiling, lit the far end of the passage. Everyone, it seemed, had gone to the temple.

He found the stairs that led to the upper level. On the bottom step, he paused, the words of the poets still murmuring in his brain, Uloi's name quivering soundlessly on his moistened lips. Step by step he climbed, and with each footfall Gestus retreated from his memory.

The lamps burned brighter in the upper halls. He paused again, alerted by a quick tread on the stone tiles. Pressing himself into a shadow, he watched Rashan exit Uloi's room and enter his own chamber further down the way. Of course Rashan, a priest of the Sun God, Savankala, would have remained behind.

Dismas moved swiftly, noiselessly, and entered Uloi's room. He stopped on the threshold, his eye caught momentarily by the shimmering trail of a dying star as it fell across the black square of the unshuttered window.

His gaze turned to Uloi. The light of a lone lamp, its wick turned low, fell upon the innocent, peacefully composed features of the face upon the pillow. Dismas moved to the bed and ran the back of one finger lightly over the stubbled beginnings of a blond beard on cheeks that no longer seemed quite so boyish.

The sleeper woke. Lids opened slowly, and blue eyes fired with an unconcealed longing greeted the gladiator. Dismas bent and kissed lips that yielded readily to him. As if moving through a liquid dreamscape, he straightened and pulled away the sheet.

Uloi rose from the bed. In the wan lamplight his limbs no longer seemed puny, nor did his ribs show through his skin. His body appeared well-formed, graced with sculpted muscle. When he moved toward Dismas, there was no weakness in his step.

Dismas extended a hand. "Are we going down to the Red Foal to watch the starfall again tonight?" he whispered.

Uloi nodded as their fingers intertwined.

They walked side by side into the corridor and descended the stairs quickly. Dismas led the way across a common hall, through the peristyle, past the aviary that housed Chenaya's hunting birds. Their footfalls made no sound, though they took no particular care now. Out onto the lawn they strode, and Dismas drew in a deep breath of sweetly scented air.

A high recently built wall surrounded the Land's End estate. In the northeastern corner stood the stables, the practice arenas, and barracks for Chenaya's trainees. Dismas avoided those. Keeping to the shadows, he set a course that followed the southern wall to the River Gate.

Though tensions were mounting between the Rankan Empire and Sanctuary, Chenaya had not yet set permanent guards on her gates. Dismas unbarred the wooden doors. He and Uloi eased quietly out.

❋

It was still some slight distance to the river. The grounds of Land's End extended all the way to the Red Foal's banks and southward to the sea, encompassing two great houses that once had been separately owned. Beyond the protecting walls stretched broad, rolling grasslands with isolated patches of woods. The trees along the river swayed and rustled in the salt-tinged breeze. Low on the horizon, barely visible through the leaves, a half-moon floated.

They walked without speaking, heading for the sea. Dismas glanced up at the sky from time to time. The stars seemed to hold their places tonight, he noticed. Perhaps the cosmic show was ending. Yet from the corner of his eye he saw a faint streak slice the darkness.

They stopped on the same low hillock where he and Gestus had lain the night before. He squeezed Uloi's hand. The vast sea undulated, its surface dappled and glittering as it reflected the immense, star-spangled canopy of night. Dismas' heart swelled, and the breath caught in his throat. He felt dwarfed, suddenly insignificant, in the presence of such majesty.

He turned to Uloi. Their chests touched, they stood so close. Their hands joined again. Dismas had never seen anyone so beautiful, never wanted anyone so much. He leaned his cheek against Uloi's soft beard and lightly kissed the place where ear and neck met. Uloi responded, murmuring softly in his own language, his breath sweet, his words strangely musical.

Dismas thought he had never known such heady joy, and yet he began to cry as, in some dimming corner of his brain, he thought of Gestus— boyhood friends, thieves together, prisoners together, then gladiators, always lovers.

Uloi's kisses turned passionate. They burned Dismas' lips, his mouth, his face.

Who would not risk hell's hottest fire
For one night of passion and supreme desire…

Dismas heard the poem somewhere deep in his mind, sung with Uloi's voice, the same voice that had reached up to him from the chasm of his dream. Uloi's touch tingled on his skin, thrilling him in ways he had never experienced, not even with Gestus. He caught Uloi's face in his hands and kissed him.

The moon rose finally above the trees in the east. Its light fell upon

Uloi, lending his skin a glow, shining in the fine blond beard and hair, igniting eyes that reminded Dismas of someone else.

He stepped back, freeing himself from Uloi's embrace. "I can't," he said. An overwhelming clarity suddenly filled him. Whatever Uloi offered, it was Gestus he loved with all his heart and soul. He backed another step, trying to catch his breath, trying to master the desire that still propelled him toward the other.

Uloi stared with a hurt expression as he extended a supplicating hand. Dismas stood his ground, and yet a trembling seized him. Was it a trick of the moonlight? He knew that wounded look most intimately. It didn't belong on Uloi's face. Yet it fit there perfectly.

"Who are you?" he asked. "What are you?"

A dark seam appeared in Uloi's body. His chest and belly opened. A squirming mass of unnamable horror spilled out, unfurling, reaching across the brief distance to embrace Dismas. A part of him recoiled, but another part met Uloi's soft gaze, took in the naked, muscled curves of his arms and shoulders, heard the promises in his murmurings.

The chasm of his dream yawned, and the voices that called from it drew him down deeper and deeper into a black abyss of submission. Wet writhings burrowed over his flesh, wormed under his clothing, caressing, penetrating him, stroking with an insidious sensuousness. They filled him with a shuddering, unearthly pleasure.

Through it all he stared into Uloi's eyes. They shone like blue stars, burning with a longing and need and a shadowy love, all beauty and desire written plainly on a face that was not his own, all horror and terror glimmering on scarlet lips. He swayed seductively, sang to Dismas in a voice sweet as flowers, hypnotic and delightful, compelling. He drew Dismas to him.

Dismas shivered with revulsion, senses reeling, flesh crawling with a terrible dark rapture. Wet, warm things slithered over him, within him, unlocking sensations, exploring his lips, his mouth, deeper, knowing him.

The murmuring voices faded from his brain, leaving nothing but a churning black sea of unending arousal. He raised his arms, parting the living sheath of pale worms, to embrace the velvet flesh of Uloi.

From across an immense gulf, he heard his name. Uloi turned, and Dismas slowly turned. A veil seemed to lift from his eyes. Gestus and Chenaya stared in eye-widened horror. A curse broke from Chenaya's lips. Gestus reached for his sword.

The mass of tendrils shifted, stirred. Languidly, Dismas pointed a finger. "Go away," he said, voice thick. "Leave us alone."

Gestus screamed. His sword flashed from its sheath. Maddened, he struck at Uloi, struck and struck.

※

"It came from the stars," Dismas told Chenaya. He lay under a sheet in his room on his own familiar bed. The Lady of Land's End stood over him as they spoke privately. "Or from the sea. I'm not sure. The voices were indistinct and seemed to use the words interchangeably." He swallowed and hid his face in his hands as he remembered.

Chenaya took a chair next to the bed. Picking up a cup of hot broth from the bedside table, she pulled his hands down and pushed the steaming vessel between his palms. "Wherever it came from," she said. "It's dead now. It won't hurt anyone else."

He sipped the broth, barely aware of taste or temperature, his eyes staring past the foot of the bed, indeed far beyond the confines of that square apartment. "But it didn't hurt me," he answered. "Not exactly. I don't think it meant to hurt anyone." He looked up at her, appealing for understanding, then looked away again. An infinite misery filled his voice. "It wanted me to love it. It needed me to protect it, to be its defender." His voice dropped almost to a whisper. "It gave me…" he swallowed again and squeezed his eyes shut. "…pleasure to win me, to convince me never to leave it." He sipped the broth once more, then set it aside. "It changed itself, its very form, to become my ideal lover."

Chenaya caught his chin, drew his face around, forced him to meet her gaze. She spoke with deliberate care. "It looked just like Gestus. Do you know that?"

He nodded slowly. "I love him."

A hint of exasperation crept into her voice. "Then what have you been moping about these past weeks?"

Dismas struggled not to shout. His words hissed between his teeth. "I can't live this life anymore, Chenaya!" he said. "This senseless fighting and killing in the guise of a game! I've wrestled with it, and on that hill it came to me clear and sharp as crystal. That creature! There was no violence in it, no anger, no hatred, no bloodlust!"

He threw back the sheet suddenly. Rising to his feet, he flung up his hands, then let them fall to his sides. His head drooped. "And there's none left in me. I'm tired of it all, Chenaya, tired of it in my soul."

Chenaya reached past the unfinished cup of broth and picked up a slim book. She turned it over in her hands. "You always were more of a poet."

"But what of Gestus?" he asked, taking the book from her and sitting down again on the edge of the mattress. "If I leave the arena, what will he do?"

Chenaya fixed him with a stern look. "Are you such a fool?" she asked. "He would give you his life."

Dismas pursed his lips and slowly nodded. Yet a sadness and a fear dominated his spirit. "He mustn't know what I've told you," he murmured. "Let him think he killed a monster."

Chenaya sat unmoving, watching him, her brow furrowed. Plainly, she also thought Gestus had killed a monster. She still didn't understand, not completely. Why should she? She hadn't stood in Uloi's embrace.

"There's something you're not telling me," she said.

The room seemed to vanish, and a dark abyss opened before Dismas. He stood poised on its edge looking down, knowing how easy it would be to fall. The whisper of alien voices called up to him. "Uloi stirred things...awakened sensations...in me." He tried to look across the abyss and saw Chenaya as if at a great distance in a tiny, dim pool of light. "Things that frighten even as they entice me," he continued. With an effort, he forced the darkness away and the abyss to close. He realized Chenaya had once more leaned forward and taken his hand.

She forced an anxious smile, and for long moments they just sat there

THE STARS ARE TEARS

like that, holding each other's hands. Finally, letting him go, she got up, crossed to the door, and opened it. Seated on a stool in the corridor, Gestus looked up with a worried expression. She beckoned him into the room.

"Let Gestus help you," she said. "You'll work it out."

He held his hand out to his lover as Chenaya left them. Yet as the door softly closed, he wondered if he ever would.

DESIRE

BY

KIM ANTIEAU

*I*n this quiet, compelling tale Kim Antieau gives us a woman, battered by and thoroughly estranged from life, who heals herself— mind, body, and spirit. She has help, though: a cat, some ghostly role models, the lonely setting of a lighthouse on the Oregon coast.

— N.G.

※

Oct 10, 1994

Should I begin this with Dear Diary? I haven't kept a journal since I was a girl of twelve. It feels silly, yet essential now. I am here, on the Oregon coast, living in the old lighthouse keeper's house. My first day. Millie, the caretaker, has left for her vacation after she assured me the house isn't haunted, despite the rumors.

"I've lived here four years and never heard a thing!" she said, giggling. Strange to see a grown woman giggle. She waved, got into her Volkswagen and drove away, leaving me with a spectacular view of the cove, the

Pacific, and the deep dark black-green forest that surrounds three sides of the keeper's house. From here I can't see the lighthouse that the Coast Guard still uses.

Inside the house, all is quiet and empty. Like me? Some metaphor for my life. Ah, I can't start feeling sorry for myself yet. I only just got here. And it was my idea. I have dreamed of this house for so long; it was time I came.

They all think I'm doing research on lighthouses and the women living in them in the nineteenth century.

But I am here to meet the ghosts. They have been calling to me all my life.

Oct 12, 1994

I slept through the entire night, can't remember dreaming. I had to put the cat in the other part of the house—this house is really two residences. The lightkeeper and his family shared the structure with his assistant and his family. The two huge twin apartments are separated by a door. The southern apartment is empty; the northern is empty except for the few rooms Millie uses: bathroom, kitchen, library, bedroom. The cat is not happy, but I'm allergic to cats. I waved to her through the beveled glass in the separating door. She promptly ran outside and tried to come in the back door. It's not going to be a pleasant three weeks for her.

Sorry, kitty.

It's midafternoon now, and I'm sitting outside on the porch. The cat sleeps at my feet. Apparently I am forgiven. The house is so quiet. I came here for a rest, for silence, to be away from all the horrors of the world, yet inside the house I am disturbed by the quiet. I played the radio yesterday and all morning.

The ghosts haven't shown themselves, if they exist at all.

It has been years since I heard one of them speak; maybe I imagined them. Maybe I was "touched" only when I was a child, and now it's gone.

Mercy I'm tired.

I haven't heard my own voice in 24 hours. Actually, I'm not certain I've ever really heard my own voice.

Oct 13, 1994

I dreamed I was stuck in an elevator. I couldn't get out, so I graded student papers. I was completely resigned to the fact that I was stuck in that stupid elevator.

For breakfast I cooked pancakes, potatoes, eggs, and sausage. Yes, me, the vegetarian. I let the cat in and fed her the sausage. She loved it.

Outside, wind strokes the house. The ocean laps on the beach below. I cannot see the parking lot or the path that leads up to the house; for that I am grateful. So far I've only seen a few tourists. They've all heeded the "no admittance" sign, however, and haven't tried to get into the house. The president of the Historical Society—they own the house—called to see how I was doing. I hated hearing my voice. I like the silence. The house creaks all around me. As yet, I have not walked up to the lighthouse.

Oct 14, 1994

I heard fireworks. As if it were the Fourth of July. They woke me. I went out, stood on the porch, and saw nothing. I heard them exploding all about me. And the lawn was silvered as if with moon light, yet it was new moon.

I think the ghosts have finally talked to me. I am still touched.

When I was a girl, ghosts always talked to me. I could walk into any place and hear conversations where there were no people; sometimes I saw people where there were no people. My mother took me to the doctor who said I was probably schizophrenic. My mother and father wept night after night. Until I went to the home of people I had never known and an Aunt Betsy, who wasn't really there, leaned over to me and said, "Tell my cousin Charlotte that I left the pearls under the floorboard in the back closet." I said it out loud. The woman Charlotte screamed and ran to her closet. She came back with a necklace of pearls, fake pearls, but pearls nonetheless. My parents took me to a priest next for an exorcism. He told them to leave me alone. I was just a troubled child in a troubled world. He winked at me as I left. I listened to the ghosts for a few years after that, trying to see if any of the chatter had anything to do with me. It didn't. Gradually, I stopped listening, until I no longer heard.

I grew up. Worked too hard. Got married. Divorced. Separated—from myself. Funny hearing Millie giggle. As if she had done something wrong. It wasn't that. It's just that I've forgotten how to laugh. I've been feeling too tired and sick for so long.

I had to put the cat out again. She left me wheezing. I vacuumed the entire house. That left me exhausted. Hopefully I got all the cat hair and didn't vacuum up any spirits.

Oct 16, 1994

Before I went to bed, I looked through the beveled glass of the adjoining door to say good night to the cat. She was nowhere in sight. On the other side of the stairs, however, someone stood in the parlor. A woman, dressed in white. I wasn't frightened. Only mildly curious. The ghosts had asked me to come to this house, hadn't they? Interrupting my dreams for months. Now I was here. I opened the door and slipped into the southern apartment. I tiptoed in the darkness across the foyer, past the stairs, to stand at the entrance of the parlor. I stared at the woman.

She looked so real. Her reddish brown hair was piled on top of her head, just barely, most of it was trying to fall down. She held something in her hand which I could not see. That wasn't unusual. I remembered when I was a child that I would often see only parts of things, people, places. A tableau with missing pieces. She tipped her hand and drank whatever I could not see. Her eyes were green, her cheeks flushed red. I could almost taste what touched her lips—dry white wine. Her dress went up her pretty neck, touching her chin, and down to her shoes. She was trying to dress up, yet she appeared disheveled. She was not made for the parlor. I could see her running outside amongst the trees. In the forest.

The forest where I never went.

She turned to me but did not see me. She smiled at some secret thought and I stared at her face. Yes, this was why I was here. This woman. I knew her. Had known her long ago. And she took my breath away.

The cat meowed. I looked down as she rubbed my legs. When I looked up again, the woman was gone.

Bridget. That was her name. I was certain of it.

Oct 17, 1994

I could hardly sleep. All I could think of was Bridget. How did I know her? Who was she? I twisted and turned and finally fell to sleep. This morning I feel strangely rested. I think I'll take a walk up to the lighthouse.

The path to the lighthouse is almost overgrown. They keep it clear enough for the Coast Guard to service the now automatic light. For a while, as I walk along the path, the wind is blocked, and I hear the distant roar of the ocean. Close by, birds call to one another, and to me, I suppose. I look to either side and the forest grows black-green and seemingly silent, until I stand still and listen. Life flourishes all around me. Ferns reach out to stroke my hands as I pass by. Briars are heavy with blackberries. I lean to pluck them from the vine, and then I hesitate. Maybe these berries have been sprayed; they would not be safe. I want them, yet I don't want to risk an allergic reaction.

I sigh and continue my walk. When did everything become so unsafe? As if the world is shot to hell and we're all left standing, battered, bruised, possibly dead, and we just don't know enough to fall down. Not "we." Me. Me. I'm tired of being the walking wounded. I'm tired of trying to figure out what is wrong with me. No doctor seems to know for certain. No therapist can untwist my inner being. I am exhausted by the struggle.

Ahead of me, the forest opens to green grass. The lighthouse beacon revolves in the autumn sunlight. Behind me the forest sings; beyond, the ocean rolls against the sand. I sigh and sink to the earth. Mother, I'm tired of trying so hard. Of being so sick.

I slept. Out under the sun, the ocean my lullaby. When I awakened, Bridget lay on the grass near me. She stared up at the sky. Her hair lay in a halo all around her, red and curly. Her dress was loose, exposing her neck and part of her chest. She was singing, but I could not hear the words. She looked more real than she had last night.

"Bridget?" I said.

She continued to sing quietly. She stopped suddenly and sat up. I followed her gaze. Coming down the path was another woman, dressed in black, a parasol shielding her head from the sun. She was pale, her hair black and pulled completely away from her face. She smiled slightly when she saw Bridget, mouthing her name, but her face remained lined with grief. I knew this woman. Her name was Suzanne.

Bridget ran to her and flung her arms around her neck. Suzanne dropped her parasol and gently embraced Bridget. Suzanne was slight, or appeared to be, bound by her grief and the corset she wore. It seemed she could hardly breathe. She reminded me of myself. What a contrast she was to Bridget, whose waist was not cinched, her hair flowing across her bare shoulders.

"Sister!" Bridget whispered.

I could hear them!

Suzanne pulled away from Bridget. "I am glad to finally be here, but I am tired. Your brother doesn't like to stop to rest, and I am reluctant to ask."

"He is stupid," Bridget said affectionately, linking arms with Suzanne. "Let me take you back to the house. I didn't expect you this soon, though I am glad to have you. I have been alone for weeks."

"And they let you stay alone?" The two women turned to walk down the path again. "I am surprised, though I shouldn't be. You have always been able to do as you please. It is your burning desire to be thoroughly free."

"My Annie, Suzannie," Bridget whispered. "I have never heard such tiredness as I hear in your voice. I will take care of you."

I jumped up to follow them, but when I reached the head of the path, the forest had swallowed their spirits.

I went back to the keeper's house. I looked through both apartments for the ghosts and found only a lonely cat. I went back to the northern house and turned on the radio. I found a station that played sad songs, and I turned up the volume while I made cookies. The cat stood on the windowsill outside watching while I kneaded dough. I thought of Bridget. How alive she seemed, even though she was dead a hundred years or so. More alive than myself. When she moved, the forest moved with her. When she moved, she was in her body. I bet she loved her body. Loved the feel of it. Made love to herself and enjoyed others making love to her.

I couldn't even remember the last time I had had sex: alone or with a partner. I hadn't expected marriage and had been equally surprised by the divorce. Now relationships seemed too frightening, or something. All that passion, on the part of the other person, and then there was me. I always felt as though I was on the outside looking in. Except for a few years between the ages of seventeen and nineteen. I had been very sexual then, before the world knew about AIDS. Then, and for a few years after, I was happy and unafraid.

And then what?

I shaped the dough into cookies and put them in the oven. Then I had started getting sick: allergies, sinus infections, depression. I looked at the world and did not like what I saw.

I guess one could say I withdrew.

Just let me get through this life and move on to the next.

Jesus. That is pathetic. When did I become this depressed and depressing woman? 40 something and I'm ready for the scrap heap?

I burned the cookies and started to cry. I cried until my eyes swelled and I got sick to my stomach. Then I threw up the burned cookies. All in all, a stellar evening. No wonder I don't date much.

OCT 18, 1994

I awaken near three and go down into the parlor of the south apartment. Bridget sits next to Suzanne, who looks ill. I kneel in the entrance and watch. A man stands with them. His features mimic Bridget's, yet he is older, without her sense of humor, dressed in a military uniform of some sort. Ah, he must be the brother, the new lighthouse keeper? His arm is across the mantel as he talks to the women. Bridget rolls her eyes and smiles at Suzanne. Suzanne hides a smile.

"Brother, can't you see your wife is tired?" Bridget says.

"Bridget—" Suzanne begins.

"I'm sorry, but he cannot expect you to run this huge house by yourself in your condition."

"What do you mean?" brother says. "In what condition? My wife is no longer with child, I thought you knew."

Suzanne gasps and quickly gets up and leaves the room. I hear the swish of her skirts. The air moves as she runs past me and up the stairs.

"Benjamin Kelly," Bridget says, standing with her hands on her hips. "You are an insensitive idiot. Your assistant and his family will not be here for another two months. Hire someone from the village to help here. In the past year, your wife has administered to the wounds of soldiers, lost a child, and moved from her childhood home all the way across the country. Give her time!"

And then, suddenly, they are all gone. I am alone, sleepy, and ready for my own dreams.

Oct 19, 1994

Today is beautiful. The sky is clear except for some strategically placed clouds which take the glare off the ocean. I sit on the grass near the house and bathe in the sun and the sea air. Both feel like gentle strokes of someone's hands.

Near to me, Bridget and Suzanne lounge. Suzanne does not look quite as ill. Today she is dressed in blue. The parasol shades only part of her face. I brush my hair and watch as Bridget gets up to stand behind Suzanne. She takes down Suzanne's long black hair and begins to gently braid it. She whispers as she braids; I can almost feel Suzanne's hair in my hands. The ocean wind takes the sound of their voices away. Suzanne's face is relaxing. Tears slowly stream down her face; she smiles as if she doesn't know they are there. Beyond them, Benjamin gives orders to a stable boy. I see stables where before I only saw rundown garages.

Their world has become my world. I have unplugged the phone. Occasional tourists walk by, but I ignore them, and they don't seem to see me. Perhaps I really have slipped into the other time.

It is all right with me.

I want to be near Bridget.

Later, I am inside, sitting at the entrance to the parlor. Bridget is there, her hair up again, as she feigns propriety. Suzanne, her face still lined, sits near Benjamin, who stands at the mantel. Occasionally, Suzanne touches her breasts, as if in pain. Gradually, another man appears. His hair is longer than Benjamin's, a bit grayer, wilder, his beard long and untidy, a big man who fills the room with his laughter and voice. I smile. Bridget likes him; she has heard his stories before but listens with pleasure. She glances at Suzanne, who smiles at the new man. Dobson, Bridget calls him.

"Mr. Dobson will visit us every few months," Bridget says. "Sometimes with his crew, sometimes not. He brings us our supplies."

"I have heard you are a fine tender," Benjamin says. "A fine tender!" Benjamin tries to be jovial, but he doesn't have the spirit for it.

The scene shifts as the cat rubs my legs. I lean down to pet her. "You're always spoiling the good parts," I whisper.

Oct 21, 1994

I went up into the woods today. Barefoot. Yes, I did. My feet hurt, yet it was glorious to dig my toes into the humus. I felt like the Goddess Diana running through the forest, crying for my hounds. I stopped at the briar patch and plucked ripe succulent blackberries and dropped them into my mouth. My body liked it all. Listen to me, talking about my body as if it were separate from me. *I* liked it.

When I came out of the woods, I nearly stumbled over Bridget and Dobson, walking arm and arm. She rested her head on his shoulder as they walked and he squeezed her waist.

"Where is that brother of yours?" Dobson asked.

"He's at the lighthouse, shining up the brass. He'll be gone all day."

"And your sister-in-law?"

"She's asleep, poor thing. She lost a child less than a month ago. Her heart and body still ache for the child."

Dobson took Bridget's hand and pulled her toward the stable.

"I don't want to hear about anyone but you, lass," he said. I ran to follow. "I've missed ye these past months!"

Bridget laughed and followed him into the stable. She backed into a wall and pulled Dobson toward her. They started kissing. She pulled at his shirt, he stroked her breasts. I went closer. She was breathing heavily, laughing, murmuring. She lifted her dress. My breathing quickened. She moved toward him, he pushed into her. I gasped and fell to my knees. I could feel him in me. Could feel her. Moving together. Moving. Finding pleasure. I could feel the wood against my back, Dobson inside Bridget, me. He knew how to please her. They cried out, shuddering and pushing together. An orgasm moved up through me, out my hands, feet, and head.

They disappeared, and I was left alone lying in the grass, in plain view of anyone who cared to see, quivering with orgasm. I curled up on the grass, luxuriating in the feel of it, rubbing it against me. I didn't care if anyone saw. It was about time the world saw the face of a happy woman or two.

Oct 22, 1994

I felt silly and blissful all day. Bridget. She was amazing. She had called me to this place to remember her. Remember how much I loved her. Remember how I had loved her body.

I had loved my own body at one time, I suppose. I must have. We come into this world all love. But something happened. It is sometimes difficult to remain loving and clear and strong in the face of so much—I'm not certain there's a word for it—so much hatred? We are not held in high esteem in this world. I thought I'd fix that by teaching women studies courses, making certain young women were strong and able, able to see themselves as whole beings. I always told my students to connect with other women, yet I had neglected to do that myself. It had seemed safer just to work, write, and be by myself.

Now I'm not certain I was even with myself. I was totally alone. Disconnected from others *and* myself.

I need to find that connectedness again.

I think the orgasm helped a bit with that.

I am giggling as I write this.

Oct 23, 1994

Suzanne sits in a huge bathtub while Bridget pours steaming water over her. She is a small pale woman except for her breasts; they look heavy, almost distorted. She cradles them gently.

Bridget sits on the floor behind Suzanne and begins brushing Suzanne's hair. The morning sunlight christens the room gold.

"You should never have married my brother," Bridget says.

"Don't say that," Suzanne says. "I have known him all my life. He is a good friend."

"You married him because you were tired," Bridget says.

Suzanne nods and looks at her breasts. "It is true. The hunger strikes exhausted me."

"Did you think that would really get women the vote?"

Suzanne nods again. "Yes. It will happen. Women are dying so that it will happen. And then the war." She stops.

"I know, sister, I know."

"You don't know what I saw." Her eyes fill with tears. My chest hurts. "They were just boys. Blood soaking into the Earth. We had to beg the doctors to get them to let us help."

"Maybe if women didn't help men during war, there would be no war," Bridget says.

Suzanne stiffens and blinks away her tears. "Do you really think so?"

"No, no, I'm sorry. If you hadn't helped, more boys would have died; that is the only difference it would have made."

"Now it's over, and I wanted to have child after child, to make up for the ones who died. Their body parts were scattered all over those hospitals. Legs here. Arms there. Do you think—do you wonder how their souls ever survived? Did they leave parts of their souls with those lost limbs? We're all so scattered."

Even back then? I feel scattered every day. Pieces of me littering the path I've taken.

"It hasn't always been like that," Bridget says. "It will not always be that way."

"Truly? The child that grew within me couldn't stay. My grief killed her. She could not bear it, so she let go of me. I killed my own dearest child."

She weeps openly now; Bridget strokes her hair and keens quietly.

After a time, Suzanne stands. The water drips from her naked body. Bridget gets a towel and gently helps her out of the tub. Neither woman seems embarrassed by Suzanne's nakedness. She drapes the towel over a chair and sits on it.

"My breasts ache so for my child," Suzanne says, her voice choked with tears. "I cannot let her go, buried in the Earth though she may be; my breasts long for her mouth." The grief lines her face again. She will be scarred for life by all that she has seen.

Bridget kneels at Suzanne's feet. Her hair is spread across her bare white shoulders. The sun shines through her night dress, silhouetting her body. She cups Suzanne's breast in her hand, leans forward, and puts her lips around her dark nipple. Suzanne strokes Bridget's hair, leans back and weeps silently as the other woman suckles her. I taste the liquid, mother's milk, sweet and bitter at the same time, like nothing I have ever tasted or felt, except maybe like the humus under my bare feet. Tears stream down Bridget's face and into her mouth, mingling with Suzanne's milk.

I close my eyes and weep out loud.

I wander from house to house. Outside it rains. The cat follows me, imitating my restlessness. I have loved Bridget forever, I know that now.

I am desperate to see her again, but the house remains empty save for myself and the cat. We turn on the radio and dance to strange music. I dance; the cat watches. I twirl around the empty house and laugh at the cat watching me. My laughter reminds me of Bridget.

I go into the modern bathroom and take a long bath. When I get out, I dry myself and then walk from room to room, naked. How wonderful to feel the air against my skin. I put a blanket down in the middle of the empty parlor and give myself a massage. I don't know if I have ever before touched every part of my body. I like the feel of my own butt, my breasts, even the flabby skin on my arms. The cat licks herself.

I get up, tingly from my massage, and dance naked around the parlor.

I find Bridget and Suzanne in my bed. Suzanne's black hair is spread out behind her. Black and gorgeous. Hair everywhere. Bridget's red curly hair. They hug and squeeze their breasts together. Suzanne flinches slightly and Bridget leans over and kisses Suzanne's breasts, one at a time, her tongue lingering on one, her hand moving up Suzanne's thigh. I lie next to them, feeling their hands on me as they stroke each other, feeling their orgasms as they move against each other, arms and legs twined around the other, their skin like beacons in my dark room. Contentedly, I fall asleep beside them.

OCT ? 1994

I have followed them for days. Or they me. I watch them squat on the Earth, naked, running from house to house, loving each other, pretending not to when others are around. The grief falls away from Suzanne. She becomes beautiful with love. Even Benjamin seems to relax. Flowers fill the parlor, kitchen, and bedrooms. Briars crawl up the sides of the house. The women wear their hair down, their feet bare. At night, they play in the ocean.

I am with them. A ghost to the ghosts. I am glad Bridget had a great love, was loved by a woman like Suzanne. And vice versa. When Bridget laughs, the world shifts. Things change. I love them both, but Bridget is who I have always wanted to be.

In just a few days, I will have to go home and leave them behind.

OCT 31, 1994

The cat and I decorated the house for Halloween. My favorite holiday. It has been decades since I celebrated. How could I have forgotten how fun it was? I dressed in a long silvery dress of Millie's. The cat tried to eat pumpkin seeds and quickly spat them out. I laughed at her; my laughter filled the house and my body, and the world seemed to change.

The entire house transforms as we put the Jack-o-Lantern out on the porch. I notice for the first time that the cat sees the ghosts, too. She watches now as they flit to and fro, dressed in costumes of one sort or another. Did they invite some of the villagers in for a party?

Suzanne is more beautiful than I have ever seen her, clothed in a purple low cut dress, a purple mask over her eyes. She dances with Benjamin and he whispers in her ear. Dobson is there, bellowing and flirting with every woman near him. When Bridget enters the room, everyone stops, for a moment, because she is so beautiful. She is the fairy queen, dressed in a green dress that matches the design of Suzanne's. Her mask is green, too, darker than her eyes, highlighting her long red hair. She carries a wand in one hand.

Tomorrow I leave this place. Tomorrow I leave Bridget.

I go upstairs to an empty room and sit on the floor. I came to this house sick and depressed. I have learned to feel again, to rejoice in my body, the land, all that is around me. I am myself again. The cat licks my hand and I start to cry.

"Who is that keening as if there be no tomorrow?"

I look up. Bridget stands in the doorway looking down at me. She holds her hand out to me, "What's troublin' ya, love?"

I stand and take her hand. I can touch it! Feel it. As real as my own hand.

"Will you be havin' a dance with me?" she asks.

"I'd love one," I say. I put my arm around her waist. I feel her move beneath her dress. She is so free. Nothing holds her in, back. She is a goddess, a queen. My love.

"Sweetheart," she says, as our dresses swish across the floor, "this is your last night. It is supposed to be a celebration."

"You know about me?"

She laughs. The world shifts as always when she laughs. I recognize her laugh.

"Of course I know about you," she says.

She laughs again. I *know* that laugh—I *remember* her laugh. It is my own. My laugh! She smiles as we dance. It is myself I see in her eyes: it is myself I have always seen in her eyes.

I step away from her and she smiles.

"That's it, sweetheart," she says. "You'd just forgotten who you were and who you are." She touches her lips gently to mine, and then she is gone and the house is quiet. I twirl around the empty room, smiling, laughing. I am in love with myself. Finally.

Nov 1, 1994

I cry and kiss the cat good-bye. Millie giggles as she hugs me, and I laugh. I wave good-bye to the house and all my ghosts. The cat watches me drive away. I am ready to go home: I am myself again.

YOUNG LADY WHO LOVED CATERPILLARS

BY

JESSICA AMANDA SALMONSON

*D*uring a six week period when I was particularly
angry with the world, Jessica Amanda Salmonson
kept me sane: I read a few entries from her
scrupulously researched The Encyclopedia of
Amazons *every night and fell asleep thinking that any world which had
contained such women—and those in times past who could believe in their
existence—could not be too bad a place.*

*Salmonson tells us: "The young lady who loved caterpillars was a real
person who lived in 11th century Japan. I always intended to write a story
about her, and now I have." It is an elegant paean to that ever appropriate
sentiment: carpe diem.*

—N.G.

❋

There lived at the Mikado's court a young lady who loved insects. She
was the daughter of a minor palace official. Next door there lived the
daughter of the provincial inspector in service of the royal court of Heian-
kyo. The inspector's daughter would gaze at times into the garden next
door, observing the girl who loved insects and thinking absurd thoughts
about her. If anyone asked why she was always gazing moonstruck at that
strange young lady, she would laugh and make it a joke, saying, "She

doesn't pluck her eyebrows! What an absurd girl she is!"

As to the young lady who loved insects, her parents' devotion to her was such that you might say they spoiled her. They never discouraged her great fondness for insects, and she was always in the garden collecting them. She considered herself a scientist. She constructed all sorts of cages and boxes so that she could see how insects grew and changed from one form into another. Day and night she would watch them with her forelocks pushed behind her ears, when any proper noblewoman would have her forelock combed and hanging neatly from her temples.

Caterpillars especially fascinated her, not because they changed from funny furry things into splendid butterflies, but because they seemed so pensive, like herself. She would cup them in her hands and watch them crawl about. She fed them bits of tender leaves which they devoured in a careful and methodical manner. It was for love of them that she stopped plucking her eyebrows, as was done by all proper court ladies. She thought her eyebrows looked like two caterpillars, and, no matter what others said of it, she felt they made her appear rather studious and clever.

The other young girls in attendance were scared of worms and bewildered by the girl who loved them. But the girl who lived next door slowly began to overcome her shyness and asked the names of all the insects in Young Lady Caterpillar-Eyes' collection.

Although the girl who loved insects knew a great deal about their natural history, she had no books about them, and did not know their official names. So she had given each one its own personal name like Willow Hopper, Peony Petal Chomper, Under A Rock Squeezer, and Sweet Smelling Slimy Fellow. Her girlfriend next door was delighted by these tiny pets, and by their names, though she was unwilling to touch them.

Now Lady Caterpillar-Eyes' parents wanted to say something about her erratic behavior as well as her new friendship, for the court ladies gossiped no end about a proper girl and the strange one always together looking at bugs. But when her mother and father spoke to her about her eccentricities, she contradicted them strongly and demanded to know why they would remonstrate with her. She insisted that humanity had a noble purpose, and achieved it by contemplating little things. She said that she was honored to have such a pupil as Kodayo, who visited her daily, and there was no reason for anyone to complain about anything.

Her parents said, "You may be right, but people are talking. If you could hear what they say about your ghastly caterpillars!"

"Why should I care what people say of me? How childish they are! Things have meaning only when we inquire into them. What is so ugly about a caterpillar? They are furry like a red fox. They turn into butterflies with wings more beautiful than court kimonos. When people talk, tell them their silk kimonos were spun by just such things as these!"

At this her parents were dumbfounded and continued to let her have her way. But when the other court ladies heard of it, they said, "She talks cleverly, but has such horrible playthings. Does she think she will turn into a butterfly someday? Her kimono has garden soil on it, and her hair is always stringy. And that Kodayo! What kind of girl is it who constantly waits on another girl?"

So Kodayo began to feel a lot of pressure. Even though she was of the court next door, the gossip spread. At first she said, "Young Lady Caterpillar-Eyes is pleasing like a shrine-clown or an acrobat. Don't you enjoy a funny show like that?" But nobody fell for such an excuse, so Kodayo began to say, "You shouldn't make fun of her. She is like a Buddha, contemplating little things the way Buddha watches us!" But when the girls of both houses began to call her Bug Disciple, she was ashamed, and stopped visiting Lady Caterpillar-Eyes.

So absorbed was Lady Caterpillar-Eyes in her studies that at first she hardly noticed something was wrong. She would be watching a colorful spider crawling about in a chrysanthemum, but her eyes would wander to the garden path where Kodayo usually came strolling from next door.

After a few days, her parents noticed she wasn't eating, and that she had grown very pale. She had gathered up her collection of insects to take with her into the screened bamboo enclosure that was her bed area, and she stayed in there all the time, only going into the garden long enough to gather the things her pets liked to eat, and surreptitiously looking up and down the paths for Kodayo.

No one knew what bothered her. The court ladies suspected they were the cause of the poor girl's suffering, for they had teased her so horribly. They began to feel a little guilty about her. So they would get together just near enough for her to overhear what they were saying, and they had conversations that were intended to be conciliatory toward Lady Caterpillar-Eyes.

"How enviable!" they said. "Others speak of the same old flowers, but our court buzzes with news of caterpillars!"

"Tell me, Hyoe, how do you think I would look with caterpillar-eyes? If I stopped plucking my eyebrows, maybe they would keep my face warm this winter."

"Our mistress has made inquiries that are most profound. Who else would display caterpillars and remark that they are butterflies?"

Despite their good intentions, the girls could not help but titter, and shuffled away with their fans held over their mouths.

Lady Caterpillar-Eyes had not heard them in any case, but sighed deeply, watching one of her pupa. A butterfly was emerging from it. Now this newborn butterfly, still crinkled and awkward, had previously been her favorite caterpillar, and she had told it all her secrets and troubles. When it first became a pupa she was sad, as though it had departed permanently. And she had to admit, now that its wings were drying out and it became, before her very eyes, as fine and beautiful as a proper court lady with well-arranged kimono, she could not speak with it from her heart as formerly.

She was sad, too, because she knew that butterflies were the most transient of friends. They never ate, but only lived to mate once, then died. The court ladies should ponder that as they arranged themselves so prettily! If they thought of themselves as nothing more than pleasing things to gaze upon, then what would they think of themselves when time robbed them of youthful good looks?

So now her favorite caterpillar was a gorgeous butterfly ready to fulfill its destiny. She let it go free from her bamboo enclosure, so that it could fly into the garden and find others of its kind.

But the butterfly had its own plan. It flitted from the hallway to the porch and across the garden to the neighboring court, then flew across the porch and down the hallway into the room where Kodayo was reading a pillow-book. The butterfly lighted on the pillow-book and moved its wings slowly up and down. Kodayo was delighted by its unexpected appearance. She said, "Why, how are you today, little butterfly?"

"I am quite fine," it said.

Kodayo was astonished. "My! I never knew that butterflies spoke!"

"I am a Buddha of my kind, and watch over the small things from paradise. I have been born into the world for a single day to tell you that your mistress suffers, and in time will die without you. Think of my short life, then think of yours. Think of the lives of all the court ladies, whose chance at love is very slight and of a superficial kind. If they could find someone besides themselves to admire, their whole lives would be rewarding. As it is, they will someday be sent from the court to return to their various families, and have marriages arranged for them with strangers, and spend all the rest of their days regretting the loss of their few glorious years at court."

Kodayo set the pillow book down carefully, and, as the butterfly-buddha lingered, she bowed to it, her face to the mat. When she looked up, it was gone.

Now Kodayo sent servants to fetch her a dozen cricket-cages, and she spent the rest of the afternoon in the garden, where she found a mantis, a snail, and a hairy caterpillar, each of which was a particularly fine specimen with something unique about it; and she found a green beetle, a red inchworm, and a yellow millipede. She put these, and other lucky discoveries, in the quaint little bamboo cages. She gave each one food that it liked, and arranged the cages in a nice display.

Then she wrote a letter that said, "Come and see my little family, who I've named Kerao (Mole-cricket-man), Hikimaro (Toad-man), Inagomaro (Grasshopper-man), Ambiko (Millipede-woman), and others who are living happily with me. Some of them can sing, as my heart is singing, to see again my precious Lady Caterpillar-Eyes."

And she ended with a poem, that read:

> "Crawling, I shall follow you,
> And be at your side forever.
> As long as I am without end,
> So is my heart yours forever."

Kodayo never plucked her eyebrows again. The two girls were known, to the ends of their lives, as Big Caterpillar-Eyes, and Little Caterpillar-Eyes. When they were old, they lived together in a forest cottage near a shrine. People visited them in great numbers during the springtime, to see their caterpillars emerge as butterflies by the thousands, whirling about the cottage and rising into the sky like a papery rainbow tempest.

IN MEMORY OF

BY

DON BASSINGTHWAITE

*T*he very first short story White Wolf ever bought, back in
1993, was from Don Bassingthwaite for our Book of the
Damned anthology. I've read almost everything Don has
written. His work is an excellent cross between action and
introspection. Here he gives us a look at brotherly love and vengeance. Bragi is
something of a composer and Fenris is a wealthy playboy. Why are they rivals?
Why do they hate each other? How might it play itself out?
— S. P.

※

"What do you think, Bragi?" Anthony stood in front of the big iron-
framed mirror and considered his reflection. He wore briefs, white cotton
bright against deep tanned skin, and heavy socks, gray wool sagging slightly
around his ankles. Bragi slid his arms around Anthony's muscular chest.
He rested his blond beard on Anthony's shoulder, and considered their
reflections in the mirror. He was half a head taller than Anthony, hairy
where Anthony was smooth, fair where Anthony was dark, muscular by
nature where Anthony spent hours at the gym. He thought Anthony

had the better end of the bargain. He would have liked to experience the deep, ecstatic ache that Anthony felt after a workout, but he never would. The equipment at the gym simply wasn't enough; he could have used it without stop for an entire day and felt nothing. Of course, he could never tell Anthony that. Anthony wouldn't understand. Anthony was a lawyer. Bragi was a musician and a songwriter.

He kissed Anthony's neck. "I think," he said, "that I should just tie you down and not let you go out tonight."

Anthony laughed and pulled away. Bragi let him go. "It's just a bunch of the guys from the team, Bragi. We won the tournament, remember? I seem to recall that you came up for air long enough to notice that. I'm sure I saw you at the party." He picked up a pair of jeans and slid them on.

"I carried you home. I think you probably saw two of me."

"I could never see enough of you." Anthony tweaked Bragi's chest hair. "Come on. One night won't make a difference. Your deadline isn't that tight."

"It is. I need to finish this score." He watched Anthony pull a tight, white T-shirt over his head. "Why so much trouble for just a bunch of guys from the team?"

"I'm gay, Bragi. If I don't at least try to look good, they'll take away my queer card. Whassa matter? You don't like?" He posed, pouting, lips pursed in a Marilyn Monroe pucker. Bragi tried to hold back a snort of amusement, but couldn't. Anthony shifted, posing again and again, mugging shamelessly, until Bragi collapsed onto the bed with laughter. Anthony fell down on top of the bigger man. "Please come."

Bragi sighed. "I can't." One hand groped over the edge of the bed, feeling for Anthony's boots. He shoved them at him. "Here. Hurry up. Your ride's going to be here any minute." He pushed Anthony to his feet. "One more week. I promise. Then we'll go out. Just the two of us."

"Verbal contracts are binding." The telephone rang. Anthony grabbed for it. "Hello? Hey, Mark." Bragi watched him as he hopped and twisted, trying to pull on his boots and talk on the phone at the same time. The exchange was brief, and he hung up. "Mark says hello. He's down in the lobby. His car's at the curb."

"Say hello back. And sit down before you fall over."

At the door, he kissed Anthony. "Have a good time. Be careful."

"I will. Don't worry." Then he was gone. Bragi waited by the door for a few more moments, then went out onto the balcony. A dozen stories down, Mark's Jag idled. After a minute, Anthony emerged from the building and got in. The car pulled away, down the street, and around the corner, vanishing from sight. If he strained his ears, Bragi could still distinguish the distinctive grumble of the car's engine, but it was just one sound in the roar of the city night.

There was a full moon rising. The light of it blotted out the stars and cast a depthless blue glow across the city.

Among the orange trees in their silver pots, certain nobles of the court met each evening. Those in attendance at the gatherings varied from night to night, depending upon their duties or their pleasures. The artificial orange groves were a pleasant meeting place, an escape from the heat inside the palace and, more importantly, from the smell. Versailles stank, a hundred odors mingling in its trapped air: human, animal, good food, bad food, wood smoke, tallow smoke, tobacco smoke, too much perfume, too much incense. The scents of the breeze (when it didn't come from the direction of Paris) and of the orange trees were far more agreeable. Unfortunately, those very qualities made the trees attractive to many members of the court, and the groves were crowded. That didn't bother the gathered nobles, however. Their meetings were hardly secret (and barely meetings). Anyone could pause and join in their conversation. Acceptance into what court gossips called their "brotherhood" was more select and not for the timid or those who feared the frowns of the Church.

"Have you noticed that young Tuscan who arrived last month?" The Comte de Vermandois drew on his pipe. The tobacco glowed red in the shadows, glinting off the silver chasing worked into the long stem. The pipe was a gift from the king, a mark of favor for one of his bastard children.

Callot grinned. "Giovan? Have you been away, my lord? You could pave a path with the courtiers willing to lie down for him."

The Comte sucked on his pipe again and blew a stream of smoke at his friend. "My attention has been otherwise occupied with heavy matters, Philip."

"As heavy as two oranges, or so I'm told." The abbé of Beaurain reached up to cup a ripening globe overhead. "If the branch was worthy of the fruit, I'm sure your attention was focused on allowing it easy passage."

His comment drew laughter out of the other nobles around and a sharp flare from the Comte's pipe. "My title," he retorted, "is the result of my eminent father sowing his seed in my mother, and not an Eminent Father sowing his seed in me." A chorus of renewed laughter roared out and this time the abbé flushed. He owed his position partly to his father's wealth, but mostly to the favor of a certain cardinal, and he disliked being reminded of the fact. The Comte settled himself more comfortably against the edge of a silver pot. "But about Giovan. Is he still the pet of that poxy old Roman?"

"He's been emancipated." Callot's ever-present grin grew wider. "But you're too late. He's already sold his soul."

The Comte cursed. "To who?"

"To me, my lord."

The nearness of that voice, rough like the coarse velvet that blanketed the king's best horses, made the Comte choke on his smoke. Helpful hands reached out to pound at his back, but he pushed them away and turned to look at the big Dane with the blond mustache who stood behind him. "Sometimes I think you are a sorcerer as well as an astrologer, Master Loksson."

Loksson inclined his head humbly. "I am as good a Christian as any at Versailles, my lord. The abbé excepted, of course."

More laughter, even from the abbé himself this time. "You reek of holiness and Hungary water, Loksson. What's in the stars?"

"A full moon rises in the house of Sagittarius." The Dane shielded his eyes dramatically and looked at the horizon. "And Saturn descends in Virgo." He swept his hand down and smiled. "My lords, I have someone with me I would like to introduce into your august company." He gestured. Giovan stepped out of the shadows and made a smooth bow, a gesture marred only by the white-haired cat that twined around his ankles. Loksson clicked his tongue at the cat and it stalked over to him.

"A sorcerer, indeed," observed the Comte. "You produce the very subject of our conversation—and you keep a cat."

"As much kept by the cat as keep him." Loksson picked up the animal and cradled it in his arms as he began formally introducing Giovan to the French nobles under the orange trees.

Bragi put down his pen and looked out the window at the moon, a pale ghost in the black sky. Maybe he should have gone with Anthony tonight. Not that he didn't trust him. Not that he didn't think a couple couldn't spend time apart. Anthony had his own friends. Bragi wouldn't interfere. He didn't have that many friends of his own—he was a loner. He had made Anthony promise not to try and drag him out to social engagements when he didn't want to go. Natural extroverts like Anthony didn't always understand why it was important to be alone sometimes. Bragi needed time to break with the world, to listen to his inner voice, to recharge.

And then there were the times when part of him craved noise and excitement. He considered the staff paper before him. The staves were half-filled with scrawled notes. A stack of completed pages lay on top of the piano. He hadn't touched the ivory keys in an hour and half, relying instead on his memory and imagination to tell him what the music would sound like. Bragi scratched his jaw beneath his beard, then shoved a hand through his hair. The moon was beautiful tonight. The sound of the last note he had written hung in his mind. Suddenly it seemed flat. Dull.

Anthony was right. He had been working on this score for too long. He needed to go out. He needed noise and excitement, an atmosphere of stimulation. Quiet solitude could recharge, but it could also lead to stagnancy. Bragi pushed himself away from the piano and went out onto the balcony once more. The air was cool, and it smelled sweet, as though the wind was pulling the air of the upper atmosphere down closer to earth. He stretched in the moonlight. The full moon always seemed to bring a rush of energy. He kept meaning to keep track of the moon phases and compare them to his moods, but had never gotten around to it.

Somewhere out among the glittering lights of the city, Anthony laughed and drank and danced with Mark and the other members of his team. Bragi wasn't sure where they had been going tonight, but it wouldn't be hard to find out. He brought Anthony to mind, remembering everything about him. The way he looked, from shining hair to sleek skin. How he looked naked. How he looked clothed. Specifically, how he looked tonight. The way Anthony smelled. The sound of Anthony's voice. The feel of Anthony's hands against his body, the feel of Anthony's body under his hands, the feel of their two bodies pressed together. He built an image of Anthony in his mind, as perfect as he could make it. He remembered Anthony just as he remembered the sound of the piano and wrote music without playing. Memory wasn't static.

Something about the image of Anthony shifted, transcending memory, matching itself with reality. New details filled themselves in: the way Anthony looked right now, what he was doing, what was around him. Bragi smiled. What was, is. The Art of Memory had always come easily to him. He recognized Anthony's surroundings. A dance club just on the shady side of downtown. Mark and the others were with him. Colored lights flashed across his face. To judge by the flush on Anthony's cheeks, he'd had just a little too much to drink just a little too quickly. He was smiling, too. If Bragi hadn't already reached a decision, that sweet, licentious grin would have forced him to one. He went back inside to change.

Giovan shifted sleepily. The white-haired cat leaped to the floor, vanishing in the shadows, as Loksson slid back into the bed. The night was warm, even more so inside the palace, and Giovan slept with the thin sheets down around his waist. He lay on his back, one arm up over his head. A few stray leaves of rosemary clung to his sweat-damp forearm. A particular blend of the herb and four others sprinkled over the bedclothes and the ticking, together with frequent airings, made Loksson's bed the sweetest in the palace. The herbs, the airings, and Giovan, that was.

Propped up on one elbow, the Dane traced the muscles of his lover's chest. Giovan stirred. Loksson licked the end of his finger and gently caressed the sleeper's nipple. Giovan twitched. His lips curled. Loksson blew across the slick skin. Giovan moved his arm to look up at him. "Back so soon?"

"I can't spend all night looking up at the stars." Loksson smiled. "Sometimes I have to return to the heaven under my very nose."

Giovan's arm unfolded, and he reached out to smooth Loksson's thick, blond hair. "I had a dream."

"Did you leave a mess on the sheets again?"

"Not that kind of dream." The arm came down. Giovan turned onto his side so that he lay face to face and chest to chest with Loksson. "I dreamed that there was something at our window." He nodded past Loksson at the narrow window of the bedchamber. They were fortunate to have it. Many of the cramped apartments in Versailles had no windows at all. "A raven, trying to get in. It wasn't being noisy the way ravens usually are. It was quiet, tapping on the glass with its beak. After several minutes, you came in from the sitting room. You were completely naked."

"Was I?" asked Loksson playfully. He touched his fingers to Giovan's lips. The young Tuscan smiled but pulled back.

"I'm not finished. You opened the window and let the raven into the room. It flew into the sitting room. You turned to follow it, but first you looked at me. It felt like you were staring at me forever—you know how time is in dreams." He smiled. After a moment, Loksson smiled back.

"I know. Then what happened?"

"You were gone. As if I had blinked and while my eyes had closed, you had left with the raven. Actually," he admitted a little sheepishly, "I think I just woke up."

"You say that as if there were something wrong with waking up."

"It seems like such a...dull ending to a dream."

"A dream is only a dream, no matter how it ends." Loksson pulled Giovan close to him. "But let me tell you what I saw tonight. The Marquis d'Auch—"

"The Marquis' chambers are practically under the eaves! How did you manage to see in there?"

Loksson hushed him with a kiss. "I have my ways. And I didn't say the

Marquis was in his own apartment, did I? He was in Louvaine's chambers. With Louvaine's second daughter, the one with the rosebud mouth, and some old hag from the kitchens. The hag had a large wooden paddle." He grinned. "Louvaine's daughter had a bowel movement. Both marked the Marquis."

Giovan hissed in disgusted amusement. "If that story was known, it would be enough to drive d'Auch and Louvaine away from court, and Louvaine's daughter to a convent."

"Wouldn't it? And Mademoiselle is betrothed as well, I believe." Loksson tweaked Giovan's nipple. His other hand slid down beneath the sheets. "Let me tell you what else I saw."

By the time he had finished, the sun was rising and both he and Giovan were sweating from more than just the heat. Giovan lay curled against him. The white-haired cat sat on the window ledge, watching them. Loksson kissed Giovan's neck. The Tuscan sighed. His eyes were practically closed. "I remember something else from my dream," he murmured.

"What?"

"You had no mustache." He pressed himself against Loksson. "You were more handsome than I've ever seen you."

"Was I?" asked Loksson.

When Anthony came off the dance floor, Bragi was waiting for him. Anthony started to grin, started to say "You came after all," but stopped. He frowned in confusion, then burst into laughter. "You shaved!"

"Do you like it?"

Anthony stepped closer, reaching up to feel the smooth line of his partner's jaw. He touched the pale skin delicately. "Yes. Very much." He slid one hand around Bragi's waist. The other continued to explore his shaven face. "But your beard?"

"It will grow back if I let it. I decided I wanted a change—and I thought you might like it, too."

"I do." Anthony kissed him and pulled back smiling. "I never wanted to mention it before, but sometimes it was a little uncomfortable."

"Like when?"

"Like in the summer. Like just after I'd shaved. Like in the shower. You wouldn't believe what it felt like when it was wet." He smiled fondly. His other hand went around Bragi's waist and he began to sway back and forth, rubbing against Bragi. He tugged him toward the dance floor. "Come on. They're playing our song."

"I didn't think that was our song."

"It could be."

Bragi smiled. "All right. But only one dance. Then I want us to get out of here."

"Why?" Anthony stopped. He looked pained. "You just got here. Me and the guys haven't been here that long. We're having a good time."

Bragi kept smiling. He bent his head down and whispered in Anthony's ear. Anthony's eyes went wide, stunned, then suddenly he crumpled. Bragi held him upright easily. Half-carrying him, he began to make his way toward the door.

Giovan lay asleep in the moonlight streaming through the window. Pale radiance turned his skin to marble as it did on so many nights. He was beautiful. More than beautiful. Somehow, in spite of the lustful advances of courtiers and the easy decadence of the games of court, Versailles hadn't corrupted him. He was Galatea, a statue brought to life but still retaining the unchanging perfection of stone. A hand moving as if of its own accord reached out and touched the living marble.

Giovan woke. Liquid eyes shone dark in the moonlight. He didn't seem surprised. "Is this another dream?"

"No."

"Then you're real?"

"Yes." He didn't move, but just stared down at the young Tuscan. He shouldn't do this. It was wrong. But he had watched Giovan for so long and he couldn't bear to simply watch any longer. His mouth was dry suddenly, like burlap. He swallowed. "Would it matter if I weren't?"

Giovan was silent. "A dream," he said, "is only a dream. But it can be a wonderful dream." He pushed back the bedclothes and slid over, making room. "Do you have a name?"

The sheets were smooth, rustling beneath him as he sank down beside Giovan. His hands touched the marble of Giovan's body again. Giovan's face was close to his. He hesitated. Giving his name made this treachery seem worse. If he didn't have a name, it would be easy to pretend that this was nothing. That it was only a dream. But he didn't want it to be just a dream. Giovan's eyes said that he wanted it to be more as well.

"Bragi," he breathed finally. The inches between their faces vanished. Their bodies merged in the moonlight. There was urgency to their lovemaking. Both were aware of what little time they had. And yet in spite of urgency, there was tenderness. Skin and lips and bodies and muscles moving slowly, smoothly; moving together. Sounds were sighs, not gasps, not cries. Afterward, they lay twined together, face to face. Giovan looked into Bragi's eyes.

"You're not like—"

Bragi put a finger to his lips. "Don't say his name. Please"

Giovan nodded. "You're not like him. You're gentle." His arms tightened. "He has a temper."

"I know." Bragi began to pull himself away from Giovan. "You must never tell him about this."

"I know." Giovan held onto his hand. "Wait. Who are you? Tell me who you are."

Bragi tugged his hand from Giovan's grasp, then smoothed his hair, pushing his head back down onto the pillow. "No. I can't. Remember this as a dream. It will be safer for you." He stepped away. "Close your eyes." Obediently, Giovan's eyes slid shut, but Bragi watched a moment longer. The Tuscan's eyes cracked open again. Bragi shook his head. "Keep them closed."

When he was sure that Giovan had obeyed him, he turned silently and, with three swift, long strides, left the bedchamber for the sitting room. He cast one look of sweet regret back at the moonlit bedchamber. Then he Changed.

And the next thing he saw as the darkness of Change ebbed away from his eyes, was Giovan peering around the doorframe from the bedchamber, face paler than even the finest marble.

Bragi leaped, Changing back as he did. He grabbed Giovan by the shoulder and slammed him against the wall. "What did I tell you?" he hissed.

Giovan's eyes were wide. His mouth moved, but only a rasp came out. Finally, he swallowed and tried again. "You...what are you?"

Bragi grimaced. "I can't tell you. You can't know." He grabbed Giovan's chin and forced him to meet his gaze. "Listen to me, and this time do what I say. Never talk about what you saw. Never talk about me."

"But—"

"*Never!*" Bragi leaned forward and kissed him fiercely. "I love you, Giovan, but your sanity—perhaps your life—depends on your silence. Do you understand?"

Giovan nodded slowly, then blurted out, "Is Loksson like you?"

Bragi growled a word. It was a word that an elder had taught him, a word that was remembered only by his kind, a scrap of First Speech. The power of that word, a simple command, was enough to stun Giovan. Bragi lifted him, replaced him in the bed, brushed his eyes closed, and drew the sheets over him. Then he Changed again, though this time he didn't leave the room. There was no point now. Giovan had seen him. Bragi could only hope that the young man had the sense to obey his command of silence.

The white-haired cat jumped onto the window ledge and curled up, waiting for the raven to come home.

"Hey Mark!" Bragi pushed his way through the crowd in the club. Mark turned drunkenly, searching for him. "Mark!" He clapped Anthony's friend on the shoulder.

"Bragi!" Mark wobbled, thrown off balance by even that light impact. "How's Anthony?"

How? Maybe Mark meant where. "I don't know. I'm looking for him myself. Have you seen him?"

Mark grinned. "He got away from you, eh? Probably wanted to keep dancing." He twitched his hips out of time with the music. "That guy would dance on a broken leg. He sure looked like hell though. I didn't think he'd even had that much to drink."

Bragi blinked and frowned. "What are you talking about?"

"I saw you carrying him out a while ago. Anthony looked like he was half-unconscious. Sorry I couldn't get over to help, but it looked like you had everything under control."

"I just got here."

"Bullshit," Mark laughed. "Before he went belly-up, Anthony was all over you." He squinted at Bragi suddenly. "Fuck, maybe I should knock off the beer before I end up like Anthony. I could have sworn you'd shaved off your beard before."

Suddenly there was lead in Bragi's stomach. No. "Mark, are you sure Anthony wasn't just all over some other guy?"

Mark snorted. "Like he would cheat on you?"

Molten lead eating through his guts. "If he would, I'd know he was safe." Bragi whirled, thrusting himself through the crowd. People yelled at him angrily, more than one of them splashed by spilled beer. He ignored them. He ignored Mark yelling after him. When a big man refused to let him by, Bragi picked him *up* and threw him aside. People got out of his way fast after that. The club was too hot and too loud. He needed quiet to concentrate. He wanted cool air.

Outside, he closed his eyes and summoned up his memories of Anthony again, desperately working the Art. The image refused to become steady. It shifted, unstable. One moment it was Anthony. The next it was a young Tuscan in the courtly dress of the late seventeenth century. Then Anthony in courtly dress. "No," Bragi murmured. He opened his eyes and scanned the skies, searching for the stars behind the harsh glow of the city lights. The Art of Memory was largely internal, but it could be influenced. Someone commanding the Art of Hours could interfere with it. Bragi had never really followed the Art of Hours. His talents in that area were little better than those of a newspaper astrology columnist. Though too few stars were visible to tell him anything useful, he knew what he would have seen. A full moon in the house of Sagittarius. Saturn descending in Virgo. A strong new lover taken, an old and wasted lover cast aside.

Lead still burned in Bragi's stomach, but angry fire moved into his heart as well. "Fenris." Bragi flung back his head and roared at the sky, a bellow that echoed off buildings. The right person would hear that roar halfway around the world. "Fenris! Answer me!"

Echoes died away into silence. Then, in the distance, a wolf howled. Grimly, Bragi sprinted for his car, fumbling his keys out of his pocket as he ran.

Loksson grabbed the sleeping cat, snatching it out of the warm puddle of sunlight so quickly that it barely had time to yowl in alarm, and hurled it against the wall. Bragi Changed in midair, absorbing the impact with his bigger, tougher human body. It still knocked the wind out of him and he gasped for breath. Loksson Changed too, the transformation shredding his fine clothes. A huge gray wolf leaped at the naked man. Bragi managed to get his arms up and catch the wolf's jaw and throat, holding it back. "Fenris! What's wrong?"

The wolf growled, then Changed. Loksson, the identity Fenris has chosen to adopt in this place and time because the sinister implications of his own name were too well known, glared balefully at him. "You know!" he shouted. "Cuckolded by my own brother! How many times, Bragi?" He slammed a fist into Bragi's stomach. "How many times have you fucked Giovan?"

Breath whistled through Bragi's clenched teeth. "How did—?"

"What? You thought I wouldn't find out?" Fenris pushed himself away, standing up to tower over Bragi. A few scraps of clothing clung to him. He brushed them away. "You were there when he told me about that first dream. I knew it was you."

Bragi tried to climb to his feet as well, but Fenris pushed him down again. Bragi looked up at him sorrowfully. "I'm sorry, Fenris. I couldn't help it."

"How many times?" Fenris snarled.

"Just once. More than a month ago."

"Once was too many. He saw you Change too, didn't he?"

Bragi nodded. "Yes."

"You should have killed him."

"I couldn't!" Bragi thrust himself to his feet, this time shouldering aside his brother's efforts to keep him down. "I love him, Fenris. He's a plaything to you, but I love him. I couldn't just kill him. I told him never to mention it again."

Fenris snarled. "He's as stupid with curiosity as any human. When you haven't been around, he's been telling me about more of his 'dreams.' He says he's dreamed of me turning into a raven, or me flying into the bedchamber through the window, or me perched outside the Marquis d'Auch's chambers, peering inside. I thought maybe he was just sensitive and I didn't say anything, but today..." He drew a deep breath. "Today he said he dreamed of me turning into a cat. And the way he looked at me, I knew he was testing me, trying to see if I could take the same shapes as you!" He snatched something out of the ruins of his clothes. A locket. He thrust it at Bragi. "And then I found this in his things. I gave it to him so that he could keep a lock of my hair inside. Open it."

Bragi did. Fenris' hair was as blond as his. The hair in the locket wasn't even human. Nestled inside the golden trinket was a little clump of white cat hair. Bragi looked at it for a moment before Fenris slapped the locket out of his hands. "He's going to keep asking questions, Bragi! Humans can't help themselves. And he's not going to be satisfied until he knows the whole truth and sees it with his own eyes."

"But I warned him." Bragi swallowed. "Fenris, I—"

"Don't say it," Fenris spat. "Don't say anything. It's too late. You took him away from me. You destroyed him." He stalked into the bedchamber and flung open the window. Then he Changed. The raven flew away. Holding his breath, Bragi watched it hurtle up into the air before arching back toward the palace and vanishing overhead. Bragi closed his eyes and sought Giovan with the Art of Memory. Horses. He was surrounded by horses. He was in one of the great palace stables. The direction in which Fenris had flown.

The wolf continued to howl intermittently, mockingly. Bragi knew that Fenris was guiding him. His brother wanted to be found. Bragi simply prayed that Anthony was all right. He doubted that his prayers would be answered.

He pulled up by the gates of a construction site. The skeleton of a new office building leaped into the sky. There was another vehicle beside the gates, a fiery red sports car. The gates themselves had been torn open, the chain holding them shut snapped. Bragi slipped through and into the night-frozen chaos of the construction. A cement mixer. Piles of girders. Drums of rivets. The detritus of the construction crew. No sign of Fenris or Anthony. Fenris had fallen silent. Bragi stalked through the shadows.

"Bragi!"

The call came from high up in the skeletal construction, the voice more powerful than any human's. Bragi's head snapped up, searching the moonlit steel. "Here!" called Fenris again. Bragi spotted him, maybe a dozen stories up or more, standing casually on the edge of a girder. Then he saw Anthony.

His partner was hanging in space, feet on a narrow bar, clinging to a cable that snaked down from a hoist beside Fenris. Anthony must have been able to see him, too. He stared down, though he didn't say anything. He seemed to be unharmed, but his face was so pale and pinched that Bragi knew he was too terrified to do more than remain absolutely still. Bragi's face twisted. "Let him go!"

"Gladly." Fenris gestured downward. "But look there first."

Rust-brown concrete reinforcement rods clustered like a thicket under Anthony. A twelve story fall to the ground would certainly injure him, but he might live. A twelve story fall onto those rods would impale him. Fenris' hand was on the release lever for the hoist. "You have several choices," he shouted. "One, try to stop me from throwing this lever. But I don't think even you could be that fast. Two, let him die." Bragi heard Anthony whimper. Fenris grinned. "Three, Change, then fly up and catch him."

Bragi flushed. Fenris laughed. "But you can't, can you? To fly, you would have to Change to your true form, and the sight of you would drive him crazy. Too bad. Now me, I could Change to some other flying form, one that wouldn't necessarily make him insane." Fenris flickered, Changing. A huge wolf with immense raven wings perched on the girder for a moment, then Fenris was back in his human form. Bragi ground his teeth.

Fenris could show off with impunity. He had no way of reaching his brother before Fenris could throw that release lever. "Of course, even if you could do that—you should have developed more Changed forms instead of just that stupid cat, Bragi—loverboy would be full of questions afterward. How did you do that? What are you? Who—"

"I think he's going to have enough questions just from meeting you," Bragi said tightly. He avoided looking at Anthony.

Fenris smiled again. "No?" he asked. "Really? Imagine that. You know how curious humans can be. You won't have a moment's peace until he finally persuades you to tell the truth. And then he'll end up just like Giovan."

Bragi's heart froze and burned at the same time. "I wasn't the one who revealed myself to Giovan."

"You might as well have been." Fenris' voice was flat.

Horses were screaming as Bragi raced into the stables. Some were still thrashing in their stalls, breaking themselves against the wood. A crowd of nobles, courtiers, and servants was gathering. Grooms and stablehands were rushing around trying to calm the horses. A few people were screaming, too, some staggering aimlessly, some bashing themselves against walls and stalls as the horses were. Four men were holding down a noblewoman who ranted and struggled violently. There was blood on the woman's hands. A child lay nearby, unmoving.

Bragi ignored them all and they ignored him, even dressed as he was. He wore only a shirt and breeches, snatched up as he ran from Fenris' apartment. His feet were bare. He was intent on only one thing: finding Giovan.

And he found him. He had thrown himself onto an iron pitchfork in his madness. The tines protruded through to his back. Fenris was with him, just turning his body over. Bloody foam dripped from Giovan's mouth. His eyes were bloody, too, as though he had tried to scratch them out.

All around them, the straw on the ground was disturbed and the wood of beams and stalls broken and splintered. As if something very large and very strong had occupied this space not long ago.

Fenris dropped Giovan. The Tuscan's body landed on its back, the handle of the pitchfork sticking up into the air like a proud flagpole. Fenris looked at Bragi. "He knows everything now. But remember who prompted him to start asking questions." Fenris Changed into a raven and streaked out of the stables, leaving Bragi alone with Giovan.

He was alone for only a moment though. The raven's flight must have attracted someone's attention, because suddenly there were people all around him, shouting and pointing at Giovan, and the Comte de Vermandois was asking questions of "Master Loksson." Bragi simply turned, numb, and walked away. When he was, for a moment, out of sight of the crowd, he Changed into the white-haired cat and vanished into the shadows of Versailles.

He hadn't taken human form again for fifty years.

Fenris watched him carefully, then shouted down, "He drops on ten." His face was as flat as his voice. There was no further preamble. There was no need for one.

"Fenris, don't!"

"One."

He would do it, too. Bragi knew that. He bit his tongue, thinking, desperately, even as Fenris counted two and then three. He swallowed. Fenris had set this up too well. He'd had three hundred years to plan his revenge. Let Anthony die quickly or save him and condemn him to the madness that had claimed Giovan. Either way he was going to lose him just as Fenris had lost Giovan. Unless…"Anthony!" Bragi shouted desperately.

"Four," counted Fenris.

"Close your eyes, Anthony! You have to close your eyes and whatever happens, keep them closed!"

Five. Anthony screamed in terror. "Bragi!"

"Trust me, Anthony! Close your eyes!" Six. Bragi didn't look to see if Anthony had obeyed him. He simply leaped and Changed, embracing his true form for the first time in centuries. Immense, leathery wings caught the air, struggling to attain swift flight. A long, sinuous body cut through the shadows. Moonlight shone on silver-white, scaly hide. Seven. Eight. A loud clack as a lever was thrown prematurely. Big, taloned claws lashed out.

The dragon caught Anthony before he had even begun to fall. Still, Anthony screamed again, shocked at the huge, cool grasp that held him. Bragi soared up into the sky. Below him, Fenris roared and Changed as well. A second dragon, identical to the first, swept up into the night. Bragi swerved, protecting Anthony with his body as Fenris flashed past. His breath was like a howling blizzard. Ice crackled and burned along Bragi's back, tearing a bellow of pain from his throat.

Then Fenris was gone, Changing into the less conspicuous form of a raven and vanishing into the night before a quarter of the city glimpsed the maddening glory of his true dragon shape. Bragi settled quickly to the ground for the same reason. The sight of a dragon was enough to drive humans insane. Mocking raven laughter echoed out of the dark distance. Bragi ignored it. He Changed back to human form and wrapped strong arms around Anthony, hugging him to his naked chest. Anthony's arms went around him as well, mostly automatically. Bragi gasped as they touched the raw injuries on his back. He didn't say anything though. His partner was shaking and sobbing, but he still had his eyes shut.

"Bragi?" he asked tentatively. "Are you...that is you, right?"

"Yes. You can open your eyes."

Anthony did and looked at him. "What happened? What was that? Who was that? Were you—"

Bragi sealed his lips with a kiss. "Don't ask." Fenris had been right when he had said that even if Anthony didn't see his true form, he would be too curious not to ask questions. Sooner or later, he would ask too many. "Anthony," Bragi said, "I'll always love you." He whispered the word of the First Speech in Anthony's ear and carried his sagging body back to the car. He drove back to the apartment building slowly, watching Anthony's face the whole way, committing it to memory one last time. Outside the apartment building, he stopped and parked the car, then leaned over to kiss Anthony on the cheek.

Humans were curious. Anthony would ask too many questions about what had happened tonight. Bragi couldn't have let him die, but he couldn't let him go mad with the truth, either. Anthony wouldn't be able to ask too many questions if there was no one around to answer them. Fenris had his revenge. Anthony would live and that was something, but Bragi had lost him as surely as if he was dead.

Bragi made himself numb, pushing his love for Anthony away, bundling it up with his memories of Giovan. Fenris was out there somewhere. Rage at his brother filled the vacuum. Bragi opened the car door. A white-haired cat jumped out onto the cold asphalt and vanished into the shadows of the city.

IN MYSTERIOUS WAYS

BY

TANYA HUFF

I have been a major Tanya Huff fan since I first read one of her books. If you have not read her Blood books, I recommend you do so. (After you have finished this book, of course.) I was very happy to read this story about Terizan, the thief who is so exceptional that her guild suggests she steal the gem from a god's shrine. How can Terizan not tick off either the guild or *the god, either of whom could skin you alive....*

—S. P.

"You want me to steal *what?*"

"The Eye of Keydi-azda."

Terizan stared at the Tribunal in disbelief. Her question had been rhetorical; she'd heard them the first time. "Keydi-azda is a god."

"One of the so-called small gods." Tribune One cocked her head and raised a slender brow. "Do you have a problem with that?"

"Actually, yes. People who steal from gods spend the rest of their very short lives in uncomfortable circumstances then they endure a painful eternity of having their livers eaten by cockroaches."

Tribune Three snickered.

One ignored him so pointedly his cheeks reddened. "You're saying you don't think you can do it?"

"No. I'm not saying that." Terizan spread her hands in what she hoped was a placating manner—the last thing she wanted was to irritate the Tribunal. Actually, the last thing she wanted was to steal the Eye of Keydi-azda, but not irritating the Tribunal came a close second. They weren't particularly fond of her as it was. "I'd just rather not."

Tribune Two's pale eyes narrowed and thin lips opened to make a protest. A sharp gesture from One closed them again.

"Very well. As you don't seem to *approve* of this job…"

Terizan winced, realizing that the Tribune's choice of words had not been accidental and reflecting that she really had to learn to keep her opinions to herself.

"…you may go."

A little surprised it had been that easy, Terizan bowed gratefully. She had her fingers around the heavy iron latch that secured the door to the Sanctum when One added, "Send in Balzador, would you?"

"Balzador?" She whirled around and swept an incredulous glance over the three who ran the Thieves' Guild. "You're going to send Balzador to steal the Eye? There's no way he's up to something like that."

"Then who is?" One asked, steepling long, ringless fingers and examining Terizan over the apex. "If you are unwilling, who do you suggest we send to the Temple of Keydi-azda in your place?"

Who indeed. Mere days before she'd joined the guild, Terizan had found herself on a narrow ledge that lead nowhere. To go back meant almost certain discovery and her head adorning a spike in the Crescent. To go on meant trusting her weight to an ancient frieze of fruiting vines carved into the side of the building. That feeling of having no choice but a bad one had been remarkably similar to what she felt now.

The only sound in the Sanctum was the quiet rustle of fabric as Three shifted his bulk into a more comfortable position. Even the lamps seemed to have stopped flickering while they waited for her reply.

She lived again through the moment when the carving crumbled under her foot and she plummeted two stories down, only luck keeping her from finishing the fall as a crippled beggar.

The guild took care of their own, but at a price.

"You've already accepted the contract?" she said at last.

"We have."

"To steal the Eye of Keydi-azda?"

"Yes."

"I'm going to need more information than that."

Three picked up a narrow scroll from among the junk piled high in front of him and began unrolling it. "We assumed as much."

"You assumed rather a lot," Terizan muttered, sinking cross-legged down onto a stack of recently acquired carpets.

One smiled, her austere expression growing no warmer. "Yes," she said, "but then, we can."

Terizan walked slowly down the Street of Prayers, grinding her teeth. She hated being backed into a corner and she really hated the smug, self-satisfied way Tribune One had done it. When an orange-robed follower of Hezzna stepped into her path and attempted to hand her a drooping palm frond, she glared up at the veiled face and growled, "I wouldn't."

Behind the orange haze, the kohled edges of the acolyte's eyes widened. Holding the frond between them like a flaccid green sword, he stepped back out of her way.

Feeling a little better, Terizan quickened her pace. Traffic picked up in the late afternoon and she didn't want to waste the anonymity the crowds provided. At the top of the street, junior priests, robed in pale blue, stood on the four balconies of the Temple of the Light and sang out the call to the sunset service. At the bottom of the street, junior priests, wearing identical robes of dark gray, stood on the balconies of the Temple of the Night and did the same. Up and down the Street of Prayers, the people of Old Oreen hurried to complete the day's business. Very few of them were heading to either service. As far as Terizan could see, none of them were praying.

According to the Tribunal, Keydi-azda's Temple shared a wall on one side with the imposing bulk of the Temple of the Forge and on the other with the building where the Fermentation Brotherhood held their weekly meetings. Two stories high but only one room wide, its fronting built of the same smoke-blackened yellow brick that made up most of the rest of the city, it was an easy temple to overlook. A weather-worn eye carved into the keystone over the arched door gave the only indication of what waited inside.

The door led to a short hall and another door. Drawing in a deep breath and reminding herself that she was only scouting the job, Terizan stepped over the threshold.

It was quiet, dim, and smelled of sandalwood.

At one end of the rectangular room, shelves rose from tiled floor to painted ceiling. Petitioners could either leave an offering or remove an item they felt they needed. The shelves were half empty. At the other end of the room stood a small altar where a cone of incense burned in a copper dish.

Above the altar was a second carving of an eye. More ornately carved than the exterior eye, it also boasted an iris of lapis lazuli centered by an onyx pupil.

Keydi-azda was the god of comfort. After a meal, fat men would loosen their belts and sigh, "Bless Keydi-azda." Terizan had murmured the blessing herself on occasion when a good night allowed her to pay for more than bare necessities. Everyone knew the name of Keydi-azda.

Not many, it seemed, came to the temple.

Terizan sang Long-Legged Hazra quietly to herself. Twelve verses later, she was still alone.

"*The priest is old,*" Tribune Two had said, "*and sleeps soundly.*"

"Must be napping now," Terizan muttered, walking silently toward the altar, hair rising off the back of her neck with every step. She'd just have a closer look and be gone before anyone noticed she was there.

The Eye sat loosely within its collar of stone.

If I slid a blade behind it, it'd just pop off into my…

"…hand."

Surprise, as much as the unexpected weight, nearly sent the disc crashing to the floor. Although barely larger than her palm, it curved out two fingers thick in the center of the onyx and was heavier than it looked.

Heart beating so loudly an army could've marched through the temple without her hearing it, Terizan slipped the Eye under her clothes and sashed the flat side tight against her belly. Braced for contact with cold stone, she found it unexpectedly warm.

Then she turned and walked out.

No one tried to stop her. Feeling slightly separated from the world as she knew it, she made her way back to the Thieves Guild and handed the Eye of Keydi-azda over to a grinning Tribune Three.

It was as simple as that.

Even Balzador could've done it.

A triple knock jerked Terizan up off her pallet, heart in her throat, and propelled her halfway out the narrow window before her brain began working.

Constables didn't knock.

"Get a grip," she told herself firmly, drawing her leg back over the sill and rubbing at the place where her knee had cracked against the edge of the sandstone block. "It's probably just Poli wondering if you want to go to the dumpling maker's with him." The sun suggested it was past noon, late enough for Poli to be up and thinking of his first meal of the day.

Tugging the worst creases out of her tunic, she limped to the door, drew the bolt, and swung it open.

One artificially arched brow arched even higher as Poli's critical gaze swept over her and around the tiny room. "So, you're alone." He sighed and shook his head, the gesture carefully choreographed so as not to disarrange his hair. "And here I was hoping to catch you curled up in a sweaty heap with a strange woman you'd picked up after too many cups of ale, brought home, and were now wondering how to get rid of."

"What are you talking about, Poli?" She stepped aside to give him room to enter.

He patted her cheek as he passed. "I knew it would come to this; it's been so long you've forgotten."

Terizan rolled her eyes and closed the door. "No, it hasn't."

"Oh?" He looked intrigued.

She ignored him. "I slept badly. I must've woken up a hundred times last night."

"Guilty conscience." Removing a pile of clothing from the only chair, he sat and smiled beneficently. "Nothing a little food won't cure. Do try to wear something that won't embarrass me."

"Like there's a lot of choice," she muttered, dragging her only clean pair of trousers down off a hook. Shoving one foot into a wide leg, she caught her toe in the thieves' pocket above the cuff, bounced sideways, tripped over the tangled blanket, and fell to the sound of ripping cloth, missing a landing on the pallet by inches.

As she swore and rubbed her elbow, Poli surveyed the split seam and shook his head. "You've got to start shopping off a better quality of laundry line, sweetling. Wear the dirty ones before we starve to death."

"The worst of it is," Terizan sighed, doing as he suggested, "I didn't steal them. I bought them from old man Ezakedid and he told me they were only second-hand." She shoved her feet into her sandals and bent to pull the straps tight. Without straightening she looked from the piece of broken strap in her left hand, to Poli. "This is not starting out to be a very good day."

The dumpling maker had sold out of cheese dumplings so Terizan rolled her eyes, ordered lamb, and bit through her tongue while trying to chew a chunk of gristle soft enough to swallow. She spit out a mouthful of blood and picked up her cup.

"There's a dead fly in my water."

"Not so loud," Poli advised, wiping his fingers on the square of scented cloth he was never without, "or everyone will want one." Leaning forward, he lowered his voice. "Do you see the young lady in the yellow scarf? There by the awning pole? I think she's trying to catch your eye."

Terizan refused to look. "The way my luck's been going today, she's probably an off-duty constable."

"I don't think so, but if she is you could always play lock-me-up-and-throw-away-the-key."

"Poli, I'm not interested." She shifted in place and slipped a hand up under her tunic to scratch at her stomach.

"You're not harboring a broken heart are you, sweetling? I did warn you not to pursue a relationship with a mercenary."

"Warn me? You practically threw me into her bed."

"Nonsense. Besides, *she's* been gone for months and *you're* still sleeping alone."

"I like to sleep alone."

"If everyone in the city had your libido, I'd starve." His lazy tone sharpened. "Can I trust that the itch you're chasing is not caused by some sort of insect infestation?"

"I have no idea but it's driving me crazy." Fleas would be just what she needed.

"Let me look."

Figuring that the little Poli didn't know about skin could be inscribed on a grape with room left over for the entire Book of the Light, Terizan leaned away from the table and lifted her tunic a couple of inches.

"It's just a rash," he announced after a moment's examination. "Most likely caused by something you've leaned against—something circular from the look of it. I don't think it's dangerous, merely uncomfortable."

Something circular.

Through the sudden buzzing in her ears Terizan heard her voice tell the Tribunal, *"People who steal from gods spend the rest of their short lives in uncomfortable circumstances."* She hadn't meant *uncomfortable* literally but why not; Keydi-azda was the god of comfort after all. And it certainly explained the way her day had been going.

"All right, sweetling. What have you done?"

She shook herself and pulled down her tunic. A quick look around the dumpling maker's cantina showed no one sitting close enough to overhear. "I did a job for the guild...."

By the time she finished, Poli had paled beneath his cosmetics. "You stole the Eye of Keydi-azda?" he hissed. "Are you out of your mind?"

"I can't see as I had much choice."

"They gave you a chance to send someone else. Any other thief would've taken it."

She laid both hands flat on the scarred table top and leaned forward until their noses were almost touching. "I'm not any other thief."

Poli closed his eyes for a moment, then he sighed. "No, you're not, are you. Well, there's only one thing to do. You've got to put it back."

"I can't. I gave it to the Tribunal. I don't know who has it now."

"Can't you find out?"

"Sure, I mean the guild always insists on a written contract for blackmail purposes. All I'd have to do is break into the Sanctum and steal it."

Poli ignored the sarcasm. "Good."

Terizan opened her mouth to protest then closed it again. *People who steal from gods spend the rest of their short lives in uncomfortable circumstances.* A short, uncomfortable life. She'd planned on a long life. She had too much to do to die young. "Oh bugger," she sighed. Although she'd certainly intended to challenge the Tribunal's authority, she'd expected to have a little more time to strengthen her position in the guild. Fighting the urge to scratch, she dipped her finger in her cup and traced a circle within a circle on the table—driving a splinter in under the skin far enough to draw blood. "All right, you win. I'll find out who has it and I'll steal it back."

"Your guild encourages freelance work," Poli reminded her.

"I doubt this is what they had in mind," she muttered around her injured finger.

He waved a dismissive hand. "Then they should have been more specific."

"You're not helping, Poli. First problem, there's always at least one member of the Tribunal in the Sanctum."

"Don't they trust you?"

"We're thieves, of course they don't trust us." Eyes narrowed, she stared down at the rapidly evaporating sketch. "I think I can get rid of the Tribune, at least for a few minutes…."

The herbalist Terizan decided to use had a small shop facing the cramped confines of Greenmarket Square. As it wasn't an area she frequented, personally or professionally, she hoped she'd be neither recognized nor remembered. Ignoring sales pitches as wilted as the vegetables, she made her way around the edges of the square and, just outside her destination, stepped on something soft that compacted under her sandal.

It turned out *not* to be a rotting bit of melon rind.

The dim interior of the shop smelled of orange peel and bergamot. Bundles of dried herbs hung from hooks in the ceiling and were packed into stacks of loosely woven baskets. Bottles and boxes crammed the shelves along one wall. In one corner, a large terra cotta jar sweated oil. Dust motes danced thickly in the single beam of light that managed to penetrate the clutter.

As Terizan entered, stained fingers parted the beaded curtain in the back wall and an ancient man shuffled through the opening. "How may I help you?" he wheezed. "Women's problems? Powders to help you find a man and keep him…" Rheumy eyes managed to focus on her expression. "Powders to help you find a woman and keep her."

"I can find my own women," Terizan muttered. "I'm looking for cazcara zagrada powder."

"Ah, constipation." Cavernous nostrils flared. "I should have known from the smell."

"That's on my shoe!"

"Of course it is. Two doses, one monkey."

"I need four."

"Four?" Shaking his head, he lifted a stained basswood box onto the counter, opened it, and spooned the coarse brown powder onto a piece of fabric with an amazingly steady hand. "Be careful," he told her as he twisted the corners up and tied them off with a bit of string. "I don't care how backed up you are, just one dose of this will put you in the privy blessing Keydi-azda. And that's no laughing matter, young woman!"

"Trust me, I'm not laughing." Wiping the snarl off her face, Terizan handed over the two copper coins.

The large antechamber outside the Sanctum smelled strongly of onions. Peppers would've been better but onions would have to do. Terizan traded jests with a group of thieves playing caravan then made her way across to the pair of kettles steaming over small charcoal fires, the four doses of cazcara zagrada palmed and ready. "Is it done yet?"

"Is it ever done before sunset?" Yazdamidor growled. He'd been a thief until a spelled lock cost him the use of one arm. Now, he cooked for the Guild.

"Look, Yaz, I'm in a hurry…."

"Meeting some pretty bit of fluff, are you?" He snorted, not waiting for her answer. "No, course you ain't. You got that mercenary captain, Whats'ername on the string."

Terizan refused to rise to the bait. There wasn't a thief in the city who didn't know Swan's name; the mercenary captain had helped her to get the better of the Tribunal and that wasn't likely to be forgotten. "I just want something to eat. You don't need to know why."

Scooping a bowl of barley mush out of the first kettle, he thrust it at her. "There's always someone what can't wait. Go ahead, just don't blame me if it ain't cooked through."

She doctored the stew as she scooped it onto her mush, stirring in the powder with the ladle and hoping that she'd got as little of it as possible into her own food. Unfortunately, the way things had been going, she expected an uncomfortable evening. The meat *was* cooked through but, since the goat had probably died of old age, she couldn't see as it made much difference.

She finished before anyone else started. As the caravan players filled bowls and moved to join her, she clutched her stomach, muttered a curse, and hurriedly left the room. Racing up the stairs, only partially faking, she heard Yazdamidor laugh and shout, "Told you so!"

Now it was all a matter of timing.

Most thefts were, patterns being easier to break into than locks.

In order to join the guild, thieves were expected to make their way through the guild house to the inner Sanctum. The rumors that reached the city of deadly traps and complicated protections were exaggerated but not by much. Terizan was the first thief to have ever made it all the way. Since no one had done it since, it was safe to say she was also the *only* thief to have made it all the way.

As a member of the guild, her access to the House had improved since that afternoon and, this time, it wasn't necessary to enter through an attic window. Even avoiding the dogs, she only had to cover half the distance. Disconnecting the wire set to ring warning bells inside the Sanctum, she pried up a tile and laid an iron bar—removed from a trap she'd disabled a few moments earlier—across the opening. She uncoiled the rope tied to the middle of the bar as she chimney-walked down the narrow chute to the trap door at the bottom. Easing it open a fingerwidth, she listened.

Nothing.

The Sanctum was…

Then she heard the scraping of a horn spoon against the side of a wooden bowl and hurriedly rebraced her feet. Regrettably, since she'd already begun to move, the angle was bad and she wouldn't be able to hold her position for long. As the muscles in her lower back began to cramp, she wondered if the Tribune about to be so abruptly visited from above would believe she was just reliving past glories. Probably not.

It didn't help that her stomach felt as though fire ants were nesting just below the surface of her skin. She squirmed to ease the itch and her left shoulder slipped.

Oh crap…

As she fell, she grabbed the edge of the trap door and used it to swing out past the net waiting to scoop up those who entered without proper planning. A summersault in midair and she landed facing the Tribune's table.

The empty room echoed to the sound of footsteps pounding up the long flight of stairs used to bring clients unseen into the Sanctum. It was the only direct route into the heart of the guild house and the upper end was both trapped and guarded. It was also the most direct route to the privies.

Silently thanking whatever gods she hadn't pissed off, Terizan wiped sweaty palms on her thighs, vaulted the table, and jerked to a stop in front of the shelves of scrolls. There were a lot more than she'd noticed from the other side of the room.

Think, Terizan, think. They have to have a system or they'd never find anything themselves. There appeared to be three sections. *One for each Tribune? Why not.* She moved to left. Tribune One had given her the job. *Okay. This happened yesterday, it's got to be right on top.*

It wasn't.

Terizan couldn't read but she figured she'd recognize the hieroglyph for the Eye. Nothing looked familiar on any of the scrolls she opened.

I don't believe this…

"…eats anything. It's no wonder he's made himself sick." Tribune One's unsympathetic observation drifted down the stairs.

If the Tribunes caught her in the Sanctum, they wouldn't just throw her out of the guild, they'd throw her out in little bleeding pieces.

Heart pounding Terizan leapt up onto the table and jumped for the hook that supported the near end of the net. Something moved under her foot and she almost didn't make it. Glancing back, she saw she'd crushed the middle of a scroll as big around as her fist.

Bugger, bugger, bugger…

Blood roaring in her ears, she dropped back onto the table, scooped up the scroll, stuffed it down one trouser leg, and jumped again.

"Look at that, he's left the door open."

Her fingers closed around the end of the rope she'd left hanging and, knees tucked up against her chest to avoid the net, she transferred her weight. Her swing forward reopened the trap door. She scrambled into the ceiling, braced herself against the sides of the chute and flicked the rope up out of the way so the springs could close the door again.

"What was that?"

One snorted. "Probably rats."

"Four legged or two?"

High overhead, pulling herself out into the corridor, Terizan missed the answer.

She couldn't take the scroll back to her room—if the information it contained was important enough, the Tribunal would hire a wizard to search for it—so she took it to the only safe place she could think of.

Although there were three lamps lit, the temple of Keydi-azda was deserted—no petitioners, no priest. A linen cloth hung over the empty socket that should have held the Eye. Fully intending to leave the scroll on one of the shelves, Terizan leaned against the wall under a lamp and unrolled it. If it came to a confrontation with the Tribunal, any information she could glean might help to keep her head on her shoulders.

Within the outer sheathing, a number of parchment pages were attached to the upper handle. Nothing on the first page looked familiar.

"I've got to learn to read," she muttered. Centered in the top of the

next page, the Eye of Keydi-azda stared out at her. "I'll be fried...."
Remembering the near fall that had ensured she pick up this particular
scroll, she glanced toward the altar and added a quiet, "Bless Keydi-azda."
Just in case. She couldn't make out who'd paid for the job so she turned
another page.

"The Staff of Hamtazia?"

And another page.

"Amalza's Stone?"

Altogether, since the last dark of the moon, seven icons had been stolen,
all from small gods. Two days ago, Terizan wouldn't have much cared, but
she was beginning to realize it was the small things that made life worth
living.

The hieroglyph on the bottom of the last page had to represent the
people who'd hired the Guild for all seven thefts. Unfortunately, it was
an incomprehensible squiggle as far as Terizan was concerned.

"May I help you, child?"

She hadn't heard the priest approach. His quiet question provoked a
startled gasp and a few moments of coughing and choking on her own
spit. When she finally got her breath back, she wiped streaming eyes
with the palm of one hand and glared at him.

"Oh my, that didn't look to be very comfortable at all," he murmured
sympathetically.

All things considered, Terizan bit off a rude reply and shoved the scroll
under his nose. "Do you recognize this?"

"Oh yes. It was made by one of the priests of Cot'Dazur. See the three
points and the dots below…"

"Who?"

The priest sighed and folded his hands over a comfortable curve of
belly. "One of the new gods. There's a huge temple in the new town, all
painted plaster and lattice work. Very stylish but not much substance,
I'm afraid."

Scratching thoughtfully, Terizan frowned and wrestled these new pieces
into place. "How does a god *get* substance?"

"Time." He smiled a little sadly. "Those who believe build it up, over
time."

"Suppose you didn't want to wait?"

"You wouldn't have a choice, child. It isn't something you can suddenly acquire." Over their heads, the lamp sputtered and went out. "Oh my, I'd best get more oil." He patted her arm with one soft hand and waddled off toward the altar.

Uncertain of how to address him, Terizan took a step forward and called, "Your worship?"

"Yes, child?"

"I've heard that the Eye of Keydi-azda is missing."

Together they glanced over at the linen drapery.

"Yes, I'm afraid it is."

"You don't seem very upset."

"I have been assured it will be returned."

"Assured? By who?"

"Why by Keydi-azda, of course."

Terizan sighed. "Of course," she repeated, laid the scroll on one of the shelves beside a small clay cup, left the temple, and ran into half a dozen of the Fermentation Brotherhood just leaving a meeting. As they attempted to stagger out of her way, one of them puked on her foot.

Cot'Dazur turned out to be the god of nothing in particular although there seemed to be a divine finger stuck in a great many pies.

"Is your business not what it could be? Are you suffering from a broken heart? Do you want to impress an employer? A certain someone?" Colored flames from half a dozen flickering torches throwing bands of green and blue and gold across her face, the priest leaned forward and pointed an emphatic finger at a plump young man. "Would you like to have an application considered by the governing council?" She leaned back and spread her arms, her voice rising, her volume impressive. "Why run about to half a dozen different temples when your problems can be dealt with under one roof." Music started up inside the building. She stepped aside and gestured through the open door. "Come. Petition Cot'Dazur."

It was a catchy tune and Terizan, hidden in the crowd pouring up the steps, found herself moving in time to the beat—until she stubbed her toe and the pain distracted her.

344

Inside, lamps burning scented oil fought futilely against the smell of fresh paint mixed with half a hundred unwashed bodies. Had the ceiling not arced better than two full stories high with a row of open windows running below both sides of the peak, the combination would have quickly overpowered even the most ardent supplicant.

Painted into the plaster over the door was a representation of Cot'Dazur with features so bland they seemed designed to appeal to just about everyone. From where Terizan stood, the paint looked wet. *When the priest of Keydi-azda said this was a new god, he wasn't kidding.*

Pushed up against a stucco wall, she scowled and brushed fresh plaster off her shoulder. A good thief avoided stucco—it not only crumbled easily, it also marked those who came in contact with it. Tonight it looked like she wasn't going to have a choice.

Most of the crowd had broken into smaller groups, each clustered around a red-robed priest. Somehow, even though the music continued in the background, the noise never quite rose to unbearable levels.

"Would you like some sweet-dough?"

Terizan eyed the tray of deep fried dough and her lip curled. "No, thanks." Grease and stucco combined would be just what she needed.

"A cinnamon tea?"

"No. I'm, uh, fasting."

The acolyte smiled down at her. "This is your first time, isn't it?"

Since she didn't seem to expect an answer, Terizan didn't bother giving her one. Glancing around the temple, she saw that all the acolytes, men and women, shared a similar bland prettiness—they were young and cheerful and completely interchangeable. The priests, who had to be at least a little older, seemed much the same. In fact, they all looked rather remarkably like the painting of their god.

"You seem uncomfortable." Placing her tray down on a convenient table, the acolyte gripped Terizan's shoulders between strong fingers, turned her around, and began to knead. "Here," she purred, "let me help you relax."

As the soft, yielding warmth of the acolyte's breasts pressed against her back, Terizan choked and leapt forward.

"Oh my. It *has* been a long time, hasn't it?"

Terizan tried very hard not to grind her teeth and almost succeeded. "Do I have number on my forehead saying how many days it's been?" she snarled. "Is that what this is all about?"

"Uh, no…"

"Fine. Then let's not talk about it. Let's talk about, oh, I don't know, money." A trio of dancers began preforming on a small raised dais. Terizan forced herself to look away from the long legs of the natural redhead. "How much does all this cost?"

"Nothing at all to you," the acolyte assured her, smile back in place. "But donations are gratefully accepted."

Which explained the empty copper pot in the middle of the tray of sweet-dough. And the rosewood boxes carved with the hieroglyph of Cot'Dazur scattered strategically about.

"Too bad I haven't got a monkey on me." She almost had to admire how quickly the acolyte disengaged and moved on. When her attention seemed fully occupied by a petitioner with a little more coin, Terizan worked her way toward the front of the temple.

There was the expected small door beside the altar. She waited until a particularly athletic solicitation drew most eyes then slipped through it.

The sudden quiet made her ears ring.

It took time for a god to gain substance and first impressions suggested this lot wouldn't care to wait. If they planned to use the stolen icons as a shortcut to achieving divine power then all seven would have to be grouped together at a focal point somewhere in the temple. Inside the altar was the most obvious spot but not even the best thief in Oreen could get to them until after the crowd ate its fill of sweet-dough and went home.

A short flight of dark stairs lead to a narrow room lit by a single lamp. Street clothes hung neatly on hooks over polished wooden benches and a large wicker basket probably waited for dirty robes. Terizan squirmed into the darkness below a bench and settled down to wait.

Laughing voices woke her.

Feet flickered past her hiding place, shadowed shapes against the shadows by the floor. Most of the conversation seemed to center on how full the collection boxes had been and on how much sweet-dough had been eaten. The smell of fresh varnish made her want to sneeze but that, at least, was a discomfort she was used to.

When the laughing voices left, she thought she could hear two, maybe three people moving quietly about the room.

"How much longer?"

"Patience, Habazan, patience."

Terizan recognized the voice of the priest who had drawn the crowd into the temple. She had an unmistakable way of pronouncing every word as if it came straight from her god.

"But we have the icons."

"Granted, but even small gods will be able to hold their power for a while."

"I thought if we took the symbol of their power we took their power."

"We did. The small gods and their icons have become one and the same in most people's minds. With the icon gone, the people assume that the god is gone and will stop believing. When enough of them stop, the gods will end, and their power—through the icons—will be ours."

"Will be Cot'Dazur's."

"Of course. That's what I meant."

"But how much longer?"

"Not very."

Not very, Terizan repeated to herself as the priest and her companion took the lamp and left the robing room. *Not very long before the small gods end.* She lay where she was and scratched at the rash on her stomach. She didn't have to do this, didn't have to risk anything to return the Eye of Keydi-azda. If the priest of Cot'Dazur was right, in not very much longer Keydi-azda would be unable to affect her life. All she had to do was endure a few discomforts and soon it would end.

Keydi-azda would end.

Terizan sighed and slid out from under the bench. Any other thief would let it go. Wouldn't risk it. But as she'd told Poli, she wasn't any other thief. *I've never killed anyone and I'm not about to start now.*

She slipped on one of the dirty robes, started down the stairs and cracked her forehead on the edge of a metal lamp bracket.

...which doesn't mean I'm not tempted.

The altar had been carved from a solid piece of the local sandstone. It might have been hollow underneath but Terizan's instincts said otherwise. There was always the possibility that the priests had hired a wizard to sink the icons into the stone, but from what Terizan had overheard, she didn't think that had happened.

So they had to be hidden somewhere else.

Somewhere in the temple.

Somewhere that could be used to focus the power from the seven gods onto Cot'Dazur.

Hugging the shadows at the base of the walls, Terizan made her way toward the doors. In the combination of moon and starlight that spilled through the open windows, she could just barely make out the painting of the god.

Wet paint.

Cot'Dazur couldn't possibly be *that* new.

The collection boxes were lighter than she expected. She only hoped they'd hold her weight. When she had them stacked as high as her head, she made a bag out of the robe, tucked her sandals under her sash and climbed carefully to the top of the pile. From there, she stepped onto the lintel of the door.

The plaster was still wet enough to cut with her longest lockpick. She sliced out a careful square, slipped it into the bag, reached through the lattice work and groped about the hole. Her fingers brushed the familiar cold curve of the Eye of Keydi-azda. Some of the other pieces were a little harder to find and by the time she'd finished, she'd destroyed most of the painting.

She was just about to step back onto the boxes, bag tied to her back, the Staff of Hamtazia shoved awkwardly through the knots, when she heard voices approaching from outside.

"I'm sure I left it up in the robing room. I'll only be a minute."

Oh crap. When they opened the door, the boxes would go flying. Balanced on the lintel, Terizan measured the distance to the closest window and realized she had no choice but to attempt it. If she couldn't go down…

Stretching her left arm out and up as far as she could, she drove her longest pick into the wall, swung out on it, kicked holes in the plaster, changed hands and did it again with her second longest pick. The Dagger of Sharidan, Guardian of the Fifth Gate, would have worked better but she couldn't take the time to dig it out. As she crab-climbed up and over toward the window, the returning acolytes pushed open the door.

The sound of collection boxes crashing to the floor, some of them bouncing, some of them smashing against the tile, covered her involuntary curse as the second longest pick proved too short and began to pull out of the wall. Desperately scrabbling for a toe hold, she ignored the shouting from below as the astonished acolytes stumbled over bits of broken wood demanding that somebody bring them a lamp.

Her fingertips caught the bottom edge of the window.

A new voice shouted from deep inside the temple.

Shit! I should've known there was a caretaker! She'd been incredibly lucky so far but unless she got out the window before the caretaker came with a light that wouldn't mean much. Under better circumstances, she'd have used her grip on the window as an anchor and moved carefully around the corner onto the side wall. Under these particular circumstances, she jumped.

Her right hand gripped the ledge safely but lost its grip on the pick. As the steel spike began to fall, Terizan jerked her head forward and caught it in her mouth, somehow managing to hang on in spite of a split lip. Anything left behind could lead a wizard right to her.

Muscles straining, she got the upper half of her body over the window sill, wrestled the Staff of Hamtazia out the opening, and lowered herself onto the steeply angled roof. *If I can make it to the ground before they figure out which way I went,* she reasoned as she began to slide, *they'll never catch me.* Most roofs in Oreen were flat or domed—it wasn't until she noticed how fast the edge was approaching that she realized her danger.

That's a story and a half drop! Flipping over onto her stomach she dug in fingers and toes but the clay tiles overlapped so smoothly there was nothing to grab. Then her legs were in the air. Her body began to tip while she tried grab a handful of roof.

Her hip hit a protrusion of some kind. Then the knotted robe slammed up under her chin and her left arm pit and she found herself hanging between two of the decorative wooden beams that stuck out from under the edge of the roof, dangling half throttled from the jammed Staff of Hamtazia.

It's about time something went my way....

Since her hands were free, she quickly returned both picks to the seams of her trousers, pulled herself up enough to free the Staff, then dropped. By the time the hue and cry began, she'd lost herself in the shadows.

In the temple of Keydi-azda, the same three lamps burned unattended. Although Terizan half-expected something to go wrong, the Eye fit back into the stone socket as easily as it had come out. The other six stolen icons she set carefully onto the shelves, where they'd be found by those who needed them. Then she knelt, folded back the robe, and pulled out the last item it held. The first square of damp plaster she'd cut out of the wall—the face of Cot'Dazur, miraculously in one piece in spite of everything.

"I'm a thief," she told the watching Eye of Keydi-azda. "I'm not a judge, and I'm not an executioner. I've never killed anyone and I'm not about to start. If the priests of Cot'Dazur need their icon back, they can find it here with the rest."

The silence was absolute but Terizan hadn't expected an answer. She didn't need a god to tell her when she was doing the right thing. Brushing bits of plaster dust from her clothes, she left the Eye to keep watch alone.

"So what did the Tribunal say?"

"What could they say?" Terizan bit into a cheese dumpling and sighed in contentment. "The priests of Cot'Dazur complained that the stolen icons had been stolen back and the Tribunal pointed out that they'd fulfilled their part of the contract and what happened to the icons after they were handed over was not their problem."

"But they don't have the contract."

"The priests don't know that. If they did, they'd cause trouble. So, as much as they'd like to come down on the thief with both feet, the Tribunal is not going to do anything that may push whoever took the contract into telling the priests that it no longer exists. Although they *have* nailed shut the trap door in the ceiling of the Sanctum."

Poli studied her from under darkened lashes. "So they suspect it was you?"

"They've never liked me much. They think I'm ambitious." Her grin pulled to one side by her swollen lip, her expression seemed more disdainful than amused. "You know, Poli, this whole thing was a setup from the start. The Tribunal had no reason to send me after the Eye, anyone could have done the job. But, even pinched and prodded by the god, no one else could have stolen the contract out of the Sanctum or gotten the icons back from Cot'Dazur."

Equal to the announcement, Poli nodded calmly. "Of course, the Tribunal planned on double crossing Cot'Dazur all the time."

"No, I don't think so. Had any other thief stolen the Eye, Cot'Dazur would, this minute, be absorbing the power of the small gods. I think I was *their* solution."

"You think you were the gods' solution?" Poli reached across the table and patted her arm. "Think highly of yourself, don't you, sweetling."

"Actually, yes. But it's also the only explanation that makes sense. The way I work it out, seven gods owe me a favor. Eight if you consider that I didn't destroy that pretty picture of Cot'Dazur when I had the chance."

Poli sat back looking a little stunned. "Eight gods," he said at last. "All owing you a favor." He blinked twice then managed to recover his poise. "Well, I suppose that it's a good thing they're small gods."

Terizan flashed him a triumphant smile. The rash was gone, her bruises were healing, and the immediate future looked bright. "But there are eight of them."

"Should I be worried?"

"You? No." She took her time eating another dumpling, savoring the moment. As Tribune One had implied, there were a number of things about the guild that had never met with her approval. They were small things, for the most part, but it was, after all, the small things that made life worth living.

She winked at the young woman sitting by the awning pole.

Bless Keydi-azda.

IN THE HOUSE OF THE MAN IN THE MOON

BY

RICHARD BOWES

G rowing up gay or lesbian can be a bleak prospect: no one to turn to, no one who will listen, none who understand. Add to that the intense feelings of alienation we all go through during adolescence and it's not surprising that the suicide rate of lesbian and gay teenagers has been estimated to be as much as six times greater than that of their straight counterparts.

Rick Bowes gives us the story of Bobby, who made it to adulthood; whose unique talent may have saved his life—or may have led to the House of the Man in the Moon in the first place.

—N.G.

✖

1.

On a blazing Fourth of July afternoon, Jax watches the stocky white man in a baseball cap point across an airfield on Long Island, New York. "Those big hangars were Republic Aviation. In the summer of '62, I'd flunked out of college and worked the three to midnight shift assembling

F-105s for $2.75 an hour. Two thousand males and every one of us straight. Including me and I'd had sex with more guys than I could count. I was eighteen, Jax. Over a third of a century ago!"

"Robert, you're just a nostalgic old cold warrior." The big African-American with the round face and shaved head leans against the hood of a dark blue rental Toyota. He wears khaki shorts and is careful not to let his skin touch the metal.

Robert closes his eyes like he's trying to remember a taste. "Until that summer, I'd lived in New England my whole life. The nights down here felt soft, subtropical. And everything, houses, streets, shopping centers looked like *Leave it to Beaver* and *Ozzie and Harriet*. Everything was so brand new and clean. Until I met a guy I called The Man In The Moon it almost seemed like I had outrun the Grace."

Jax pays full attention. A couple of times recently, Robert has mentioned the Grace. He's been full of surprises. Until he proposed this trip the other day, Jax never knew Robert had lived on Long Island.

"In one place where we lived when I was about seven, in Watertown outside of Boston, a livery stable had burned down years before. I only discovered that years later when I went back. Retraced my steps. Like I'm doing now. All I knew then was that I'd wake up at night screaming about fire and horses. From the nuns I knew anything as scary as what I felt had to be a gift from God. So I called it 'The Grace.' Naturally, I never told anyone."

"Naturally," says Jax.

Robert turns from the fence, walks over to the car and slides behind the wheel. A firecracker volley comes from somewhere beyond the horizon. "I'll drive," he announces, adjusting the seat. Jax shudders but gets in. The Toyota runs east on the Hempstead Turnpike past major fast food franchises and carpet warehouses, buildings full of dentists and animal hospitals. Robert speaks almost as if it's to himself and Jax hangs on the story.

2.

One night early in that summer, Terry, a guy I worked with at Republic, gave me a lift home in his Corvair.

We'd had some fast beers at a place outside the Republic gates. We held frosty cans of Rhinegold. From Manhattan, forty miles down the road and in another dimension, the Shirelles sang, "Oh, My Little Soldier Boy…". Back then, this stretch of the turnpike was undeveloped.

Terry was my age with high cheekbones and a blonde d.a. He turned me on, talking about junior high jerk-off contests. He held the can on his crotch and slapped his wrist with the fingers of his other hand. My prick pressed against the band of my jockey shorts. Terry stopped and for a long moment we sat in the dark. He waited, silent, not making a move. But coming on to guys was one of the many things I didn't do. I said, 'See you Monday,' and slid out the door.

Of course, walking home, I imagined Terry and me driving along Route 66 with our hands in each other's pants. Sprinklers whirred and an occasional dog barked that night. The TV was on in my parents' living room. Not wanting to disturb anyone, I came around to the back.

Then I noticed the cigarette tip glowing in the dark. My father said in a low voice, "Get over here." And my hard on instantly disappeared.

3.

"What street are you looking for?" Jax asks. Robert is obviously searching for a sign. Suddenly, without slowing or signaling, Robert says, "Shiloh Road. That's it," and hangs a left into the oncoming lane. Jax covers his eyes. But traffic is light and they sail onto a shady street lined with split levels.

"My parents lived right around here," Robert tells him. "Forty-two Gilead Lane." It takes a few tries before he finds a white colonial surrounded by flowers. "It looks a lot nicer now. The development was only a few years old. The houses were still identical. The carports and dormers and extensions have sprouted since. The trees were saplings." Robert starts to get out of the car, saying, "I need to go around back."

Jax sees an older lady with ash-blond hair watching them uncertainly through the screen door of the house. "Hold on. Take off your hat," he tells Robert. "Smile for her." Then in a warm, melodious voice he says, "Excuse us ma'am. But you may recognize Carroll O'Connor, the television actor. He played Archie Bunker and that nice redneck sheriff on *Heat of the Night?*"

"Oh yes!" She beams at Robert.

"Well, we're going to be making a movie here on Long Island and he wants to get the *feel* of a peaceful neighborhood like this. Would you mind if we were just to walk around your lovely property?"

She watches them from the window as they stand in the back yard. "Why did you have to tell her that? Archie Bunker, for God's sake!"

"That resemblance is what I first loved about you. Do you think she'd be so happy if I had said, 'Hi. You think I'm a nightmare, but actually my name is Louis Jackson, Manhattan D.A.'s office. And this is my boyfriend Robert Logue. You may have heard of him, the guy who sniffs out mass graves. He'd like to poke around in your rhododendron beds.'"

"Rhododendron!" Robert says. "What kind of a faggot are you? Those are azaleas!"

Jax does not doubt that for a moment. Robert knows an amazing amount. And he cracked serial and mass killings. Regularly. It made sense, the two going together. But as he got close to this man, Jax felt that his lover's knowledge was somehow a front. Almost like he solved the crimes, then created a chain of detection. Jax waits patiently. Robert stares up at the house then speaks without looking his way.

4.

My parents moved down here to New York at the end of my senior year of high school. The summer before, I had a job in Boston and stayed with relatives. Then I had lived in the dorms. So I hadn't really been around my father for over a year.

Working nights meant I didn't run into him much. He sat out on a lounge chair drinking whiskey. I stood just out of reach. Things hadn't been real good in the few days since he got the letter saying I'd lost my scholarship and wasn't quite ready for college. Like my mother's family, I'm not tall, and then I was skinny too. My father was big. Six feet. He had fought in World War II and still wore a close crew cut.

"You come to any decision on the army?" He blew smoke my way. My father wanted me to enlist immediately and not wait a year and a half for the draft. I wasn't going to do it. I'd survived high school after I butted, bit and kicked my way through a couple of fights. Enlisting sounded like another three years of that. The draft was far in the future. Besides, I was afraid the army would do to me whatever it had done to my father. I just shrugged and turned to go in.

Then he asked, "You do anything at school except grow that Goddamn hair? Tomorrow, I want it all off." Déjà vu twisted me. This couldn't be happening again. The start of each summer and any time I was in disgrace had always seen me forcibly and thoroughly shorn. "You know the rules."

The Saturday before, my brother Neil, fifteen, talked back when told he was going to the barber's. Our father dragged him into the bathroom, punched him around, took the mildly hoody clothes he wore in imitation of me right off him.

That night, Neil had to appear at the dinner table, red faced, in sneakers and shorts, with his hair cropped just like our old man's. That look's hip now. Then it was like a brand that told the world your parents owned you body and soul. Neil had to choke out an apology for causing trouble.

My sister Jessie, ten, bowed her face to the table. My mother sat like this wasn't happening. Asked much later, she'd say it hadn't. My father watched my reactions with a tight smile. Helplessly I recalled exactly the same thing happening to me right before my senior class photos were taken.

Friday night, the old man was lit and wanted me to give him an excuse to explode. Then he could wake everybody up and have an audience for his drama. Careful not to say anything, I turned and walked toward the house.

If he followed me, I was in for a fight I wouldn't win. Then I'd have to leave home. I wondered where I could go if that happened. I had a little money saved. But I'd worn out my welcome in Boston. And New York City, on my short visits, terrified me. I was too crazy to live anywhere but with the people who had raised me.

When I opened the back door, my father was still in his chair. If my luck held, he wouldn't remember this incident tomorrow. In the living room, the TV was on with the sound off. My mother's voice was muffled. "Honey there are sandwiches in the refrigerator." My throat was full of bile. I wasn't hungry. When I was little, I wondered why she let stuff like this happen to me.

She lay on the couch, pale face, dark hair, pale robe. Mostly, we get along really well. But since I'd screwed up in school, my mother wasn't happy with me either. I had sometimes wondered if the point of us kids was to distract my father from her. She asked, "Could you turn that off?" When I did, she and the Late, Late Show disappeared. "Goodnight," she said and I was too angry to answer.

My year in college got spent in a haze. That spring they sent me to the school shrink. I mentioned that the reason I couldn't make it to biology class was that I felt great pain when I went near the building. The death of a million frogs saddened me so. He seemed real interested.

So for the first time in my life, I explained to someone how certain places made me real unhappy. Emboldened by that, I told him my other big secret, how I earned pocket money. At that point, he recommended that I seek help. That semester I flunked every course.

Late that night in my parents' house, I slipped past the bedroom where Jessie slept amid stuffed animals. In the room Neil and I shared, he said, "Hey," half asleep. "They've retired the asshole trophy. The old man gets to keep it for good."

I knew he'd heard us outside. My little brother was already taller than I was. We slept in our briefs. I stripped down, rubbed his head for luck. I worried that I was drawing fire, that my presence made things harder for Neil. "Fuck him. I'm not doing it." This sounded brave and I hoped it worked.

I grabbed my biography of Arthur Rimbaud and headed for the bathroom. That summer, I was hung up on getting a tan and on Rimbaud. My French teacher first semester had told me I looked like him.

It wasn't his poetry but the pictures that caught me: a photo of the slit-eyed teenager about to discover Paris and get gang raped; a group portrait of hairy, dusty, poets and the angelic kid in the corner; the painting of the hollow-faced youth propped up in bed shot by his lover Verlaine. It

IN THE HOUSE OF THE MAN IN THE MOON

seemed to me the Grace was, maybe, poetic inspiration and that my life was kind of an ass-backward version of Rimbaud's.

I'd always looked a few years younger than I was. Maybe because of trauma. Looking in the bathroom mirror that summer, I finally saw the tanned kid, hip, a bit hoody, with great hair, that I'd wanted to be at sixteen. Feeling trapped, needing some kind of control over my life, I decided that instead of jerking off, I'd go into Hempstead the next day.

My father came into the house and talked to my mother. They didn't sound happy. When I was little, because we moved around Boston and vicinity a lot, I thought they were spies. Then I thought maybe we were all Martians. Actually, the mundane secret was that my father was a mid-level public administrator who liked to drink and had trouble holding jobs.

In the years since, I've tried to figure out where the Grace came from. Neither Neil nor Jessie showed any sign of it. My mother, of course, would deny having it no matter what. It's too late to ask my old man. Lots of things got him mad. He took his anger to the grave with him. But the way he went after me, I wonder if he didn't sense something. I know that's how it worked with the Man In The Moon.

Saturday when I got up, my father wasn't around. And I knew I was safe for the moment. I put on tight, black chinos and ankle boots that made me look taller, walked down to the Turnpike and hooked a ride.

Sometimes, I went to the station and took the train into Manhattan. All I could find was Time Square and Third Avenue, which seemed cold and tough. But Long Island, for a city kid without a car or even a driver's license, was a formless maze of ranch houses and malls, towns of twenty-thousand people that had been potato fields ten years before. I hitched rides a lot, which was one way of meeting people. Then I discovered Hempstead.

5.

Robert looks around the back yard one last time and seems ready to leave. Jax hooks the car keys out of his pocket. "Let me drive." The lady of the house appears at the back door. "She's ready to give us the tour," he says. "When she asks for your autograph, remember there are two l's in Carroll."

A bit later that afternoon, they roll east toward Hempstead with Jax at the wheel. Robert beside him watches Levittown Plaza and Hofstra go by. Jax raises soft jazz on the radio, waits for whatever comes.

He loves the guy and tries not to think like this, but their excursion has begun to feel chillingly familiar to a D.A. It's like those times when someone needs to confess. When that happens, there is no stopping them. Jax has seen guys ferried from place to place, reliving the deeds committed by the killer inside them.

"I don't know what the town is like now," Robert says. "But when I found it, Hempstead had blocks of shops, department stores, a movie house that showed foreign films, a black ghetto, a bus depot and train station, pedestrian traffic, a low background hum almost like a real city. Being a traditional town, action went on in a couple of men's rooms. And on a block of dingy stores with a bar and a bus stop was a minor league Strip."

The town they drive into features public housing, empty store fronts and a park with black and Spanish bums on the benches. Miniature urban blight. Everything looks bleached and dried out, oddly Southern and mostly deserted on this midweek holiday. At the center of town, a couple of blocks of buildings are being leveled for a parking lot.

Across the street from that is a slatternly bodega, a store selling new and used furniture, a club called the Venus Lounge and an abandoned video arcade. A kid, Spanish, maybe thirteen, in shorts and a Knicks T-shirt stands with his foot against the wall. When Jax slows at the corner, the boy glances at them. Then seeing them as cops, he looks away.

Up ahead is a big, two story building. The ground floor houses a Nassau County betting office closed for the holiday. "Can we park over there?" asks Robert. As they do, a bum rises from a doorway. Jax takes some change out of his pocket, rolls down the window. "This building used to be Arnold Constable's, a kind of classy department store," Robert says. Jax will not interrupt no matter where the story takes them. Robert understands that, looking straight ahead and talking.

6

I was about the same age as that Hispanic boy back there, the first time I got picked up. The guy was in his mid-twenties. He stopped me in a subway station in Boston, looked at me with these burning, curious eyes and said, "Hey, I know you."

He put his arm around my shoulder, led me into a back alley, took down my pants. He seemed surprised that I had pubic hair. He felt it, then he gave me a blow job, stuck some money in my pocket and said I was a good kid. Until that moment, I hadn't known what a blow job was, let alone that it meant money.

That summer, the Boston papers had a story of two local kids, brothers eleven and twelve, who disappeared. First they found the bodies, stabbed and raped. Then they found the guy. From pictures in the *Globe*, in the *Record*, I recognized the eyes of the one who had done me. It came out these kids were not the first ones he had killed.

That gave me pause, you know. I understand it's possible that my life was spared because he only killed prepubescents or some other mad whim. But right then I thought it had something to do with my Grace. That it's what he saw when he thought he recognized me and was the reason he didn't kill me.

Anyway, by then I was having big trouble at home and in school. Subway Man slipped back out of my mind. I'd already let myself get picked up a few times for pocket money and thrills. Imprinting we call it. An endless replay of that first encounter.

I was a sad kid with these two huge secrets, since nobody figured them out. I thought that made me smarter than anyone else. What happened, though, was that five years passed and hustling was the only social skill I had learned.

Hempstead, the summer I hung around, was a low intensity scene, no more than a couple of kids looking like they might be waiting for a bus. One boy about my age was small, blond, good-looking except that under bangs, his hair was thin. There was a light-skinned black kid with eye makeup and a guy who had, maybe, played high school football and appeared more like a bum as time went on.

Looking real young was my big attraction as a piece of meat. I had no trouble getting picked up that summer. Guys would honk and sometimes just the idea that I had been chosen was enough for me. I'd shrug and walk away.

When I got in a car, a lot of times the guy, wanting to believe he'd found an actual hitchhiker, would ask, "Where do you go to school?" I'd say I was a dropout. He'd think that meant from high school. "A good-looking kid like you must have girlfriends."

I'd squirm, mumble, "You got to have money," and we'd get down to business. One guy took me to an empty boat house, undressed me and gave me a little massage before he got to work. It felt real good. I imagined him adopting me and my going back to high school and being a big social success. I couldn't manage to grow up.

Through the half-open door, I felt a warm breeze on my skin, saw bright sunshine and blue water. In my brain, I ran images of Rimbaud and felt tragic, misunderstood. My life made no sense. But as long as an older guy was down on his knees, I was in control. The money was the talisman. His handing it over meant he was a pervert and I wasn't.

One afternoon, a shabby gray Ford two-door slowed. The driver beeped his horn and looked my way like he knew me. Something made my skin crawl and I shook my head. The sedan cruised up the block and the boy with the thinning hair stepped forward.

To chase my sudden chill, I needed a drink. The legal age in New York was eighteen. But lots of times bartenders and store clerks decided my draft card was fake and wouldn't sell to me. Near the bus station was a sleazy bar where they never even asked for proof. I did a lot of drinking there and at a couple of other places. It kept me away from home, helped me avoid the old man.

At Republic around August, the foreman, a big droopy-eyed guy, came up to me and said, "Bobby, we're letting you go next week." He put his hand on my shoulder. "You don't belong here. Go back to school. Don't be like me and the rest of these guys. Strong backs and weak minds." I had lasted about six weeks.

That's when I got a job as a stock boy at Arnold Constable's in Hempstead. It didn't pay like Republic but it was convenient. I told the fat, bald buyer in ladies' shoes that I was going to college nights.

After work one September evening, I saw a kid, maybe twelve, standing on my favorite corner. He was a dark-haired child with worn-out sneakers who stared fixedly at oncoming cars. Thinking he was lost, I asked, "You waiting for someone?"

"My daddy," he said and never took his eyes off the traffic. Like an idiot, I started to tell him this wasn't a good place to hang around. Then a horn beeped. The gray Ford two-door I'd seen a couple of times had stopped. The driver met my eyes and nodded. His face was pale and flat as the Man In The Moon's. I froze and looked away. But the little boy went over with no hesitation, opened the passenger door and talked price.

At work, I kept my bright, college kid act together about as long as it would have taken to turn a trick with the shoe buyer. After that, I floated in a daze. Remembering where the size 6A Brockman pumps were stashed was beyond me. One Saturday was Rimbaud's 108th birthday. That Monday, Kennedy was on television telling the world about missiles in Cuba.

The next week was tense. At the store, a radio played in the stock room. An American destroyer intercepted a Russian freighter. In the paper were pictures of guys my age at their inductions. Reserves got called up. The draft age fell fast. They would be calling me in a few months.

"Honey, what are you going to do?" my mother asked. "I want to know what the hell your plans are," said my father. I was now so obviously fucked up that it made the two of them nervous.

Then Krushev backed down. Shortly afterward, the shoe buyer said I was through. I didn't tell my family at all. Instead, I went into Hempstead every day and hung around. My legs hurt from standing. Long Island in November doesn't get really cold. But for professional reasons, I wore a short jacket and no underpants. I tried to get home so late that nobody would be awake.

Guys now had no doubt they were picking me up for sex. Lots of stuff I wouldn't do because I wasn't queer. Sometimes when things didn't work out they got mad. One guy dumped me in the middle of nowhere. Another didn't pay.

Rimbaud gave up poetry when he was about the age I was then. His later life was empty and bleak. He knew no peace, died a bitter failure in his thirties. I couldn't imagine living that long. The town library had no books on Rimbaud. I read magazines but that kept me off the street and I needed enough money to make it seem like I was still employed.

And to drink. I drank up anything I had. One rainy afternoon in a bar where there sometimes was action, I bought an old black guy a beer. We watched a police car drive by and he asked if I'd ever been in the slam. I shook my head and he told me, "When that happens, you choose the toughest stud you can find who don't look like he wants to slice you up for kicks. You be his boy. 'Cause otherwise a baby like you will be turned out for the whole cell block." He never doubted I was going to be locked up.

That evening when the air was chill and damp and I felt zits developing and my hair was gritty and my socks were wet because my boots now had holes, the beat-up Ford slowed down. The Man nodded and stared at me. Maybe because I was so numb all the time, I felt no warning twinges.

On automatic, I opened the car door, touched my cock and said I needed twenty-five dollars. That was more than I ever got. Instead of haggling, the Man In The Moon nodded and I climbed in.

There was no inside door handle. I had to use the armrest to shut the door. That didn't tip me off. The Man was big. Pulling away from the curb, he looked at me hard and said, "I had my eye on you." For the first time in years, I thought of the Subway Man saying that he knew me. We sped out of town and in the dark I had no idea where we were going.

We went past some shopping center and the Man said, "All this was farmland. My daddy used to have a hundred acres here." He said other stuff I didn't want to know.

Then he said, "You remind me of myself back then." As he did I began to feel the Grace. It was very faint at first but I was aware of jumpy kids in this car. The man said, "When I was your age, my daddy kept me barefoot most of the time. Now get your shoes and socks off and toss them in back."

I understood that I was going to be him as a kid and he was going to be his own old man. Ordinarily, on things like that, however creepy, I went along with the john. But I was aware of a succession of boys who had played his game and found themselves half naked on the plastic seats and having second thoughts. As I'd learned to do at home, I pretended nothing had been said.

We sped along and I focused on the Grace. Some of the aura was people I knew, the boy who said he was waiting for his father, the pretty kid with the thin hair. They all wished they had never gotten in the Ford.

The Man In the Moon talked under his breath. "You think you're too old to have your pants taken down and your ass creased." This was too close to real life. Again, I acted like I hadn't heard. "NO PANTS, YOU LITTLE FAGGOT!" He grabbed my belt and unbuckled it. "DON'T MAKE ME TAKE THEM OFF YOU!"

Once he did, it would be hard to escape. And suddenly I wanted that real bad. I knocked his hand aside and yelled, "STOP THE CAR!" I tried to open the door and found I couldn't. There was no way even to roll down the window.

His right hand shot out and I took a hit on the side of my face. My eyes lost focus. He had his attention off the road. Breaks squealed. He lurched to the left, almost sideswiped a truck. All I could see out the window were headlights. Someone in another car yelled. Horns blared. He steered onto an exit and reached under his coat.

From the Grace, I sensed that the Man In The Moon would draw a knife and pull up on the side of the road. Not wanting that, I kept my eyes down and whispered. "I'm sorry, Daddy. I'll be good. Don't do this out here in front of people. Wait until we get home. Then you do what you want. Please." This was awfully close to appeals I'd had to make, agonized pleas to my father not to punish me in public. Somehow, I still imagined the Man just wanted to screw me.

It worked. He grunted under his breath. "Thought you were so fucking smart. I knew about you that first time." He concentrated on his driving, hung a right without slowing and another. I was tensed to move. Then, all of a sudden, I saw the inside of a garage. The Man killed the headlights and stopped so suddenly I got jerked forward. The door closed behind us. In the Grace, I felt the little boy hope that the guy wasn't going to hurt him too badly.

The Man In The Moon pounced. With a practiced move, he grabbed my jacket, sweater and T-shirt, pulled them in a bunch over my head, blinding me, binding my arms. Twisting the clothes tight, he dragged me head first out of the front seat, yanked my pants down to my ankles without opening them. And I was caught just like the others.

He hauled me to my feet and ran his free hand all over my body like he was inspecting livestock. He squeezed my scrotum and prick. When I cried out, he said, "Shut up or I'll cut them off." I felt the Grace all around like it was enveloping me. I pissed myself.

The Man threw me face down on the hood of the car. He put his fingers way up my ass and twisted hard. "Little faggot, I got you trussed like a fucking pig!" I'd freed my head so I could see. Arms pinned behind me, legs hobbled by my pants, I was frog marched to a side door, held against it as he got his keys out.

"Wait and see what daddy does!" The house vibrated with pain, kids whose tendons had been severed, who had no tongues with which to cry out for their mothers. The lock clicked. The Man In The Moon leaned forward to turn the knob.

His free hand was near my head. The door swung open. He loosened his hold. On instinct I bobbed down and bit him. "FUCKER!" His blood was in my mouth. I butted him in the chest. The Man fell back and drew a hunting knife.

I stumbled over the threshold. He lunged at me. I got my arm free and slammed the door. It had a bolt lock which I threw. Gasping for breath, I pulled up my pants. They were wet. I got my T-shirt back on and wrapped my jacket and sweater around my left arm.

I was in the rumpus room of a split level house. A dim light was on. Nearby, a box overflowed with sneakers, high school jackets, jeans, socks. Beyond that stood an exercise horse with chains on it. On the wall above the light, with glass eyes in the sockets and lank hair, was a stuffed head of a kid. As I took that in, the garage door rolled open quietly.

That's when I caught the reek. Instinctively, I recognized blood and shit. It came from the cellar. Down there, kids roiled forever in the bathtub where they had bled to death. I vomited. Then the front door creaked open. The Man In the Moon was inside his house, stalking me silently.

So, I unbolted the lock to the garage, ran past the gray Ford sedan. I felt the agony of a tongueless, castrated kid who had made it this far before being dragged back. The garage door was open a couple of feet. I rolled under it.

And the Man In The Moon was right on top of me. He slashed and I blocked with my left arm. I felt his breath on my skin as I scrambled to my feet. Street lights were behind him. I spun around. A line of dark trees lay that way. Beyond them, I heard a familiar rushing like a river. I ran down a slope, stumbled on roots and burst into the light.

Cars honked, drivers caught a glimpse of a crazy, half-dressed kid, dodging traffic as he ran across the parkway. When I got to the other side and looked back, the Man In The Moon was gone.

Putting on my jacket and sweater, I found they'd been slashed. My arm was cut, not badly. My nose bled worse. I leaned against a tree, shivering, sobbing. I stank of urine and vomit.

Then I went through the trees on that side of the parkway and onto a suburban street. Completely lost, I walked past rows of identical houses, saw TV's on in living rooms, heard families. I couldn't catch my breath. Once I saw a gray car and hid behind some bushes. Hours later, I found my way home.

After that, memories run together. My parents heard me come in. The next day, my mother saw the cuts and bruises. I said I'd hurt myself at work. She decided I had pneumonia. A doctor came and shot me full of something. Everything I'd worn the night before got thrown away.

Music from the radio swirled in my head. The number one songs were "He's a Rebel" and "Big Girls Don't Cry." I got chased through woods by a guy with a knife. Not the Man In The Moon, the Subway Man. I got tangled in my clothes and he started carving me. I woke up with Neil holding me and saying, "It's only a dream, Bobby."

My sister Jessie modeled her Thanksgiving pageant costume for me. I never went outside. Once, when no one else was home, I called the Nassau County Police. I didn't give my name. I babbled stuff about a bathtub full of blood and the Man In The Moon and hung up afraid they'd trace the call.

My parents took me to a psychiatrist who got the doctor's file from school. That winter at Creedmore State Mental Hospital, I sat in pajamas in a row of zombies waiting for electroshock treatment.

Maybe my folks saw Creedmore as a compromise between the army and college. They were right. It made me tough and taught me a lot. I got zilched a few times that winter. I lost my spontaneous memory. All I had was the here and now.

That and the Grace. If I had told anyone about it, I would never have gotten out of there. But fear, despair, blighted lives, death, permeated every inch of the hospital. I felt like I was drowning. To save my life, that's when I learned to control the Grace, or at least to live with it.

When I came home that June, my parents were talking about moving. Everything was at a remove. My reactions were something like, "Oh, this is my father. 'Hi dad.'" My father in a weird way now respected me. Which I now understood meant he felt a little fear.

So he celebrated my return by cracking down on Neil, who had discovered girls and hanging out. Our old man decided he wanted to send him to military school. The poor kid was freaked by how remote I'd gotten. Like he must have wondered if this was what was going to happen to him.

7.

"This next exit, I think," says Robert. Jax drives off the parkway behind a family coming home from the beach in a Jimmy Truck. Jax looks at Robert and sees Bobby. It's only a flash but for that moment, with the hat pulled down, the eyes squinting against the slanting sun, there is a kid, tense, confused, angry, vulnerable.

Jax thinks, "Poor baby, along with everything else he gets brutally punished for being raped and almost killed." But another part of him also recognizes the kid. Jax sees him all the time in homicide work, the abused youth who kills.

In the blue dusk, Jax drives slowly through a development a little shabbier than the one where Bobby's family had once lived. They roll past a clutch of blond-headed six- and seven-year-olds sitting on the curb looking up in the sky for fireworks. Laughter, the sound of Creedence

Clearwater's Greatest Hits, the smell of charred meat, indicate a barbecue in progress in the back yards on one side of the street.

Behind the houses across the road, the sun slants through the trees along the parkway. Some of the leaves are brown in the blazing drought. The street dead ends against a fenced-in sump, a deep pit for catching ground water. It stands bone dry.

All the houses are split levels except for the single forlorn ranch bordered by the parkway and the sump. Slightly isolated, aluminum sided, its windows are dark. A weathered 'For Sale' sign stands on the brown and patchy lawn. That's where they stop. Jax knows what this has to be. He also remembers hearing his partner say it too was a split level.

Robert says, "This house is empty a lot. Nobody stays there for long." As he speaks, he breathes deeply almost like he's asleep.

8.

What I learned in the hospital came from the other young patients. My first peer group. I made friends. Andy was a nut a year or so my senior. In for mandated drug treatment because he'd been caught smoking marijuana. Curly hair like Dylan. Absolutely cool. He was gay. I was this miserable, conflicted kid. He brought me out very gently.

That summer, when we were both released, Andy showed me a whole world, a local bar called the Hayloft, Greenwich Village, Fire Island. He was going to move into the city that fall and wanted me along.

As I said, my spontaneous memory was gone. Even that awful night with the Man In The Moon didn't haunt me because nothing evoked it. Then *Newsday* ran a picture of a fifteen-year-old who had disappeared. He looked like a baby.

That night, a man chased me, his eyes luminous, his face gray and grainy like a newspaper photo. I tripped on my clothes. "Don't I know you?" he asked and cut me up.

I awoke to bone-shaking terror and unbearable pain. Miles away, in the house of the Man In The Moon, the newest victim screamed out with the others. In the stillness, I looked at Neil asleep in the next bed. It was my fault the boy in the paper had died. Made desperate by our old man, my own brother could be next.

At dawn, I was out tracking. The trail ran through empty shopping center parking lots, down suburban streets where people were just waking up, across highways. The Grace was now more precise. Also more intense. The agony of the kids twisted my bones. The warning their deaths had given me was what saved my life. I couldn't turn back.

Finally, through the woods, I saw his house. So fucking ordinary. That's what got to me. All down the block, people came out of houses just like it and drove off to work. As I watched, the Man In The Moon's garage door slid open, the gray car emerged. I froze behind a tree. The man gazed around before he drove away.

Looking the outside of the place over, I thought about how two killers had picked me up. It was more than just spotting a kid who turned them on, a potential victim. They had both recognized me on first meeting, realized I could know what they had done. Like they could sense the Grace. It was what must have scared the Subway Man enough so that he didn't kill me. It made the Man In The Moon go after me until he almost did.

The Man might have had a few bad nights worrying after I escaped. But he was back on the job. The boys he had killed cried out for comfort. They couldn't rest while he was at work. Neither could I. But I was young, a dropout, a mental patient, an outsider. If I told the cops what I knew and how I knew it, they'd lock me up again. I had to destroy a murderer.

A couple of the Creedmore kids were able to tell me about fire. Just before dawn, when the Man was asleep, the garage went up. The gas tank in that terrible car exploded and took a wall of the house with it. Kids danced, naked and mutilated, in the flames. The Man In The Moon was dead before the Volunteer Fire Department arrived.

Even a crew of clowns like the Nassau County Police managed to find the remains of three young males. There were lots of others that they missed. The Man In The Moon, it turned out, was actually named Simmons. The police decided he had set the fire and shot himself in a fit of remorse. No suspects, no investigation. Just a wave of antigay hysteria in the papers. My family was moving again. To Maryland, this time. Me, I split for Manhattan just before Labor Day.

9

Robert falls silent and steals a glance at his partner. Jax says, "As a lawman, I appreciate an investigation that ties everything up neatly like the locals did. What happened next?"

"Rimbaud's real life, his poetry, was over at nineteen. Mine began. I had a few rough passages after Andy and I hit the city. But I thought of myself as fortunate. Plenty of kids like me hadn't made it that far. And I thought the Grace had saved me for a reason. I went to school, cultivated my talents, met a cop or two I could trust, broke a case, became a consultant. I've never told anyone all of this. Since we first met, I've wanted it to be different with you."

Jax says, "I'm honored. You know I have a gorge index. Real unprofessional way of deciding what I think is a serious crime." Robert nods. "Well what the Man In The Moon did makes it rise. What you did does not." Jax kisses Robert on the mouth. "Of course, when we get home I'm going to have to hide the matches and sharp objects. Meanwhile, ready to get something to eat, Bobby?"

Robert nods and smiles at the nickname. Jax starts the car, executes a U turn. Robert waves to the kids on the curb, glances back at the house and says, "I appreciate your hearing me out more than I can ever tell you. But one thing still bothers me."

Jax wonders if there's more confession. That, he realizes, is a problem. The Grace he might live with. One learned to accept things in his business. But he could never be sure this wouldn't happen again, that some other buried crime wouldn't get pulled forth to be forgiven. Could any relationship survive that?

Then Robert catches his eye, and it's like he's followed Jax's thoughts. "I worry about the families that live on the spot. They're transients. People fleeing failure. On the move like my family was. And every once in a while, one of the kids living there wakes in the middle of the night, scared and screaming. They tell him it's okay and he knows it's not."

✖

NICOLA GRIFFITH

was born in Yorkshire, England, but was granted legal immigrant status in the U.S. in 1994 on the grounds of being an "alien of exceptional ability." (It always comes up as heavy-handed jokes in interviews, so she likes to get that out of the way as fast as possible.) Over the years she has paid the rent with the usual potpourri of jobs—singer, bouncer, laborer at archaeological digs, teacher of women's self defense, counsellor—but finds she much prefers to write. Her novels *Ammonite* and *Slow River*—with another, *Penny in my Mouth*, forthcoming from Avon—have won several awards.

Nicola lives in the Wallingford neighborhood of Seattle, where she and her partner, writer Kelley Eskridge, have just bought a house. Readers with access to the World Wide Web might want to check out the official Nicola Griffith Web page at: http://ww.america.net/~daves/ng/.

STEPHEN PAGEL

(who shortens his name to Stephe—after all, why should he spell his name with a 'v' just because everyone else does?) is a book lover who has done a bit of everything: taught high school math, managed a pizza place, and designed and programmed ATM machines for New York banks. While he was doing all that, he also fed his habit by working part-time in a book store. In 1985 he realized books were more fun and went into the book industry full time, managing a store at first, then becoming a national buyer for the Barnes and Noble/B. Dalton chains. Ten years later he moved to Atlanta to become White Wolf's Director of Sales.

Stephe also co-owns DNA Inc., a small press that publishes *Absolute Magnitude*, a quarterly science fiction adventure magazine (later this year Tor Books will publish a collection of the best stories from the magazine: *Absolute Magnitude*, coedited by Warren Lapine). DNA launched its book line last year with *Hymn to the Sun, an Imitation* by Roger Zelazny. Although Stephe lives in Atlanta, he can be spotted all over the country attending various science fiction, fantasy, and roleplaying conventions.

ABOUT THE AUTHORS:

�֍

KIM ANTIEAU

This is Kim Antieau's third White Wolf appearance. She's had over thirty stories published in various places. Her first novel, *The Jigsaw Woman,* is from Roc Books, her second is due out later this year. She writes to remember what is nature and spirit.

✖

ROBIN WAYNE BAILEY

is the author of eleven novels, most recently *Shadowdance* from White Wolf Publishing and the highly successful *Brothers of the Dragon* series from Roc Books. After earning a Master's degree in Literature, he worked as a teacher, planetarium lecturer, martial arts instructor, and sometime-musician. He's also active in fundraising for various AIDS service organizations; his special fundraising auctions at science fiction conventions in the midwest have become almost legendary. He lives in Kansas City, Missouri.

�֎

DON BASSINGTHWAITE

comes from Meaford, Ontario, but currently lives and works in Toronto. He is a graduate of McMaster University and the University of Toronto with degrees in anthropology and museum studies. He is the author of the dark fantasy novels *Such Pain, Breathe Deeply,* and *Pomegranates Full and Fine,* and the coauthor of *As One Dead.* His current project is a dark fantasy trilogy, *The Siege Perilous.*

✖

K.L. BERAC

lives in Vancouver, Canada, with a partner, a computer, and a cat, and when not writing is employed as a stripper (no, not THAT kind) at a local publishing company. The job title sometimes makes crossing the US/Canadian border an interesting experience. Immediately upon completion of "Magicked Tricks" Nikki started pestering K.L. for a novel. He's getting his way.

✖

RICHARD BOWES

was born in Boston in 1944, grew up and went to school and college there and on Long Island, New York. For most of the last thirty years he has lived in Manhattan, where, amidst various misadventures, he designed board games and had several SF novels published. A few years ago he began writing short fiction and has had good fortune especially with his "Kevin Grierson" stories which have appeared in *F&SF, Full Spectrum #5, Tomorrow, Year's Best Fantasy & Horror* and *Best From Fantasy and Science Fiction.*

DOMINICK CANCILLA

is a typesetter and sometimes horror writer from Southern California. His work has appeared in *Young Blood*, *365 Scary Stories*, and *Robert Bloch's Psychos* anthologies, as well as in many large and small press horror magazines. He hopes to one day be able to devote himself entirely to his writing, only leaving the house on weekends to visit Disneyland. Internet surfers can find him via his Web page at http://www.horrornet.com/cancilla.htm.

CAROLYN IVES GILMAN

has been publishing fantasy and science fiction stories for ten years in magazines and anthologies such as *Fantasy and Science Fiction*, *Universe*, *Full Spectrum*, *Interzone*, *Realms of Fantasy*, and a variety of others. She is also the author of five nonfiction books on frontier and American Indian history. Her last book won the Northeastern Minnesota Book Award, and she was a finalist for the Nebula Award in the novelette category in 1992. She lives in St. Louis, where she works as a museum exhibition developer.

TANYA HUFF

lives with her partner and four cats in Prince Edward County, Ontario. After spending three years in the Naval Reserve (she was a cook; no tatoos) she got a degree in Radio and Television Arts that she's never used—although there are those who say it's responsible for a certain visual quality in her work. Her most recent book, *Blood Debt*, concludes the Vicki/Henry/Celluci vampire series and she really means it this time.

CHARLEE JACOB

lives in the Dallas/Fort Worth Metroplex with her husband Jim and four cats. She is now a full-time writer but has been a restaruant cook, a laundress, an actress, and a purveyor of designer rags. She was born in 1952 and is a native Texan. Her fiction and poetry has been published in many magazines, including *Terminal Fright, Bizarre Dreams, Bizarre Sex and Other Crimes of Passion III, Prisoners of the Night*, and *Palace Corbie*. She has just finished a novel called *Dark Moods*.

M. W KEIPER

is an alumnus of the Clarion West '94 Workshop, where he wrote "Ploughshares," a story that won the 1st Quarter of the '95 "Writers of the Future" contest. His mainstream novel, "Privateers," won first place in the 1996 Florida First Coast Writers' Festival. Keiper has worked as an ironworker, bouncer, newspaper reporter, special deputy, smuggler, and, briefly, "followed the profession of Jesus." At present, he writes feature stories and a weekly column for a small town southern newspaper.

ELLEN KUSHNER

swept the 1991 World Fantasy and Mythopoeic awards for Best Novel with *Thomas the Rhymer*. Her first novel, *Swordspoint*, was hailed by Gene Wolfe as "the book we might have had if Noel Coward had written a vehicle for Errol Flynn!" The further adventures of *Swordspoint*'s two antiheroes may be found in *The Year's Best Fantasy and Horror, Vol. 5*. A longtime public radio personality, Kushner hosts a new weekly series, "Sound & Spirit: a musical exploration of the human experience," which airs on public radio stations nationwide. The Website is http://www.wgbh.org/pri/spirit.

※

HOLLY WADE MATTER'S

stories have seen print in *Argos Fantasy and Science Fiction*, *Asimov's*, and *Century*. In 1995, she was the recipient of a grant from the Seattle Arts Commission, which allowed her to complete her novel, *Belltown*. She is passionately interested in icons, the pre-Raphaelites, abandoned buildings, alternative comics, old cemeteries, and Hello Kitty. She and her husband Brad spend a lot of time photographing elaborate Victorian funerary architecture and statuary, in Pittsburgh, Seattle, and wherever they find it.

※

MARK MCLAUGHLIN'S

fiction has appeared in numerous magazines and anthologies, including *Galaxy*, *Ghosts & Scholars*, *The Third Alternative*, *Carnage Hall*, *Tekeli-li!*, *Palace Corbie*, *100 Wicked Little Witch Stories*, and *The Year's Best Horror Stories: XXI and XXII*. He has a long poem in the *Air Fish* anthology, reads his work regularly at a local coffeehouse, and is the editor of *The Urbanite*.

※

JAMES L. MOORE

has written for comics and is the author of *Hellstorm* (HarperPrism) and the coauthor, with Kevin Andrew Murphy, of *House of Secrets* (White Wolf). He spent two years as the Secretary for the Horror Writers' Association and during the same span published interviews regularly in *Inphobia*. He has also published additional interviews in *Cemetery Dance* and *Deathrealm*. His short stories have appeared in several anthologies, and he is a regular columnist for Game Shop News. James lives in Marietta, Georgia with his wife of eight years, Bonnie.

JESSICA AMANDA SALMONSON

writes poems and tales. Recent volumes of her tales include *Phantom Waters: Northwest Legends of Rivers, Lakes and Shores*; and *The Eleventh Jaguarundi and Other Mysterious Persons*. Over the last two decades she has published a handful of novels, including *Anthony Shriek* and *Tomoe Gozen*, and edited a score of story collections, including *Amazons!* and *What Did Miss Darrington See?: Feminist Supernatural Short Stories*. She is the author of *The Encyclopedia of Amazons* and is presently working on an extravagant *Philistine's Guide to Women and Goddesses of the Bible*. She has received the World Fantasy Award, Lambda Award, and The ReaderCon Award. Jessica studies Kabbalah and Saktism, is a vegetarian, and lives with several salamanders, rats, and a prairie dog.

MARK SHEPHERD

began collaborating with Mercedes Lackey on the Serrated Edge urban fantasy novel *Wheels of fire*. He has also authored novels based on the computer game, Bard's Tale: *Moonrise*, and *Prison of Souls* (in collaboration with Lackey). Other novels include *Elvendude*, an elves-in-the-mall urban fantasy, and its sequel *Spiritride*. He is a contributor to *Tapestries* and *Swords of the Rainbow*. Mark lives in Oklahoma in the aerie known as Highflight, which he shares with Mercedes Lackey and her husband, Larry Dixon, ten tropical birds, miscellaneous raptors in rehabilitation, and three cats.

SIMON SHEPPARD

Known primarily as a writer of erotic fiction, Simon Sheppard has published work in a goodly number of anthologies, including the 1996 and 1997 editions of *Best Gay Erotica*; *Happily Ever After: Erotic Fairy Tales for Men*; *The Badboy Book of Erotic Poetry*; *Switch Hitters*; *Noirotica*; and *Ritual Sex*; as well as in magazines ranging from *The James White Review* to *Drummer*. He lives in San Francisco, and traveled to Morocco many years ago.

DELIA SHERMAN

was born in Tokyo, Japan, and brought up in Manhattan. Her first novel is *Through a Brazen Mirror* (Ace) and her second, *The Porcelain Dove* (Dutton), won the Mythopoeic Award for Fantasy Fiction. She is the editor, with Ellen Kushner and Don Keller, of the fantasy anthology *The Horns of Elfland* (Roc), and, with Terri Windling, of the latest *Bordertown* punk-elf anthology (Tor). She lives with fellow author and fantasist Ellen Kushner in a lovely old house in Somerville, Massachusetts...but prefers cafes to home for writing (they bring you things to eat and the phone's never for you) and traveling to staying put.

LISA S. SILVERTHORNE'S

work has appeared in Marion Zimmer Bradley's *Fantasy Magazine*, *Sword & Sorceress XII*, and *Blood Muse*. She is an active member of SFWA and is currently working on two novels. She works as a microcomputer support coordinator in a university library. When she isn't writing, Lisa enjoys raising Oranda goldfish, gardening, and traveling to the Pacific Northwest (where her fascination with orca whales began). She lives in Indiana with her furpersons, Seville and Marshall.

※

MARK W. TIEDEMANN

began writing as a child. He wrote and drew his own comic books, then traded the typewriter for a camera in high school and worked in commercial photography for twenty-five years. In 1988 he attended the Clarion writers' workshop and soon after sold the story "Targets" to *Asimov's*. Since then his stories have appeared in *Universe 2*, *F&SF*, *Science Fiction Age*, *Camelot* (edited by Jane Yolen), *Tomorrow SF*, *Alien Pregnant by Elvis* (edited by Esther Friesner), and *War of the Worlds: Global Dispatches* (edited by Kevin Anderson). His first novel will be appearing from White Wolf in 1997. "Gestures…" is his twenty-third sale.

※

B. J. THROWER

has been published in markets such as *Aboriginal SF*, *Terminal Fright*, *Distant Journeys*, *Non-Stop* and *Asimov's*. She is currently marketing a completed dark fantasy novel, *All the Warriors in Pell*, and working on another, *The Mongrel*. With the exception of five years in Wyoming as a child, she has spent her life in Tulsa, where she lives with her husband and two daughters, and works at the University of Tulsa Law Library as Circulation/Media Services Coordinator. She is the vice-president of Oklahoma Science Fiction Writers (OSFW), and an Active SFWA member. "The Home Town Boy" is her ninth short fiction sale.

※

LESLIE WHAT

has "ghosted" a book of memoirs for a survivor of the Warsaw Ghetto, and written feature articles and a health column for an alternative newspaper. Her fiction has been published in such magazines as *Lilith, Fantasy & Science Fiction, Fugue, Asimov's, Hysteria, Japanophile, Realms Of Fantasy,* and others. She is a maskmaker and member of the Radar Angels, a rather bizarre women's art collective, whose members enjoy taking high tea, dressing up as fairies to perform at the Oregon Country Fair, and planning for the annual benefit Jell-O Art show and Tacky Food Buffet.

※

JEFF VERONA

teaches English at the collegiate level in the Dallas-Fort Worth area, including courses in science fiction literature. He writes fiction and poetry, edits an APA, bakes all his own bread, studies Renaissance-era dance, pesters his doctor wife, Marcy Fitz-Randolph, with obscure medical questions, and tries to out-compete his two cats in the curiosity department.

ABOUT THE COVER ARTIST

KEVIN MURPHY

has been an illustrator for six years. He is the winner of the 1995 World Fantasy Award for Best Epic Fantasy painting for his cover to Terry Goodkind's *Blood of the Fold*. He was nominated for the Chesley Award in 1995 for Best Nonpublished Work for his painting Void Engineers. Other past projects include the Paratwa Series from Tor and the Technocracy Series from White Wolf. He is currently working on a CD-ROM game for MTV, and several ongoing projects with Milton Bradley in conjunction with Lucas Films for Star Wars, and with National Geographic.